The Boy Next Door

A Novel

The Boy
Next Door

Irene Sabatini

Little, Brown and Company
New York Boston London

Little, Brown and Company
Hachette Book Group
237 Park Avenue, New York, NY 10017
Visit our Web site at www.HachetteBookGroup.com

First Edition: September 2009

Little, Brown and Company is a division of Hachette Book Group, Inc. The Little, Brown name and logo are trademarks of Hachette Book Group, Inc.

The characters and events in this book are fictitious. Any similarity to real persons, living or dead, is coincidental and not intended by the author.

Library of Congress Cataloging-in-Publication Data
Sabatini, Irene.
    The boy next door : a novel / by Irene Sabatini. — 1st ed.
      p. cm.
    ISBN 978-0-316-04993-1
    1. Zimbabwe — Race relations — Fiction.   2. Bulawayo (Zimbabwe) —
Fiction.
    I. Title.
    PR9390.9.S18B69   2009
    823'.92 — dc22
                                                                2009001447

10 9 8 7 6 5 4 3 2 1

RRD-IN

Printed in the United States of America

This book is dedicated to
Fabio, who never believed otherwise;
Griffin and Riordan, treasures
and my parents, who set me on my way.

The Boy Next Door

PART ONE

Early 1980s

1.

Two days after I turned fourteen the son of our neighbor set his stepmother alight.

A week later the police came. I was reading *Sue Barton, Senior Nurse* on the veranda, and I was at the part when Dr. Bill Barry proposes to Sue Barton. Daddy was busy tinkering with the Cortina under the jacaranda tree. Mummy was in the bedroom trying on her new Manyano outfit for the graduation ceremony that was going to take place at church, which would turn fifteen young women into fully fledged members of the congregation. Rosanna was helping her.

"Good afternoon, Mr. Bishop," I heard. "Sorry to disturb. We have come about next door."

The chief constable wiped his forehead with a tissue. "This heat is destroying us," he said, and from the veranda, I could see a wet dark patch on his shirt, which made it cling to his back.

It was midday and there wasn't a single cloud in the sky. Even though it was the end of January not one drop of rain had fallen in Bulawayo.

"This problem of no transport. Only walking these days for us. Ten kilometers and I am not so young anymore, not like these calves." He pointed at the other two policemen who were standing near the Cortina at attention.

Daddy said something about bulls, which made the chief constable laugh while the calves remained very rigid and serious.

Most of the brand-new police cars donated by Britain were in scrap yards; the police force had been statistically shown to have the most dangerous drivers in Zimbabwe. In fact, the chief constable, who had only recently been promoted after his white superior had tendered his resignation, had been responsible for a recent smashup against an electricity pole; Daddy hinted that he was most likely driving without a valid license.

"Are you finding petrol?" the chief constable asked, eyeing the two policemen who sprung forwards. It looked like he had jerked them into motion with string.

"A little only," Daddy replied as he gently put down the bonnet. "Enough to go to the office and back."

I knew that he was exaggerating; he didn't want the chief constable to feel free to ask him for transport.

The chief constable took out his tissue again and patted his forehead. "The South Africans are making it very difficult, Mr. Bishop."

Today's headline in *The Chronicle* was about the RENAMO rebels in Mozambique who were funded by South Africa. They had sabotaged a big section of the pipeline, which brought oil to Zimbabwe. South Africa was trying to destabilize our newly independent country.

"Let's hope we can secure the Beira pipeline from further attacks," Daddy said, while wiping his hands on his orange overalls.

Daddy and the chief constable looked at the Cortina as if they were expecting some response from it. The Cortina was gleaming proudly in the heat.

The chief constable coughed and cleared his throat. "Well, Mr. Bishop. This is a very sad business we have come about. We . . ."

Roxy, our Jack Russell terrier who had been sleeping in his kennel, came running out at full speed. He leapt and landed on a police foot and began vigorously licking the boot. The policeman hopped and skipped and wagged his foot, but he couldn't shake Roxy off. Daddy finally managed to pull him away while trying hard not to laugh.

"We are looking for evidence," the chief constable started again, once Roxy was safely in Daddy's arms. "We have thoroughly investigated the McKenzie property, and now we are checking all the neighboring land. We would like to take a look by the perimeters."

Daddy took them to the back of the house where the two juniors cupped their hands under the tap at the end of the vegetable patch and drank as though they had not seen water for a very long time. The chief constable looked at them and shook his head. He drank slowly from the glass that I had brought out to him. Then they all walked along the fence that separated our limestone pink Spanish Colonial from the McKenzie's whitewashed Cape Dutch.

Their black boots kept getting sucked in and stuck in the mud as they trudged about looking for the evidence, because Maphosa had just watered the vegetables even though Daddy was constantly telling him that watering at the hottest time of the day was a treacherous waste of a precious natural resource and that even the borehole could run out of water.

After one walk through, the evidence was still missing. The chief constable said, that was quite all right; they had obtained a confession.

He took out his notepad, like Columbo, and he asked Daddy if he had heard or seen anything strange at the neighbors on that night or before. Daddy quickly said no, not at all. And then he invited the chief constable, who was one of his best customers, for some tea.

Daddy worked for the Telecommunications branch of the post office, making sure that the phone system worked throughout Bulawayo and the rest of Matabeleland. Sometimes he got calls in the middle of the night, and he had to take off to the exchange to fix something. But he was also good with other things like radios and TVs. He had passed the City and Guilds of London Institute exam in electrical repairs. He did up the boy's kaya with electricity so that Rosanna, who lives in that small room, is much better off than the real maids and gardeners who have to stay in them: they have to use candlesticks and paraffin stoves and sometimes, they don't even have proper toilet facilities.

Last year, with the help of some apostolics, he built his own workshop between the boy's kaya and the chicken pen using asbestos roof sheeting and bricks that were made by the apostolics in their yard.

The chief constable dismissed his juniors with instructions that they should type out a report, ready for him when he got back to the station.

He stood with Daddy by the fence. "Our white people are losing direction, left, right, and center, Mr. Bishop. Independence has confused them."

Mummy, Daddy, Rosanna, and I had watched the independence ceremony on TV over two years ago now. Prince Charles looked rather sad when they gave him the British flag; his mouth was set very firmly as if to make sure that he would not cry and disgrace the queen. All the previous week *The Herald* had had a list of white Zimbabwean beauties who would make a perfect bride for him.

Mr. Robert Gabriel Mugabe took his oath, his hand firmly on the Bible . . . *and so help me God* . . . and Zimbabwe was born.

Daddy and the chief constable washed their hands under the tap.

"He was smelling heavily of smoke, shaking nonstop, you could think he was suffering from heavy-duty malaria. We have never had any problems from that place before. It seems the boy has only just come from South Africa for his father's funeral."

They went to sit under the gum tree. I started making the tea in the kitchen, leaving the window wide open. They were sitting only a couple of meters away and the chief constable had a loud voice.

"It was very bad, very bad over there," he went on, settling into his chair with a very loud "humph." "The youngster, only seventeen, came to the station, gave himself up. And you are quite sure you have never seen this boy before?"

I bit my lip and held tightly to my breath, but I didn't hear Daddy's reply because the kettle started whistling.

I brought the tray outside, and the chief constable closed his notebook and put it on the table beside the tray.

They were quiet until I was back inside.

"We found the remains at the back of the house by the boy's kaya. Eighty or so percent of the body burnt, just bone left in some parts."

I saw Daddy turn, and I quickly bent my head by the kitchen sink and pretended to be busy washing the dishes.

"But, madoda, this is a strange case. There is another woman also; the young man brought her first to the hospital before he came to us."

He started scratching his arm and then reached out for a slice of bread that I had spread with butter and strawberry jam.

"It is not at all sure she will survive," the chief constable went on, shaking his head while he chewed with his mouth open. "And we do not know the precise identity of this woman. We are not sure of her age, if she is even local. We have contacted Beitbridge Border Police for the entry documents to see if we can learn anything; the car he was driving has South African number plates."

He was eyeing the second slice, and Daddy told him to please help himself. "He will not talk about her, nothing. Tsh, he will have enough time to think about all this in the stocks."

The chief constable scratched his head and drank some more tea. Some spilled on the saucer, and he poured this back in the cup.

I stood there in the kitchen the chief constable's words creeping inside me.

"Lindiwe . . ."

The glass dropped from my hands.

"Rosanna, you gave me a fright," I scolded, bending down to pick up the pieces.

She was standing by the door, holding an empty perfume bottle. She must have been in the main bedroom all this time.

"Daydreamers will miss the Lord's Banquet," she sang roughly to the tune of The Lord Is My Shepherd, with her eyes closed. She put the bottle on the table and took the broom from the corner.

I couldn't even smile at her impersonation of Mummy. The chief constable's words had suddenly made what had happened next door real. Until now I had been reading about the events in *The Chronicle* like everyone else in Bulawayo, trying to pretend that I didn't know more. I could feel Mrs. McKenzie here, her eyes following me, watching. I was sure her presence would soon bring in the chief constable, who would open his notebook and take my statement.

"It's good that she has gone to her meeting with Mrs. Ncube. What's wrong, Sisi? Your hand is shaking; you will cut yourself. Leave this, I'll finish."

I liked the way Rosanna called me Sisi; it irritated Mummy. When we were living in Thorngrove, one of Mummy's brothers brought her from Kamativi and said that she was the daughter of so-and-so in the village who had just died.

Could Mummy please look after her? Mummy had no choice but to help.

"What would have possessed that boy to do such a thing?" Mummy asked when we were having supper in the lounge.

"South Africa," said Daddy. "Pure and simple. They pick up fast ways over there. Drugs. Mandrax and even worse."

"But," said Mummy, "to do something like that . . . ?"

I was looking at where Daddy was sitting, thinking that not too long ago that boy had sat in the exact same place, cradling a car radio on his lap, like a cat, waiting for Daddy to take a look at it.

Daddy caught me staring at him and said, "In life, anything can happen."

2.

He had rung the bell at the gate. Maphosa went to see who it was, and then he called Rosanna. Rosanna let him in because he was a white boy. He'd just brought his radio from South Africa, and the thing was already playing up. "Those South Africans," I heard him say. "They're a bunch of crooks, right skellums, not like us honest blokes down here, lights off." He sat on Daddy's chair. I was sitting across the room from him, doing my homework on the dining-room table. Rosanna went to make his tea.

"Hey, lightie," I heard, "what you're doing?"

I'm not a lightie I wanted to tell him. I'm not tiny. And, *I'm not a boy.* But his voice didn't sound as though he meant to be mean to me.

"Homework," I answered in my best European voice.

"Homework," he said, leaning forward to put the radio on the table. I thought of how annoyed Mummy would be to find it there, possibly scratching the wood. It only needed to be moved a bit to go on top of the lace cloth, but I couldn't do it.

"Talking about skellums, you should have seen what we guys got up to, how we mucked about, did fuck all at school."

Fuck all echoed inside me.

I couldn't believe that this white youth was sitting on my father's chair, his white tackies planted on the brown carpet.

I tried to concentrate on my math problem, but the numbers would not stay still.

His hair was cut in the same style as Craig Davies, the youth leader at church: very short at the sides with a little tail at the back and the front looking like the bristles of a brush. When he leaned back against mummy's doily on the back of the chair, his head made me think of a porcupine.

Craig had announced on Friday that he was heeding God's call and going to Pretoria to spread His word. Daddy said it was funny how, of late, God was targeting whites and being very specific in his relocation directions. I had overheard Craig tell one of the church deacons that there were way too many Affs now, the atmosphere had all changed. . . .

For a long time we were the only nonwhite members of the church. On our very first Sunday at church, Mummy, Daddy, and I had the whole row to ourselves and no one sat behind or in front of us. An old white lady gave Mummy a dirty look when their elbows brushed.

"Mind my language. So homework, heh?"

Rosanna brought him the tea and a plate of Marie biscuits. She looked at me as though I had done something wrong.

He gulped down the tea and munched on the biscuit. He seemed very hungry.

"You look like a boffin," he said. "What number you come in class, heh?"

I didn't want to tell him. Somehow I was embarrassed by it.

"Come on, cough up. Don't be shy."

"Number one," I said in my best European voice.

"Number one, heh."

He slapped his thigh and some tea spilt on the carpet.

"I told you so. I can spot a boffin from a mile away. Me, I was right off the scale, the other end of it."

He coughed and choked on his biscuits and tea. He went red in his face, and I could see the schoolboy in him.

"I tell you what," he said. "Since you're so smart, I'll give you a problem to solve. It's something that's bothering me a lot."

But before he could tell me the problem, Daddy came home and took a look at the car radio. They moved out to the workshop and I finished my homework. For days I thought about the problem, his problem that was bothering him so much. I wondered if it had had anything to do with Mrs. McKenzie and this made me feel guilty as if I could have done something to save her life.

Because, three days later, Mrs. McKenzie was dead.

3.

The Friday after the chief constable's visit I went to the public library. I didn't go down straight to the Sue Barton series or to the Nancy Drew shelf like I usually did; I went upstairs to the medical section. The librarian gave me a funny look but didn't say anything. She was busy chatting with a farmer, telling him all about the mobile library.

I wanted to find out how long you would have to burn to become just bone. I wanted to know if Mrs. McKenzie had burnt all night while I had been sleeping. I tried to think what I had been dreaming of. I wanted to know if something had happened in my dreams that should have made me wake up, draw back the curtain and see . . . what? Would I have seen her? Heard her? Smelt her? I tried to remember when was the last time I had seen her alive, but I couldn't see it, that exact moment. Sometimes I would think I had spoken to her or she had said something to me, but when I thought harder, I couldn't see the two of us anywhere like that. Mrs. McKenzie didn't like me. Even though I was a girl and too old, she still thought that I was one of those kids who ran down the road ringing bells and scooting off. She would send old Mphiri, her gardener, after them. He couldn't match their long skinny legs, and Maphosa would get angry and start his muttering: *That old man should be back home, but what is he doing? Look at him—boy this, boy that—with their broken Makhiwa Ndebele. Bastards, amabhunu.*

Maphosa called any white person who personally outraged him a Boer, Bhunu. Daddy said that this was probably because he had worked for a while in the mines in Johannesburg and had been thoroughly mistreated by the Afrikaners. I wondered if that's where he had lost his eye. But, would he have been accepted as a fighter in the bush without an eye?

Maphosa came to our house six months ago. He came with a small suitcase and a knobkerrie. He had been demobilized. He came from Entumbane where there was heavy fighting between the two Liberation Armies housed there. School was closed for two whole weeks, and from home we could hear loud bangs and blasts coming from that direction. Maphosa said that the Shonas were trying to wipe out the Ndebele Fighters. But the Ndebeles had the blood of the great Ndebele warriors, kings: Milikazi and Lobengula, flowing in them and could not be bothered by such little insects as Shonas.

Mummy had made him wait outside for Daddy from half past eleven to five o'clock. She only gave him a glass of water to drink in all that time. When Daddy came home and saw Maphosa waiting like that he raised his voice at Mummy. I didn't know if he was upset with Mummy or Maphosa or with them both. Daddy said that Maphosa was a relative, and he should be accorded due respect. Mummy mumbled how was she to know and keep count of every single member of Daddy's family.

Daddy has many stepbrothers and sisters.

The new Zimbabwean Army did not want Maphosa and his like among its ranks; it only had room for Shonas. He had to live life in Zimbabwe just like everybody else.

Early on Daddy tried to get Maphosa an apprenticeship with the post office. At the job interview, Maphosa said that he was not willing under any circumstances to work for a white man.

Maphosa puts Ingram's Camphor cream on his bald head,

and you always smell him before he arrives. Sometimes he doesn't rub it in very well and his scalp is covered with patches of whites. I heard Mummy remark to Daddy: "Does he think that the cream is medicine that will grow back his hair?"

To make up for the lack of hair on his head, he has a tuft of beard which he pulls at when he is upset as if he is trying to snatch off a disguise. Some days he ties a black cloth over his bad eye and he looks like a pirate.

He is the chapter president of the Baysview War Veteran's Association, which has five active members. They meet at Maphosa's room when Mummy and Daddy are not around. Maphosa cooks a pot of sadza on a fire outside his room, and they sit around and discuss the war and the failure of Independence to deliver the land. When the sadza is cooked, they eat it with some meat that Jacob has brought with him. They nyosa the meat on the fire. Jacob is a butcher boy at the Baysview butchery. He doesn't hear very well and he doesn't talk. Sometimes the association is still meeting when Mummy comes home, and the members have to sneak out at night.

The twenty-fifth of each month Maphosa goes to town to collect his war veteran allowance and his disability benefit. When he comes back, he is in a bad mood. He says that he is not at all interested in pieces of paper. This is how our people were tricked in the first place. He wants the land. That is what they fought for.

One thing that he cannot tolerate is cruelty to birds. When he sees any boys tormenting birds and nests with their catapults, he shouts and chases after them; sometimes he even throws stones at them. Then he will go and check that the birds are all right, and once I saw him climb a tree in the bush opposite Baysview Superette and look inside a nest to see if the boys had broken any eggs. He says that birds saved his life in the bush more than once. When I asked him how, he said that

there were some birds that would become very quiet when the
enemy was close. Other birds would start singing in a certain
way. Then you knew. Once a bird had flown right onto his left
shoulder and started tapping on it with its beak. He understood
the bird's message: They must prepare. The enemy wanted to
ambush them. When Maphosa tried to tell his commander the
bird's message, the commander told him to shut up. If only the
commander had listened. As the bird had warned, the enemy
ambushed and the commander and five other guerrillas lost
their lives.

He was at Rufaro Stadium when Rhodesia became Zimbabwe on April 18, 1980.

Actually, we were Zimbabwe-Rhodesia for less than a
year from June 1979 when Bishop Abel Muzorewa formed a
Government of National Unity with Ian Smith's Rhodesian
Front. Everybody said that Muzorewa was a puppet and that
he was put there to try and get international sanctions lifted
and to isolate the Nationalists. Daddy said that Bishop Abel
Muzorewa was not very able at all and that he was a laughing
stock. And, "Where have you ever heard of a country with a
surname?"

Bob Marley came to sing; he wrote a special song: "Zimbabwe."

Maphosa says that he was right out in front, and as soon
as "Zimbabwe" started, the crowd went wild and began mis-
behaving. They were pushing and trying to climb over the
barriers onto the stage to sing with Mr. Marley. He says the
little man, which is what he calls Mr. Mugabe, did not look
amused at all. Everyone knows he wanted Cliff Richard, not
Bob Marley, to be there.

The next day, after the news, the new prime minister gave
his first Address to the Nation. Rosanna, as usual, was sitting
too close to the TV, but Daddy didn't scold her this time; he
was concentrating too hard.

"Well, he sounds quite reasonable and sincere," Daddy said afterwards.

"Reconciliation is the best and only policy."

Daddy sounded as though he was trying to convince himself with good arguments. "He's a very educated man. Did you hear his Engl—?"

"He's a Shona," Mummy interrupted him.

Ever since the elections when Mugabe and ZANU-PF had shocked them by winning fifty-seven of the eighty seats while Nkomo and ZAPU had only won twenty, Mummy had been making daily predictions about what life under Shona Management would bring.

"This is their chance now. Everyone will be forced to speak Shona. Watch, he will even make his Address to the Nation in Shona.

"They will flood this place. Those jongwes of theirs will be crowing all over the Matabeleland."

Mummy was very scornful about the ZANU-PF symbol of a rooster.

Rosanna shook her head. "There is just something about him," she said. "He is too serious."

It felt as though, sitting so close, she had seen much more of Mr. Mugabe than the rest of us.

I didn't say anything. I was wondering whether, sitting in front of the cameras, Mr. Robert Mugabe had felt all those millions of Zimbabwean eyes looking at him, whether he knew how much power he must have to have everyone waiting to hear what he had to say.

4.

When I went to see Dr. Esat at Galen House, the ladies at the reception were talking about the trial which was on the front page of *The Chronicle.* They were saying what a shame it was, such a good-looking boy.

There was a big picture of him; he was looking down at his feet. The headline was "Murder!"

One of the older ladies said her son had gone to school with him and there had been something going on in that house for sure; he would come to school with welts all over his legs, even the Welfare Department had been called in, and now that he had come for his father's funeral who knows what that woman had schemed and let loose.

She was interrupted by some patients who had to fill in the Medical Aid forms. I had the *Femina* magazine open on my lap, and I was praying that Dr. Esat would be running late as usual.

And she had been talking to John, her son, she started again, how sometime near the end of Form One, close to four years now, the boy had disappeared; word was that he'd taken off to South Africa to find his mother. And that was another story, how that woman had abandoned the poor bugger, gone chasing after some sweet-talking salesman in Jo'burg, left the little mite to the house girl not even a month old. He'd been back a couple of times, never stayed too long, though. You could tell just by looking at the poor lad he'd been driven to it. And why had they put him in prison khakis; he hadn't even been convicted; yet another strategy to humiliate us whites. . . .

One of the ladies nudged her and hissed, "Shush, June."

June looked at me, and I pretended to be reading the poster on "Good Hygiene Habits" on the wall.

They started to talk about other things.

When Daddy finished reading *The Chronicle* that evening, I took it out from the basket where Mummy puts all the old newspapers so that she has an ever-ready supply of papers to line the kitchen drawers and cupboards. Mummy is convinced that the newspaper contains something that repels cockroaches. I took the front page out. My heart was beating very fast as if I was stealing. I folded the paper over and over again, and when I was in my room, I put the paper in the pink handbag Aunty Gertrude gave me for Christmas last year.

I kept thinking that if only we had moved from Thorngrove to Baysview in 1978 instead of 1979 I might have seen him. I tried to imagine how he might have looked like around about my age, what kind of boy he would have been.

Daddy said that even though Mrs. McKenzie was a racist, she was not such a bad person. No one deserved to die in that manner.

In the past year, added Mummy, Mrs. McKenzie had changed. She had even told Mphiri to give us any spare vegetables from their patch, and she had stopped complaining about the chickens. Anyway, when the municipal police had come round, they had turned a blind eye because Daddy kept them well supplied with eggs. Mrs. McKenzie had not even made a fuss about the workshop. She was not the same person who had called us kaffirs when we had first moved in and who had kept calling the municipal police and the RSPCA over.

The superintendent of the RSPCA, Mrs. Van der Klerk came on a Saturday morning, with two black inspectors. She was very tall and looked down on everyone she was speaking to, even Daddy.

"I have come to inspect the dogs," she barked. "We have received numerous complaints about mistreatment at this address. We are entitled by law to carry out a spot check on any animal's welfare in any premises within the territory of Rho . . . Zimbabwe."

She said all this very fast as if she were firing bullets, and Daddy and Mummy just stood there looking up at her. Even Maphosa who always had something to say about white people was quiet.

"Where are the dogs?" asked the RSPCA superintendent.

Daddy pointed to Roxy and Tiger who were rolling about at her feet. The superintendent looked down, down at them. She looked very hard.

I knew what she was thinking. Black people don't keep dogs like Jack Russells. They keep skinny crossbreeds, big dogs who are kept hungry so that they are vicious, for guarding property. But Daddy had bought the dogs from a white couple in Montrose after he had read an article in *The Reader's Digest* that said Jack Russells, in spite of their size, made excellent guard dogs and required very little upkeep.

"The other dogs," she said at last. "The ones being mistreated."

Daddy and Mummy looked at each other.

"These are the only dogs we have," said Daddy.

The superintendent didn't believe Daddy because she walked right past him, round to the back of the house to check. The inspectors followed, then Mummy and Daddy, then Maphosa and me. The superintendent looked and looked. She knelt down and looked deep into the dogs' kennel. She even went to Rosanna's place and then to Maphosa's. Daddy's workshop, too. Finally she gave Roxy some pats on the head and said, "You have very happy dogs," and then she left.

But still, Mrs. McKenzie was always shouting and screaming at Mphiri, calling him a no good so-and-so, and since Mr. McKenzie Senior had died, Mphiri would disappear for days on end in his room. Rosanna said that Mphiri complained of headaches and sometimes his face was a strange color with bumps and swellings. Rosanna said that he was very obviously getting attacked by the spirit of Mr. McKenzie Senior who was quite angry to be dead and gone and to have his house taken over by the witch. "Idiot," said Maphosa quite angry. "Mphiri is an old man. Can you not see that with your two ever-busy eyes? He must be falling and knocking into things. He should be back home where there is not so much concrete and walling and other unfortunate objects."

5.

For a long time, Daddy told the story of the RSPCA lady and her inspectors to anyone who came to visit. He would always conclude by telling the visitor, if only that fearsome lady had gone over to Thorngrove; she would have had her work cut out for her with Mr. Rosset and his yard full of underfed crossbreeds.

In Thorngrove (the raw coloreds called it Groove Town), I had a black dog called Rex who would disappear and come back limping and bloody; he had been attacked, once again, by Old Man Rosset's pack of dogs down by the end of the road where the stream began. Sometimes at night the dogs barked so much you would think that all the thieves in the country had descended on that one house. Some people, like Mrs. Bernie, said that Old Man Rosset had the evil eye which could strike you dead. But other people, like Mrs. Green, argued that didn't make any sense: if Old Man Rosset had such a powerful weapon, why would he need a pack of dogs? The other people would answer back, they were there for when he was sleeping, but then evil eyes were not supposed to go to sleep. . . . One day Rex did not come back. Not the next day, not the day after that, either. I thought that Old Man Rosset had kidnapped him and added him to his pack.

It was Rosanna who let out the secret: Daddy gave Rex to someone at work because he was afraid of him catching rabies.

Even though Rex was vaccinated, Daddy still didn't trust that to work against all those dogs and their bites, especially after the city council issued a health warning about a rabies outbreak.

When Daddy was a boy, a relative in Nyamadhlovo was bitten by a dog and the relative had to be tied to a tree to keep him from attacking people.

Thorngrove was a colored suburb, and we had lived in a two-bedroom municipal brick house. The Soutter children who lived opposite us used to torment me. They were always lying in wait for me when I came home from primary school with Rosanna.

"Your mother is a kaffir, kaffir, kaffir!" they would shout and throw stones.

Once, Rosanna chased them right into their house and smacked one. They said all these things about Mummy even though their own grandmother, who sometimes just turned up at their doorstep and who they made sleep in the boy's kaya, was coal black and couldn't speak any English; they tried to tell people that she was the mother of their house-girl. Also, Mrs. Soutter was always coming round to ask for "some slices of bread," "a bit of sugar, my dear, if it's not too much trouble," "a pinch of salt," "a tomato or two" because Mr. Soutter, who was a train driver, was also a world-class drunkard. Mrs. Soutter would say things like Mummy was so lucky with skin like hers, whereas she suffered so much what with the sun burning her and all; it was her Scottish ancestry that was the culprit. Everyone knew that the Soutter girls straightened their hair; once Charmaine got caught in the rain and her hair caught such a dwinch that it looked like the hair of the golliwog I had received from the Christmas hamper at church. And the Soutter boys never grew their hair; it was always well cropped, very close to the scalp so that you couldn't see how cruess it was.

The best thing about Thorngrove was Mummy's cookery classes. Every Thursday evening, Daddy dropped Mummy and Granny Joseph at the Guild Hall opposite the fire station. Granny Joseph was very big, and she occupied the whole backseat of the car by herself. After every Thursday, Daddy complained bitterly about his springs and the alignment of his car.

Mummy spent two hours cooking, and when she came back home, she had parcels of food that she would carefully lay out on the dining-room table. Scotch eggs were the best; I would eat the baked sausage meat rolled in breadcrumbs casing and leave the hard-boiled egg for Daddy.

Mummy put on weight, and Daddy would tease her and call her *isidudla*, fatty, but then she went to the doctor and they discovered the cysts.

Mummy had three big files with all her recipes, and there were also pages with drawings and diagrams of very complicated table settings. There were forks, which were 1a, 1b, 1c, 1d . . . then the spoons . . . then the plates. . . . She would save some of her personal allowance from Daddy to buy dessert spoons, forks, dessert plates, soup plates, serving dishes, and she would put them in the display cabinet in the lounge and lock them inside.

The European food Mummy cooked at her classes required special ingredients, and if Mummy wanted to cook them at home, she would add them to the monthly grocery list. Sometimes the list would be very long, and Daddy would grumble about unnecessary expenditures as he pushed the trolley up and down OK Bazaars on the End of the Month Saturday. Sometimes he would leave Mummy and me stranded with the trolley in one of the aisles while he ran across the road to check and compare the price of one item at OK Bazaars with that at Woolworths. Even if there was only a difference of two or three cents, he would get the cheaper one. Sometimes he made two or three dashes across the road.

Mummy stopped going to the cooking classes because she said she was tired of Daddy always complaining and not appreciating anything she tried to do to better herself. Her recipes and complicated table settings found their way to Daddy's workshop where he used the blank sides to draw his technical diagrams of the insides of TVs and radios.

Mummy said Thorngrove was only a little bit better than Magwegwe Township.

I don't remember Magwegwe at all because I was very small, but she says that we were living in nothing more than a glorified shack and we were paying an exorbitant rent to a businessman who owned various bottle stores in the townships. The three of us lived in one room and used a paraffin stove for cooking so the room always smelt of oil. The toilet and shower were outside, and we shared them with three other families. Some people in the township didn't like having Daddy there because he was a colored.

Whenever Daddy talks about Magwegwe he always laughs. He finds Magwegwe very funny. He will say something like, "Those Magwegwe people, masters of improvisations. . . ." And he never tells the same story twice about Magwegwe; there is always another story waiting in the wings about any subject that will make his eyes water and his body bend over with laughter. I can tell that he misses Magwegwe. Every now and then he goes down there to fix someone's radio or TV.

Mummy does not miss Magwegwe at all. She did not find it at all funny.

Magwegwe was the place of her greatest humiliation, the place of my birth. Instead of being born on the right day like any normal baby, I chose to make my grand entrance three weeks early. And instead of giving warning signs so that she could go to the hospital in good time, no, I hijacked her when she was at Renkini, the bus depot, and made her give birth right there on the concrete floor with drivers, conductors, bus passengers, thieves, crooks, rapists . . . all watching what was going on between her legs and what kind of thing was coming out. Mummy would never forgive me for that. Or forgive Magwegwe. Or even forgive Daddy for making her live in Magwegwe.

Up to a year before we moved in, Baysview was a Whites-Only suburb. Ian Smith changed the law: he wanted to show the world that his government was a reasonable one and not racist by any stroke of the imagination. He said that people in Europe and America were being misinformed by communists and their sympathizers. There was no apartheid in Rhodesia.

"We are Pioneers," declared Daddy. Because of this we had to be brave and to take everything in stride—for example, when someone left a dead snake in the letter box, Daddy carefully took it away with a stick and said that no one had ever been bitten by a dead snake and that this was the work of some mischievous boys. Later, in the dustbin I found the white piece of paper Daddy had taken out with the snake. It said, SHIT HAPPENS, TO TERRS.

Mummy had her reservations about Baysview when she first saw it.

First of all there was the cemetery that our new house was only one road behind. Even though she is a good Christian, she still believes in ancestral spirits and ghosts.

Before independence the cemetery was full of dead soldiers from all the wars the whites had fought and there were also tiny graves where dead white babies lay. Once, I walked home from youth group at church, and instead of walking up along the road, I went down and walked among all the dead people and angels. After a while I got scared and I ran all the way out.

After independence, black people joined the whites, and the whites started going all the way up to Burnside in the kopjes to try and find a place where they would be left to Rest in Peace.

Daddy says, once you are dead, you are dead. That is it.

The railway track that cuts across Baysview also troubled Mummy straightaway. Every day at about three o'clock, we can hear the train that comes from South Africa rumbling onwards to the station. She says that the train gives her headaches, and very often she retreats into the bedroom and lies down with the door shut.

Daddy says that the train is bringing goods and thieves. Services.

Mummy approves of the fact that Baysview is so close to town; she just has to catch one omnibus, which drops her after twenty minutes directly in front of the Large City Hall, instead of her getting all squashed up in two or three Emergency Taxis when Daddy is at work and can't act as her chauffeur.

Once a month we all tshena in our finest clothes, and Daddy drives us into town at night to do Window Shopping. Sometimes Rosanna and even Maphosa come, too. Daddy parks the car at the end of Selborne Avenue opposite Thomas Meikles department store, and we walk along the pavements and look at all the brightly lit shopwindows. Meikles and then across the road Edgars, Truworths, Topics, and across another road Haddon and Sly and all the little shops in between. Maphosa entertains us with his comments about the white dolls in the windows and about the other families we pass who are also tshenied and doing Window Shopping. His best, most colorful comments are reserved for the couples we bump into who are busy fondling in corners.

"This is not your bedroom," Maphosa growls.

And if he is really mad he growls in deep, deep Ndebele. Once, one man who was wearing a white cowboy hat like J. R. Ewing's in *Dallas* threatened to put Maphosa in hospital in double-quick time. Daddy had to apologize profusely to the man and also give him one dollar to fully restore his manhood, which Maphosa had attacked in some choice Ndebele proverb. Maphosa was very angry with Daddy; he said that he would have knocked down the man with no problems. Daddy told Maphosa to keep his opinions to himself in future, but this has not stopped Maphosa. There is always something for him to comment on. He does not like city women who encase their bottoms in tight fitting trousers or paint their lips with bright red lipstick. These are the two things that make him most angry when we Window Shop, and it is best to cross the road if you spot them before he does.

The other good thing about Baysview is that it is close to the Drive Inn. Daddy likes going to the Drive Inn because it is a chance to take the Cortina for a drive and check the work he has done on it during the morning on Saturday. Sometimes we will not reach the Drive Inn because he hears a strange noise and turns "the Old Lady" back. We unpack the baskets of food and blankets and watch ZBC instead.

When we *are* at the Drive Inn, my heart beats very fast no matter what movie is showing. I sit outside on the gravel, leaning against the front of the car, covered with a blanket and eating the sandwiches Mummy has brought. Most of the time I'm not watching the movie on the giant screen but the groups of young white people who are calling out to each other, kissing, laughing, talking in their style.

"Hey Mike . . . !"

"Howzit!"

"What's happening down your neck of the woods?"

"Did you check . . . ?"

They are my movie. Daddy also likes the Drive Inn because it is near the airport and it has the best view for seeing British Airways going back to England.

Now, Baysview is full of blacks.

The McKenzies were the last remaining whites on our street.

6.

Mr. McKenzie Senior died in his sleep. Rosanna said that he was having such a good time in his dreams that he forgot to wake up. Maphosa gave her a bad look and said that the only thing that was called for was for Mphiri to be finally allowed to go home and rest. That old Bhunu had died in his own home not bothered by anyone; Mphiri should do so, too.

Daddy said that it was all that running and trying to be a young man that was probably the root cause of it all. Mr. McKenzie Senior's body had got worn out and given up the struggle. An old man could not compete with young men; he only ended up making a fool of himself. What more, there was the hair dye, earrings, and leather jacket Mphiri had mentioned to Rosanna that Mr. McKenzie Senior had started wearing just before his death. The man had obviously felt pressurized.

Mummy suspected Foul Play. She had never heard of someone dying like that. What had he eaten the night before, for instance? And look how happy Mrs. McKenzie seemed. She was not even dressed in mourning.

Daddy said that Mrs. McKenzie was not even white. She was a Cape colored, and everybody said that Mr. McKenzie Senior had picked her straight off the streets. Mummy pointed out that she must be reverting back to her old ways; day in, day out, the gate was clanging open and shut, all types of men coming in and out.

As far as we could make out, there had been no wake or gathering of sympathizers at the McKenzies. Even though Daddy and Mummy had had only a very limited contact with Mr. McKenzie Senior, they went to the funeral out of respect. When I got home from school, they were still talking about the disgraceful way Mrs. McKenzie had behaved.

"She was smelling of beer," Mummy said. "She couldn't even stand properly."

Daddy said that there had been very few people there and the boy had come over and thanked him for coming. He had introduced his mother, who had also come from South Africa, to them.

"A very nice woman," Mummy said. "Very good. She even shook my hand. Sarah. Sarah Price, yes, that's it."

Mrs. McKenzie had then come pouncing on them, talking nonsense, accusing the boy of trying to throw her out of the house and already plotting to get his hands on her rightful inheritance, saying that he and his mother were spreading lies all over Bulawayo about her.

"She even tried to attack him with her claws," said Mummy. "She had to be dragged away."

Daddy went back to work, and Mummy went to rest because she had a bad headache.

I started my homework. I did not want to write about "My Holidays," the essay assignment my teacher had given us that morning on the very first day of term in my new school. I did the long division, which was easy.

I picked up my English essay book, opened the page, and wrote the title "My Holidays." I thought and thought. I had to fill two pages with "My Holidays." I knew what some of the girls were going to write about. They had already started talking when Miss Turner wrote the title on the blackboard: Natal and Durban, Cape Town, Okavango Swamps, and even

London. My holidays: 16 Jacaranda Avenue, Bayview, Bulawayo. But I wrote something else. I went *away.*

When I finished, I went outside and started reading on the
veranda. Sue Barton, Student Nurse, had just met the intern,
Dr. Bill Barry, when the commotion started. The shouting was
coming from the McKenzies. It was happening right by the
gate. Mrs. McKenzie was holding on the latch, rattling it up
and down.

The boy was leaning against the Datsun Sunny with his
hands crossed on his chest. He let Mrs. McKenzie shout and
shout, and then he got into the Datsun Sunny and drove away.
Mrs. McKenzie kept shouting after the car. Rosanna, who was
coming back from the tuck shop at the corner, said that she had
seen a white woman in the passenger seat.

Mummy who'd been woken up by all the noise said, "Look
at how she's continuing. That woman is only asking for
trouble."

We could still hear Mrs. McKenzie from the veranda, and
when I stood on the clay pot that had the elephant's ear plant
growing in it, I could see her. She was already in her dressing
gown. Her hair was all tangled up. But we didn't tell the police
any of this because Daddy said it was best to mind one's own
business; once you became a part of a police case, it was very
hard to extricate yourself out of it.

I thought that if only all this had happened during the holidays, I might have made use of it in my essay.

7

For the first day of school, Aunty Reggie had straightened my hair in her kitchen. She left the straightening cream on for too long because she was busy talking to Mummy about something that was happening at church with one of the girls who was rumored to be pregnant and so should not be graduated.

"It's burning!" I shouted, jumping from the chair and dashing to the sink.

The back of my head was covered in blisters, and when Daddy saw them, he asked Mummy, did she and her friend intend to kill his child or what? "They must see that she is a colored," replied Mummy.

At my old school the real colored girls had called me names because I was not light-skinned and I had a wide nose. My new school was a former whites only, Group A school. I had passed the entrance exam.

Daddy twisted his mouth; he didn't like it when Mummy talked about coloreds and blacks. Although everyone classified him as a colored (he was light-skinned, had good hair and a straight nose), he didn't see himself as one. He didn't talk like a Barham Green or Thorngrove colored and his Ndebele was perfect. He was proud of his mother who had brought him up in Nyamandhlovo. His father was a white farmer in the area who had agreed to have his name on the birth certificate and who had paid for his education.

Mummy made me practice all the way in the bus, "good morning," "good afternoon," using my best European accent.

We reported at the headmistress's office. The headmistress, Mrs. Jameson, smiled very sweetly when I said, "Good morning, headmistress," and even commented on my pronunciation. She called in the deputy headmistress and asked me to read some words from a piece of a paper that she pushed towards me: "The Annual General Meeting of the PTA." The words were getting entangled in my mouth with my spit. The deputy headmistress stood by the doorway smiling with her hands crossed.

"Hmmmm, that's quite a lardy-dardy accent you have there," the deputy headmistress said, "just like Her Majesty, the queen, no less. We'll have to be on our toes with the likes of you in our midst now."

The headmistress made a noise like a pig grunting.

"Okay, come along then," she said, getting up from behind her desk. She turned to Mummy and said, "You may now leave Mrs. Bishop. Linda is quite fine now."

Mummy opened her mouth to say something, but then she said something else. "Good-bye, Lindiwe. Good-bye, Mrs. Jameson."

Mummy had pressed her tongue down hard on my name, and I knew that she was trying to give the headmistress a message. I watched her turn round and walk out of the door. Seeing her leave made me feel tearful.

"Come along, Linda. You must not keep Miss Turner waiting any longer. She is your class teacher."

I followed Mrs. Jameson along the corridor and down the stairs until we reached class 1B. She tapped on the door and without waiting pushed it open. She stepped inside. "Sorry to disturb you Miss Turner, but we have a late comer. I've been assured that this is a one-off. She will apologize. Come along,

Linda. This is your new teacher, Miss Turner. Do you have something to say to her?"

I stood looking down at my shoes.

"Linda?"

I looked up at Miss Turner, and she raised an eyebrow.

"I am sorry, Miss Turner, for my late arrival."

The class burst out laughing.

"Shush, girls. You'll sit over there." Miss Turner pointed. "Tracey will help you settle. Hush now, girls."

All the girls were saying, "I am sorry, Miss Turner, for my late arrival." Some of them were pinching their noses.

"Enough girls," said Miss Turner, clapping her hands. "We have a lot of work to do. Continue reading, Dawn."

"She smells."

"Shhhh, Tracey, she'll hear"

"So what, she does smell."

"It's what she puts in her hair."

"She doesn't bath."

"Tracey!"

"Actually *they* don't bath."

"You're being racialistic."

"I'm just being honest."

I pretended that I hadn't heard. Anyway I didn't care. I made myself think of something else. Mrs. McKenzie and the funeral of Mr. McKenzie Senior, which was taking place later in the morning, came into my head.

In the three years we had known her, she had worn very short skirts and white stiletto heels. She would sit on her veranda smoking, painting her nails. Or she sunbathed. Sometimes she took the stereo outside and put the music so high that the chickens squawked and squawked. When drunk, she had stumbled towards the fence and mumbled things like, "I know you're spying on me, you blacks."

"I don't want to sit next to her. My mother said I should tell Miss Turner. It's not fair. She's probably got lice or something, all that stinky oil in her hair."

That was Geraldine with her melodious voice. In singing class she had all the solo parts. She had the Voice of an Angel. You would never think that anything ugly and discordant would come out of that mouth, but in the week that I had been her classmate, I had learnt my lesson.

My ears were burning. I sat very still. If I turned round, then she would know that I had heard her.

"Siss man."

I could see her shifting and squirming in her seat, thinking of all the lice crawling about in my hair. Maybe I should shake my head to give her a real fright.

"Girls . . ."

Miss Turner handed back the essays. I got a B plus.

She asked Debbie, Teresa, and me to read our essays out loud to the class. Debbie's was full of dolphins and beach games. Teresa's was chockablock with wildlife.

I opened my mouth. "My Holidays."

"My Holidays" burst out the whole class.

"Shush, girls, carry on Linda."

"My Holidays. Some days I stayed at my house, but on other days I went on adventures with Nancy Drew. Sometimes I visited at Nurse Sue Barton's hospital to see what was going on there. . . ."

"But that's cheating," said Tracey as soon as I had finished. "She didn't really *go* anywhere."

"Not cheating," said Miss Turner. "She was creative in her interpretation of the assignment."

"It's still cheating," said Tracey.

"Tracey, do not use that word in here. I have already said it is not cheating. She went on holiday in her imagination."

"She's weird."

"Tracey Edmonds!"

In February a new girl arrived. I watched her standing next to Miss Turner. Her skirt rose above the knee (which was against the school rules and would earn her detention), and her white shirt fit tightly around her breasts. Her hair was permed and reached her shoulders; she was wearing it in a ponytail. Her eyebrows were plucked and her lips shone with lip gloss. She was standing like a model, and when I looked down, I saw that she was wearing proper shoes with real heels and not the rubber tractor ones from Bata's school range. She corrected Miss Turner about how to pronounce her name.

"No, not like that," she said. "Bree Jet."

And Miss Turner, who had thrown a rubber duster at Geraldine the previous week for talking, actually said, "Sorry, my dear, Bree Jet."

She was born in Britain, which she says makes her more British than Geraldine and the others. She speaks real European English, which is sometimes hard to understand. All the white girls want to be her friend, but she doesn't have any time for them.

She has chosen me.

The first thing she said to me was "Why do you talk like that in front of them? Your Real Voice is nice."

Her father is a businessman with very high-up connections. She lives in Morningside in a mansion. She doesn't know Ndebele, and when I went to her house, I saw the maids exchanging looks when she said something. In Ndebele, one of them said, "Listen to the little white mistress giving us poor Africans orders."

She says that white people in Britain smell. They smell because they don't bath; they don't bath because it is too cold.

She told me her secret about her name. She changed it in Britain. Bridget was too common a name; anybody could be a Bridget. Bridgette has personality and they are few and far between.

I looked at her as if she was mad, and she laughed and said you could do anything you liked overseas.

8.

The Chronicle informed Bulawayo that Magistrate Court 101 was packed day in, day out. Even though Mr. McKenzie had admitted his crime, justice should be seen to be done. Everybody wanted to see Mr. McKenzie. The new telephone at home rang all the time. Mummy would put it down and off it would go again—*trrrring, trrrring*—all Mummy's friends wanted to have updates. Being the McKenzies neighbors, they thought we had Inside Information. Sometimes Mummy would get a bit annoyed; when she would put the phone down, she would say to the wall, "Does Ma David think that we were cherished friends with them, oh?"

Sometimes she thought that she was being accused: Why hadn't she gone out to save Mrs. McKenzie? Why had all the residents of Number 16 Jacaranda Avenue been sleeping so soundly when such a terrible thing was happening at Number 18? They were accomplices, maybe.

Her Monday afternoon Bible study group, which was at our house that week, was attended by all its members, even Mrs. Sithole who was recovering from a knee operation. They stayed much longer than usual after they had dissected the Bible, discussing sinners and the devil that could live among us, even next door. Mrs. Khumalo and Mrs. Sithole asked Mummy to show them her beautiful vegetable patch. The rest of the group followed. Prayers were said by the fence, and the house next door was all the time standing there, looking innocent and untouched as though nothing at all had happened there.

"Guilty," announced *The Chronicle* five weeks after the trial began.

When Mummy was at one of her church meetings, I took out the page from *The Chronicle* that I had put in my pink handbag. I sat on the bed and looked at his picture for a long time. I put my finger on his bent head and moved it all the way down to his feet. I looked at them. They were bare. Where had they put his tackies? I traced his foot. And then I went back up again and touched his hair.

I went outside and found Rosanna and Maphosa having a full-blown argument.

"He will not be hanged," declared Rosanna. "A white man be allowed to hang from a rope? Never."

Maphosa had been sweeping the driveway, and he was leaning against the broom. He picked it up and jabbed it towards Rosanna who was on her way out.

"You are heavily colonized" was Maphosa's answer. "White or not white, the law is the same for everyone now. He will not hang because it is relatives he has burnt. It is only a domestic disturbance, a Category B murder. If it was you or me, that white man would be leaving this world, for sure."

Rosanna laughed out loud. "What! A white man die because of killing a gardener and a house girl! You are dreaming."

Maphosa became very angry. He shouted at Rosanna. He threw the broom at her but she dodged its attack.

"You are stupid," he yelled. "An ignoramus. Fighters died during The Struggle to liberate you and look at you, completely colonized. Nobody died so you can go about mawhoring with lipsticks and short skirts and. . . ."

He saw me and went to the back, muttering to himself things in deep Ndebele.

When I asked him, Daddy said that there would be no exeution simply because the crime had been committed by a minor.

"Maphosa must go," Mummy told Daddy that evening.

She had said this many other times before.

"We have done our best," she continued with her Christian voice. "On my way back from church, I could hear him from all the way down the street, right by the shops. He must go and try something like farming. His people are always calling for him."

Then she started humming and singing The Lord Is My Shepherd.

Last month I heard her tell Aunty Gertrude, who came from Botswana in order to keep an eye on her because she was recovering from the operation, that Daddy felt guilty and sorry. He had fought for the Rhodesians. He was sorry for what had happened to Maphosa. But, she argued, what choice did he have back then? He was a man with a wife and child, responsibilities. He could not just take off to the hills. That was for young men like Maphosa and company who were quite free to do something of that nature. Daddy was a colored and he had to obey the law; he would be imprisoned if he was caught dodging his call-up and it would be very easy to catch him because the post office gave all the details to the army. And anyway, Daddy had never fired a single bullet; he was fixing radios and other equipment. And as for what had happened to Maphosa, that had nothing to do with Daddy; was it Daddy who had stuck his bayonet into Maphosa's right eye? No, not at all. And knowing Maphosa, it could very well be a self-inflicted injury. She did not trust Maphosa's heart. Not a single bit. And, what more, she strongly suspected him of taking dagga; how come his good eye was so red all the time?

Aunty Gertrude who is a midwife told her not to worry herself unduly. Things would resolve themselves.

When I was bringing the tea, she exclaimed, "Oh my goodness me, look at you Lindiwe! Last year you were only so high and now . . . and what a well-mannered girl you are, too."

From the passageway I heard her say to Mummy, "But you must keep an eye on our Lindiwe here."

As soon as Aunty Gertrude left, Mummy called me into her room and told me never to converse with Maphosa, never to go into his room, and to exercise modesty at all times.

The problem was Mummy still believed all the stories that had been in *The Chronicle* and *The Rhodesia Herald* during the war about the terrorists.

I once said "the terrorists" to Mummy and Daddy, and Daddy said, "Nationalists, Lindiwe, Freedom Fighters."

Mummy scolded Daddy, "She will go around saying these things."

"Independence is on its way," countered Daddy who did not seem at all concerned. "Mrs. Thatcher and Lord Carrington are making sure of that at Lancaster House; they will make Smith see sense."

The Chronicle said that the terrorists did barbaric things to villagers who didn't support them, like cutting off their noses and ears and burning them in huts while making people sing and dance as the flames rose higher and higher. Daddy said that this was just Rhodesian Propaganda.

At the height of the war, Uncle Silius managed to make it out of Gwayi communal lands, which are over one hundred kilometers from Bulawayo. Two of his sons had gone to the hills and he had come to town to try and find a job. He said Smith's soldiers were doing terrible, terrible things down there:

villagers were being herded into camps so that crops and cattle were dying in the lands because there was no one to look after them; pregnant women's stomachs were being slit open and their babies bayoneted; young boys were being used as mine detectors in front of army vehicles, and other kinds of things were being done to young girls, who were kidnapped when they went out to fetch water, which burnt up their insides and destroyed their womanhood for life.

Mummy didn't like too much talk about the war. She said you never knew who could be listening and on which side of the fence they might be. People had long memories. When Daddy once came back from his call-up, standing in full view outside our gate in Thorngrove, wearing his uniform, they had a big fight. Even here in Baysview, where it was all quiet, anything could happen. Garden boys and garden girls could turn out to be related to so-and-so, who had been out in the bush, up in the hills over in Mozambique, and come victory, well, better safe than sorry. . . .

Mummy is quite sure that Maphosa has an AK-47 hidden under his room and that one of these days. . . . Everybody had been talking about how the boys had not handed in all their weapons to the British and Australian soldiers at the assembly points like it had been agreed at Lancaster House. The events at Entumbane had shown that this was the case. There were countless weapons and grenades in the hands of former fighters, and there was talk that arms caches had been found in some farms owned by Nkomo.

Trouble seemed to be fermenting again.

9.

After the fire and the arrest, Maphosa tried to reason with Mphiri. I had just come back from netball practice at school when I saw Maphosa leaning over the fence. I stood around the corner, watching. I picked up Roxy and held him to keep him from barking; he started licking my face.

"Baba Mphiri, baba Mphiri!" Maphosa called.

After a while Mphiri hobbled over to the gap in the fence, which the McKenzies were meant to have fixed a long time ago. Maphosa had brought along a stool. He pushed it through the gap. Mphiri sat down and waited for Maphosa's lecture.

"Now, mudala. You can finally go back home and rest. You are free."

Mphiri whose hair is white, white said, "No, umntanami, I am quite happy here. The young master will come back. He is a good young man. He will come home again I am sure."

I could feel the strength of Mphiri's faith in his old voice.

Maphosa raised his voice. "What are you saying, mudala? That boy is in jail. He will stay there till he dies. Your children are waiting for you. You must go back to your homestead to share your wisdom."

Mphiri begged, "No, no, my son, do not be angry, but you are wrong. My children do not have need for me. I am only a nuisance, an extra mouth to feed. No, it is good and proper that I stay here. I will tend the vegetables. Do you see this jacket I am wearing? The young master gave it to me before all the problems. Brand-new. All the way from South Africa."

Maphosa kept on arguing and reasoning and arguing, and Mphiri started weeping against the fence, asking Maphosa to please forgive and understand him.

Even though I was very hungry and dying for the crunchy peanut butter sandwiches I always have after practice, I stayed where I was. My grumbling stomach disturbed Roxy, but luckily when he struggled out of my arms, he ran off to the other side of the house. My face was wet with his spit.

I saw Daddy come out of the workshop. He was holding a part he was fixing and he was obviously annoyed.

"Maphosa, leave the old man alone," he said.

Daddy waited until Maphosa moved away from the fence.

"Better in the bush," Maphosa muttered.

Mummy, who had come out of the house, heard him. "If that's the case," she said with her hands crossed, "feel free to go. The bush is waiting."

"No, no, Mama," Maphosa said. "It is not like that. It is just that matters were simple there. Kill and be killed. One settler, one bullet. Now people are even angry that they are liberated and can make their own decisions. They are grumbling that the white man took care of them and now they are being left to fend for themselves."

He stood there looking at Mummy, and then he raised his hand and started rubbing his bad eye.

I went inside the house and thought about Maphosa, how annoyed he is by the fact that white people have been given the vote.

"We did not fight for one vote, one settler," I had heard him argue with Rosanna.

Daddy told me in private that this was not strictly true. White people got much more than one vote each: Lancaster House had awarded them twenty seats in parliament even

Irene Sabatini

though there were only about twenty-nine thousand registered voters in the white electoral roll. The over two million voters in the common electoral roll only got eighty seats. And whites could be registered as voters in both rolls.

As far as Maphosa is concerned, all the leftovers should go back to England; there is no such thing as a white African.

10.

Mphiri's faith has been rewarded. Over a year and a half has passed and Ian McKenzie is going to be released. *The Chronicle* says that the verdict has been quashed because of a successful appeal. New evidence was presented to the court concerning the validity of the confession.

Maphosa and Rosanna argue about this, too. Rosanna says that definitely he will not be released because he is a murderer and he has killed a white woman; Maphosa says once again Rosanna reveals her unending ignorance: that boy will definitely be released *because* he is a murderer of a white woman. It will make white people feel very confused about the government and its intentions; they will not know which way the wind is blowing. "Let them start murdering each other," says Maphosa. "Maybe then we can have our land at last."

Daddy says that prison can reform some people; it can make them realize the error of their ways so that they make amends.

Mummy looks at him and says all she knows is that now we will have to live with a murderer in our midst and then she starts humming. This is Mummy's way of telling Daddy "I told you so." She has been urging him for a long time now to start looking for a new house in one of the better suburbs. A better suburb to Mummy is one where there are higher quality white people and no apostolics. She wants to move further north. But Daddy says that we can't afford to move; the rates alone will kill us. Mummy doesn't believe him and thinks that this is yet another example of Daddy's tightness with money when it concerns her.

After dinner I go to my room and slowly move the dressing table. I remove the lighter that I have taped to the back of the mirror. I sit down on my bed and look at it in my palm. I am breathing deeply, in and out, like when Dr. Esat asks me to as he moves the stethoscope around on my chest. I close my eyes, which makes me feel dizzy.

Roxy found the lighter somewhere in the vegetable patch. It had clinked on the driveway, and I was surprised by that because Roxy usually had a poor lizard dangling from his teeth, which would only make a dull slapping sound when Roxy flung it on the stone slabs. I stooped down, picked up the object. It was wet with saliva and dirt. And then I ran water over it and I saw what it was.

It had been months since the sentencing. He was in jail now. I chanted the old playground claim, *finders, keepers; losers, weepers,* over and over again, but the more I held it in my hands the more it became what it was, evidence. And I had it.

He came today.

We all saw him.

He stood outside the gate and looked up at the house.

He stood there just looking.

Mphiri came out and opened the gate.

Maphosa said that there will never be peace now.

Rosanna, who is pregnant, was quiet.

Mummy said he looked like a criminal. I didn't think that she was right about that.

*   *   *

He helped us push start the car. The Cortina stalled again at the gate. I got out of the car and saw him standing by his gate, looking. I felt shy to have my back turned from him, my head bent down, my bottom up, straining my weight against the car.

"I'll give you a hand," he said.

I hadn't even heard him walking up.

Our hands were side by side.

The car finally started and I got inside. Daddy leaned his head out of the window and thanked him.

"It's nothing, Mr. Bishop. Glad to help."

In the car, Daddy looked at his windscreen mirror and sighed. I was thinking of his hands. I was thinking of the lighter in them. The lighter that said Rhodesian Army on it. Hot and burning.

When I came home, I took out my diary, which was wedged in between the mattress and the headboard. I had bought it in March in Kingstons at half price with my pocket money. It had a picture of a ballerina on the cover and a lock and key. I found the date and put a big X in the space for writing. I counted; it was twenty-one days since he had been released. Then I locked it up again and put the key back in my pencil case. I wasn't supposed to have any secrets from my parents.

And then I took the lighter out from behind the mirror. I stood in the room trying to think of another place. I thought that maybe I would put it in my pink handbag, which was too childish for me now and which I kept hanging in the cupboard. I was opening the cupboard door when I heard Mummy's footsteps, and I shoved it under my pillow.

"Lindiwe," Mummy says. "Our interaction with that boy must be kept to the strictest minimum. If he comes here when there are no adults around, you must not let him in. I have already informed Rosanna and Maphosa. Is that understood?"

"Yes, Mummy, I understand."

Mummy is now treasurer of the Women's Group. Monday and Wednesday afternoons she is away at meetings.

Mphiri says that the young master is sleeping in the boy's kaya with him. Mphiri scratches his head and says that this is not right. The young master sleeps right on the floor without even a mattress. He sleeps on the grass mat. Maphosa says that maybe now Mphiri will see reason and go back home. Even white people are afraid of Amadhlozi, the spirits who want to avenge a grave wrongdoing. Rosanna does not believe Mphiri. A white person would never do that. She cannot even imagine them using the same toilet as Mphiri. Mphiri is just getting too old. White people need electricity. She cannot even think of a white man sitting down to light a paraffin stove.

Christmas passed, the new year came, and things were normal; everyone seemed to just accept his presence. Nobody made any comments about him, and nothing bad seemed to be happening to anyone. Maybe Mrs. McKenzie's spirit wasn't interested in doing anyone any harm. Maybe the heat had dried it up, sapped away all its energy (and anger), like it was doing to everything else.

Every evening, Daddy was glued to the TV rain forecast report and the graphs on the level of the dams. Hillside dam, which we had visited at school, was not even half-full. The drought wasn't showing any signs of ending. The city council tightened its water rationing measures. The use of hosepipes was completely banned, even if you were using borehole water. Maphosa had to water the vegetables with a bucket.

Sometimes he would drive out of his gate at the same time in the morning as us. Maybe he had found a job. It was funny to me that he would never overtake Daddy even though Daddy drove so slow. It was like a mark of respect. Sometimes sitting in the back, I was tempted to turn my head but I never did.

And then, it was a Saturday morning and I was standing at the bus stop, getting nervous because the bus was already thirty minutes late. I was going to be late for the netball match if I didn't leave straightaway. It was an interschools quarter final, and we were taking on the Convent Girls who had beaten us badly last year. Everybody on the team wanted revenge.

He took the corner, passing me, and then he reversed.

He rolled down his window and called out, "Do you want a lift?"

I got into the yellow Datsun Sunny.

I put my bag on the floor on top of my feet.

I put my hands under my mauve skirt, and then I placed them on my lap. I wished that I wasn't wearing my tracksuit bottoms under my skirt. I looked like a country girl.

He drove all the way down Jacaranda Road, up the bridge onto Acacia Drive, where all the acacia trees along the road were in bloom, their yellow flowers making me think of how when Daddy got called to fix a fault in Hwange National Park, he saw giraffes feeding on the flowers and said that they looked like very tall, elegant ladies ruminating about life. And then he annoyed Mummy by saying, "Not like you big Manyano ladies."

I looked straight through the front windscreen, and then my neck began to hurt so I turned and looked out my window.

There wasn't much to see because most of the houses were
behind durawalls, except for the white double story, which
was at the corner of Marula Avenue and Main Street. When
I had first seen it, I thought that it must be full of children
running up and down stairs, laughing and screaming, something like in *The Sound of Music*. But only an old white man
lived there who was rumored to have shaken hands with
Hitler.

I had the strange feeling that my head was shaking, vibrating.

"Don't be nervous. Lindiwe, isn't it?"

I was shocked that he knew my name, that he had said it out
aloud to me. I liked the way it sounded coming from him.

"Yes, Mr. McKenzie," I said.

"*Mr.* McKenzie," he almost shouted. "Now, you're trying to
be funny, heh. Ian. Just Ian. I'm not an old bally."

"Ian," I said in my head.

I didn't know why I had blurted out "Mr. McKenzie" and
why I kept thinking of him as that. Was it because he had been
in jail and had experienced things that adults do? Or was it
because he was so big and made me feel like a child who didn't
know much about life?

I didn't think it was because he was white that I was a little
frightened of him. Mummy was always telling anyone who
would listen that when I was a baby I would wail if cotton wool
or a white person happened to touch me.

We drove in silence all along Main Street, all down Fourth
Avenue, and then at the corner of Fourth Avenue and Borrow
Street, I said, "You can drop me here. I'll walk the rest of the
way."

He didn't say anything.

I opened the door and said thank you.

He said, "Here, your bag and good luck."

*　*　*

The second time we passed each other along the escalators at Haddon and Sly. He was going up. I was going down. We looked at each other. That was all.

The third time was at the Grasshut. It was dark inside, and I didn't see him until he was out front at the till paying his bill. He was taking money out of his wallet, looking right at me. I was with Bridgette and she said, "Isn't that . . . ?"

The fourth time was when it really began.

I was at the National Museum in the Minerals Hall collecting information for my science project. He was sitting on one of the benches lining the glass wall. I saw him first because his face was turned away, looking down.

Just as I was about to walk away, he turned and said, "You again."

I stood there in my school uniform not knowing what to do or say.

He got up. "Would you like something to drink?" he asked. "I'm thinking of going down to the kiosk to get a Coke."

Without thinking, I said, "Yes, thank you."

This time I noticed things about him: how his hair was cut so short it looked as if he had meant to shave it and then changed his mind at the very last minute, how his hands were bruised.

He saw me looking at his hands and said, "So did you win?"

The netball match had been weeks ago, so I didn't understand at first.

"Your netball," he said.

"Oh, yes. Fifteen to three."

I had a Coke, too, and we sat there just sipping, drinking.

After that we walked back down. We stopped a bit at the mammals' exhibit where all the stuffed animals are. He made a funny noise, as if he was trying to let out a laugh but was choking on it.

"My word, this brings back memories."

We were looking at two lions tearing apart a baby antelope. Its stomach was spilling out and blood was everywhere.

"Bawled my eyes out when I saw that. My old man gave me a good clip around the ear, a kick in the backside plus. What an embarrassment I was, a damn prissy boy. And the old man, a fricking Selous Scout. What a git."

The words *Selous Scout* echoed in the chamber so full of blood and entrails. I was glad that there was no one else to hear them.

"The Selousie," Daddy says on one of the days when he re-members the war and something takes him back there, maybe a newspaper article or a TV program. "Those guys were some-thing else, I tell you."

I can hear fear and wonder in his voice and also the way he stops a bit, his mouth moving silently as if he is arguing with him-self: Should he go on? Should he just stop right there? He has said quite enough already, but then his mouth opens and the words come spilling out. He doesn't look at anyone when he is talking like this. He looks at the war. He is talking with the war.

"You don't want to get on the wrong side of them. They are sharp. Sharp! And they know the bush. You put a Selous Scout in the bush with nothing. Nothing, no water, food, weapons, nothing, and I'm telling you that is how they are trained, dropped in the bush by helicopter and not city, town bush. Bush, bush with *nothing*. Seven days they must survive, just like that. Anyone who survives that, you can become a recruit.

Just to be a recruit. We ordinary soldiers, you meet a Scout with his FN submachine gun, you don't even look. Forget it. Those guys disciplined, sure, but anything can trigger them. *Anything.* And mind you, they don't hesitate. Trained machines. Afraid of nothing. *Nothing!* Even the boys respect them. One Selousie can take out thirty, forty, I'm telling you, in no time at all. And the African ones, the worst or should I say, best. Masters in disguise, infiltration. How many went right into guerrilla camps and took those boys out like that. And when . . ."

Daddy had stopped talking when he saw Maphosa opening the gate.

Outside, we walked through the park, all the way up to the main entrance.

"I'll give you a ride," he said.

He dropped me in South Grove by the cemetery; as he was pulling away he stopped the car and shouted through the window—"Hey, Lindiwe, meet you here tomorrow round about this time"—and then he drove away before waiting for my answer.

I took the bus the rest of the way home.

It was only later, lying on my bed, that it came to me—not once sitting there with him did I think of him as the boy who might have done that terrible thing. Not once.

11.

Thirteen missionaries have been killed in Esigodini by dissidents. The dissidents went into the farmhouse with pangas and hoes. One boy and two other people, who pretended to be dead after they had been hacked by pangas, escaped. The boy hid in the bathroom and crawled out of the window and ran all the way in the dark. The dissidents even killed the babies. The mothers said the Our Father as their babies were held high and dropped onto the floor. Just like the terrorists used to do.

Maphosa says that it is all lies. He says that this is a setup. Mugabe is trying to create trouble in Matabeleland so that he can launch a full-out attack. He is impatient to have his one-party state. He wants to crush all opposition. Look how Tongogara was eliminated; if he was still alive, he would be in charge, not that little man. Maphosa says these killings are the work of Shonas posing as dissidents. True ZIPRA fighters would only attack military targets. When I ask him how he know this, he looks at me as though I have accused him of lying. "You can believe what you want," he says. "The truth is the truth."

Geraldine Ainsley is immigrating to England. Her father says that there is no future for whites here. "They will hunt us all down," he says. "This is only the beginning. All this so-called reconciliation and working yourself to the bone adds up to a baby smashed by munts onto a concrete floor. No ways, man, are we staying here."

"We're reclaiming our British citizenship," says Geraldine, tossing her hair. "We have brand-new passports. Thank goodness for that."

During break time she hands out the invitations to her farewell party. Everyone is invited, even me. And Bridgette, of course. On the cover there is a picture of her family: Mum, Dad, Geraldine all waving and smiling brightly and the two poodles leaping up trying to catch the speech bubble that exclaims "Cheers."

"Just wait," says Bridgette. "They'll come back running when they get a dose of reality. No servants, no gardens, just some horrible poky little flat in east London, where they will have to rub shoulders with so many Indians they will think they are in India, and the cold *brrrrr!* They think that the royal family will be waiting at the airport to receive them with open arms, they've got a big shock coming. I give them two months, *mmmm,* not even that. Look at her, do you think she has the slightest idea of how to make her own bed?"

At assembly, Mrs. Jameson asks us to please say special prayers for all those who have died out in Esigodini; those poor people were only trying to do good in the world.

In *The Chronicle,* spread out across the two middle pages, are six coffins lying side by side in front of the altar inside the cathedral. Two of them, one at each end, are very small.

In the evening news we hear the priest say that only love will heal the deep wounds in Zimbabwe.

12.

"What a right cock-up," he says.

If no one will take him on here, give him a job or an apprenticeship, something in mechanics, he'll go back down south, try his luck; there are opportunities there even for someone like him; he can pick up from where he left off.

We are at the park by the aviary.

"That's a Cardinal Woodpecker," he says pointing. "That one over there, and over there—yes, that frisky one—that's a Hoopoe, now take a look at that Hadeda. You know the best place to watch birds? Down by the sewage works, over at Aiselby Farm by the Umguza Dam. When I was a lightie, my old man was the manager, and man, there were manigi birds: Cape Shoveler, Pink-backed Pelican, Pochards, Teals, you name it. It was like you were in blimming paradise or something."

He bursts out laughing. "Jeez, I'm full of bullshit. Big-time bullshit."

"Look at these poor buggers," he says. "Just like Khami."

It's the first time he's mentioned the prison.

He goes to the fence, grabs it. "Yah, just like that blimming hellhole."

He turns back to look at me. "Although, to tell the truth, I didn't spend *that* much time in there. Three months, tops. Most of it I was over at Esigodini doing fricking farming. Eeesh,

I even got promoted for good behavior. By the time I got to Khami, I had put on some major muscle what with all that hoeing and shit. Check."

He pushes the sleeves of his shirt up, bulges his arms. Then he cracks into a smile. "Jeez, man, my *This Is Your Life,* heh. So how about you, what's happening?"

"I'm going to a party," I say. "This Saturday."

"A party, heh, birthday?"

"No, a girl is leaving. They're going to England."

"And another one bites the dust. So tell me about it on Monday, heh."

13.

Geraldine's house is right on top of a hill in Matsheumhlope, carved into stones.

Geraldine says that in the topmost room you can see most of Bulawayo.

Three fountains and two pools.

Fourteen rooms and balconies.

Fireplaces.

Spiraling stairs of stone and teak.

Game room with a pool table and a TV in the wall.

Geraldine has her own lounge next to her bedroom and Barbie dolls scattered everywhere; a huge dressing table with perfumes and jewelry boxes.

Today, there is a braai and swimming and *Clem Tholet's Greatest Hits* blaring on the stereo. The girls are all in their bikinis, in the water or sunbathing, smoothing on suntan lotion. The boys are running around playing rugby; the girls giggle whenever a boy passes by. "He's nice," "he's cute," or "he's a dof," they whisper to each other. The men are by the braai, looking after the sizzling boerewor sausages and T-bone steaks, and in the gazebo where there is a fully stocked bar.

Bridgette and I are standing by the pool sipping Fantas. We didn't bring any costumes.

One of the old men at the bar calls out: "hey, you two girls,

good thing you're not taking to the water, what with those am-
abeles you'll sink like anything. You black girls are overdevel-
oped; wait, by the time you're twenty, they'll be hanging to your
knees like the grannies at the Reserves. Boy, can they flap those
things over their shoulders; give you a technical knockout if
you're standing too close.

The men laugh. The girls laugh. And the boys shriek and
hoot.

Bridgette and I go to the game room where the boys follow.
Three of them.

"Hey, kaffir girls!" the fat one shouts. "Check this out!"

They pull down their shorts, shake their bums, and fart;
they turn around and shake their things. They rush out of the
door, shrieking, their pants undone.

"Stupid idiots," says Bridgette. "If I were them, I would
be ashamed to show those things in public. Earthworms are
bigger. Now Joseph's, that's a real mamba."

"Bridgette!"

Joseph is one of her boyfriends. He is a sixth-former at
Milton. He is the only black boy on the rugby team.

"Oh, oh, Lins, don't look at me like that!"

She bends over, collapsing with laughter. She claps her
hands.

"You look like you've just had an electric shock. Oh, I wish
I had a camera. Yes, I have indeed seen Joseph's missile. Yes, I
have even touched it. I'm not a virgin, thank God."

I open my mouth but only air comes out.

My heart is beating so fast because I am thinking of Ian and
what I will tell him on Monday.

14.

The Matobo Hills have been declared a no-go area by the government. Dissidents are hiding out there and the government is going to send the Fifth Brigade to flush them out.

Three weeks or so after Maphosa came to stay with us, we took him to Matopos. Maphosa stood on Rhodes's grave, looked all around at World's View, and started singing a song from The Struggle. His singing voice was so different from his talking voice it did not sound like Maphosa at all. He was singing about Lobengula and Mzilikazi, the forgotten chiefs, who would rise up to reclaim their land. There were some whites at the statue of the Pioneer Column and they were looking at us. When Maphosa stopped singing, they started. "For we are all Rhodesians and we'll fight through thick and thin; Rhodesians never die and . . ."

Maphosa looked over at them. They were young boys and girls. The Children of Settlers. Daddy said, "We should be going now, it's getting late." Maphosa was rubbing his eye. Whenever he is very angry, his eye itches and hurts him. We walked down the hill. I could hear the whites laughing and shouting.

Later that year we went to the Trade Fair. Since independence many more countries had come to exhibit, even Britain. South Africa was banned.

We all watched the parachute jumping, the police dogs, and the police motorcycles doing tricks by the showgrounds; Mummy, Rosanna, and I went to the fashion show at the David Whitehead Hall while Daddy and Maphosa went to see the technical exhibits in Hall 1.

In the newspaper there were stories about gangs of white youths wearing RHODESIANS NEVER DIE and RHODESIA IS SUPER T-shirts, insulting and even beating up people.

Maphosa said enough is enough. "We will teach these people a lesson. They still think that this is Rhodesia."

On the last day of the fair, there was big fight near the animal showgrounds and Maphosa did not come home for three days. Mummy said that she was sure he was in jail and it was time to let him go. Daddy said, "Let us wait and hear what he has to say." When Maphosa came back, he had nothing at all to say. We all noticed the cut on his forehead, but no one said anything.

Twenty-eight dissidents have been captured. They are lined up on the TV. Their hands tied to one long rope that a policeman holds at either end so that it looks like they want to play tug of war. The dissidents look very skinny. They have bushy, uncombed hair. They're confessing. One by one. They have been working to destabilize the government. They have been killing villagers. They are under the control of Nkomo.

Maphosa is very worried. There is trouble at his rural home in Gwayi. He wants to go, but Daddy has warned him that there are roadblocks everywhere and the Fifth Brigade is on the lookout for former ZIPRA fighters. "If they catch you going there, they will accuse you of going to join the dissidents," Daddy tells him.

Maphosa says that women and children are getting persecuted. Daddy says that these are only rumors. Children and women are not dissidents.

Maphosa says that Mphiri has been behaving strangely of late. Yesterday when he passed him on the way to the shops and made his greeting, the old man looked at him without any recognition. Maphosa repeated the greeting but the old man made no response at all. "That mukhiwa boy has a lot to answer for," says Maphosa. "It is time he packed his bags and took off to South Africa." Maphosa thinks that Mphiri is in the process of being bewitched and if action is not taken the old man will die in the hands of evil spirits. That cannot be allowed to happen.

15.

He picked me up at the bus stop just at the entrance of the cemetery. He was almost forty minutes late, and I was about to cross the road and take the next bus home.

"Mind the chips," he said as I was about to sit down. "Help yourself."

"So, the party, was it lekker?" he asked as he checked the mirror.

"It was okay."

That's all I said.

He turned and looked at me. I thought he would say something, ask me more about the party, why it was just okay, but he didn't; he concentrated on his driving.

It made me feel better to see that he'd chosen my favorite flavor, Salt and Vinegar. He didn't say anything about being late as he drove, and I concentrated on eating the chips without making too much noise. In the parking lot we drank the Cokes and watched people strolling about at the station. Then he had the idea to go to the Railway Museum for old-time's sakes.

Walking up the footbridge from the railway station, he said that his best memory of school was his class visit when he was in standard one, when he was seven or so. The history teacher, Mr. Scolds, took them, and if there was ever a name to fit anyone, Scolds was it.

"Boy, could that man let rip."

Anyway, on that day, he remembers being allowed to go on his own in the yard, looking at the carriages and engines, making drawings, notes, scrambling on the locomotives to check something out.

"It felt good to be out there; I reckon Mr. Scolds took off to the bar because when he finally pitched up he was way too jolly. Heck, he even brought the whole class ice-lollies."

We are standing outside Cecil John Rhodes's private carriage looking through the large windows. The teak table gleams in the dining-room carriage. It is set with beautiful chinaware and silver, crystal decanters, and goblets, which make me think of Mummy and her collection. Everything in there looks as though it is waiting for Mr. Rhodes to come in. I keep looking towards the doorway; any moment the founder of Rhodesia might duck his head and enter his carriage. He will draw out a chair, sit down. He has a hat, which he puts on his knee, his leg outstretched. A black steward will soon arrive and start preparing the table for dinner, the dinner that is being cooked in Mr. Rhodes's private kitchen. Maybe Mr. Rhodes will turn and look out of the window, watch the countryside gently roll by. His country. Rhodesia. That must feel good. And then dinner, a cigar, a bath (perhaps), bed.

"My old man signed me up with the Cubs—what was it now?—Fourteenth South Grove Troop, met every Tuesday over by the hall near the fire brigade station; used to go camping at the Matopos. Come school holidays no schlepping round the place; the old man thought he could toughen me up a bit. Hated every shit minute of it. Bloody Scout leader, Mr. Caldwell, Mr. Fuck-Well to me, a New Zealand bloke, always had it in for me. Only joy I got out of it was when there was bugger all to do but take myself off somewhere and just sit and scribble things in the notebook. Drove my old man penga that book."

I think of Mr. Rhodes who used to stand so proudly on his

pedestal in Main Street, his hands crossed behind his back, his head leaning a little bit to one side; looking, in his wise and fatherly way at all of Bulawayo going about its business around him. And now he stands all by himself behind the museum, forgotten, his only company weeds, insects, and the birds who don't know his greatness, pooing on him. His Bulawayo, now.

I think of Maphosa finding out about this train; how it brought Mr. Rhodes all the way from Cape Town in South Africa up to Matopos, in Bulawayo. A journey of over two thousand kilometers, the plaque says. That Mr. Rhodes was dead, lying in his train, waiting to be buried up there in World's View.

I think of Mrs. Palmers, my history teacher in primary school, whose eyes became all wet when she told us Mr. Rhodes's words as he lay dying: "So little done, so much to do."

"May that be an inspiration to you all," she said, snapping shut her book.

The railway platform is full of soldiers disembarking. They are speaking in Shona.

Ian quickens his step.

"Come, let's get a move on."

Whenever I'm in the car with him, I can't relax.

When we stop at robots or intersections, I keep thinking that some pedestrian will suddenly stop in the middle of the road and look straight at me.

"Lindiwe!" they will shout out.

Their eyes will move from me to the driver and then back to me.

"What are you doing here, who is this . . . ?"

So I sit quietly, my eyes on my lap and listen to him.

"It's a pity about Matopos. I was thinking about making a trip there. Sit on the rocks and think fuck all like the good old days. Man, I hope the dissidents teach the Shonas a lesson. They're getting way too arrogant. Pride comes before a fall. They're flooding this place with Shonas to neutralize the Ndebeles. You can trust a Ndebele; the Shonas now, as slippery as hell."

I think of the soldiers on the platform. They seemed very young and their uniforms looked as if they had just been taken out from packages. Those soldiers didn't look like killers. They looked like boys pretending to be soldiers. Even the street girls who hang around by the station were not intimidated by them. They were calling out to the soldiers, "Come, boys, come; good times here, come." Maybe they were just beginning their training. Maybe when they went back to Harare, they would be real soldiers. They would know all about killing. No one would call them boys. It's funny but I don't even remember if they had guns.

"The thing with the Shonas is that they have to learn that they didn't win the war; it was a negotiated settlement. They were backed into a corner; it was a no-win situation. They had to accept whatever the Handbag and her windie, Lord Carry on Selling the White Man Down the Drain, was prepared to give. Now I think of it, who knows if the Shonas are running about all over the place because they're so blimming ashamed. Could be something in that: trying to convince themselves that they actually *won* the war, that it wasn't a Surrender. If they can't take out the white man, they're going to give it a go with the Ndebeles, for old-time's sake."

We're in his car at Khumalo. He has come to check out an old buddy of his, but I think he's having second thoughts. He keeps twirling the car window handle. We've been sitting in the car talking and being quiet and waiting.

And then he looks at me and smiles. "Yah, well, all that's straight from the horse's mouth; the Rhodesians running to South Africa. You should hear that lot yakking on. Sad. They don't know what's hit them. And the Afrikaners and the Brits can't stand them. At least my old man stuck it out. Eeesh man, what's so fricking funny?"

I don't tell him it was the "Lord Carry on Selling the White Man Down the Drain" bit. I know he meant Lord Carrington and I know that white people are really angry about the whole Lancaster thing and how Rhodesia became Zimbabwe—how Smith sold them out after he had promised them that not in a thousand years would blacks ever rule Rhodesia.

"Yah, smile now, wait till they come tshaying you. And anyway, if they want to see real racialism, they should take a trip across the border. That's Hardcore racialism. There an Aff even looks at an Afrikaner the wrong way, he's had it my boy. The Afrikaners have a cruel, mean streak. As hard as diamonds that tribe. They should think themselves lucky this lot."

I want to ask him about his life in South Africa—if he went to school, if he lived with his mother, if he has brothers or sisters.

"Jeez," he says. "I wished I smoked or something. The old man smoked like a chimney; smelt of bloody smoke big time."

He hits the steering wheel with his hands; I jump a bit on my seat.

"Sorry. Jeez, I'm jittery today. Shit, let's get out of here."

But it's too late. There's someone by the gate, and a dog barking. He gets out of the car.

The dog is a Ridgeback. He's baring his teeth and gnashing at the gate. He looks like he hasn't been fed in days.

"Hamba Zulu! Foosake man!" shouts the man, giving the dog a kick in its hind leg. "Heh, Ian, is that you man, howzit?"

"Howzit, John, long time no see, heh?"

They give each other a high-five over the gate, and then they stand there looking at one another.

"So, I thought I'd come and check you out."

"Bad timing, man. I'm on my way out. Got to hop over to the garage, some gondie having a kadenze about overcharging; you won't believe what ideas they're getting these days."

His buddy shakes his key. "Tell you what, how about Grey's Inn, six o'clock. Check out the chicks. New stock just arrived from England, come to save the natives."

Ian turns a bit. I sit in the car very still.

"What's that?" says his buddy looking over the gate to the car.

"Nothing. Just giving a lift."

"So Grey's Inn, right?"

"Right."

They stand there until Ian says, "Okay, see you then," and turns round.

In the car, on the road, he says, "The look on his face. To think we were mates. All the way through primary and now, *that* look. Didn't want me anywhere near his property. Jeez. What did he think I was going to do?"

Later, while we are waiting for some cows to pass, he says, "Can't blame him though, can I?"

The cows are moving slowly and they keep knocking into each other. There is no sign of the herd boy, who should be waving his stick about, directing them to safety.

We sit in the car for a while. Ian taps the steering wheel with his fingers. I look at the last cow that has stopped at the edge of the road and is looking back at us with very sad eyes. It looks as though his legs are about to buckle, and he will collapse right there in the heat.

"Herd boy probably rolling off in the grass, suffering from Class One babbelas. Just take a look at the skinny things, can hardly walk. It's going to be a bloody scrappy year, that's for sure. Bobs had better have his act together, get the GMB guys in order; they're exporting so much maize to Mozambique when the shit hits the fan here, 'sorry, no stocks, hapana food'—man, lots of hungry fuckers equals lots of angry fuckers. You should check out the mess in Khami."

White people had started calling Mr. Mugabe, Bob. And sometimes they put "comrade" in front. Daddy says it's a way for them to belittle him, turn him into a boy, someone manageable like their workers. In truth they are frightened of him.

I had thought of how when I was at the telephone exchange with Daddy, sometimes the whites (some of them apprentices straight out of school) whom he was training would call him Danny or Danny Boy and he would just laugh. I had also noticed that, since independence, he didn't tolerate that anymore.

I want to tell him that I'm not nervous anymore, even though I jumped a little bit before. I want to say that I don't think he is a bad person; that I like his name, Ian; that I'm not afraid of him.

But instead I say, "It's hot."

He turns to me and says, "Hey, madoda, kuyatshisa," and laughs.

I laugh back.

And I can hear Maphosa. "Bastard!" "Settler!" "Sellout!"

We stop over at the old mineshaft. I want to say to him that we had better hurry; Mummy should be almost finished with her group.

He gets out of the car, looks down at the quarry.

"Man, once when he was all boozed up, he started mouthing off about how many gondies they'd kicked into abandoned shafts, makeshift graves. Said once they cut off their tongues, threw those in first, and then the poor buggers."

He looks back at me. "Shit, sometimes I forget you're just a lightie."

"I'm not a lightie."

"Touchy, touchy."

He puts his hand on my head and then steps away. "Shit, we should be going back. Your mother is going to throw a right old kadenze."

Before he starts the car, I say, "They've captured some dissidents, over at Nkayi."

"They'll be lucky if they get off with any balls left. Word is Commies from North Korea are drilling the Shonas with new and improved torture techniques up in Inyanga."

I tell him to stop at Alton Heights. I'll catch an Emergency Taxi home. Just to be safe.

"Thank you," I say. I turn to open the door and suddenly I feel his hand on my shoulder.

"So, Lindiwe, it's good to have someone to joll with, someone who doesn't think I'm bad news."

I wait for him to say that now it is enough. To say something like thank you, good-bye, it's time to move on.

He takes his hand away, but I still feel the pressure and heat of it. I want to put my hand on my shoulder, where his was. To keep it there.

"Listen, man, we should try and arrange a way to meet."

"Like an appointment?"

"Jeez, I'm not a doctor. I mean meet like friends."

He puts his hand through his hair. "Asch man, forget it, It's just . . . I'll see you when I see you."

"You can write something maybe, put it in the letter box."

"What, so your mother can find it, no ways."

"Not if you put it in at night, anytime after six. A small piece of paper."

"With the appointment? Date, time, location." And he smiles. "Okay, works both ways, you do the same your end if you want to meet up."

"Yes."

And my heart jumps and skips.

Rosanna gives me a funny look when I come in. Mummy is still not in.

Ever since Rosanna became pregnant, Mummy has become short-tempered. The more Rosanna's stomach grows, the shorter Mummy's temper becomes. Rosanna should have gone back to the village to have the baby. But now with all the problems in the rural areas, it is not safe. When she saw Rosanna's stomach, Mrs. Ncube said that this was surely a big healthy boy growing in there, as heavy as anything, pulling Rosanna's stomach so far down. That evening Mummy gave me a clap when I asked her for the keys of the pantry so that I could get a new packet of sugar out, and then she locked herself in her room.

Rosanna will not say who the father is.

"Who is going to support this child?" shouted Mummy. "How can damages be paid when there is no culprit. Ba-Lindiwe you must throw her out."

Whenever Mummy addressed Daddy by "Lindiwe's father," it meant that a very serious request was being made and Mummy was calling upon Daddy as head of the household and my protector to act. Even though Rosanna was Mummy's relative, once she had come to our place she became part of the family under Daddy's guardianship.

Daddy said we must be charitable.

"We are not a charity!" shouted Mummy.

Mummy wanted to know where Rosanna was getting the money to buy all the fancy maternity wear and shoes from Bata. And what of all the bags she kept bringing back from Babyrama, Woolworths, and even Meikles. Mummy told me to keep an eye on her and not to leave anything lying around.

"With the excuse of this pregnancy, she is doing nothing. 'I am tired,' 'my feet are hurting,' but not too tired to go shopping."

Rosanna is fairer skinned than Mummy and her face isn't marked by dark patches because of using Ambi Fade skin lightening cream. Rosanna doesn't wear a glossy black wig like Mummy, but her short hair is neatly plaited in rows. She is also taller than Mummy, and before she became pregnant the boys at the shops called her Miss Coca-Cola and made smooth movements with their hands to illustrate the shape of her figure. Rosanna didn't pay them any attention.

"I don't like her change of attitude at all. She is acting as though she is the mistress of this house. When Mrs. Ncube came yesterday and I asked her to fetch a glass of water, she actually started saying 'but I'm . . .' and I gave her such a look that she thought better of it. Even Mrs. Ncube was surprised. That's what happens when you act in a Christian manner, people take advantage. She must watch out. I won't stand for any nonsense."

We are at Chipangali by the lion enclosure. The lions have been fed, and they are lying down, their jaws matted with blood, sleepy eyed, content. But they still make me nervous. Something, anything might provoke them.

I have the lighter in my pocket. I want to give it to him. I want him to know that I am on his side.

This is the furthest we've driven off and we met one road-block. The policemen told us to get out of the car. They checked the boot and under the seats. They asked us where we were going. They said we should not go any further than Chipangali.

I told Mummy and Daddy that I was at the public library studying.

There is no one around but us and the animals.

"I wanted to be a bloody vet," he says. "Jeez luck, didn't even get round to sitting my O levels; had to get away from that house. Education, that's the key. The be-all and end-all."

He sounds a bit like Daddy.

"What are you smiling at?"

"Nothing."

"Asch, I'm sick of looking at these lazy fossils. Let's go and get a drink."

In the gazebo it is very cool and we can hear the birds chittering away. The lady serving behind the counter looks at me and makes a face. Ian orders two Cokes and some buns and chips. We sit at a table in front, and I put my hand in my pocket to get a tissue out to blow my nose. The lighter makes a tinkling noise on the stones. Ian bends down to pick it up. The lighter is in his hands. He turns it over, sees "Rhodesian Army" on it. His face changes. Splotches of red by his cheeks, on the side of his head. He squeezes the lighter in his hand.

"So, what's this," he says, looking at me.

A cold weight is pressing hard on my chest.

"Something from your dad, a souvenir?"

Too late I realize I could lie. I could say yes.

"No, I . . . I found it in the vegetable garden. The policemen came, they were looking for evidence, they said . . . I wanted to give it to you, today."

"Man, so you think I . . . that that's what happened, that I . . . You've had it all this time, why?"

I don't even know why, but I start crying, tears just falling on my cheeks. I wipe them away.

He looks at me, and then he starts drinking his Coke. He puts the lighter on the table. I can't drink, eat; I sit there looking at the lighter.

He gets up. "Let's go," he says.

He leaves the lighter on the table.

We don't talk on the drive back.

He drops me by the cemetery, and I walk the rest of the way home.

17.

On the last day of term, Bridgette throws up in the toilets. I help her clear up. She starts crying and stops.

"My dad is going to kill me," she says.

After school we go to Grasshut. Every Friday we meet up there and we exchange news. She's my best friend (Bridgette says we're "mates"), and because of this, I don't really care what the other girls say—that I'm a bookworm, a teacher's pet, a goody-goody. Bridgette calls them losers, losers with a capital *L* and attention seekers.

We sit right at the back in the dark. We share a toasted cheese sandwich; I have a Coke and she a cream soda.

"I told him, and you should have seen how scared he got, Lins. He said he had nothing to do with it, as if I'd done the whole thing by myself like Mary. He doesn't want me around anymore. Can you imagine, a grown man acting like such a coward and one of Daddy's good friends, too. He gave me forty dollars. It's something, I guess."

She says that she will find a way to get rid of it.

I try to think of a baby inside Bridgette's stomach. I try to put the biology drawings inside Bridgette. We are sitting here and Bridgette has a baby growing inside. The baby has a head, eyes, ears, a mouth. The baby has arms and legs. The baby might have a penis.

"You know, last time we were here, we saw that guy, that white guy."

"Yes," I say.

"He was really looking at you."

I don't say anything.

"Do you know him? I mean, do you talk to him?"

"No."

"Why do you think he did it?"

"I . . . I don't know. But he was cleared, remember?"

"Aren't you afraid living next door to him?"

"No, not really. I don't think about it."

"It would give me the heebie-jeebies, for real."

I don't tell Bridgette that I lie on my bed and imagine him next to me. The two of us, side by side, on my bed.

18.

Day after day, I keep opening my new diary; the pages all flick past empty. I try to write things, like how I started off last year, when I was so excited about finally having my own diary. Things about what had happened in school or at youth group. But I've stopped writing because what I want to write now is too big to be safe in there, even if I do have a lock and key. So I just put *X*'s, my secret secret.

The days are long, ugly blanks.

Christmas is very quiet. We don't get any visitors, and Mummy doesn't make anything special like she usually does. Maphosa didn't have to kill the biggest chicken, and Rosanna didn't sit outside the kitchen with the chicken in the green zinc tub, pouring hot water over it until the feathers softened and could be easily plucked from the skin. "Come, Lindiwe, don't be so shy; come and help me," she would tease me, laughing when I ran away. And Mummy didn't put the chicken on the kitchen table and experiment with her stuffing. One Christmas, Aunty Gertrude even brought some crackers.

After we come back from the morning church service, Mummy shuts herself up in her room and stays there for the whole day. Daddy gives me an envelope with thirty dollars inside and goes to the workshop. Rosanna stays in her room.

She is seven months pregnant now. I go to the veranda with a pile of magazines from the Book Exchange, where you can buy secondhand ones from South Africa for twenty-five cents.

I walk to the gate. But he isn't anywhere in sight. Because he parks his car at the far side of the house, I don't even know if he is around. Maybe he is at Grey's Inn celebrating with his friends. And then suddenly a thought shoots through me. What if he has gone back to South Africa? What if he got so angry or he just wanted to be with his family there? I shake my head. I won't think about that.

I will be in Form Three this coming year, almost a senior.

Bridgette phoned yesterday and I could hear music in the background. She sounded a bit drunk and later there were funny noises like she was crying.

She is always trying to get me to go to the late-afternoon sessions at Talk of the Town Nightclub. The only discos that I go to are the ones organized by the church youth group. Bridgette says that's so boring, even though she hasn't been to one. "For a start," she says, "there's no alcohol."

I've told her a little bit more about him. And the last time, when I spoke a bit too freely, she came out with, "you like him, don't you." I laughed and told her not to be stupid. She pinched my arm and said, "Faker." Then she went on about her new boyfriends and how good or bad they were. She said that no one had the complete package, so you had to get a bit here, a bit there.

She didn't say anything about her problem.

I sit on the veranda trying to get interested in the beauty and fashion pages of *Fair Lady* and *Femina*. And then I go to the problem pages, which are usually entertaining.

But actually, I am waiting for something to happen.

19.

I'm closing the letter box when a noise makes me jump.

"The postman is making very late deliveries these days."

Maphosa is standing so close to me that I can feel his breath on my neck. I stand very still, the piece of paper scrunched up in my hand. The only light comes from the street lamp across the road; it flickers dimly.

I'm supposed to be outside at the back by the kitchen, topping up the dogs' plates with our bones from dinner. Very soon Mummy will be calling me for her tea.

"Watch out."

I move only when I hear him walk away.

I open the note in the bathroom, the door locked. I read it over and over. I trace his words with my finger, and when I come out, I put them in my diary and lock them inside.

He is standing by the foot of the stairs outside the public library.

"We need to talk," he says.

As simple as that, as though it has only been a couple of days ago since we last exchanged a word and not a month almost.

I don't say anything but walk next to him.

He offers to take my bag, but I shake my head.

Anyone could see us. Daddy who might be out on a call from the exchange. Anyone from school. Mummy who might be doing some shopping.

We walk down Main Street, then left along Leopold Takawira.

"This will do," he says.

We go into the Art Gallery. He pays for us both. We go up the stairs and then he starts.

"So what exactly are you playing at, Lindiwe?"

Around us there are stone sculptures. On the walls, batiks.

"Did you hear me, what exactly are you playing at?"

He reaches out, grabs hold of my wrist, pulls me to the window.

"And don't put on that fucking quiet act. You don't know what you're messing with."

He lets go of my arm.

"I just kept it," I say.

He leans his hands against the frame of the window. I can hear his breathing. My arm hurts.

He turns, faces me.

"I'm going to tell you something. I'll say it this one time and it's finished, all right?"

"Yes."

"I'm not joking. I don't want to hear anything about it after this."

He is standing there, his hands crossed on his chest, looking down.

"I didn't do it," he says.

That's all he says.

Walking out of the gallery, I bump into Mrs. Ncube.

"Lindiwe, what are you doing here?"

"I . . . I'm just researching for school."

"School these days, too much to learn, my child. That is good. Anyway, tell your mother I will be coming round to-morrow to discuss the patterns for the costumes."

"Yes, Mrs. Ncube."

I see him, between cars, crossing the road, his hands in the pockets of his jeans. When he's over at the pavement on the other side, he looks back, and even though he sees me, he walks away.

20.

Bridgette says that she's managed to find someone who can take care of her problem. She says if she was still in England this would be no big deal. Everyone has abortions. There are even advertisements of special clinics stuck on the walls in the underground where the trains go through.

Bridgette says the word "abortion" so casually as if it is any other word like *eat, food,* or *run.*

Abortion is a sin. It is murder. You are killing a baby.

Bridgette says that this person has experience. She's done it lots of times. It's nothing for her and she is not so expensive.

Bridgette's house girl gave her the name.

"I'm going tomorrow," Bridgette says. "Will you come with me? The woman is over at Lobengula. She can do it in the afternoon, after school."

I say yes.

I am going to help her commit a big sin.

She squeezes my hand.

"Thanks, Lins."

We walk together after school, all the way across town, zig-zagging up and down the avenues and streets, and first we are talking about this and that, trying to make each other laugh about things that are happening at school, like how today

Michelle said that she still believes in fairies; but very soon we are quiet.

We hear and feel Lobengula Street before we reach it. African music is on at full blast.

Bridgette keeps looking down at the piece of paper with the address and the diagram. We get lost twice and we have to ask some pavement vendors the way. I've never been to Lobengula by myself and passing all the men standing in corners, making comments about us, one even grabbing my arm, is not nice.

This is not the exciting and wonderful Lobengula that Daddy takes me to whenever he goes on a Saturday to Old Man Patel to get his new trousers adjusted. In that Lobengula, Daddy stops in the middle of all the loud music and blaring hooters, greeting so many people along the shop fronts, sometimes picking up a radio, even a TV set that needs fixing.

Old Mrs. Patel always gives me a brown paper bag sticky and oily with Indian koeksisters, and I marvel at the ripples of her midriff's brown flesh, which her sari reveals. Daddy and I wolf down all the koeksisters and wash them down with Fantas from one of the roadside stalls before we get home; otherwise, Mummy will throw them away because she says that Indians are dirty and heathens. Old Man Patel is always talking of going back to India even though it's years and years since he left.

There's the pitter-patter of little Indian feet running between the counters as some relative or other has come visiting, and sometimes different ages of Patels are shouting from one end of the shop to the other in an Indian language, while Ndebele and English are mixed together by the black assistants and customers, adding to the commotion.

Once a customer came in with a baby goat and wanted to exchange the goat for the two costumes that they had put on Lay-By. Daddy scolded the man for his shortsightedness, saying in his loud lecturing voice that this was the problem with black people. A goat will be food for time to come. And clothes? They will only get old. People can survive with nakedness, but can they survive without food? Daddy told the man to think about the welfare of his children. The man said that his wife was wanting those costumes very bad. Daddy said was he sure it was his wife and not a girlfriend. The man looked down at his feet while the goat started sniffing some bales of cloth. Finally the man walked out of the shop with his goat. Old Man Patel and Daddy had laughed and laughed.

But on this day there's only Bridgette and me, and Lobengula Street is not an adventure.

The place is in a block of flats. I don't want to go into that dark passage that even from the pavement smells of urine and vomit. I want to tell Bridgette that we should turn back. We can think of something else, but she steps into the dark and I follow her.

There's no lift so we walk up the stairs, all the way to the fourth floor. The stairway is dim, and there are strange banging and crashing sounds coming from behind doors. On the second floor we hear a man shouting "bitch," and then the door opens and the man pushes against me and says "bitch" again; he bangs on the door, tries to open it, but now it's locked; he shouts "bitch," kicks the door with his foot, and then stumbles down the stairs.

I'm scared.

We keep putting our feet into puddles, but I don't look down.

Finally, we arrive at room 403B.

Bridgette and I stand for a while getting our breath back. There's still time for us to forget about all this, to be two schoolgirls again out in the sun, walking on the pavements of Lobengula Street. We can stop at one of the canteens and buy a Coco-Cola and bun. But Bridgette knocks on the door.

"Who is it?" someone demands. "What have you come for?"

The woman is speaking Ndebele, and I have to translate for Bridgette.

"I've come for the special thing. Joyce sent me," she says to the closed door.

I say it all again in my broken Ndebele.

The woman must be suspicious because she takes some time to open the door.

All we can see is her face, which looks swollen as though someone has beaten her. I hope that she shuts the door again; we will have to go home. But she opens the door wider and we step inside.

There's only paraffin light, so everything in the room is shadows: a shadow of a chair, a small table that has some things on it.

"Which one?" the woman asks.

She's looking at us like pieces of meat or something like that, something you pick and choose, decide which is good or bad.

"It's me," answers Bridgette.

Her voice is so weak, it doesn't sound like her at all.

The woman flings out her hand. Bridgette takes out her purse and puts the notes in the woman's hand.

The woman slaps the money on her palm, and then she counts it, licking her fingers between notes. She doesn't seem too happy, but she finally shoves them deep into her bra.

She takes a cup from a table. She puts her fingers in it and takes some things out which look like a piece of bark and roots.

"Drink," she commands Bridgette.

Some of the liquid spills on the table.

Bridgette takes some sips.

"Hurry, hurry," says the woman. "There are other customers."

Bridgette takes a long drink, and when she tries to swallow, she starts coughing.

"Take off your skirt and underpants," says the woman. "Lie down there."

Bridgette undresses. She goes to lie down on the floor.

I'm holding Bridgette's skirt and underpants. My hands are shaking. I stand against a wall. I want to stand looking at the wall. I don't want to see the woman pick up the knitting needles from the table or to hear Bridgette's screams.

"Shut up," says the woman. "Quiet."

I help Bridgette get dressed. She's trembling, shivering, and her body is moist. She takes the four Panadols she brought with her. We walk very slowly down the stairs. All the way to the bus stop, we have to take stops every few steps. I want to tell her that we should go and confess everything to an adult, even if the woman warned us about telling anyone. "You will go to jail for many years," she said.

I help her get up on the bus, sit down. I wait for the bus to leave, looking at Bridgette's head, which is pressed against the window. And then I go away because I am already very late.

21.

He picks me up outside Jairos Jiri Crafts Centre. I haven't seen him for eight days. There was his message in the letter box: "Jairos Jiri, 2 o'clock."

"How about we joll over to Ascot Plaza, get something to eat. No chances of bumping into your mum that end, is there?"

My heart is beating so fast.

"Ascot? My uncle used to bet on the horses."

"Used to? What, he stopped?"

"Yes, his wife beat him when he lost a whole month's salary; since then he doesn't."

He makes a whistling sound. "Sounds like one tough Ndebele mama."

"She runs a beer garden in Makokoba. No one ever tries to leave without paying."

There is a packet on the dashboard. He slides it towards my end.

"I got you something."

I put my hand inside the plastic bag and feel a small hard box. I take it out, put it in my palm.

A jewelry box. *Kings Jewellers.*

"So, open it."

They are shining. Earrings. Flame lilies. The national flower of Rhodesia, Zimbabwe.

"I was a bit harsh the other day," he says. "Bygones be bygones, heh?"

I don't know what to say.

"You're not going to turn on the waterworks now."

The box is warm in my hand.

"Thank you."

"So, what you're reading there? *Animal Farm*. Isn't that banned?"

"Yes."

I got it from the library and Mrs. Grange just stamped it. She couldn't care less. She's emigrating. The final straw was the farmers up at Filabusi who were killed. In cold blood. Hands behind their backs. Kneeling down. She had been telling anyone who stopped by for a chat. The country was going down to the dogs.

He picks up the book, riffles through its pages.

"That's Zimbo land for sure, one giant *Animal Farm*. How old are you, anyways?"

"Sixteen."

"Sixteen, huh?"

I don't tell him that my birthday was five days ago, and that Mummy gave me a little talk about keeping myself clean.

"Bad shit is happening over at Matopos. They've sealed the whole area off. Nothing moves after six. Did you hear they say Nkomo's gone toodling off kitted out in women's gear, undies and all, only in Zimbo land I'm telling you."

Maphosa has disappeared, too. He has gone with some of his friends from the association to investigate.

"Shit, it's hot. We should get a room or something. Air-conditioning. Come on."

The lady behind the desk looks at me and says, "Will you be staying for the night, sir?"

"No, no, nothing like, just want to get out of the heat, an hour or so, max."

"We don't do hourly rentals. You will have to pay for the whole day."

"How much is it again—thirty dollars, no discounts? Okay."

"You'll have to write her name, too."

He writes something in the book. The lady gives him the keys. Room 201. We take the lift to the second floor. Room 201 is the second room on the right.

We are here.

The last and only time I was in a hotel room was in Francistown. Daddy took us on a trip to buy spare parts for the Cortina. We stayed in a hotel used by prostitutes and truck drivers. Daddy, Mummy, and I shared one room. The sheets were so dirty we slept with our clothes on. In the morning a fat man squeezed my breasts and offered me ten pula if I went to his room. We were served tongue for breakfast. It looked exactly like a tongue on the plate. And we all got lice.

"That's more like it," he says. "I was getting fried out there."

He is lying on the bed, his hands under his head. His shoes are still on.

"Come on, I won't bite."

I sit down.

"You know, you're not half bad-looking. Why do you put so much grease on your hair? You should check out some of the Afrikaner chicks. As ugly as anything, but they all think they're in the running for Miss South Africa. You should cut your hair. I can do it for you."

"No, thank you."

"No worries, but you'd look good with short hair. Short back and sides. Army style. Miss Africa. Miss Zimbabwe."

I don't tell him about the first days of school.

"Not being racialistic or anything, but heh, some black people stink as hell. You don't."

"I'm colored."

"Colored? You don't look like a goffle. You've got more black blood than white. Look at your mother; she's as black as . . ."

He gets up from the bed.

"Asch man, people get so touchy. Let's just drop it. Soon as a whitey opens his mouth he's being racialistic."

"She thinks I'm a prostitute."

"Who? Oh *her,* down there, *that* fossil. And I'm the king of Sheba. No, I'm a sugar daddy. A skint sugar daddy. That would be a first, heh."

He turns around, goes over to the picture on the wall.

"Blimming Kariba. Have you ever been there?"

"No."

But at school we've just finished learning about the construction of the dam in the 1950s; the biggest man-made dam in the world. We watched a film about Operation Noah when all the animals had to be removed from the area before it became flooded; how elephants and lions were tranquilized by brave and determined rangers and released back into the wild. Mr. Stewart, the geography teacher, said that it was a true testament to Rhodesian grit, labor, and expertise. He didn't even correct himself.

"Not missing much. Bloody hot. Come October, forty-five, fifty degrees easy. No wonder the Tongas got shit for brains; damn things got fried. Rhodie Central up there. Boats and fishing and big talk—who caught what, who saw what. All that fricking water, and you can't even take a dip to cool down. Mahobo crocs and hippos. You should see the jaws of those things. A hippo will crush you, drag you down into the water, and that's it, friend."

He stands against the window, and I wonder what he can see out there.

"Now Victoria Falls, that's something. Scared myself shit-less on Knife Edge Bridge. Halfway got soaked, full-on spray. Better views from Zambia. A bloody monkey bit me in the rain forest, had to get rabies injections, and boy do those things hurt, and one chappie got his leg chomped off by a croc."

He turns, looks at me.

"I'm off down south. Got to get my act together. Come next week I'm old news, Lindiwe."

"What about the dissidents, the Fifth Brigade?"

"Checked it out. All clear as long as you stay on the main road. I'm not going off camping in the bush and sticking my nose where it's not wanted. No worries."

I want to say, you can't go.

He says, "What I wouldn't give for a Castle now. Should've brought something up."

He sits on the bed again and starts punching the mattress.

"Have you even been to Ascot during race day?"

"No."

"You've been to fuck all, haven't you? The old man would work himself into a palaver. Betting, and ten times out of ten, he'd put his dosh on some cripple everyone else knew had zero chance of even finishing the race, and, my word, later there was hell to pay, like it was me who made him . . . so anyway, where've you been?"

I can feel his eyes on me, waiting.

"We went to the Drive Inn."

"The Drive Inn. That's lekker. What, with a boy?"

"With the church youth group."

"Don't tell me you're a happy-clappy. That lot drives me up the wall. Jesus this, Jesus that . . . so, what did you watch?"

"*Cannonball Run.*"

"Was it good?"

"It was okay. I liked *Grease.*"

"*Grease?* Is that the one with the moffie guy? I'm out of touch with movies and shit. I'll catch up down south. Though to tell you the truth, I lose interest halfway. What the hell am I doing watching some moffie prancing around? I end up asking myself. And they're all moffies over there in Hollywood. Like all the guys over by REPS Theatre. So your church group, is there anyone you like there?"

"No."

"Don't run a fast one over me. It's not all praying and praise the Lord, is it?"

I get up from the bed.

"I must go," I say.

By the garage, opposite the bus stop, are three police trucks and soldiers.

"I can't drop you off here. I'll drop you at the turning."

The soldiers are smashing the windows of the garage shop with their rifles.

The garage belongs to ZAPU.

The Herald and ZBC say that arms caches have been found in Nkomo's farms throughout Matabeleland; the Ndebeles are planning to wage a campaign to destabilize the democratically elected government of Zimbabwe. Mugabe warns that they will be taught a lesson that they will never forget; he will send down the rains that will wash away the filth; the people of Matabeleland will soon come to know the meaning of the word Gukurahundi.

"Old Smithie should have been smarter. If he'd played his cards right, he'd still be top dog here."

22.

Rosanna and Daddy are whispering in the kitchen.
"I will tell her," says Rosanna.
"No," says Daddy.
"You must tell her," says Rosanna.
Mummy comes into the kitchen.
"Tell me what?" she asks.
There is silence everywhere.
Then Mummy says, "No, no."
"Mama," cries Rosanna.
Daddy tries to hold Mummy, but she pushes him away.
She pushes past me in the corridor.
She goes into the bedroom, locks it.
Daddy knocks on the door. There is no answer.
Rosanna goes to her room, outside.
I stand still in the corridor, holding my breath tight inside.

Mummy has not come out her room for two days. Daddy stands
outside begging and asking for forgiveness. "I have told Rosanna
to go," he says. "It was a mistake. You must come out. Please."
He puts water and food outside. She does not touch anything.
When I come home from school, I knock on the door, wait. On
the third day, Daddy says that he is going to force the door open.

*   *   *

Bridgette does not come to school.

Mrs. Jameson says that she has some very sad news. Bridgette is very sick. She is at the Bulawayo Central Hospital in the intensive care unit. She has had an accident. She has lost a lot of blood. We must keep her in our prayers. And then she says, "Linda, will you please come with me?

"If you know anything at all, it will help Bridgette. You are her best friend. You mustn't keep anything from us. It's the only way you can help."

I stand very quietly in the office, my legs shaking.

At last, she lets me go.

On my way to the bus stop, I go into Woolworths. I stop at the sweet counter. I think of Sophia and her gang always coming back during lunch break, their fists full of marshmallows, licorice sticks and fudge; I had watched them dare each other before setting out on their expeditions to see who would get away with the most stuff. They thought it was all very funny, and they would sit there in the quadrangle giggling and chewing away, thinking that they were oh so very clever and smart. Bridgette said they were posers, out for a cheap thrill.

The girl at the counter is busy with her reflection, patting down her newly permed hair.

I swoop my hand in the jelly babies.

I shove my hand in my pocket, the jelly babies in my fist.

I walk outside, making sure that my feet stay on the pavement and do not start flying off, running, my heart beating and bumping, waiting to hear the security guard calling out behind me, "Thief! Thief!" his baton knocking on my shoulder.

I smell the sweat under my arms.

I keep my hand in my pocket all the way home, the jelly babies, warm and sticky, safe.

There is whispering in Mummy's room.

Mrs. Ncube comes out.

"Lindiwe, Don't worry now. Your mother is quite all right. How is school, my daughter? How is your research?"

I say "fine" and go in my room.

I take the jelly babies from my pocket. I squeeze them in my hands till they are almost melting. I put them in my mouth and spit them out on the bedspread.

I look at the mess.

I take out the box with the earrings and put it next to me on the bed.

I lie down on the bed and I think of Ian, driving away.

When I come out of the room, Mrs. Ncube and Mummy are in the lounge. I go and ask them if they want tea.

Mrs. Ncube gets up and says, "No, no, thank you, my child, I am just going." She turns to Mummy, "Bye-bye, Ma Lindi."

Mummy says bye-bye quietly. She does not get up. Her hands are folded on her lap.

I take Mrs. Ncube to the gate.

When she is outside she adjusts her head scarf and says, "Your mother will get better, my dear, don't worry; these things happen.I find Mummy sitting on her bed. The big Family Bible with the gold lettering that Daddy is paying for in monthly installments is open. Her hands are flat on the page. She looks up.

"I tried everything for a boy. Everything."

She looks down at the pages again. The Family Tree with all the branches she cannot fill.

I know that she is thinking about the two babies who died inside her.

One of them was a boy.
I wait for her to say more.

When Daddy comes home, he goes to the lounge and waits by the door. Then he goes to the workshop where he stays all night.

23.

I go over to the McKenzies. I crawl under the gap in the fence. Anyone could see me, but I don't care. I go to the boy's kaya and knock. No one comes. I push open the door. The room is dark and smells of paraffin oil and smoke. My eyes begin to see things in the dark. There is only a straw mat on the floor. This is where Ian sleeps. I lie down on the mat and wait.

Mphiri and Ian do not come.

I crawl back under the fence.

The house is quiet. I go outside to Rosanna's room, and I find her lying down on the mattress holding her stomach. "Are you okay?" I ask her. She doesn't say anything. Maybe she is sleeping.

The light in the workshop is on. I start walking; I should ask Daddy if he wants anything to eat. And then I change my mind. I turn and go to Maphosa's room.

I open the door and I can smell Maphosa. There is a thin mattress on the floor, a tin cup, a tin plate and saucer in a corner. There is a paraffin stove and an old dish towel. There is a vegetable crate upside down. On the wall there is Bob Marley. I lift up the mattress. There is no AK-47. I think of the soldiers by the garage. I think of Maphosa and his friends, whether they have gone back to the bush to fight, if a new war is starting all over again, so soon.

I think of Daddy, Mummy, Rosanna, Bridgette, Ian.

In my room I take out the newspaper article from the pink handbag. I look at the picture and then I lift the paper up and I put my lips gently on his hair.

24.

"You wouldn't believe I was with a chick last night. A fricking expat. I was over at the curry munchers, Naiks down at Lobengula, trying to pick out a shirt, and she just comes over and says that the blue one really brings out my eyes. These European chicks as forward as you like. And hairy as hell. And the curry muncher is standing there, grinning like a fricking monkey, 'yes, yes, the lady is quite right, quite right.' So I buy the thing and head out of the shop, and can you believe she is standing by the door asking if I want a drink. Jeez, man. No chance I'm saying no to free booze. Heh, what's the matter with you? Anyways, over at her place she starts telling me that there's hobo shit going on at Matopos. She's Swedish and working with one of these NGOs, development something or the other, one of those fundies running around. And the waterworks start flowing when she starts on about how the Fifth Brigade is busy tshaying people left, right, and center. Speciality: broken ankles, wrists. Man, even talk of bodies dumped in Antelope mine."

We're at Mzilikazi Arts and Crafts Centre. We're sitting on a bench under a jacaranda. He's chewing a biltong.

"Jeez, luck, and she lays it on thick how nice it is to meet a white Zimbabwean who isn't—what was the word she used again?—'prejudiced,' that's it, prejudiced. What a bunch of dunderheads these, 'I've come to save Africa' whities. So I go on about how I'm a farmer trying to contribute to the new

Zimbabwe, and boy, does she lap it up hook, line, and sinker. For fundies man, they can be dwaas."

He takes out a strip of biltong from the packet. "Here, do you want some?"

"No, thank you."

"Fricking good, impala."

"A boy tried to kiss me at the youth group."

"Did he manage or did you tshaya him good?"

"Where's Mphiri?"

"Mphiri? What's that to you?"

"I—I just haven't seen him around lately. Is he all right?"

"I took him to Renkini some days ago. I told the mudala I was hightailing it out of here and he had to go back to makhaya. Talking about waterworks. The fossil starts crying and saying why am I chasing him away, has he done something bad. I say, 'Look, Mphiri, I am leaving, you must leave, too.' He says that he will take care of the place. So I try to get through to him that the place is for sale, that there will be a new baas, I felt like a real wally, you don't know what that man has done . . . anyways I put him on the bus, with a letter in case he gets stopped at a roadblock."

"Are you selling the house?"

"Not that anyone's queuing to buy the dump. Hey, maybe your old man could take it, expand his business. I'll give him a damn good offer. Super discount. I should have a word with him before I take off. You know the history of the two places, don't you?"

"Which two places?"

"For an educated chick you're slow. The two houses, what else? They used to be one lot. Oupa, Grandpa McKenzie, thought it was fricking genius to have the two houses facing each other. He stashed Grandma McKenzie over at your end and carried on like a fricking bachelor at the other end. You check the goffles hanging around the bottle store, all McKenzies I reckon."

He makes a noise like something is stuck in his throat.

"But then my old man must have needed cash and he sold the place. I reckon it was the bitch who got him to. Shame, I used to have a lekker time at your place, used to hide out there when the old man got hobo drunk or when the bitch. . . ."

"You mean your father sold it to my father?"

"You're slow, but at least you're catching on."

I try to remember the big day when I came with Daddy to the house. I try to remember the white man who stood by the gate giving Daddy the keys and papers. Was that Mr. McKenzie Senior? But all I remember is Daddy sitting in the car crying. We didn't even go straight into the new house that day. Our new house.

"Hey, I think I caught sight of your war vet down by Queens Bottle Store. He looked as mad as hell. Ten or so of them shouting, clenched fists, kicking dust. He should watch out. He'll end up where the sun don't shine."

On our way back he suddenly stops the car.

"A little detour," he says.

He does a U-turn and we drive towards Belmont.

I think of Uncle Robson who works at the Lobels' factory down one of these side roads; whenever he comes to visit, he brings us two or three loaves of bread, which have not risen well or are slightly burnt, and some buns.

We pass the industrial sites (in my head I say out loud all the names of the factories along the road) and finally he stops at a gate.

He shows the guard some papers and says his name and then I hear, "Sarah Price."

I read the sign on the guard post: WELCOME TO INGUTSHENI MENTAL HOSPITAL.

After checking the papers and names on sheets of papers on his clipboard, the guard unlocks the gate.

Ian parks the car in the visitors' section.

"Wait here," he says. "And keep the doors locked. I won't be long."

I sit in the car and watch him walk up the dirt path, jump up some steps, and wait at the door.

I watch him disappear inside.

On the dirt path there is a man mumbling to himself and twisting his hair. Every now and then he throws his hands in the air and clutches at it as if he is trying to catch butterflies or flying ants. Then he goes back to mumbling and twisting his hair. I turn my head and watch the woman sitting on a bench suddenly jump up and stamp her feet on the ground. And then she bends down and starts scratching at it with her fingers. I see attendants in white walking along paths, and over by the walls, there are men, women standing. I am hot in the car. I unwind the window. The air is so still and quiet. One of the attendants looks at me and waves. I wave back. I put the palm of my hand on the metal of the car. It's burning. I look by the bench again and see the attendant who waved pull the woman from the ground and call out to the men and women by the wall. There are cars and trucks outside, but this place seems to make everything silent, a world in itself.

"Shit, I hate this," he says when he comes back. "I'd rather be dead than . . ."

And then he's quiet.

He drives for a long while, holding the steering wheel so tight as if he wants to snap it in two.

At a robot he says, "When I've made some real dosh I'll find something better, private. I'll sort it out."

He is talking to himself, making plans, and then he remembers me. "Now you *really* know Bullies, warts and all, heh."

He looks at me and tries to smile. I look out at the robot and watch it turn green.

For a long time we drive without talking until I say to him, "Do . . . do white people get put in there, too?"

He brakes hard and for a while there is just his breathing.

He opens the door, slams it, and stands outside.

"I'm sorry," I say. "I didn't mean . . ."

He is punching his right palm with his left fist.

"No problem," he snaps, looking at the stray dog that has stopped to take a look at us. "Just a question."

But he doesn't answer it and I don't ask him again.

25.

I can't sleep.

I go to the kitchen and I take out the Histalax cough mixture. I take the bottle to my room. I put it on my lips. I open my mouth. I drink and drink.

Geraldine always carried a bottle with her at school when a test was coming. She said it calmed her nerves. She would take swigs of it in the toilets.

I put the bottle back in the fridge and I go back to my room. I lie on my bed. I see Ian standing. He's wearing a blue shirt, which brings out his eyes. He's swaying this way and that. And he is saying something I can't hear. And then, it's morning.

The room smells of chloroform and the frogs are lying on the white sheet waiting. The frog makes me want to cry. He should be out jumping and croaking, but he is here waiting for me to cut him up, to show off his heart and lungs, pin them on a board. I don't want to do it. But I have to. I pick up the scalpel and I press it on the frog's stomach. I can't remember how I'm supposed to start. All the way down, all the way up? I look sideways and see Theresa pushing the blade in; I copy her.

Afterwards I sit on a bench in the quadrangle. I take out my peanut butter sandwich and feel sick looking at in my hand.

I think of Bridgette and I try to stop. I try and try not to remember.

"Eeeeee . . . !"

I look up and see a bunch of girls who've come back from Chicken Licken, pushing and shoving each other, laughing and shouting, their hands clutching paper bags streaked with oil, full of chicken burgers and chips, knocking against their thighs.

I see Sophia turn around, see me. I see her whisper something to Brenda, give her a high five. I see her walk over, throwing her head back, laughing at something one of her friends has called out. And here she is now, hands on hips, chewing gum, ready to have some more fun.

"Everyone's saying your friend killed her baby, shame."

She blows a big bubble and pops it. She takes the gum out of her mouth, stretches it out and rolls it into a ball again, puts it back in her mouth.

I think of how she got a week's detention because Miss Turner caught her reading *Lace* in class. The blockbuster was on her lap, her exercise book on top of it.

Ever since the book became hot news, Sophia and her gang have been calling other girls "bitches."

I think of Bridgette and me right at the last table in Grasshut, Bridgette reading the juiciest bits to me using a small torch because it was so dark, sucking her chocolate milk shake in between.

"Stop, I don't want to hear anymore; shush, you're too loud."

Some of the words made me feel funny.

"Lins, don't be so squeamish. You can learn lots from her."

Her was the film siren Lili, who was looking for her mother who had abandoned her a as a baby.

She would skip over the boring bits and go to the parts where something juicy was happening.

"Lins, look how you can give yourself satisfaction without a man."

"No, Bridgette, stop!" And we would end up giggling, the two of us.

I look up at Sophia and my head is sore with Bridgette.

"She thought she was so smart. They'll put her in jail, you know. Maybe even you. If you confess . . ."

"Oh, shut up," I say, getting up.

She stands there with her mouth wide open.

I hope she chokes on her bubble gum and dies.

There is a bomb alert at Woolworths. Someone has left a suitcase in one of the aisles. So I cross the road to OK's and get a bunch of Cadbury's Flakes. The Fawcett's security guard looks at me and I walk right past him, right out the door, and I do not turn my head once to check if his eyes are still glued on me.

I sit on my bed and break the chocolate into tiny, tiny pieces. I lick my hands and stick them in the chocolate, and then I start licking it off my hands. I do this until there is no more.

I go into the bathroom. I lock the door. I look at my face in the mirror. I watch myself put my finger in my mouth; I push my finger as far back as it will go. I hold my hands on the sink and watch it fill with chocolate.

I go out of the house, over to the back.

Rosanna is lying on the mat, making a strange noise.

"The baby is coming," she gasps. "The ambulance. Call the ambulance, Sisi."

I stand there and then I run back into the house. I cannot think of the phone number. I cannot think of where the phone book is. And then I remember Daddy has all the emergency numbers on the wall above the phone. I dial seven, one, seven, one, seven. The phone rings and rings. No one answers. It rings and rings. I put it down and dial again. It rings and rings. No one answers. I run out of the house. Rosanna is moaning and crying. I run out over to Number 18 shouting, "The baby, the baby, Rosanna!"

Ian walks out of the boy's kaya. He's rubbing his eyes as if he's been asleep. He's wearing a blue shirt, the buttons done up wrong.

"What the . . ."

"It's Rosanna, the baby's coming, I don't know . . ."

"So call the fricking ambulance."

"I tried; no one's answering."

"Jeez man."

He jumps over the fence and stands outside the door.

"Jeez man, she's in a bad way. We'll put her in the car. Take her to the hospital. Try the ambulance again."

I go back to the house, try, but still no answer.

Ian tries to lift Rosanna, but she starts to scream. "No, no, oh, oh . . ."

"The baby's head, it's fricking huge."

I look and I see it. The baby coming out.

"Put your hands under, Lindiwe. You don't want the little bugger to get concussed or something."

Rosanna is pushing and pushing and then, just like that, all of the baby is out, in my hands.

The baby is wet and slimy and crying.

"Put him against her stomach, so he gets some heat or something. Does she have a blanket?"

I put a blanket over the baby.

"I'll go and get an ambulance," he says.

I stay behind.

Rosanna is shivering.

I look down at the baby.

Someone comes into the room.

It's Mummy.

She looks up at Rosanna, then down at the baby.

"It's just a girl," she says and goes away.

The ambulance arrives. They take Rosanna and the baby away.

I look for Ian, but he's gone.

I go in the kitchen and Mummy is there. She is humming. The Lord Is My Shepherd.

"Lindiwe, my child."

"Yes, mummy."

I wait for a bit and then I say, "I have to go and study."

"You are a good child. Don't study too hard."

I wait for Daddy by the gate.

When he comes home, I tell him about Rosanna and the baby.

He goes in the lounge and sits there with Mummy.

I go in my room, and I think of Rosanna and the baby.

The baby who is my sister.

Half.

26.

"*So you were* born in the boondocks, heh? Kamativi. Me, I'm a city boy through and through. Mater Dei. Jeez, that little bugger was as ugly as hell. Did you check the nose of that thing, like a blimming hippo?"

"She's just a baby."

"Yah, yah. I don't mean anything. Just commenting. Anyway, babies are funny looking full stop: white, black, yellow, curry munchers, porcs, the whole lot of them."

He gets up from the grass and tosses away the stick he's been hitting the backs of his hands with. He stretches his arms and yawns. He comes and sits with me on the bench, and we both look out to the fountain that isn't spewing any water because of the drought.

When he was on the grass, talking, I could look at him without being shy; it wasn't staring. While he was talking, I was thinking that he didn't look like any white guy I had ever seen in Bulawayo. I was trying to work out if that was because I was getting to know him. If I didn't know him, if I saw him in the streets, would I think, Oh, there's a Rhodie. I was trying to think what made him different to me, what I liked about him, trying to list things in my head. But it was hard to make a list because it seemed that I kept coming to one thing: he's Ian, the boy from next door, the person I'm beginning to know. It was like asking myself why I liked Bridgette. I couldn't really answer that except to say, she's my friend, we get on well together; she's Bridgette.

"I got my rands today. And the fossil at the bank giving me such a hard time about it like it was his dosh I was taking. Hey, the old man worked for it fair and square."

I stretch out my leg and he stretches his out, too. He slings his leg over mine.

"Leg wrestling. Jeez, man, you're weak. And you've got Ndebele blood in you. You need to eat more sadza and relish."

And then he picks up my hand from the bench and puts it on his thigh. I hold my breath. He puts his hand over mine.

"Jeez, you're a midget."

I look at all the scars on his hand. He lets me look. And then I take my finger and trace the scars. He lets me do this.

I've seen him smack his keys on his hands so hard there was actually blood. I've seen him gnawing at them with his teeth and that really frightened me because it looked like he wanted to get right into his veins.

"She'd take my hands and put fricking polish on the nails," he said once when I had the courage to say, "Please, don't."

"Fricking pink, too."

And that was all.

He laces his fingers over mine, lifts both our hands so that his elbow rests on his thigh.

"I can't believe how light you are," he says, letting go of my hand. "And your wrists . . ."

"Could you give me a lift?"

"A lift? Now? Where to?"

"When you leave for South Africa. You can drop me at Gwanda."

"Gwanda! Are you penga? What the hell do you want to do in Gwanda?"

"Can you give me a lift? It's on the way, or else I'll just hitchhike."

"Then hitchhike. I'm not . . ." He looks at me and shakes his head.

"Please, I . . . I have a message to give Rosanna's aunt."

My face is burning and my mouth is dry. I try to keep looking at him, but I can't hold his eyes. I look at the mermaids of the fountain.

"Lindiwe, there's no ways I'm—jeez, man I've got enough on my plate."

"Please, I'll go and come back the same day. I'll take the bus home. Please."

I don't like the sound of my voice.

And then I feel the tip of his finger on my nose. I turn my face to him, dislodge his finger onto my lips. I feel the gentle pressure of his flesh, and my heart is thumping so hard I am sure he can hear it, feel it.

"I'll think about it, okay."

I don't tell him of Mummy's shouting and her silences. I don't tell him of how Daddy is trying so hard not to love his new daughter or even notice her. I don't tell him of school; how the girls there are bored with me, how they ignore me completely. I don't tell him how much I miss Bridgette, how she's been sent away. I sit in the car keeping everything inside like I always do. And the most important thing I don't tell him is that he is the only one, the only one, who truly knows I exist.

I don't tell him that it's not Gwanda where I intend to stop.

There's an army truck outside the gate. Daddy tells me to go in my room, lock the door.

From the window I can see two soldiers coming out from Maphosa's room.

27.

Two days later he picks me up at the Holiday Inn.

I changed from my school uniform in the toilets at Haddon and Sly.

"Nice earrings," he says.

I put my hands on my ears.

"You're a hard case," he says. "A fricking hard case."

But he's smiling.

I want to tell him so many things. How Prince Charles shook my hand outside the City Hall when he came for independence. How proud Mummy was and how Daddy scolded her for taking me there into the crowds where anything could have happened, like getting squashed to death by overexcited would-be Zimbabweans. How I looked and looked at my hands afterward to see if they were any different because Mummy said I had shaken "the hands of a prince." Or how, last year, I got stuck at the Eisteddfod public speaking competition, and I stood on the stage in front of hundreds of people, including Mummy and Daddy, also Uncle and Aunty Wesley, my mouth opening and closing, opening, hoping that words from the air all around would somehow enter and give me once again the power of speech; how I could hear every single noise in the hall, every whisper, giggle, cough, except what I was desperately looking for, my words, until finally the Master of Ceremonies led me away, and just as I got behind the curtain, the words came, "In

Praise of Silence," my speech. How Mummy and Daddy greeted me with silence, and Uncle Wesley, who had just come from Canada where he had done a doctorate in aeronautics and who Daddy respected very much, made Daddy take us all to Eskimo Hut, the Kings of Ice Cream, where Uncle Wesley brought me a double ice cream cone and Aunty Wesley said that in Canada she had seen grown men shaking in front of podiums and she had heard someone say that the best approach to public speaking was to think of your audience with no clothes on. Aunty Wesley was like that. She said some Very Interesting things. Or how I had four full scrapbooks of Lady Diana, now Princess Diana, and how I had written her a letter telling her all about them. How I thought Björn Borg was a great tennis player and maybe he (Ian) would laugh and say. "Jeez, man, you've got one heavy crush on him" (which was true) or . . .

I want so much to impress him. I want to give him something.

"Mummy doesn't know, but Daddy killed someone during the war."

It comes out of me so forcefully that I am out of breath.

"Shit. A gook? A terr?"

"No. There was an ambush. He started shooting. It was a baby on a woman's back."

"Cross fire, shit. Shit. That's really heavy shit. How do you know?"

"He told me."

"Just like that."

"It was the time I was sick with malaria. He thought I was sleeping. He was praying, I think, asking for forgiveness. It was a big mess; his unit ran into an undercover operation. Next thing they were under fire. He told me once that the war was full of secrets. Full of bad times but good times also."

"Yah, one thing the old man said was, once you got in the

bush and the grass and sky were shitting bullets, every man found God and then, shit, lost him in double quick time once he was safe again with his mates and downing lagers and telling mahobo tall stories about kills. Worked like a charm, he said, every fricking time."

I sit in the car next to Ian thinking of the pocket money I saved up, which is rolled in a sock at the bottom of my schoolbag, how much rands it can buy.

I sit in the car next to Ian, thinking of the note I've left behind for Mummy, Daddy, or Rosanna to find. I think of what I've left behind. I try to think of what there is to come. Of how everything can be different, new.

"So, did he kiss you?"
 "Who?"
 "The youth group chappie."
 "No."
 "I knew it. You tshayad him good, didn't you?"
 "I wasn't interested."
 "What, he was ugly?"
 "He was white."
 "No shit. An expat?"
 "No. A Rho . . . A Zimbabwean."
 "Now, that's a first. You know, I reckon my old man killed mahobo gooks."
 "What are you going to do down south?"
 "Who the fricking hell knows. The rands will tide me over for a bit, and then I reckon it's mind over matter, got a couple

of connections there. You still haven't told me what you want to do in Gwanda. Fuck all there. Jeez, check how dry it is. That Swedish chick says that no drought relief is being allowed in dissident areas. She reckons people are dying like fricking flies. Bob, shit, he's hard-core. Shit, *now* what? A fricking roadblock."

I look out of the window

"Jeez, did you see how that gondie looked at you. I thought he was going to drag you into the bush and do God knows what, what the Swedish chick hinted at—it's like fricking World War Three; me, I'm sticking straight on the tarmac, no fricking adventures, you hear me."

"So, I'm your sister."

"Quick thinking, heh, half sister. Thought he was going to drag me into the bush when I came out with that, almost did a double take myself. Shit. You check those gondies in the cattle truck? Where the hell are they taking them? You see the look in their eyes and the smell, shit. Fear. That Swedish chick says that they've made camps. Balange, Balangwe, something like that over at Matopos is where the main indaba is. Bob has it in real good for you Ndebeles. Shit man, gondies versus gondies, had to happen."

"Why do you keep saying that?"

"What?"

"Gondie."

"Gondie, now don't you start that racialistic shit. Gondie, Aff, helluva lot better than kaffir, munt, muntu, toey in my book. You can call me honky, no worries."

"Boer. Bhunu."

"Now, that's a bit far."

"Gondie. What does it mean?"

"Shit, I don't know, just another way of saying Aff. Anyway, in forms and shit what racial group do you tick?"

"Colored."

"Colored. Yah, well, different strokes. Me, African. No two ways about it. Pure and Simple. Born and bred."

I think of Maphosa. What he would say to this African here.

"Boy, did I hate that Clem Tholet song, 'Rhodesians Never Die.' Don't even get me started on that one. The old man would tune that stuff, what was the other one, yah, 'It's a Long Way to Mukumbura,' and the whole house would be like a fricking Rhodie sport's club come Saturday evening. . . . You should check how all teary he'd get listening to Troopie's Request on the radio. Come six o'clock, he was downing scotch. 'My boy,' he'd say. 'Come, come here, my boy, just listen to her, Sally Donaldson, you have no idea how much comfort that voice gave us troops out there in the bush, no idea.' I even found a picture of her from *Look and Listen* in his bedside drawer, would you believe."

"My father also liked her. He said that she even played requests from African soldiers."

"Give me 'Nkosi Sikelel' iAfrica' any day. Yebo mama, God bless Africa. One thing you can say for sure is gondies—what? okay, okay—Affs can sing. Now I think of it, I bet that chick's been with a gondie; they're all into gondies. Third World groupies. You check them walking in town, hand in hand. Not being racialistic or anything, but it just doesn't look right. You can tell even the blacks want to tshaya the gondie. And then you get all the goffle kids."

I think of the white girls at school, how they pulled faces when they had to learn "Nkosi Sikelel" from Mrs. Moyo and how they copy her accent and wave their hands over their noses when she passes them. How they inch their bodies away from her when she walks around the class.

"So, what's she going to call the little bugger, heh?"

"I . . . I don't know."

"And no blimming sign of the father and so, what's new. Are you sure your war vet hasn't been . . . Anyway, better a mother; one thing for sure, no lightie needs a *step*mother. Once she caught me with a *Scope*. You know that South African magazine with chicks? Boy, did she throw a major kadenze. Wasn't she pretty enough, all this shit, and when the old man gets home, she gets him to give me a right good hiding, and afterwards she's all 'come luvvie, show me where it hurts.' Jeez, man, it's fricking hot. Best years of my life, I reckon, must have been zero to seven. Remember fuck all but *she* wasn't around. Plain downhill after that."

I try and remember Mrs. McKenzie, what she looked like. She's been dead for two years now, and she's only someone in people's heads, stories. She only comes alive then.

"She got rid of Mavis, the girl who was looking after me, and she told me mahobo lies about my mother, how I'd been abandoned and all that shit. When I got down south and found her, boy, did the truth come out; how he used to beat her, showed me the scars from the knives, and anyway, he chased her out, made her leave without me. I shouldn't have let her come back with me. Shit."

He suddenly claps his thigh.

"Man, too much gloom and doom."

"What school did you go to?" I ask him.

"Baines, primary, Gifford, secondary, one term only, though."

"Baines, Baines, have no brains."

"Yah, they're still blasting that one? First year there was a real bust-up at the interschools' sports day. The Baden Powell kids start blasting that from the stands, some senior boys donnared them good, and then all the fossils get involved. Shit, they had to call the police—two of the boys in hospital, broken noses, ribs, the works. They were tshayad, that's for sure, no brains but hobo brawn! Every time I drive past that school now, its looking like a real dump, the grass is growing up to here. Funny to see black lighties running around there. Where did you go, primary?"

"McKeurten."

"Shit, that's some rough goffle school. So I guess you *are* a goffle. You see a McKeurten kid, you cross the road, whitey or not: *ek sê that, ek sê this, I'll tune you.* . . . So you like it?"

"No, not really."

I don't tell him how Mummy had to pretend to be the house girl when she would come to pick me up from school; otherwise, they would have kicked me out because Mummy was too black and the headmistress was always going on about standards.

"Shit, not another one?"

"It's the Fifth Brigade, look at their . . ."

"Yah, yah, I've got eyes, haven't I? What the fuck do they want now? Check the look on this one now. Chill."

I sit quietly, not moving, wishing that I was at the back, like a good house girl. I do not look up at the soldier who has thrust his face in Ian's window, filling the car with smoke.

The cigarette dangles from his lips, and he speaks through it.

I look down at my lap and concentrate on nothing but Ian's voice. "Identity, sure, look. No, I've got my passport. She's my sister, half sister. No, I'm dropping her off in Gwanda. Yes, yes, I have my passport. Me, South Africa. But I have to go today. How can the road be closed . . . okay. Thank you. Thank you."

"Nothing like rands to open up a road, heh? Good thing I hid the rest of it in my shoe. I thought that chick was laying it on thick, but shit, those guys look like they could do anything. And what's with the red berets? Their heads must be frying under there."

He drives on for a bit, whistling.

"How come you've got your passport?"

He gives me a look, waiting.

"Jeez, man, you're not thinking of crossing the border. Are you penga? As soon as we get to Gwanda, you getting off."

He looks at me again, waiting.

"Lindiwe, for your information, there is apartheid in South Africa. What the heck do you think you'll do there, if they'll even let you through, man? God, you're dwaas."

"I can go there; there's no law."

"Lindiwe, be reasonable; there's no ways you're going, not a chance."

He shakes his head, looks at me again. "Open the compartment, yah, get a cassette out, the one with the black chick.

"Sweet, yah? Ella Fitzgerald. American. No ways a white chick could sound like that . . . what the fricking heck was . . . shit . . . we've blown a tire . . . hold on . . ."

"You okay?"

"Yes."

"Lucky I wasn't belting it, otherwise we'd be roadkill."

We get out of the car.

"The last thing I feel like doing is changing a fricking tire. Shit, I could use a Castle."

The slamming of the boot makes me jump.

And then he is hitting the lid with his fists. "Shit. Shit. No spare tire. I've got no spare tire. Shit."

I watch him kick the ground with his feet until finally he sits down on a boulder, his head in his hands, tired out.

I stand for a moment in the heat, and then I go to him.

"I reckon it's thirty, thirty-five K's to Gwanda," he says, shading his eyes. "We can walk it."

"It's hot."

"Yah, it's hot, any suggestions?"

"We could wait for a lift."

"Do you *see* anything moving on this road? Remember, it's *closed* and I don't want to be picked up by no gondie, no red beret, Fifth Brigade Commie gondies. And no fricking water; where the hell did we think we were jolling to, shit. Come, let's get a move on."

But he doesn't move. He just sits there. The sun is right on him. He doesn't care.

"Ten thirty, and it's already baking bricks."

He still doesn't move.

I go to the car. The metal burns my hand. I take out my bag, and after I think about it, his too. I think some more and push the cassette out; I open the compartment and take everything out; I find a Meikles plastic bag and I put everything in there. I walk past him.

I walk on the side of the road. I look up all the way along the road and I think how long and glittery it is.

I walk and I think of Mummy and Daddy.

I think of Rosanna and the baby.

I think of Maphosa and Mphiri.

And Bridgette.

I walk and I don't hear him behind me, but I don't turn around. The bags are heavy, but I don't put them down. I just walk and think.

I think of him.

Ian.

I say "Ian" softly.

I think of him sitting on the boulder by the edge of the road.

I think of him in the car, driving.

I think of him chewing biltong.

I think of him, his new blue shirt, the buttons all done up wrong.

I think of his hair, his eyes, his ears, his nose, his mouth.

I think of him, my brother.

My half brother.

And I just keep on walking.

"You better slow down or you'll be kwapulad by the heat in no time."

"Finished sulking?"

"Don't get smart-alecky with me girl."

I watch him take the bags off me.

"Thanks," he says.

"No worries," I say.

And he laughs.

We've been walking for so long when I see Bridgette standing there, holding a calabash in her hands. She tilts the calabash forwards and water spills to the ground.

Even though I know it's not real, that it's a mirage, I say, "Bridgette, don't. Don't waste it," and I begin to walk faster towards her, towards the water before it all spills to the ground.

"Hey, stop running!"

Even though I know Bridgette is not real, the water is not real, I keep thinking, please, please, don't waste it, and I can hear myself panting, running.

"Hey, what's up with you? Stop running."

I'm on the ground now, the hot burning ground.

"We need to get out of the sun, look for cover."

And he heads off into the bush.

"No, Ian, no. Ian! I'm not going in there. Please, stop."

"Just for a while, we're not going in deep. There, there's a tree, not much shade, better than nothing."

"They're going to find us, in the bush, in here. I'm not going . . ."

"Listen, we need to rest. Just sit down. Shit, it's hot."

He clears a space with his foot, puts my bag on it. "Sit. Here, have some of this."

From his pocket he takes out a slab of chocolate, a naajitshe. I watch him break the chocolate, peel the naajitshe. I take one bit of naajitshe, suck out the juice. He gives me another one.

"We'll save the rest," he says.

"You should have something."

"I'm okay."

He sits down on his own bag, and he shakes his head.

"Man, to think I was a fricking Boy Scout; survival guide in the bush went through one ear, came out the other."

He twists his head.

"Do you smell that? Like burnt. The grass is so dry, must be mahobo fires."

"We can drink water from aloes."

"Yah, that's right; plenty of that stuff over at Masvingo by the Zimbabwe Ruins."

"Great Zimbabwe."

"Don't start again, it's too fricking hot. They're ruins, aren't they? You can't change history."

"Whites said they were the work of Europeans, Africans couldn't build something like that; it's only recently that archaeologists have . . ."

"Jeez man, okay, okay, Great Zimbabwe Fricking Ruins, happy now? Shit, the smell. It's coming from that end."

"Where're you going?"

"Just stay there. I want to check out this smell."

"People get lost in the bush. They start walking in circles. They lose their bearings."

"Yah, yah, now you're a fricking scout. I'm not going far. There's a track here."

"I'm coming with you."

"There must be a kraal round here; might be able to get some water. No fences here, not commercial farming area. TTLs, communal lands. Just gon . . . , Affs."

"We're going too far. We can't see the ro—"

"Shit man, look at this."

They're burnt.

The huts, some of them still smoldering.

And the smell is there, everywhere.

It goes right inside me.

The smell I did not wake up to a long time ago.

The smell, he knows.

I look over to Ian. He is so still. His legs wide apart, his hands on his side, his fists clenched. Then I see his teeth chewing inside his cheek.

I look at the old man, bent picking.

I look at Ian who is watching the old man.

"Mudala," he says, "what has happened here?"

The old man does not turn around. He continues picking through the ash, settling the bones to one side.

Ian goes right up to him, gets down on his haunches.

"Mudala," he says, "what has happened?"

The old man stops and looks at Ian.

He does not seem surprised to see a white man suddenly there.

Ian puts his hand on the old man's shoulder.

"I will help you, mudala," he says.

And I watch him pick through the ash.

His hands move gently, quickly, sorting.

And then he turns to me, and I wonder if he knows what I am thinking—if he thinks I believe he is like the men with the red berets, the men who have come here and done this.

When they are finished, the old man looks around; Ian takes the Meikles bag, empties it, and gives it to the old man, who puts the bones, one by one, inside.

I watch him get up.

He says to Ian, to me, to the bush, the bones, his children, "We have suffered this day," and then he walks away into the bush, deep, deep into the bush.

Ian turns to me.

He wipes his face with his hands.

He looks down at his hands, then up at me.

"You okay?"

"Yes."

We stand there in the bush.

The two of us, listening, waiting.

"I woke up," he says, "and she was burning."

He looks right at me, through me.

"I let her burn."

That's all he says.

"At least they won't get any ideas that we've been sticking our noses where they're not wanted."

We've walked back to the car. Thirst burns my throat.

"Those goons are probably coming back to clean up. Best they find us here. Hopefully, it's a lift that turns up first. Shit, I could use a drink and a shower."

The lift turns up. A white pickup with zebra markings. Zimba Wildlife Lodges. In the driver's seat a white man and, by his side, a black Alsatian.

"Hi, what's up?" the man asks, opening the door. The dog starts barking and scrambling to get out. I move closer to Ian. the man says, "Quiet, boy," and pushes the dog back on the passenger seat.

"Burst tire, no spare," says Ian.

"Can give you a lift till the lodge. Finally got through the roadblock, a waste of a day and a half. I wish they would do whatever they're doing and move on. We can tow your car, get it fixed up tomorrow by our boys. Who's she?"

"She's with me."

"She'll have to hop in the back."

"Thanks, man."

"Jeez man, I'm knackered. You're still up? The man talked and talked. Acute verbal diarrhea, that's for sure. Didn't tell him about that shit in the bush, kept my answers short, to the point. Lindiwe? What, are you crying? Lindiwe, don't . . . You're shivering, what . . . Lindiwe, Lindiwe, don't . . ."

In the morning I wake up first.

I pick up my clothes scattered on the floor.

I stand still in the bathroom.

I look in the mirror and it is me.
I wash my face.
I get dressed.
When I come out, he is gone.

The car is fixed.
He is going on, setting off just now, off to Beitbridge.
Without me.

I stand by the car.
Waiting.

"So, Lindiwe," he says, "you heard the guy, the road's all clear now; they've moved on, you'll be all right."
He doesn't even look at me.
"I'll write, send you some cool postcards."
He is already so far away.
"Lindiwe," he says, and then he turns away.

I wait for the car to stop somewhere near, far.
I wait for the car to turn around, to come back to me, for me.
I wait for him to get out of the car.
To stand just right here.
But the car moves on and on until it is nowhere, gone.

On the bus I think of his hair, his eyes, his ears, his nose, his arms, his hands.
I think of my face in his hands.

My head pressed tight against him.
I think of never seeing him again.

So you're at varsity now, always thought you were a smart aleck.
Good thing I caught you before you took off. Sociology, Social
Anthr—what the . . . I see you're going to be one of those fundies,
make lots of dosh sorting out Third World Issues. Me, you know,
I'm just hanging. I miss the shit out of Zimbo, would you believe.

*So since you're becoming a fundie and all, no more letters to us
numbskulls, heh? No worries. Heard there's rioting and shit at the
varsity, hope you're steering clear of it.*

Lindiwe,
    At last I get something. So you got kwapulad. Well, not to be
harsh, I hope you learnt your lesson. Just concentrate on being a
fundie and leave the politics well alone.

Lindiwe,
    *Thanks for the philosophizing. I got caught up in a demo
downtown, some fricking whities sporting* FREE MANDELA, ANC
T-shirts. Lots of heavy shit happening in Soweto and in the hostels.

So now you're hanging around Frenchies and Italians; hope you
don't get Je taimed, and remember, the Frenchies, they eat frogs.
Talking about Italians, you know that they got buried alive in the
Kariba wall; the Tongas called their spirit to tshaya them good
for driving them out of the land and the dam flooded and the
workers got caught. Nice, heh?

I'm a Domestic Engineer. Would you believe, I'm fixing fricking fridges.

Lindiwe,
    I thought you were trying to pull a fast one. So, you're going

to the Tongas to do your, what do you call it, research ... the
effect of forced migration on the intra ... and you're saying I
gave you the idea, yebo mama. Just wear a hat, a good thick bush
hat, so that your brains don't get scrambled. And don't upset
those Tongas; they might be thick but they have one powerful
sekuru up there.

*What, now you're touring? I thought you were studying. With
the Frenchies. Yah, I told you the Vic Falls was lekker. What? You
camped? Can't the Frenchies even afford a hotel? They're rolling in
forex, aren't they? Me, I'm keeping a low profile. I hooked up with a
bird last night, would you believe.*

So, now you're a feminist. Must be hanging out with all the
expats that's causing severe brain damage and Frenchies called
Jean, for that matter. Jeez, man, a chick's name. So, I'm racialistic
and unfeministic ...

Chauvinistic, yah, yah. I knew that was the word.

Don't laugh. I'm sitting my O levels. Night classes over at the
Polytech. May as well get educated.

*Malaria, shit. Didn't you take your pills, man? No wonder you were
so quiet. I thought you were giving me the silent treatment. Shit,
you're lucky it didn't go into your head, then your brains would be
scrambled for sure.*

You wouldn't believe, but now I'm taking pictures. I was
messing around with this old Kodak and I sent the pictures to
The Star for a competition. Next thing I've won and I'm hanging
around, doing apprenticeship, with a hard-core photo journo
who's seen it all. Never too late to teach an old dog new tricks,

heh? Off to Soweto, tomorrow. Beats fridges in the burbs, that's for sure. Get to be in the Great Outdoors and to see The Great African Wildlife, up close. Hope I don't get clobbered; reckon I should get hold of one of those T-shirts.

I GUESS YOU'VE CHECKED OUT THE NEWS . . . THEY'VE FRICKING RELEASED MANDELA.

Sorry about the old man. Do you have a phone number? Here's mine. I move around a bit. Anyways here it is . . . Word of warning, if the Rhodie picks up, put on your European accent or else he'll hang up.

Shit, your voice brought back mahobo memories.

I'm taking a break. I'll be in Zimbo Friday next.

PART TWO

Early 1990s

And there you are.
  There *we* are.
  Here.

He skips up the stairs and gives me a hug, and I hear "Lindiwe" against my skin. It is a warm, gentle brush of air.

It's so unexpected to be like that, in his arms, against his body, that I feel myself stiffen, draw breath.

"Asch, I'm too rough. It's just that . . ."

There's a flurry of movement up ahead to the left: the afternoon cinema crowd getting out, stopping by for refreshments, or rushing across the car park to Scoop, the ice cream parlor, or next door to Nando's.

"The Italian Bakery, heh," he says while drawing out a chair. "Your preferred hangout these days? Classy."

I can't tell if he is being sincere or if he just finds the whole setup silly.

"No ways like Haef's Bakery over in Bullies. Hey, nothing washed down better than Haefeli's Hot Cross Buns and Coke when we were lighties."

Inside, I smile at that word.

I watch him take a look at the tables with their marble tops, their curlicued wrought iron legs, the tiny ornate chairs, and the well-heeled clientele sipping delicately at their cappuccinos.

We're sitting on the veranda, but when he pulls himself forward, he can see the glass cabinets filled with Italian pastries and paninis and the croissants stuffed with Nutella and vanilla cream and a long marble-topped counter, lined with six high stools, where the old regulars hang around conversing in Italian with the owners.

If we're still here at six, a queue will start forming that sometimes stretches down to the stairs for the different types of bread straight out from the ovens. In the queue there are maids from Avondale and Mount Pleasant in their starched, checked uniforms, diplomats' wives, gardeners in their patchy blue overalls, black businessmen in shiny polyester suits, and women in viscose outfits. It's a democratic queue where everyone patiently waits their turn.

"Come on, don't start."

His eyes settle back on me. And for some moments we are both staring openly, taking each other in.

How much I've forgotten. The length and breadth of him.

"Jeez man, you've grown."

"And you too."

"How many years?"

"Six, almost seven years."

"Jeez."

"I was wondering if I would ever hear that again."

"So, where's the Frenchie?"

"Don't start. Be nice."

"Seriously, where is he?"

"At work."

"Does he know you're meeting me?"

"Yes, of course."

"Interesting."

"Tell me."

"What?"

"Come on, tell me anything."

"It's great to see you, Lindiwe. You're sure your brains didn't get cooked out there with the Tongas?"

"I'm sure."

"Just checking I'm not talking to scrambled eggs."

"You're a photojournalist."

"I'm just taking pictures. Asch man, what's this?"

"Cappuccino."

"Cappuccino, heh?"

"Yes, *what?*"

"Now, you drink Italian coffee. Are you sure you come from Bullies?"

"Yes."

"Shouldn't it be Frenchie coffee?"

"This isn't The French Bakery. We could have gone to the Alliance, I suppose."

"Different strokes."

"What's *that* supposed to mean, Ian?"

"Nothing. Man, it feels good to hear you say my name."

"Come on, show me your pictures."

"No."

"Why not?"

"I'll take pictures of you."

"No thanks."

"Jeez man."

"Jeez man, to you too. You look tired."

"Yah, it's a long drive. I stayed a couple of days in Bullies. Still as sleepy as ever."

It's a shock to hear that he's been back there. I wait to see something in his face, something that will tell me if he might know.

"How is it like, down south?" I ask him.

"Not looking good. The security forces, the Zulus, the right wing, the ANC, the Commies they're butchering each other like . . . Asch, let's get out of here, too hot. Let's take a hike somewhere, you and me."

"A hike?"

"Yah, out of Harare."

"I . . ."

"Don't tell me the Frenchie has you on a tight leash, won't give his permission. I thought you were a feminist."

"Leave Jean out of this."

"Jean."

"That's not how you say it. Jean. Where do you want to go?"

"Anyplace. Just out. How about The Great Zimbabwe Ruins, heh?"

And we both smile at that.

He drives us to the Botanical Gardens, where we sit on a bench up at the savanna.

I follow a soldier who is walking briskly down the path, a plastic carrier bag hooked on a finger, his eyes fixed solidly on the paved stone. There've been irate letters in the *Independent* from white Zimbabweans with pseudonyms like "Nature Lover," and "Concerned Citizen" protesting how the army has appropriated chunks of the gardens, hacking down rare species of trees. There are all kinds of stories about what goes on in there behind the barbed wire, the MILITARY AREA — KEEP OUT signs.

"Come on, Lindiwe, tshaya me with some stories."

What could I say?

I could "hit" him with my first couple of months on campus; my frantic, heady dash into all that liberation, away from the oppressive atmosphere at home: Daddy's sudden sickness, Mummy's righteous forbearance of all things including my sins, the stains on my character.

The friends I had been swept up with for a while.

At the foreground, Cynthia, who I got to know because we shared a cabin in the train on that momentous journey from Bulawayo to Harare; I had sat on the top bunk bed, my back pressed against the wall, as she leaned out the window laughing, calling out, clasping hands, receiving yet one more package through the narrow window, and finally waving good-bye to the large group that was on the platform, two boys breaking off and running after the train calling out her name, just like in the movies. No one was there to see me off, and I thought of how I had taken the taxi to the station, holding the picture, smoothing his face with my finger, until finally I put it away in my purse. As soon as the train had gained full speed, Cynthia had slumped onto her bed and brought out a bottle of brandy from her handbag.

The first time I ever tasted an alcoholic drink (and got spectacularly drunk). The occasion, my birthday: Cynthia and me at the cinema on a weekday afternoon while watching *The Last Emperor*; she used her stiletto heel to somehow dislodge the cork out of the Vat 10 wine bottle because we had no corkscrew and we spent the time huddled at the back in the empty cinema swigging and giggling at the movie.

My tries at smoking up on the roof of the Student Union with Cynthia.

There was also Vumisani, Cynthia's cousin, and Edmond, Vumisani's roommate and first-year law student, who once he had learnt a bit of legalese would amuse us by talking in jargon.

Fridays and Saturday nights, after the government had paid out our grants and loans spent at Circus Nightclub, which we would walk to from campus, usually singing at the tops of our voices while taking nips from whatever alcoholic beverage someone had brought along (once from oranges that Cynthia and I had injected with vodka as there were rumors that police were patrolling the university neighborhood on the lookout for public drinking) so that by the time we arrived we were in very high spirits and ready for yet more. And sometimes we would pack into a rundown Emergency Taxi and head over to Playboy in town to catch Ilanga, the band of the moment, play live, our frenzied, drunken dash onto the crowded dance floor as soon as we heard the first few chords of "True Love," or even more down market to Jobs, which at month end was teeming and reeling with prostitutes and soldiers, flush with their loot from Mozambique, fights breaking out sporadically on the dance floor to the beats of Oliver Mtukudzi, Thomas Mapfumo, the Bhundu Boys.

Edmond's good-humored attempts to bed me.

The hangovers on Sundays, the habitual chilling-out trek to the university swimming pool, our bodies sprawled on the grass catching the sun while overhead the boys jeered and called out insults from the Student Union until we finally gave up and left. The undertone of violence always present.

And then meeting Jean on the last day of the first term. A kind of growing up again. The big fight with Cynthia, my friend spouting out the same kinds of things as Maphosa. I was selling out.

What could I say?

Jean has asked me to marry him. Yesterday, on this bench. And the word *yes* was there on the tip of my tongue, but I said instead, "I have to finish university." And his response, "bien sur," and we left it at that.

I don't tell him anything about Jean Pierre Roulier. How they seem to be the very opposite of one another. That Jean, who was born in Algeria, is a doctor in a mission hospital and has lived most of his life in Africa, but wouldn't call himself an African; that he would think that an act of great arrogance and pretentiousness.

I imagine Ian looking down at his small, compact body, taking in the pensive, weary look in his eyes, and drawing his own hasty conclusions.

"Still as tight-lipped as ever, heh?"

"What exactly do you want to know?"

"You're serious aren't you, about the Frenchie bloke?"

"Is there no other subject?"

"Just answer that, serious, yes or no?"

"Yes."

I think of how I found out about his wife, a brilliant doctor who had been killed two years ago in Brazzaville by bandits, and how he was only now starting to recover.

"Be gentle with him," I was told on a veranda out in Rusape by Marie, the brittle wife of one of his oldest friends, Herbert Molyneux who was the project coordinator of a French non-governmental organization, which had been trying for four years to set up a network of rural markets in Manicaland.

"You should have seen him before. He was finished. A wreck."

Jean and Herbert had gone out to pick up some crisps and some beers.

"He is a saint. Maybe you are too young to appreciate his love. But do not play with him, promise. No games. I will kill you if you do that, I promise."

She had laughed roughly, whirling smoke into the cool air.

I had only known Jean for a few weeks, and I felt the weight of responsibility as I lay next to him that night. I couldn't respond to him. I was afraid to touch him. To be touched.

"What troubles you, Lindiwe?" he asked me at last.

"I . . ."

"Lindiwe!"

Ian grabs my hand, shakes it. And then he knocks gently on my forehead.

From here we can see the pond. There's a couple walking hand in hand. They stop and watch the ducks.

I don't tell Ian that I walk here from the university; when I'm feeling desperate, I come here and sit on this exact bench. That I watch the gay white men walking gingerly around the pond, making contact. That if we stay here a bit longer, they'll be here and Ian will have something to say about their tight shorts, their tight vests, their limp wrists. Sometimes there are schoolboys making fun, wiggling behind the men, calling out, "Hey, pansy; hey, pooftah."

"Anyways, I hope you're not thinking of doing anything stupid."

How stupid would it be to give yourself to someone who wants to take care of you? And everything that comes with you.

"So, the old man?"

"Dad? He's paralyzed on the left side."

"Shit. Your mother?"

"My mother has the Lord. Stop looking at me like that."

"It's quiet here. It's like coming to fricking paradise. Zimbo, I mean. Everybody calmly going about their business. Looks like things are looking up."

"Oh, don't be fooled; we've had our dramas. The corruption scandal. Willowgate. You haven't heard? The illegal selling of brand-new cars at exorbitant prices by members of government, not a very socialistic practice. A minister killed himself over it. And plus Mugabe is mad as hell at Mandela for stealing the limelight, for getting himself released."

"Tame stuff. When you think what's happening down south. Shit, those guys really know how to . . ." He lifts his hand, touches my head. "I told you you'd look good with short hair."

I don't tell him that I had it cut just yesterday.

That Bea at the salon at Fife Avenue Shopping Centre kept saying, "Are you sure? are you sure?" over and over again. "But you've got such lovely, thick hair. The time and work we've spent. Look, it falls on your shoulders. Are you sure? Are you sure?"

And the other customers were looking on in horror as all that hair fell, wasted.

"Cut it shorter, shorter," I said, ignoring Bea's fit.

"But you won't be able to perm it. You'll look like you've just stepped off a rural bus."

"Cut it, Bea."

I don't tell him that I like his hair this new way, a bit long, and I wouldn't dare tell him that it makes him look bohemian, artistic.

I don't tell him that everything I'm wearing is new.

The first guy has come. A regular. Tall with a slight paunch. His shorts are shiny blue joggers digging into his crotch. His hair, as ever, is thick, glossy, the curls lapping his shoulders. He is standing, facing the water, his hands on his waist. I wait for Ian to say something.

"News flash, Lindiwe, I'm not as racialistic as before."

"Oh, so you're still *a bit* racialistic."

"Jeez, let me finish. I think racialism is always there; I've toned down."

"That's something."

"I think it's seeing dead bodies, white, black, brown, yellow; in the end they all look the same and that gets you thinking. . . . Heh, is that a mof . . . ?"

"Don't start."

"Start what?"

"Yes, he's a homosexual man, and he is on the lookout for other homosexual men. One will probably turn up. Homosexuality is illegal in Zimbabwe although lesbianism isn't;

I guess the powers that be don't think that's a dangerous enough offense to the nation's morals. Actually, I'm wrong; strictly speaking it's sodomy that's illegal. Let's see: as long as you don't practice what can be deemed a homosexual or an 'unnatural' act—I guess that includes women, too—everything should be fine. So, let's not give him a hard time, okay."

"I was only making a comment. What's wrong with you?"

"I'm tired, too, Ian."

I want to tell him so much, what it means to have him suddenly here, with me.

"Show me your hands," I want to say to him.

We're quiet for a while watching the gay man. He bends down, dips his hand in the water. When he gets up again, someone is there. Another jogger. The tall guy touches his hair, flings his head back. The other guy pats him on the leg.

"Looks like he's happy."

"Good for him. Let's go."

"Lindiwe . . ."

His hand is tight on my arm.

I turn around, look up. I've forgotten how tall he is.

I'm standing at the museum in Bulawayo. He wants to know what the hell I'm up to. His hand is tight on my arm.

"Sorry," he says and lets go.

I don't ask him what he's sorry for—for grabbing my arm or something else?

I step back from him. I want to take his hand.

"Where are you staying?"

"The Bronte."

I don't tell him that that's where Jean and I go when he is in town.

"We should go up north, Ian. Inyanga. I also need to get away from the heat and all this studying. I think there's a National Parks office at the back. We can rent a cottage super cheap." I *want* to get away. With him.

"You sure?"

"Yes, I'm sure. Why, you've changed your mind?"

"Me. Never. Your Fren . . . ?"

We meet up again at Second Street Extension for dinner at The Mandarin. We have a seat by the window with a view of the car park, and we can just make out the car under the streetlights. Ian got into a lively discussion with the young tout about looking after his car and making sure its radio and other accessories didn't magically disappear in the course of our meal. "Yes, baas," the tout finally said, waving us off with his cleaning rag, and Ian looked at me and shrugged helplessly.

"Vegetarian, heh?"

"Yes?"

"Only vegetables."

"And fruits."

"Vegetables, chete. Some of your gray matter *did* get cooked. Which reminds me, the Tongas, how were they?"

"They're incredibly resilient, very artistic; you should see the weaving they do for baskets. Anywhere else they would be making a very good living. What are you smiling at?"

"You sound like a fundie, an expat fundie. Shit, don't sulk."

"I'm not sulking."

"So, how does it work here?"

"You get up, get a bowl, and pick whatever you want to eat; put it in the bowl; choose the sauce; and give it to the cook who stir-fries it in front of your very eyes."

"And there's meat?"

"Yes."

"Very sophisticated. And I can take as much as I want?"

"As much as the bowl fits."

"How big is the bowl?"

"Could you get up and go and see for yourself."

"Asch man, it's not a big bowl."

"Do you want to ask the kitchen for another one?"

"Shit, I want proper food. I'm hungry."

"So maybe we can go downtown and get a plate of sadza and relish."

"That's more like it. Come on, I'm playing, Lindiwe."

"Not bad. How can you just eat a plate of mush?"

"They're called vegetables and noodles."

"Yah, mush."

"So we set off early tomorrow. Seven, eight o'clock."

"Yes, baas."

I watch him join the queue again. The solid bulk of him. As if he knows what I'm doing, he glances back, gives me a wink.

There's lots I could tell him. Secrets. One by one. All of them. I want him to come back. I want to see his eyes. Find out exactly what shade of blue they are. I want to ask him if he still has that blue (the buttons all done up wrong) shirt.

I watch him pile up his bowl, splosh in the sauce, hand it over to the cook, say something to him that makes him laugh. I can guess what he said: "Jeez, shamwari, I'm hungry." I want to look at his hands. His hands that were bruised blue the first time I saw them. The hands that held my face that one night.

He drives me back to the university and he parks outside Swinton, the female Hall of Residence.

"How's life in here?"

"It's okay."

"The guys and girls are separate?"

"Yes."

"The guys don't get, you know?"

"They do, especially after Pay Out, I mean when the government grant has come through. Then the Student Union becomes a no-go area for female students. The first year I was here I was . . . anyway, for some reason beer is subsidized."

He turns on his seat. "You were what, Lindiwe?"

"Nothing, just some stupid guy locked his room and tried . . . Nothing happened. I screamed like a madwoman. He opened the door, that's all."

"Shit."

"It gets out of hand."

"Too much jolling."

I open the door.

"Lindiwe."

I turn to him, and before I know what I'm doing, my hand is resting on the side of his face, gently there, feeling the warmth of his skin. He puts his hand on top of mine.

"I'll pick you up tomorrow, outside your Italian Bakery, eight o'clock sharp."

"Righto."

In my cubicle I open the drawer of my desk. I take out the box, which is right at the back. I open it. *Kings Jewellers*. Flame lilies. *Thump, thump, thump* goes my heart, telling its own impossible story.

2.

I'm late.

"Thought you chickened out."

"No. One of the boys beat up his girlfriend. I had to take her to the clinic."

"Jeez man, Lindiwe. You should move out."

I don't tell him that Jean says the same thing; that he's offered to pay for the rent.

"This is what I miss. No traffic. No fricking billboards."

We don't talk much all the way up to Marondera, and then as we're leaving the city center, he says, "In case you're wondering, I've got a spare tire and water and food, not taking any chances this time round."

I try to laugh but I can't.

Up to Rusape we talk a bit more. He tells me about taking pictures; the black people he has got to know in Soweto; the family who've taken him under their wing.

"First days on the job and I make the cardinal mistake of going down there on my own, and I end up wandering around roads, dirt tracks, shacks still burning; get lost like a real shit and there's a vibe in the air, bad. The place is deserted like I never

seen; anyways, this old chap comes out of his house, tells me not
to head into the hostels today, I'll be killed in no time. Those
boys in there once they've locked the place down got no time
for journalistic what-whats; they smell blood, that's it; so he lets
me hole up in his place, which turns out to be two blocks from
the hostel. And you never seen such a scene, Livingstone, his
wife, three grown-up kids, six grandchildren, an aunt, uncle all
in that matchbox and whoever else drops by from back home.
And you see the love in there, the way they are trying to hold
everything together, it just makes you think."

Hearing, listening to him talk like this in the car, I am
brought back again to what must have struck and touched me
as a schoolgirl, the gentleness at his core.

"We've had braais together on that patch of dirt at the front
of his house; of course, the whole street soon joins in. Man can
Livingstone eat. I thought I was one greedy bugger. They lost
a son in Sharpeville, fourteen years old. And you try and find
the bitterness there, nothing, anger, yes, and this desire for justice. You know for the first time I can actually see myself on
the same footing as blacks; I'm in their home, I'm a guest. I see
all the bullshit of yesterday, of our fossils. 'Ah, the blacks that's
how they live; they've just come out of the bush. They don't
understand European things. They're just like that; they don't
mind no electricity,' all that shit. When you see a family, decent
people, trying to get by then it really donnars you. You've been
thinking one way for one hundred percent of your life so far,
and then, *bam,* you start to see, and it hits you hard. . . . Anyways, people change, that's all I'm trying to say."

He's quiet for a long time after that.

We stop at The Crocodile Motel in Rusape to stretch our legs,
have a Coke. There are some children playing in the pool.

"Do you know that guy?" Ian asks

I lean over, and for a moment, my heart must miss a beat.

Under one of the umbrellas, there's a man looking directly at us.

There is a shameless scramble in my head for words.

"He's been eyeing us since we walked in. What the hell is his problem?"

"Yes, I know him. He's, he's a friend, Herbert."

"*Air-bair.* Let me guess, Frenchie?"

"Yes, he works for a French NGO that's based here. I'll just go and say hello."

I get up. I am conscious of Ian behind me, watching as I walk towards Herbert, Jean's good friend.

"Lindiwe," Herbert says. "I thought it was you."

He stands up, pushes himself away from the carcass of the T-bone steak, and gives me a kiss on the cheek and a hug.

He smells heavily of the Galois cigarettes he chain-smokes.

"As beautiful, as always," he says.

"I'm . . . I'm . . . with a friend."

How guilty and imbecilic I sound.

"I told Jean I'd be going away." *Guilt, guilt, guilt.*

"How is Marie? Tell her I say hello."

"In Cape Town to get some culture."

Herbert shrugs.

Last time I saw Marie she was in a rage, screaming at him about how sick she was of living like a rat. Later we had sat outside on the veranda where she told me that sometimes she feared she was losing her mind and that she would not be good for anything. She needed civilization, culture. Books. Theater. Art.

"I am harsh, no," she said. "So much poverty, hardship here, and I want these things. I think I will leave Herbert. Go back to France. But then I think, France, I am a small insect. I will get trampled on, poor little me."

"I pick her up from the airport tonight. And your friend, you are visiting this sleepy place or you're passing by to Inyanga?"

"No, yes, and . . . it was good to see you, Herbert."

When I come back, Ian is up on the veranda fiddling with one of the table games there.

We both watch Herbert get up, wave, and leave.

"One of your expat friends," Ian says.

It is a matter-of-fact statement. Almost. A statement of fact. Almost.

"Yes."

"He's a big guy."

"Yes."

"Looks a bit like that *Lethal Weapon* guy."

He looks at me and then he says, "Let's go."

"If you want I can drive."

"You can drive?"

"Yes, don't look so shocked."

"I have to get used to you like this."

"Like what?"

"Grown."

He's driving. I'm in charge of navigation.

"We turn off here, I think."

"You think?"

"Well, it's the only turnoff. Yes, I'm right, that signpost says Nyanga National Park."

As soon as we leave the main road and get onto the gravel, something seems to happen. It's as if the car has slid off somewhere and is floating, weightless, carrying us with it. I know he feels it too because he turns and says, "Jeez, man, *now* I feel lekker." We dip and turn, dip and turn, and ahead of us as we rise, the mountains ripple away in waves, the mist snatching bits of them away. I open the window, put my head outside. The air is cool and scented with pine. Then we're in a forest, the trees sometimes so close to the road I can touch them, the breathless eeriness of us, the car, on this pass almost makes me want to cry.

"I hope you brought a jersey," he says.

"Yes, I did."

We stop at Juliasdale to buy some groceries. We both take a basket. He fills his with a carton of Castle beer, a loaf of bread, cheese, biltong, chips, a packet of T-bone steaks, Nestlé coffee, sugar, Marie biscuits. I fill mine with milk, tomatoes, pasta, onions, toothpaste, carrots.

At the counter he looks over at my basket and says, "Healthy living, heh?"

"At least I won't die of a heart attack."

"No, you'll die because of a lack of *food*. How can you live in Africa and swear off meat. You must be penga."

The lady at the counter smiles.

"Are you paying together?" she asks.

"No," I say, taking out my purse.

"Yes," Ian says and pushes past me.

In the car I say, "Thank you."

"What for?"

"For paying."

"Don't be stupid."

I close the window and I listen to the sound of the car moving. We catch a glimpse of the falls.

"We'll check them out tomorrow. I hope you like hiking. What kind of shoes have you got?"

I lift my foot, show him the Bata tackies.

"They'll do. You really need a pair of veldt skoeners, farmer's shoes, if you're going to be serious."

It's three o'clock when we arrive at the lodges. Ian gets out of the car to get the keys from the warden at the gate. The warden walks around the car, takes a look at me, and says to us, "No hooting in the park, please, and drive with due respect."

The cottage is right deep in the park, and it takes us another twenty minutes to find it. There are no other cars around. I stand outside and feel for one moment, looking at the still water of the lake, absolute peace. I look up to catch Ian watching me.

"That's a picture I could take," he says.

Inside, the cottage is simple and clean. Two old-fashioned sofas with sunken seats facing the fireplace. Four chairs, a table with a formica top, like the one in the kitchen in Bulawayo. One main bedroom with twin beds and a tiny one with a single bed. Ian throws both our bags in the main bedroom. Then we look at each other.

"Right," he says.

"Right," I say.

"Beer."

He's drinking a beer on the veranda.

"Come on, sit," he says.

I drag the chair next to him.

"Want some?"

I shake my head, then change my mind. "Yes."

"I'll go and get you a glass."

"It's okay. I'll just take a sip. Okay, you can pour it into a glass."

"Jeez, you're complicated. Just take a sip. You don't have herpes, do you?"

"The question is, do you?"

"Check." He purses his lips towards me. I laugh.

"It looks safe."

He gives me the bottle. I take a sip.

"You don't drink much do you?"

"No, I don't like the taste."

"I should have picked up a bottle of wine."

"No, that's okay."

"Look, look, over there, look at that."

Two large brown eyes in a clearing. Then another two.

"Waterbuck," he says.

The two animals look at us intently, and then they skip off into the mist.

Sleeping arrangements.

I'm standing at the door with my bag.

"Good night," I say.

"Where're you going?"

"The other room."

"Why?"

"Because."

"Because what?"

"I'll just feel better, I mean, more comfortable there."

"Really?"

"Really. Good night."

"Come on, Lindiwe, stay here. How am I going to talk with you if you're right at the other side?"

"We're supposed to be sleeping, and it's right next door."

"Just for tonight."

"Why? No."

"Lindiwe, I just want to have someone, you, with me. Jeez, it's coming out funny. Like friends, we're friends aren't we? It's been a helluva long time, six, seven years. . . ."

"Yes."

"So, come on. Look, I'll move the beds way apart. Check."

"Okay. No, okay. Just for tonight."

"Yebo mama."

I wake up in the middle of the night.

"What?"

"I'm cold."

"It's all the vegetables."

"What?"

"Move over here."

"What?"

"Body heat."

"What? I just need a blanket."

"You've already got the two blankets."

"Oh, sorry."

"Push your bed here, and we'll warm each other up."

"What?"

"Jeez man, not like that. I mean, it's warm my end of the room, just move. Come on, I'll even push the thing for you."

"Better now?"

"No."

"Give it ten minutes."

In the morning I wake up; my head is on his shoulder.

"You've got one heavy head, Lindiwe," he says, shaking his hand. "What the hell is in there?"

"Gray matter."

"Heavy-duty lead, more like."

"So why didn't you move it?"

"No worries."

"You look cute in those pyjamas."

I can't help it, I start smiling.

"What's that for?"

"It's my birthday. I'm twenty-three today."

"Lindiwe, why didn't you . . . ?"

"Thank you. Being here is really great. Thank you."

"Don't start the waterworks. Wait, stand there, like that."

"No."

"Yes. You look lekker. It's a great picture. Tell you what. I take you out to a real fancy dinner tonight. Troutbeck Inn. I reckon they have vegetables there."

"No, you don't have to. This is fine. More than fine."

"Troutbeck Inn."

"Look," he says pointing to the map. "We can walk to the falls. Slow and easy."

We're drinking coffee and eating toast inside. Outside, a shroud of mist covers the lake. I rub my shoulders.

"Cold?"

"A bit."

"I thought you had a jumper."

I point to what I'm wearing.

"That? Here, take mine. It will get warmer soon."

"It's okay."

"Take it, woman."

"Thanks."

"Twenty-three. I can't believe."

I want to tell him something. Some thing. I want to

begin. I want a word. A single word. A way of saying it.
"Ian, I . . ."

"Yah?"

And I can't do it, I can't.

"Nothing."

"Don't get cross now, but why aren't you celebrating with
your Frenchie?"

"He's working."

"Working, on a Saturday?"

"He's a doctor. He works with the Tongas."

"Shit. So how did you two, if he's way up there?"

"At the Alliance Française. I go for French classes. There's a
café there and I bumped into him, spilt his coffee all over him,
and so that's how we met."

"A doctor, heh?"

He starts drumming the table with two fingers.

"He must be a bit older than you. Doesn't it take yonkers
to train? Cough up, Lindiwe, how old is the fossil? I can tell
you're mahobo embarrassed."

"It's none of your business."

"Yah, yah, how old?"

"Forty-five."

"Jeez man. Old enough to be your . . ."

"Shut up."

He leans back on his chair, his hands under his head, a broad
smile plastered on his face.

"You look very satisfied with yourself."

"I bet he's got white hair and I reckon bad teeth."

"Could you leave it please."

"Touch touchy."

"Okay, tell me about your—what do you call them?—birds,
all those suburban madams throwing themselves at your feet."

"Few are chosen."

"Few want."

Then he becomes serious. "I reckon I'll never get tied down."

"Why?"

"Way too many spooks on my back."

And that's all he says.

"Tired?"

"A bit."

"Worth it though, huh?"

"Yes."

We're standing at the foot of the falls.

The light catches the water as it splashes and spills over the stones, and yellow butterflies slip and float out of the streams of falling water. I read in one of the pamphlets from the national park that the air in Inyanga has been described by well-heeled travelers as "dry champagne"; I've never drunk champagne, but standing here now, I think I must know what it tastes like.

Elixir, I say quietly to myself and imagine a knight from King Arthur's Round Table standing there a goblet in his hand; Maid Marian sitting languidly on the grass, the pale mauve flowers grazing her legs.

I think of Ian laughing out loud if he knew what was in my head.

"Jeez," he might say, "you're full of mush, Lindiwe. Lead *and* mush."

I imagine running, stripping myself of clothes, and diving into the wide pool, skinny-dipping, yelping and splashing about, something I'm sure young white people, exuberant and fearless, do when they come here, playing games. I watch Ian duck his hand into the water. I watch him lift his shirt from his body, tug and pull, and I wonder if he will be one of those white people. He stands there, bare chested. And I see that there is nothing wasteful about his body. I notice the flick of a scar on his right shoulder blade. And I quickly look away.

I watch him soak in the sun; its rays fall on the hairs of his chest, glisten gold.

He bends down again, splashes water over his head, onto his skin.

I think for a moment that he will not be able to resist it. He will let himself go, dive smoothly into the cold water; already his jeans are wet up to his calves.

He turns to me with a grin, flicking water at me. "You should try it."

He shakes the water off his head. "Nice. I needed to cool down a bit. That was quite a hike, huh?"

And I think of how many times he took my hand, helped me over a log, a rock, a ledge, cleared the path for me, as if it was the most natural thing in the world. How we both stood still when we came to a little meadow with a stream running through, and just as he had done with the birds so many years ago, he named the flowers and grasses for me. The ferns and orchids at the edges of the crystalline water. Bushes of sweet peas, traveler's joy, purple lassandria, and the sugar pink Rhodesian creeper with its fragile bell flower. (When I said *"Rhodesian,"* he charged back, "Jeez, Lindiwe, when I was a lightie they *were* Rhodesian.)

He pointed out to me the woodland of dwarf msasa trees further away on the slopes of the mountain.

And birds, so many of them, calling out to each across the rolling hills and granite cliffs.

Blue duiker and samango monkeys, he told me, only found here.

There was a quiet pride and satisfaction in his voice. I could tell he felt home.

He flings his T-shirt over his shoulder and rubs his hands. "So, stand there, picture."

"Oh please!"

"Oh please what? There. Done."

We sit on some rocks, under the shade of a tree, eat our cheese sandwiches, drink some water.

"Tell me about the six years. What have you been up to, Lindiwe?"

I think of the letter I wrote at the end of that Christmas day. I'd spent the whole day hoping and hoping. Hoping and fearing. That I would hear a car at Number 18. He would be there standing beside the yellow Datsun Sunny, looking over the fence at me. And then he would know. But he didn't come. He didn't come for six years.

"School, studying, that's about it."

There is everything that is unsaid between us. He knows it, feels it.

"So," I say. "Let's talk about the next six years."

Which, of course, is a mistake. I want him so much to know. And not to know.

"Jeez man, who the hell knows? Could be jolly well dead."

Where (from whom) did he pick up that word, *jolly?*

"What kind of fundie are you going to be when you finish, when is it, next year?"

"Yes, I don't know. I'll have a bachelor of science in psychology. I don't want to get into personnel which is what most people are doing, and I don't know if I even want to practice as a psychologist."

"So why the hell are you studying this stuff?"

"I'll probably go into personnel actually. That's where the money is. I've got a part-time job with an advertising company, three afternoons a week. Last week I had to go around Harare looking for a dozen doves."

He looks at me in a way that suddenly makes me feel shy.

"And what you're reading these days?"

"Reading, oh, for pleasure you mean? *She Came to Stay* by Simone de Beauvoir."

"Simone de who?"

"A feminist, a French feminist, she wrote the first real book about the condition of being female, *The Second Sex,* how women are born under subjugation and . . ."

"Does this chick even have a boyfriend?"

"Yes, a guy called Jean-Paul Sartre, who wrote *Nausea* and *Being and Nothingness* about the existen—"

"Another Jean, man, these Frenchies . . ."

"Jean."

"Yah well, they're everywhere, your Frenchies, huh?"

I choose to ignore the comment. I think of the look on his face if I let on that it was Marie who introduced me to Beauvoir.

"You were always into your books; I reckon the library in Bullies misses you a lot."

Before I know what I'm saying it's said. . . .

"Please, tell me, what happened that night?"

It's so quiet here between us.

I think of the lighter falling on the stone, the look on his face then.

"Jeez man, Lindiwe. Jeez."

We are alone here. A man. A woman. Anything can be said, done. But I am not afraid. I want to tell him that whatever happened, we are connected; we will always be connected. I want him to trust me with his secrets; I have my own to tell him.

I was sleeping, dreaming while Mrs. McKenzie burnt.

"Why, why now? Like I told you, Lindiwe, I woke up and she was burning."

"Because I'm not fif— sixteen anymore."

He looks at me.

"Because I'll believe you."

I fill my head with the sound of the water falling over leaves, on the stone.

"I went to the police station to tell them what had happened. The next thing I know is that they're arresting me. On suspicion, they keep on saying. On suspicion. They hadn't even checked out the house, didn't know what was what, but they had a white boy in the stocks and they were pleased as hell. I reckon there were some CIO guys that day. Then they finally go down to the house, talk to Mphiri, and they come back and say that I am no longer under suspicion, and I'm thinking I told you what happened and next thing I'm under arrest for murder. And then it's, 'I've made a confession,' and they change everything to sound like I did that, I did this, and all the time these guys—the ones I think are CIO—are tshaying that they have me for sure, how nice it's going to be to see a white neck in the noose, the first whitey that is going to hang, that maybe if I cooperate they can do something, appeal for mercy in view of my age, for my mother's sake, so by this time I'm scared as hell and there's no talk of lawyers and rights like on TV. I'm alone with these blokes, who look as fierce as hell, and then they start about how a small, white boy like me will have many admirers in the stocks, big, strong African men who have not seen a woman for years, decades even, how they will enjoy, and but if only I cooperate they can organize a special cell. So I sign the paper. And that's how it is."

I watch him push and grind his palms on the rock. I remember that day at the museum when I saw that his hands were bruised.

He looks up, his palms flat on the stone. I move my hand that little bit across the stone, put it on his.

"She'd told Mphiri that she wanted him out of the house. That she knew he was stealing. She was hitting the old chap. She'd lock him in the boy's kaya, hit him with sticks, belts."

He lifts our hands off the stone.

I watch him wipe his palms with a tissue, see the streaks of blood there.

"He snapped, that's all. He must have got her while she was sleeping. Poured the paraffin. I told the police it was an accident. That she tripped on a paraffin stove. They weren't interested."

He gets up from the stone, sways a bit. He looks down at his hands and then up at me. I force the words out, unsparing and cold. I have waited so long. I cannot look at him, though. I look down at the stone, the stone that has particles of his flesh, blood.

I try to imagine Mphiri doing something like that. The old man with paraffin in his hands bending over the sleeping woman. I try to think of how much Mphiri knew, what he saw in all those years there in that house. I think of Ian, the small boy, running away from his stepmother into the boy's kaya, a safe haven from the shouting, the beatings. The picture wavers in my head, and it is replaced by something else.

"What about the other woman?"

I look up, up at the vast sky, following the arc of a bird, waiting.

"What other woman?"

He is standing there, his hands tucked in his jeans.

"The police said that there was another woman who got burnt. They said you took her to the hospital before you went to the police station."

I watch him watch me.

"You know who it is, Lindiwe, my mother. Sarah Price. I went to Ingutsheni yesterday. I haven't been to see her since I left, not once."

His eyes are steady on me.

I think of my pink handbag with the page from *The Chron-*

icle. "Guilty," it said. I touched his head with my finger, and when I looked down, I saw that his feet were bare.

"And now I'm here. With you."

The first time he said my name, the way he said it: no exaggeration, not a hint of exasperation at having to pronounce an African name. My name was there, perfect in his voice.

"I wanted to sort myself out."

He is standing by the gate, looking up at the house, until Mphiri comes to open it.

"I kept telling them that I could look after her; that we could move to the house or go back south but nothing. The psychiatrist on her case was on a real power trip, a real pompous windbag—she was his responsibility; I had just been released from jail, no guarantees, couldn't take the chance—on and on he went when I got the nerve to go to that place, you must know how it goes, Lindiwe, it's your field."

He is sitting on Daddy's chair, the car radio on his lap like a cat, white tackies on his feet.

"Once they found out she was my mother they reckoned they had it all locked up. The two of us there. A domestic dispute, incident: premeditated."

Our hands are side by side on the car. He is helping us to push it.

And here he is, wiping his hands on his jeans.

"Okay Lindiwe, can we leave it for now? I just want to chill."

On the drive to Troutbeck Inn, we listen to a homemade tape of a South African band, Stimela.

"You should see them live. They're going to be hot. Check out Ray Phiri on the guitar and vocals."

The road, enveloped in mist, unwinds down the mountain; sometimes we are so close to the edge of the escarpment that one moment's inattention and we could disappear below. I don't tell him that I'm nervous about the drive back in the dark.

"What music do you like?"

"You'll laugh."

"Come on."

"Dire Straits, UB40, Bruce Springsteen, Culture Club . . ."

"Jeez . . ."

"It gets worse. Until recently I was really into the New Romantics, you know, those British bands with lots of eyeliner and lace, Spandau Ballet, Duran Duran . . ."

"You're a fricking Rhodie!"

"And, and Julio Iglesias."

"Julio who?"

"Julio Iglesias, he's Spanish. Don't tell me you haven't heard 'Hey!'"

"No. Hey, what?"

"Just 'Hey!' It's all in Spanish and I don't understand any of it, but it sounds so romantic. Yes. Yes, I even have the album."

"Christ!"

"Oh, and Richard Clayderman."

"Rhodie fricking Central for sure. Culture, my child, culture. You should check out Lovemore Majaivana and those township blokes. They can really belt out a song; you can really feel the emotions, all that shit about the ancestors, it's all there. . . ."

I watch him roll the window down, and I listen to his voice as it is carried away into the forest.

He rolls the window up again, looks at me, his fingers tapping the steering wheel to the song in his head.

I look at him with my mouth wide open.

"Yah, yah, it's a honky voice. No need to look like you're going to cry. Not that bad."

"It was beautiful, Ian."

"When I was a lightie, ten, eleven roundabouts then, over at Matopos, I checked out a rainmaking ceremony like you never believe. I was hiding out in the bush, scrammed away from the troop, went right up. . . . And there the saddest—you want to hear beautiful, that was beautiful—scared the life out of me. Then they start blowing on the gourds and shit, the air is carrying that sound, vibrating with it, like everything is waiting, calling on God. . . . If God is going to be anywhere, it's in the African bush all right."

I watch him turn the cassette over, press the play button and hold my breath as the car is flooded with Louis Armstrong and his magical trumpet.

On and on we drive.

"You know he came to Bullies in the sixties?"

"No, really?"

"Played over at the Queens Cricket Ground. I would have loved to see that. The guy belting out the classics, "Mack the knife," "When the Saints Go Marching In." Past his prime but still delivering the goods. The place was packed, black, white. Listen. Sweet."

Because we're early, we sit outside, having drinks. I look about and an image of Troutbeck Inn before independence fixes itself on me, just like this one: the white golfers teeing off around the lake, the anglers fishing, the wives nursing children here at the patio, the black waiters carrying trays, weaving in and out of tables, *good evening, madam, sir*—yes, just like this, except, of course, I wouldn't be here getting looked over by wives, nannies, and waiters. And I can hear Maphosa all right; his anger still fresh and raw, "Amabhunu" and then right at me, "Sellout." I look at Ian and see "the

White Man," "the Oppressor," "the Settler," "the Colonizer," for the first time really, and wonder if he would accuse me of being racialistic.

"What's the matter?"

"Nothing, I'm just going for a walk."

"You don't like it here?"

"No. I mean, yes, I like it. I'm just going for a short walk."

"I'll come with you."

We find a signposted trail just over the lake, and we go into the forest. We walk without talking until we reach a clearing and find ourselves at the trout breeding farm. I sit down on a log bench.

"I know what that was about," he says. "You shouldn't care so much what people think."

And suddenly my anger is so hot and fierce.

"You don't know anything!" I shout. "You're white, how would you know?"

"Shit," he says, "it's your birthday."

"Forget my birthday. I don't care."

"We've all been fucked up good. Shit man."

And the anger evaporates. And he is just Ian again.

"It's beautiful out here," I say.

"You eat fish?"

"Yes."

"Now, correct me, but last time I checked, fish was not a vegetable."

"That's right."

"And next you're going to order chicken."

"Yes."

"Exactly what kind of vegetarian are you?"

"I just meant to say that I don't eat red meat anymore."

"Why?"

"Just . . ."

We're at a table a little bit away from the fireplace. Ian has a view of the fire. I have a view of the other diners. I want to swop seats, but I don't want to cause a scene. I'm trying to find a sentence that will come out naturally: *Ian, do you mind changing seats, I want to see the fire (I don't want to see them).* He'll see through that. And I can't imagine saying his name in here. As if he were a boyfr—

"Hello, anyone home?"

"I just OD'd on red meat."

Secrets. I don't tell him it's because of that day. The old man in the bush going through the ash, gathering bones.

"You're one strange chick. I reckon it's all the Frenchies you're hanging around with."

"French people eat meat."

"And snails and frogs."

"Yes, and you guys eat raw dried meat; Ndebeles eat macimbi and flying ants; Shonas, well, I don't know what their speciality is, but I'm sure it must be pretty interesting, every culture has its—"

"Yah, yah, now we are the international food fundie. Biltong, one thing; even dried mopani worms, no worries, you can chuck those things in your mouth like popcorn; as for amahlabusi, man, those were the days. Come the rains, I used to joll to the bottle store and join the picannins by the streetlight just opposite. Boy, did we catch those buggers, and boy, did I get bawled out by my old man, hanging with picannins and all that, but yuck man, frogs, those things live on flies, only Frenchies."

"You might not be racialistic, but you really are xenophobic."

I must have spoken a bit loud: the lady at the corner looks up sharply and whispers something to the man sitting opposite her. He turns round, fixes me with a stare. Ian stares back.

"Zeno what? . . . Hey, some of us didn't finish secondary school."

"Which reminds me, did you do your O's?"

"Nope, got caught up by events."

"You're going back on Monday?"

"Yah."

The children at the table are staring. One of them, a chubby little boy, sticks his tongue out. I smile. He starts pulling his ears, rolling his eyes. The two girls start giggling. The mother looks up at him, slaps the boy on the arm. "Shush," she says.

"We'll check out World's View tomorrow."

"Another one? Don't tell me, The Very Honorable Mr. Cecil John Rhodes is at it again."

The lady at the table on the left of ours chews very slowly, her raised hand with its knife still in the air.

"Yes, he's been here too. Liked the place. Built a grand house, which you now know as the Rhodes Inyanga Hotel."

"Very interesting, Ian."

He looks over my shoulder. I can hear the wheels of the trolley.

"Dessert time," he says.

"Happy birthday, madam," says the waiter, lifting the cake from the trolley.

"No," I say.

The waiter confused, hesitates.

"Oh yes," says Ian, nodding and rubbing his hands.

The waiter smiles, puts the cake on the table.

It's chocolate with one candle.

"I reckon you chicks are so sensitive about your ages better not give too much away."

The waiter lights the candle.

"Make a wish," Ian says.

I close my eyes, blow.
My single wish lights up the room and is then, gone.

We don't go back to the cottage; we check in: a double room with a view of the lake.

It is the longest kiss.
The longest, sweetest kiss.

In the morning I wake up, lift my head from his hand.
"Where are you going, Lindiwe?"
He lifts his hand, pulls me back to him.
"Lindiwe," he says, "it's different. This time, it's different."
Secrets. And there it is, here it is, the moment for me to tell him the truth.
"I know."
That's all I say.
I go back to sleep in his arms.
I wake up in his arms.

We are late for breakfast so we have sandwiches on the patio. Like yesterday there are the golfers teeing off around the lake; the anglers fishing; the wives, children, nannies here; the waiters weaving in and out of the tables, *good morning, sir, madam,* looking me over, but today, none of that matters.
"Lindiwe . . ."
"Yes."
"You keep tuning out. One minute here, the next gone."

"I'm here."

"So we'll stop over at World's View, then head back to the cottage; should we spend another night here or do you want to go back to Harare?"

I don't want to go back. I want to stay. I don't want to move from this place. I want us to be here, together, forever.

"Lindiwe . . ."

"You have to be in Harare by Monday."

"We can leave early Monday morning; I'll just belt it down to Jo'burg."

"That sounds fine."

"Are you all right?"

"Yes, more than all right."

After a bit of a scramble, Ian pulls me up and finally we're on a smooth expanse of rock, looking out at a view of the world. Far, far away the mountains shade into purple. I'm embarrassed by my heavy breathing, how unfit I am.

"Not bad," he says, turning to me. "Are you okay?"

"I think I've had the exercise of several lifetimes."

He smiles and comes to sit down next to me.

We watch some Japanese tourists busy photographing each other leaning against the observation tower, looking away from the view towards the car park.

"I'm going to start jogging when I get back or play tennis, squash, anything. The university has courts."

"How about netball?"

We look at each other and both smile as the shared thought of our younger selves settles between us.

"Man, I was confused."

"Confused? About what?"

"You, Lindiwe, you."

He bends over and kisses me, his hand warm and strong against my neck.

And then he points out the different types of sunbirds and warblers darting among the trees, perched on the rocks.

On our way back to the car, we pass the vendors' stalls lined up away from the warden's hut. Ian lifts a stone sculpture. A Zimbabwe Bird. He lifts another one, holds them in the palm of his hand.

"One for you, one for me."

He hands both of them to me and he takes out his wallet, looks inside.

"Do you have any change, Lindiwe?"

Without thinking, I say, "Look in my purse."

He takes the purse from my backpack that he has slung over his shoulder and it's only when he opens the purse I remember.

"Ian, no . . ."

But he's already found it.

The little picture. He takes it out from the purse, looks at it.

"What's this?" he says, but he already knows the answer.

"Ian, I . . ."

"Don't say anything, just don't."

I get out of the car. I walk all the way back to the observation tower. I climb up the stairs, and standing there, looking out at a view of the world, I know that whatever had begun is finished. Done.

*　　*　　*

"What's his name?"

"David."

"David."

And that's all he says.

We drive all the way back to the cottage. Without a single word.

He sits at the table, the picture there.

"Why didn't you . . . ? Why, Lindiwe? Why?"

I don't know what the answer is. I don't know where the answer begins. The room in the lodge? The bus ride home? The missed period? The months out of school?

"You could have written. On the phone, you could have . . . Why?"

Because Mummy loves him like her own. He is her own. He is hers. Only. Because she is his keeper. The Chosen One.

"David," he says. Over and over again.

In the morning he says, "I'm going to see him. We're going to Bulawayo."

Just like that.

I know that there is nothing for me to say, nothing I can say. We will go to Bulawayo.

We will do as he says. We will see the boy, his son.

3.

He drives as if he is possessed. He *is* possessed, by the Holy Son. I want to prepare him. I want to warn him. I want to tell him the power Mummy holds. But he has powers of his own. Nothing will stop him. I see this. And as he drives, I see him all those years ago.

"He's not bad looking for a Rhodie," Bridgette said that time at the Grasshut. "He doesn't have that look of theirs."

And I think of Mummy with the boy, hand in hand, waiting, for us. I think of her lips pursed, her hand squeezing his. I think of the boy looking up at her, loving her.

I look at Ian, and anger's silent litany starts. What right do you have to accuse me of anything? To judge me? You weren't there. I was the one who had to put up with everything. Who do you think you are? You don't have any idea what it was like, all those years by myself.

I came back from Gwanda to Mummy's terror. She waited for me to enter the house, and then, within its walls, she dragged me by the hair, slapped me over and over again. But that wasn't enough. She spat at me. She went out and took a belt from Daddy's closet and beat me. I lay on the floor and let her. And when finally she was done, she told me to get up, get out of her sight, that from now on she did not have a daughter.

I think of those nine months, the look on Mummy's face as my stomach grew. She tried to convince Daddy to send me off somewhere. I wasn't allowed to go into town, anywhere out of the property, and even then, when she had her Manyano group over, I was to stay in my room.

I think of those years when I had to go to Speciss College with all the other failures to do my O and A levels because none of the schools would take on a girl who had been pregnant, the bad influence she might have on others, the contagion she might spread. The girls I would bump into from school, who would look at me up and down, pass comments to each other, words like *cheap, slut, baby dumper* tossed from one lip-glossed mouth to another. How I had shut myself off; hours in my room studying, draining bottle after bottle of Histalax to quell my attacks of anxiety, loneliness.

And always the boy kept from me, bound tight in Mummy's godly arms.

She didn't want me in the house before five o'clock. I left at seven thirty with daddy to go to college. When I came home, I would get busy with the cooking, the cleaning, and ironing. Mummy and the boy would eat in the lounge, the door closed; Daddy in the workshop over whatever it was he was fixing, and me in the kitchen, standing up. I missed Rosanna who had been thrown out when the boy was only three months.

Mummy took him everywhere.

I look out of the window, watch the Bata factory in Gweru recede, and I know that in two hours we will be in Bulawayo. I think of that Saturday after Pay Out when I went into town to try and find something for him; the two pairs of Bubblegummers, one red, the other yellow, in the drawer in my room on campus, lying neatly in their boxes waiting for his tender spongy feet. I agonized over them in the Bata store on First Street. Which one? Which one? What size? What color? What type? I couldn't decide if I should just post them to Bulawayo, send them with someone, or wait until April, a whole three months away.

And will Mummy let him wear them at all? Will she throw them away once I'm gone?

Ian turns the radio dial on, then off, then on again. I watch him chew the inside of his cheek, scratch behind his ear. These things give me comfort. He is nervous.

I think of the last time I was home, Christmas, only a few weeks ago. He wriggled out of my arms and called me "aunty." Mummy, always standing near, watching with her hands crossed said, "What do you expect? You are always away." And I saw her pleasure when he called her "ma." It's just short for "grandma," I told myself, but I knew it wasn't so. And Daddy there, locked in his room, alone.

But I had managed to take him with me just once. I lied to him and said that we were going to meet Grandma in church (Mummy had been called before sunrise to a Manyano member's house to commiserate over her husband's sudden death), and then I drove into town to take him to see Father Christmas in his cave at Haddon and Sly with Jean who had come with me from Harare and was staying at The Selborne. Jean brought a Lucky Dip full of plastic soldiers and toffee, which Father Christmas was supposed to hand over to David. Father Christmas sat in his throne and beckoned to David. "Come, my boy, I see you've been a good boy. Come and get your gift." David's eyes had opened wide and then he'd started shaking, tears rolling from his face. He called out for Mummy, his chest heaving, and he'd banged his little fists against me.

He wouldn't let me touch him during the rest of my stay.

WELCOME TO BULAWAYO.

*   *   *

I think of how she won't let him go to school. Excuses after excuses.

Those children are dirty and rough in Baines. It's just blacks now. They hit him. He's too sensitive to go there. Anyway, I'm teaching him. He already knows his alphabet and his two times table.

We pass all those familiar places. Alton Heights. South Grove. The graveyard. The garage that is now a deserted shell, the bus stop, and then we turn and, we have arrived.

And there she is, Mummy, waiting for us. God has warned her, prepared her for our onslaught. There she stands by the gate, her white Manyano cap starched to a peak pointing heavenward. There she stands in her red blouse, black skirt, and black lace-up shoes, God tucked under her arm.

Ian looks at me. He sighs. He gets out of the car leaving his door open.

"Hello, Mrs. Bishop."

Mummy holds on to the gate, looks past him, to me.

"You remember me, Mrs. Bishop. I'm Ian, Ian McKenzie, from next door."

Of course she remembers him, knows him, has lived with parts of him for all these years.

"I have . . . we . . . Lindiwe is here with me. We've come to visit, to see my . . . my son. I've just found out, Mrs. Bishop. I . . ."

She has already turned away, is walking back into the house. I watch Ian watch her. I watch him lift the latch of the gate, follow.

I get out of the car, call out to him, "Ian, Ian, wait, wait."

He waits.

"Let me go first, okay. I'll talk to her. Wait here for a moment."

He doesn't say anything. He doesn't move. So I rush past him, into the house.

It is quiet and dark in the passageway. And then I hear the murmur of voices.

Mummy's: "the Lord is my shepherd I shall not want."

His: "he leads me not into temptation."

And I wait there in the dark until they are done. "Amen. Amen."

Mummy is getting off her knees, settling herself into the couch. He is standing, looking up at me.

"David," I say.

He looks up at his grandmother who tells him nothing, something.

"Mummy," I say, "he's come to see his son."

"He cannot enter this house. I will call the police."

"Mummy, he has to see his son. If you want, I can take David out. Come, David."

Mummy jumps out from the couch, shrieking. "No! No!"

She snatches the boy.

"No!"

"Mrs. Bishop, he is my son. I have a right . . ."

I step out of the doorway and Ian stands there, looking, watching, waiting.

A tableau. A terrible tableau. I can't bear it. I leave them. I go to Mummy and Daddy's bedroom. I knock. I open the door and find him there lying, curled up on the bed.

"Daddy."

"Daddy."

And his eyes flicker open, then close.

I sit on the bed, take out his thin, shrivelled hand. I sit there with him for the longest time, until the dark comes.

*   *   *

Mummy is in the kitchen sitting at the table, staring at the wall. The back door is open and I can see out to Rosanna's place. I close my eyes and think of the day when Mummy chased her away, throwing all her things out the gate, and how people on the street came to watch, some of them laughing, clapping their hands. And Daddy was trying to calm Mummy down, trying to pull her by the hand, but she shook herself away, screaming and shouting that enough was enough. She had been disgraced enough. "Look at what has happened to your own child," she shouted, beating her chest, pulling her hair as if she was possessed. And then she lifted her dress and showed him her scars, how much she had suffered. "For what? For what?" she kept demanding until he gave up and shut himself in the workshop, leaving Rosanna and my sister, half, to fend for themselves.

Rosanna waited outside by the gate with her belongings until Daddy came out and took them to Uncle Silius, who was now living with his family in Pelindaba township. I know that this is what happened because the next time Uncle Silius came to visit, Daddy gave him some money and a packet of baby blankets.

Later Mummy picked up my baby, and I found them together on her bed, fast asleep, her arm so tight around him I feared that she would break his fragile bones.

I open my mouth to ask her about Rosanna, about whether she has been in touch with her, but as if she knows my intentions, she gets up and walks out of the back door, shutting it behind her.

I find the boy lying on his bed. I look around the room and

see evidence of Mummy's residence there; her perfumes, her nightgown, her handbag, her slippers. I sit on the bed next to him, feel his body grow rigid, see the panic darting in his eyes. I look down at his bare feet. The shoes will fit.

"David," I say. "David."

He lifts his eyes to me, the panic flickering, on, off. I raise my hand. He flinches. I get up from the bed. I stand there looking down, the words in my throat, twisting and turning.

"I love you, David."

That's all I say.

I think of that long bus ride home when he was already in me, the cells fusing, growing, becoming him. I stand there thinking of the night before, in that room, in that lodge, in Gwanda, where Ian and I . . .

"I want Ma," he says.

He springs up from the bed, scoots past me, shouting, "Ma, Ma, Ma . . ."

I crawl under the fence. I go to the boy's kaya. I stand outside and look out at the main house. The kitchen door is open.

I see the woman in flames, rushing about, now here, now there in the house, and then out, whirling and twirling in the garden, screaming, and he standing there in the doorway, watching.

"Lindiwe. What are you doing . . . ?"

His touch surprises me.

I look again and the door is closed.

He closes his arms around me, draws me against him, and I hear his words pressed on my head.

"It's a lot. A lot to take in, Lindiwe."

And I hold myself still in his arms.

"I'm sorry, Ian."

4.

David sits there at the back, his voice hollowed out, the screaming quieted; he sits there shaking, shivering, whimpering.

Ian drives, jaw clenched, looking straight ahead.

This feels like a kidnapping, an abduction; something wrong, fatal.

I look at the side mirror and see Mummy still running after the car. Perhaps she will run all the way to the police station opposite the graveyard; perhaps she'll tell them of the crime that's been committed; she'll tell them of the boy who was stolen from his bed, and I look at David, shaking, shivering, whimpering in his striped pyjamas and I am guilty.

"Keep the doors locked," he says. "I won't be long."

And he gets out of the car and walks on the dirt path, jumps up the steps, waits at the door, and disappears inside. The echo of these things envelops me: when I was a girl and I waited in a car for him in this place; here I am again, a woman now, a woman with child. And the child sits at the back, brokenhearted.

"David, David, please . . ."

We wait in the car, the two of us.

I twist the knob of the radio, then twist it off again.

I look out and I'm taken by the emptiness of it; not a single person outside. A month ago there was an article in the paper about malnutrition among inmates in state mental facilities, how there were suspicions that food was getting diverted elsewhere.

"Ma, Ma, Ma . . ."

There is nothing I can offer, give him. There is only me and Ian now, his tormentors.

How small he is. I could, despite himself, scoop him in my arms, hold him against me, the miracle of him, like that first time.

Rosanna was the only one who helped me in those months. Mummy wouldn't talk to me. Daddy was bewildered. Aunty Gertrude came and said that I had disappointed everyone. It was Rosanna who made sure that I ate well, who took me to the clinic. And it was Rosanna who was there when the time came, and I was so scared in that ward with the overworked, impatient nurses who looked at me as if I was a loose girl.

"You can do it, Sisi," she said. "Look, the head is already out. Push now. Push."

And then, there he was, all at once, in my hands.

Daddy drove us home: me and the baby (my baby) at the back with my sister, half and Rosanna up front.

Mummy wasn't at home.

I started awake and there she was sitting on the armchair Daddy had moved to my room. She was holding the baby in her arms. I didn't see it at first, but the baby flopped its head back and I saw Mummy's breast, her nipple glistening.

Mummy looked up at me. "He is hungry," she said.

She gave him to me and I waited for her to leave the room. The baby started to cry. His face pushed against my breast.

"Feed him," said Mummy.

I unbuttoned my blouse and fed my baby.

Mummy stood over me all the while, and when I was finished, she took the baby from me and left the room.

And that's how it was. How my baby became hers.

"Ma, Ma, Ma . . ."

At last Ian comes back. He yanks the door open and he sits in the car, his eyes closed, his head pushing against the head-rest, taking gasps of air.

I put my hand on his arm. "Ian, how is she?"

He looks at me and there is the shock of his glistening, red eyes.

"She's not crazy," he says. "They just put her there."

He is about to say something else, but then the boy moves and he stops.

He starts the car and we leave.

We've just driven out of the city limits when I turn and see the boy curled up on the seat, his body quivering.

"Stop the car. Ian, please."

He gives me a look and then swings over to the lay-by, gets out of the car, bangs his hands on the boot.

"David," I say, twisting around. "It's all right. We're going on an adventure. The three of us. We'll come back to Granny, promise."

I reach out my hand, touch him with my fingertips.

I don't know how much of me he can take. If he'll allow me to hold him. When we put him in the car and I tried to keep him still in my arms, he kicked and punched and only calmed when I left him alone.

Ian gets back in the car, looks over at me then at the boy.

"Isn't that right," I say, looking over the boy to Ian. "This is an adventure."

"That's right," says Ian. "We're off on an adventure; lots of interesting things out there."

"I don't have my Bible," the boy sniffs. "I want my Bible."

I look at the boy, then at Ian.

"It's all right," I say. "We'll get you a new one in Harare. One with pictures."

That seems to calm him; I feel his body relax, his breathing change tempo.

"I'll see Jesus," he says.

"That's right."

"And Mary. And Joseph. And Peter."

"Yes, that's right."

"And heaven. And hell, too. A very, very ugly picture. The devil will be there roasting and toasting sinners, like Grandpa."

There is a quietness in the car. I look at the boy and out the window. There is nothing there to get hold of.

"Because Grandpa did something very bad and God strike him down, and Grandpa was communing with Satan."

Ian starts the car and I am grateful for the smell of diesel, the sound of the engine, distractions.

The boy sits there appeased.

We drive on and on.

I look out of the window and cling onto the passing of things.

Ian makes a wrong turn, drives right into Gweru city center.

Here we are, stuck at the robots, the early lunchtime crowd jostling by.

I watch a woman stop, tuck in better at the sides the fabric that is holding her baby on her back; two men walking, fingers loosely laced, likely Shonas; a man rummaging in a plastic bag from OK Bazaars bump into a schoolboy.

There is the former Cecil Hotel owned by a ZUM opposition candidate, who got shot in his private parts by ZANU-PF thugs just before elections and is now disabled.

I watch the Bata factory float away, and I think of the Bubblegummers in the drawer in my room on campus waiting for his spongy little feet. Now, sitting at the back, he is barefoot like a Rhodie kid would be.

"Are you a Christian?"

"A Christian?" I repeat, turning my head back.

"Ma is a Christian. I am a Christian. We love God."

"Are you hungry?" I ask him. "You haven't had breakfast."

"Ma makes me porridge with butter and milk."

"If you're hungry, we can stop and get something to eat."

The boy doesn't answer.

We drive on and on.

The boy doesn't say anything else, all the way up to Kadoma where we stop. Two more hours left.

We sit outside in the garden of the Kadoma Ranch Motel and order three toasted chicken sandwiches, two Cokes, and a glass of milk.

There are two peacocks sauntering on the lawn. I look at the boy to say something to him but his eyes are squeezed tight and my words, *Look at those two show-offs, aren't they beautiful,* disappear.

Ian says he's going to the toilet. He asks the boy if he needs to. The boy doesn't answer. Ian waits for a moment and then leaves.

The boy sits cross-legged on the wire chair, his pyjamas, his bare feet, a rebuke. I see the sleep at the corners of his eyes. I look at the reddish tinge in his hair and wonder once more of the Irish, Scottish stock that lies there. I look across the other end of the garden where the passengers of the luxury bus company Tenda are lining up for their buffet lunch. A woman in red plastic stilettos walked past us just now and almost fell into the pool because she couldn't stop gawking at the sight of the three of us. And here is Ian coming back with something in his hand. A giraffe. A wooden giraffe. *Oh, Ian.* He must have picked it up from the curio shop at the entrance. Did he even go to the toilet?

"Look what I found," he says sitting down, showing the boy the animal. "He's yours."

The boy does something that surprises me. A shy smile lights up his face; he reaches out his hand and then he remembers something, collects himself, takes his hand away.

In my head I hear Mummy's stern voice, "Thou Shall Not Covet."

Ian doesn't make a fuss.

He puts the giraffe gently on the table and says, "He's all yours, my boy."

"Lekker," says Ian, wiping his mouth.

I see the boy wonder at that word, *lekker.*

"He means 'great,'" I say.

"Yes, your mother is the fundie around here."

"He means 'expert,'" I say.

"Maybe you should run a translation service," Ian says and I catch the testiness in his voice.

The boy looks up at me, at Ian, over to the giraffe, and he must decide that the giraffe is the sanest, safest one of us three because he doesn't take his eyes off it until we leave.

As we're walking away a waiter runs up to us.

"You forget this," he says, holding out the giraffe and it is the boy who reaches out his hand and takes it.

"Thank you, very much," he says slowly.

I go into the gift shop. I buy a pair of socks with frogs on them, an orange T-shirt with a giraffe and ZIMBABWE on it in the rich colors of the flag and a pair of shorts. I show these to the boy and ask him if he wants to change.

He says, "No, thank you."

I put the bag next to him in the car.

Just as we reach Chegutu the boy falls asleep. Ian pulls over and lays him across the seat. The boy holds the giraffe tightly to his chest.

Driving, Ian begins to talk.

"We can make it work," he says. "We can do it."

I don't ask him what "it" is. I let him talk.

Ian looks at me; he wants me to say something but I can't.

"He'll grow used to us."

"He'll grow to love us," is what Ian means.

"What are you going to do?" I ask him.

What I mean is, What are *we* going to do?

He looks at me.

"I'll rent a place, something. For now I'll get a bigger room at the Bronte and then, we'll see, that's all."

I know at this moment he's thinking about the Frenchie, how the Frenchie is going to get in the way, mess things up, I know it.

I try to think of Jean but I can't.

"I'll find something," he says.

I look outside, concentrate on the truckload of pigs in front of us, and I feel Ian's eyes on me, waiting but I don't know what to say.

WELCOME TO HARARE.

We drive all the way up Samora Machel Avenue, and as we are turning up Fourth Street, we hear the sirens.

"Pull over," I say to Ian. "It's the president."

Ian keeps on driving.

"Ian, someone got shot dead, last month."

He stops.

"Shit," he says.

"You have to pull out of the road; you have to switch off the engine."

"Jeez man, he's coming down the *other* side."

"Ian, they want all vehicles off the road. Just do it."

I can hear the boy moving behind me.

Ian pulls over, off the road, but he keeps the engine running. We watch the presidential motorcade zoom by. The road vibrates with the surge of police motorcycles, open-topped Jeeps packed with heavily armed soldiers, unmarked cars, ambulance, Peugeots filled with intelligence operatives, presidential Mercedes (or decoy vehicle with look-alike president, who knows), and behind that, more police motorcycles, more open-topped Jeeps, this time carrying youths wearing ZANU T-shirts shaking their fists, more Peugeots until, finally, the road is clear.

"What a load of bullshit," Ian says. "Bob and the Wailers. One thing for sure, Ian Smith wasn't so fricking para—"

"Ian, *David*."

Ian looks over.

"You're awake, my boy," he says.

We drive along Fourth Street until we reach Baines Avenue and there, at the corner, is the Bronte, nestled in immaculate gardens.

The boy keeps stopping and staring at the stone sculptures dotted among the jacaranda trees, along the path; mythic creatures from a lost world. Ian strides ahead, onwards to reception.

"That looks like a hippo," I say.

The boy stands there holding the giraffe close to his heart. He looks at the would-be hippo, which is about his height.

"Why don't you feel him," I say, and I watch him gingerly raise his right hand and put it gently on the stone. I imagine the shock of the coldness of it going through his little fingers.

*   *   *

We find Ian at the patio with the key in his hand.

"It's a garden suite," he says. "Two bedrooms, lounge, and bathroom, ideal for families, and a veranda."

He says all this as if he has read the brochure and memorized it or he's put to memory the receptionist's spiel.

I don't say, "I have to go. I have to go back to campus."

I don't know if he's asking me to stay or if he has already made up his mind that I'm going to stay or if he's just hoping or maybe it's not even about me; he needs space, room. I think of the money he's spending. But he sits there seemingly unconcerned, pleased with himself, the great provider. We both look out into the garden, at the boy, who is watching the mythic creatures, introducing them to the giraffe.

"He needs to go to school," I say.

I want Ian to see what he's taking on, that it can't be something he can do on a whim.

"We should take him back."

"No ways, Lindiwe."

"My mother . . ."

"Your mother's feeding him a whole load of bull. I don't want him to . . . Jeez, Lindiwe, he's yours too. . . . Don't tell me it doesn't cut you to see how wound up he is. Look at him over there. He's starting to relax."

I look out at the boy, watch him circle the stone and then gently stroke it with his free hand.

"I love this place," I say and regret it once the words are out of my mouth. I think of Ian thinking, How does she know this place so much that she loves it, who's she been here with, oh, the Frenchie . . .

So maybe that's why I add quickly, "I only have a tutorial in the afternoon tomorrow. I don't need to get back till then."

He nods.

"Let's go and check out the digs. It's that one over there in the corner."

"David, come," I call out.

The boy bids farewell and comes.

There is a double bed in the main room, a single bed in the other.

I look at the boy.

"This is your room, David."

I feel his breathing change, his body tense, so I quickly add, "But if you want, in the beginning, until you're comfortable, you can sleep over there with us, or we can bring that bed over here."

I look up at Ian.

"Or one of us can come over here and sleep with you. Whatever you like."

The giraffe is pressed so tight against his chest that I'm sure it will leave marks on his skin.

At last I say, "Maybe you want to watch a cartoon."

"Ma says TV is the work of Satan."

Ian lets out a whistle and mutters, "Penga."

I open all the bedside drawers and I can't find the slim volume of the New Testament. It *has* to be here. There *must* be a copy. There's always one in hotel rooms. *Somewhere.* Ian stands there watching me.

"Lindiwe, relax," I hear. "We'll get it tomorrow. You can tell him a story from the Bible."

"I . . ."

And suddenly I'm just tired. I slump down on the bed. I listen for a sound coming from the bath.

"He's so quiet in there."

"He's okay, Lindiwe."

"We should telephone Bulawayo. We have to let her know that we're, that he's safe. She must be worried sick. Whatever she's done she loves him."

"Phone her then. Don't tell her where we are."

I wish I could speak to Daddy. I dial the Bulawayo number and listen to the phone in the passageway ring on and on. I put my phone down.

"She's not answering."

I try again. This time, as I'm putting the phone down I hear, "Hello."

But it's not Mummy. It's a voice that comes from a far place, such a long time ago I can't believe it.

"Hello," the voice says again.

"Hello," I say, "who is this?"

"This is Rosanna," the voice says.

Rosanna!

"*Hello,* hello. Hello, Rosanna, it's me, Lindiwe. How are you? I would like to speak to Mummy please."

"Sisi! Hold on. I am fine, thank you, Sisi."

Rosanna, I keep saying to myself, Rosanna, how can she be . . . ? What is she doing . . . ?

"Hello, Sisi Lindiwe, Mama is resting; she is lying down."

I can tell Rosanna is trying to find the right words. Mummy doesn't want to speak to me.

"It's okay, Rosanna. Just tell her that we are all fine."

"Yes, Sisi. Okay, bye-bye."

It is only after I put the phone down that I think I should have asked about her daughter, my sister, half.

"Rosanna's there," I say to Ian.

*　　*　　*

"Are you ready to come out?" I ask the boy.

He takes the giraffe from his perch on the bath's ledge and cradles him.

"Would you like me to bath you or maybe you want Ia—your father?"

His small body rocks in the bath, and I try to catch what he is murmuring.

Of course.

"The Lord is my shepherd, I . . ."

I pick up the small hand towel, rub soap on it.

"It's better if you stand," I say.

I wait for him.

He stands still in the water.

How small and skinny he seems.

"Good," I say and take his free right arm which feels so weightless to me, and begin to scrub as gently as I can. He keeps at The Lord Is My Shepherd, all the way through the scrubbing of his body, and it is only when I'm done and look up at his face that I see the tears.

"David, what's wrong? What's the matter?"

My questions seem to release something because the silent crying becomes heart-rending sobs, and I watch stunned as his fragile little chest heaves in and out, the tender bones of his ribs threatening to snap any moment because of the pressure of his anguish.

"David, David."

I hear the panic, desperation, in my voice and hate myself for it. What is he doing here? What are we doing to him?

"Hey, what's wrong, little man?"

I step back from the bath, leave the boy to his father. I listen out in the lounge, and soon the sobbing subsides and I can hear Ian's voice, "Jeez man, you've got a good pair of lungs on you, that's for sure."

I sit down on the couch and wait.

Ian comes through carrying the boy, who is wrapped up in a white towel, in his arms.

"Should we order some sandwiches or go to the restaurant?" I ask Ian.

"Just order some sandwiches and chips," he says. "This fellow's finished for today."

"Off to bed," says Ian and off they go, the two of them, in the small room with the single bed.

I can hear Ian's voice, rising and falling as he tells the story of Jonah and the whale.

I must doze off because the next thing I'm on the couch with a plaid blanket over me.

"Hey there," I hear.

I sit up and see Ian with the TV remote in his hand.

"What are you watching?"

"A documentary on Mandela," he says, rubbing his eyes.

I don't ask him when he'll go back, how long he'll stay, what this means, us, here.

"I'm going to have a bath."

"Lindiwe," he says, reaching out for my hand as I walk past him, "don't worry yourself penga; everything will sort itself out, promise."

I try to hold on to his words. To believe.

5.

Sitting at a table at the Alliance Française, I write a letter to Jean. I do the one thing Marie warned me not to.

I think of the one trip we made to Bulawayo together, during the Christmas break. We drank beers on his balcony, watching Bulawayo ambling along in its leisurely way. Jean said that he could never get over all the colonial architecture of the city. "Look at this place," he said, pointing at the arches and all the teak furnishings. "It's like a movie set. What do the English call them? Period pieces."

He had wanted for me to stay. "I can't," I told him.

He shook his head. "Not I can't," he said. "I won't."

And I had laughed and told him how good his English was, all thanks to me, and I went away.

I was afraid of how much he wanted of me, of who he thought I was.

I'm not good enough for you.

I put the letter in the envelope, seal my words in.

I get up and start walking.

I make myself think of Ian and the boy. Of the cottage Ian has just rented in Avondale.

I walk slowly.

I cross the road and watch the learners maneuver the cars between the drums in the grass field. Further on I watch the trainee security guards practice their drills. I walk on and on, all the way up Herbert Chitepo Avenue, all the way up Leopold Takawira Street, past Parirenyatwa Hospital, where Jean says what is happening there is criminal, the AIDS patients dying all along the corridors and the nurses and doctors who won't treat anyone suspected of having the disease.

On and on I go, under the shade of the jacarandas lining either side of the road.

I step into Avondale post office and buy the stamps I need. I lick them and put them on the white envelope. I stand outside and look at the red postbox, which waits patiently.

Someone says "excuse me," and I watch an elderly white lady put her letter through the slit.

And then I do it, put my letter in, let go.

I stand still for a moment, watching the tremor in my hand.

I walk through the parking lot up to the Italian Bakery, and before they see me, I see them. David and Ian and a young woman, white, a Rhodie. Ian has his head back laughing and the woman is slapping his arm. The boy sees me first, then Ian, then her. I pass one, two, three tables.

"Hi," I say.

"Hey, Lindiwe. Just bumped into Heather here, the sister of a mate of mine I used to joll with in Bullies."

And he has become, just like that, a Rhodie again. Heather gives me a weak smile.

"Hello," she says. "I have to go now. Nice seeing you, Ian."

"Yah," Ian says, getting up. "It was good to chew over old times, catch up on what's what."

I watch Heather walk away and I sit down.

"She's pretty," I say.

Ian shrugs. I look at the boy, the giraffe on the table looking at him.

And then I look at the boy's father who is looking at me.

"I'll get my stuff from campus. Can you help me transport it?"

"No worries."

6.

"*Ilo Peretti, Lindiwe.* You have to see the place. It's magic, straight from the pavements of downtown Harare into another era. The guy's got prints all the way back to the thirties man, all up on the walls—Egypt, Morocco, Ethiopia. I stepped in there and man . . . his back room, boxes and boxes of negatives, who knows what he's got stashed there. When he saw I was interested he said I could go down there, go through the stuff, take whatever I want."

It's good to see him so excited.

"What's he doing down there? Shouldn't he be somewhere more upmarket, Newlands, Sam Levy's?"

"The guy's got quite a story. He was part of the whole Mussolini thing in Eritrea. You know, in the thirties when they Italianized the place? Anyway, he went absent without leave and went jolling all over the continent, got hold of a camera and just went about taking pictures. Worked his way down here, late forties. Some of them are real beauties. Got some shots of the construction of Kariba, some of the Tongas, by the way. Man, to think he's stuck there over by Rezende, in one of those shops opposite the post office; you can lose all track of time looking at what is on the walls. He's got one picture up, and I'm not lying, you could swear he'd taken a shot of Lawrence of Arabia, and then some really soft ones of this girl and you know it's someone he had big feelings for. He's been around for ages on the street. The man's an institution. He has a flat up-stairs."

I hate to break into his good news, especially because of the hard time he's been having trying to find photographic work. How he has had to start doing work as a mechanic, his name on a part-time roster at an employment agency. The way he's been humiliated at job interviews, made to wait for a whole morning sometimes to see the young, black, upwardly mobile, politically well-connected entrepreneurs who're moving into white-held businesses. After one of these interviews at a car showroom, he came back and smashed his hand on the wall, spraining his wrist; his would-be boss had, after keeping him hanging around for two hours, casually flung his legs on the teak desk and asked him to please polish his shoes in the toilets.

"The guy actually takes off his shoes, crocodile, and hands the things to me, and then the laughing when I took off. Lindiwe, I was ready to turn right back and hit the git. Shit, wait till they run the businesses to the ground. Then we'll see what's what. Man, they're driving around with the latest import Mercs with all the trimmings, and they're just out of their fricking twenties."

I was pressing ice on his hand.

"Asch, the goffle lady at the agency warned me, showed me the drawer stashed with unemployed whities. She said two, three years ago they had no whites in their books, everything was through the network, not that I would have been networked even then."

"So, it's okay to discriminate as long as it works for you?"

"Lindiwe . . ."

And I know he's said no to Heather's husband's offer to work for him.

"No ways man, he's a friend now. I'm not *that* desperate."

And now for him to have stumbled on this treasure.

"Ian . . ."

"And can you believe, to top it off, after we've been talking all morning, the guy gives me a set of keys, any time I want to come in and do my own stuff, says it's good to have someone take an interest, now the only thing people are interested in is instant color . . ."

"You should take me there. He must be old."

"Yipp, easily late eighties but as sprightly as hell; he's still running a studio, can you believe, taking the pictures himself and one guy helping with the developing. Only in Zimbabwe."

"Ian, the school phoned."

He's turning the old camera in his hands, another find.

"Ian . . ."

"Yes, the school phoned and . . ."

"They want David to take some tests, they . . ."

"What tests?"

"I'm not sure, she didn't go into details. She's set up a meeting for us this afternoon."

"They need to leave him alone. He'll come out of his shell in his own good time. He's not stupid."

"Ian, they just want to help him."

"You're the fundie, Lindiwe, but I don't want them to start tuning that he has to be in a fricking special class. He's gone through a lot. They should hold their horses."

I know he's right; this is my forte, testing and assigning scores to thought, behavior, emotions; I know all about labeling, but I'm worried about David. Maybe it's guilt. It's been two months and the only thing he seems attached to, to have any confidence in, is the damn giraffe. A sudden thought crosses my mind—perhaps we can get a puppy, something alive and warm for him.

"We can hear what she has to say, Ian."

"Who's *she*?"

I take a deep breath. "The government psychologist."

"Christ Lindiwe, he's not getting ambushed. He's already making strides with us, he's starting to trust, when I was that age . . ."

And then he stops.

I go to the meeting alone and find myself steadily getting angry by the tone of the professional. How she seems to have already made up her mind, given the drawings that have been forwarded to her by the teacher. I refuse to sign the concession form. She gives me a stern look, shakes her head, and says that he shows all the symptoms of emotional abuse, and unfortunately, there are no clear-cut laws to protect children from this or else she would . . . I'm shaking by the time I leave her office.

I decide to walk all the way down to the school to pick David up from his art club.

At the school gate I watch David walk slowly down the steps, the giraffe peeking out from his backpack. I watch a boy try to push the giraffe deeper inside the backpack. David turns around and the boy steps to one side. The giraffe is in David's hand now. I take the backpack from him and we walk silently side by side. I take his hand, and we cross the road and catch an Emergency Taxi home, him sitting on my lap, squashed in between five, six people in the aged Peugeot 504. I twine my hands around his and the giraffe.

"How was school today?" I ask him when we are in the cottage, and he is sitting by the table, having a cheese sandwich, a glass of milk.

He looks up, shrugs his shoulders.

"Hey, guys," Ian shouts cheerily when he comes in. "Hey, little man," he says, ruffling David's hair. "Ready for the trip?

We'll have to take care of your mother here, make sure she doesn't get hassled by monkeys."

For the Easter holidays, which are still a month and a half away, Ian is organizing a whole Camping in Great Zimbabwe Experience somewhere by Lake Mutirikwi. Perhaps that's what David needs, the three of us together, relaxed, our first holiday.

David looks at me his mouth full of bread and cheese, a milk mustache on his lips.

When finally he swallows and has wiped his mustache with the sleeve of his T-shirt, he says, "Yes, Dad," and Ian and I look at each other across the top of his little head, and Ian can't resist mouthing, "See, I told you so."

7.

I'm on campus in the lecture hall when the trouble starts. Students have been gathering at the vice-chancellor's and administration offices demanding their Pay Out. It's been due for a month. I come out of the hall to find a mob chanting and the vehicles in the car park getting stoned, and there are windows already broken in the administration block. Students are running around with branches and bricks. Some are rocking the vice-chancellor's car. I know it's only a matter of time before the riot police get called in.

"Looks like you're going to be in for a long holiday," Ian says when I get home.

The university has been closed indefinitely.

During the impromptu closure, I work four afternoons a week at the advertising agency, and on one of my lunch breaks, I find Ilo's studio squashed in between a shoe repair stall and a tailor, several meters inside a narrow passageway. If I wasn't looking for it, I would have missed it. I open the door and I see what Ian means. The old black and whites on the wall, some on matte, some on gloss, giving the whole place an old glamorous movie-like feel. I turn around and I go to one wall which is covered with different studio images of one woman. What did Ian call them? Soft. I lift my hand and I'm startled by a discreet cough behind me, and when I turn, there is a man in a white dustcoat. He's just a bit taller than me and there are sprigs of hair on his mottled bald head. He rubs his glasses with his sleeve and puts them back on. He looks at me, then he gently takes my hand, pats it.

"So you are the one," he says.

He takes me to the back room and there, hanging on a string from one end of the wall to another, are images of me.

And I see that Ian's been experimenting with lighting and texture. With stillness and movement. With the whole and parts of the whole.

I stand there taking it all in.

"Un uomo innamorato."

And I understand.

When I come back from helping with a shoot at a housing site for a building society's advertising campaign, after having lugged film equipment over rubble, getting my new skirt covered in red dirt, thus fulfilling my job title of production assistant, also known as General Dogsbody, I come back to the office to find Ian sitting on my desk and Leeann, the receptionist, in an apparent state of rapture.

"Jeez man, Lindiwe, you look like you've been out and about in a war zone."

I look past Ian at Leeann who is all shiny, pink and scrubbed and has her eyes latched onto Ian's head.

"I came to take you out for lunch."

There's a sigh from behind Ian and he turns around.

I think of saying a Leeann kind of thing, "Oh, luv, I have to go into the ladies room and freshen up."

Leeann smiles at him, and I'm delighted to see that despite her continual tweaking and touching ups, there is a smudge of red on one of her pearly whites.

"You're such a gentleman," she exhales.

Mr. Poll, the agency director, comes over and dumps a bag of gigantic prawns on my desk.

"Have to clean the whole lot of those before four. Need them for the Bon Marché advert."

Another sigh coming from the usual direction, accompanied by the tip-tap of a pencil on a pad.

Ian slides off the desk.

"She's got plans this afternoon," he says, picking up the bag and dumping it on Leeann's desk.

"Ian, it's fine."

"Lunch, Lindiwe."

And he pulls me along with him.

We walk into town, up into Barbours department store to the restaurant on the terrace. We take a table right at the far end, away from the bustle of people coming in, going out.

"Privacy," says Ian. "I've got major news."

"And I thought you just wanted to take a girl out."

"Just wait for it."

The waiter comes, and I order a Coke and a cheese sandwich; Ian, a Castle and a steak roll.

"So, what is it?"

"I got a visit from someone today over at work."

"Yes."

I've only been up once to TV Sales and Hire since Ian's been taken on full-time; I caught him in his office looking as though he had just woken up from a nap, and I could smell Listerine on his breath, which meant that he had been drinking.

Despite his distinct lack of enthusiasm, he has been rapidly promoted to manager.

"Yah, Lindiwe I know," he said when he came home with the tag on his blue shirt. "What can I do? I'm just benefiting from the system; we need the dosh. What am I going to say, 'No, thanks, please, please promote Charles there, your loyal black employee who's been at his job for years and knows it like the back of his hand'?' It's how the world works. And anyway, I give Charles lots of time off, paid; I reckon he's collecting two paychecks. I'm doing the bloke a favor, trust me."

"I'll ask Charles next time I see him," I said and regretted it as soon as the words came out of my mouth. Ian had finally managed to tap into the old boys' network care of Heather.

"Better than actually *fixing* the fridges," he told me. "I supervise the fixing of the *fricking* fridges. To be honest, most of the time I'm bored shitless. It's a job."

Ian gets through the Castle in a couple of dregs and signals the waiter for another one.

"So this chap, he comes right up to me and starts on about my old man, the good old days, and he's talking full blast. Anyway, he was reeking of booze, really down-and-out, and he kept swaggering about the shop, talking 'your old man this, your old man that.' You should have seen the blacks that were there, enjoying the sight like hell. So I'm trying to steer the guy through the door when he starts struggling, like I want to beat him up or something, but he just wants to take something out of his pocket. 'Look, look,' he keeps telling me. 'For old times' sake you must help me. Your father would be proud . . . ,' and he shoves a picture in my hands, look."

Ian takes the picture from his pocket and gives it to me.

"It's a battalion, Lindiwe, my old man's up front, second from left."

I find Ian's father. His face is brutally serious, glaring into the camera. It looks chiseled in stone. It makes me want to drop the picture. I look up at Ian.

"Yah, he looks like a scary shit all right. Your old man's there, too, Lindiwe. Look, right at the back there, right at the end."

I look at Ian as if he's talking gibberish, and I look at the picture there and he is right, my father is standing there his face turned to one side.

"They had Coloreds and Indians serving in some of the white battalions of the Rhodesian Regiment."

"They were in the same unit, battalion . . ."

The words seem impossible in my mouth. "But I . . . I thought your father was a . . . a Scout."

"That's what he says. Anyways, even if that was true, they used to select the Scouts from the regular regiments, the best of the crop. Funny how when you think about it, the Selous Scouts were the only fully integrated unit—black, whites, if you could do the job, you were in, end of story."

I look down at the picture again.

"You think that's why he sold the house to my father?"

"What, for old times' sake you mean?"

I don't answer him for a while. It's as if I'm trying to grasp something just out of reach.

"Maybe. I mean, no one else would sell to my dad once they found about Mummy being black. Maybe your father . . ."

"Had a soft spot? Not happening, he'd have accepted cash from the devil. Your dad must have offered him a good deal, that's all."

"I feel like I'm missing something important, like, I don't know, it's crazy, your father and my . . ."

"Yah, I gave the old drunk some change for the picture, as happy as . . . you know, I reckon the guy was drinking home-grown brew."

I look down at my father again, at his head turned to one side. I wonder if he was embarrassed, angry to be there, ashamed. I look at Ian's father. At his steely expression and the gun so firm in his hand, and I go over to my father again and look at how the gun rests in his hand and I think it's as if he were holding Roxy in his arms. The gun doesn't belong there.

"I need some air, Ian."

We take a detour to Africa Unity Square. Sitting on the bench looking out at the fountain, Ian beside me, I am brought back to Ian and me at Centenary Park, *leg wrestling.*

On this bench, in this city, Ian takes my hand.

"You're quiet."

"I'm shocked. I keep thinking of what my father must be carrying inside himself because of the war. You know, your father looks like he was meant for war, I don't . . ."

"What, you're right."

"Daddy, my father, whenever he came back from his call-ups, the first couple of weeks, he would be really talkative, about anything, you know, as if he was trying to fill up the space . . . and sometimes when I would wake up in the middle of the night to get a glass of water, I would find him in the kitchen in the dark, sitting there wide awake."

"My old man drank. But I reckon he was drinking because he was bored of the home life. He wanted to go back to the bush."

"Then he would become argumentative. Anything would work on his nerves. The arguments he would have with my mother. He would accuse her of spending too much money— who was she trying to impress? what was she doing when he was not there?—and you know, once he actually told her to pack her bags and get out of the house."

"Did she?"

"Yes. I don't know where she went, but she was gone for a week. We were living in Thorngrove and Rosanna had just arrived."

"Picture, picture, for the lovebirds."

I look up at the young photographer whose hopes have leapt up at the sight of this murungu with his black girlfriend.

"Twenty-four hour delivery," he says, adjusting his camera.

"No, it's okay, shamwari. I also take pictures."

The photographer's eyes widen at Ian's accent, his Shona.

"But I will take an excellent one, of you and the pretty lady, shamwari, door-to-door, express delivery."

I get up from the bench.

"Sorry, my friend, next time," says Ian. "But you are right, she *is* a pretty lady and I'm a lucky bastard."

The photographer beams him a smile and wanders off towards the Meikles Hotel to try his luck with the five-star guests.

"I *am* a lucky bastard," he says, bending to kiss me.

We walk along the pavement, and the flower vendors who've been sitting about arranging their wares leap into action; they start gesticulating to Ian and holding out flowers. Ian stops and picks out a bunch of yellow roses.

"Very good choice!" cries the vendor who looks much older than the others.

"Thirty-five dollars. A very good price for you, sir."

Ian bargains the price right down from thirty-five dollars to eleven dollars ("Look, man, I'm a local. No ways I'm forking out that much, daylight robbery. Come on, be reasonable now . . .") "How very dashing, Ian" is on the tip of my tongue, but I swallow hard.

I take in the rows and rows of wreaths and crosses: colored tissue paper mounted by wire on polystyrene "kaylite" boards. The brisk economy of AIDS has swiped away any African taboos and superstitions about selling such items in the open. I wonder what the foreign businessmen staying across the road make of this when they venture out.

I take the flowers back to the office and arrange them in a chipped jug while Leeann looks on.

"You know," she says finally, "we're ordering orchids and long-stemmed roses for the wedding from a *proper* florist, Interflora, no expenses spared."

Of course not, I think. Not with the groom being a tobacco farmer's son and the farm having what, two or more lakes, and the bride's head filled with ideas of the beauty parlor that she is going to set up on the farmhouse veranda that will bring the finesses of make-up application and hairdressing to the farmers' wives stuck out there. "You don't have to look like a frump. I'll show them how to apply foundation . . ."

"And the prawns are waiting in the fridge, you better hurry."

A one-syllable word starting with *B* flashes red in my head.

8.

"This is it. Sikato Bay Camp." Ian turns round and whistles to David, who's asleep at the back. "Wake up, my boy. We've landed."

I get out of the car, stretch out my legs. What I wouldn't give for a nice, firm bed, clean sheets, a duvet, a warm bubble bath. I look at the dirt clearing before us, the campsite. A few meters back, the ablutions block. There are three tents pitched and a group unloading from a minivan. I can smell boerewors on a braai.

Ian sniffs.

"Great, huh?"

I look around me, buttoning up my jersey.

Ian's been building this trip up, going with David to the National Parks office, then off to an odds and ends shop downtown to get a secondhand tent, army-style sleeping bags, gas cookers, torches, fishing rods. Back to his Boy Scout days. He's been showing David how to fit the gas cylinder on the stove; he caught me with my wry smile. "Relax now, wait till you have to cook on this thing, girl," he said. He teased me about black chicks and camping, and then he must have remembered my postcards and his face tightened and he said, "Yah well, it'll be lekker."

I don't know how I can let him know, see that I'm not comparing him with anyone or keeping tab of things.

I found him this morning, sitting outside on the veranda, putting some pictures away in a cardboard box. When he heard me, he got up, the box in his hands, kissed me, and asked me what I was doing up so early. I said, "I missed you in my sleep." "You're a poet," he said. He put the box on the crate we're using as a side table, and he lifted his T-shirt, that I was wearing, off me. Later, when I looked, the box was gone.

"Are you sure it's safe out here, Ian? It looks so open."

What I mean to say is that I'm cold and would like to get back in the car and go home.

"Man Lindiwe, relax, there's maybe a rhino or two, tops."

David wakes up and Ian gets busy working on the tent. One of the men from the minivan comes over.

"Hi mate, need some help?"

"No, cheers, thanks for the offer."

"We're setting up a braai. When you're ready, join us, plenty of beers. We've got some kids, the boy can muck around. You can bring your girl if you want her to keep an eye. Where's the old lady?"

"What, yah, thanks."

When he's left, I look at Ian.

"What?"

"'The girl,' Ian, the *girl*."

"What, oh *that,* Lindiwe, I wasn't paying attention. I didn't get what he was going on about . . ."

"Ian, you just let him. He assumed I was the maid, of course . . ."

"Lindiwe, I've been on the road for what, close to five hours? I'm knackered, I wasn't listening to the guy . . . why do you have to always suppose the worst from me? You want me to go there and tell him you're my chick? Fine. You want me to shout it out? Okay. 'She's my chick!' Happy now? Oh and 'she's not my fricking house girl!'"

And he hits me with a kiss right there.

"There goes the fricking beers," he says when he finally lets go of me.

I hit him on his side.

"Do you think we should stay here?"

"What now?"

"Vibes, Ian."

"Lindiwe, just get the food out the back. Make sure it's covered, otherwise we'll really be attacked by monkeys."

"Ian, where's David?"

I have a moment of panic until I find him by the toilets.

As Ian puts the last peg on the tent, the minibus guy comes over.

"Invitation still stands," he says. "It would be an honor to have you and your chick over."

Ian looks at me. I look at him.

"Ian McKenzie," he says, holding out his hand. "This is Lindiwe Bishop and my, our son, David."

"Clive Jenkins. We're here with my brother from England. He's pissed off with yours truly, putting my foot in it, my uncultured bushman self."

He takes a bow and despite myself I find him rather engagingly silly.

Ian smiles, looks at me, gives me a little prod with his eyes.

"Thank you for the invite. We'll come later," I hear myself say.

"You have to give people a chance," Ian says when we're alone, and I'm fully expecting him to add his seal of approval: "well done, Lindiwe, good girl."

"Ian, he still calls black women girls, okay, and don't tell me there's nothing wrong with that. It's the tone, it's what he meant by it."

"It only hurts if you feel it. Chill."

* * *

The braai is in full swing when we get there. Beer flowing freely. Ian's brought along a crate and two packets of boerewors and some steaks. There are some boys fishing over by the lake.

"Heh Ian, good to see you."

I stand there next to him feeling like a *lightie*.

Clive does the introductions.

"Lindiwe, the girls are over there, setting the table."

"The women," says Ian, "as in, the wives and girlfriends."

Clive throws up his hands in either self-defense or defeat.

"Yes, *those* girls."

I make myself walk over towards the trestle table.

And I stand there like an idiot.

There are four of them arranging plastic plates and cups.

"Hi," I finally squeak out.

Four pairs of eyes latch on me.

"Oh hi, Lin, Lindiwe, isn't it?"

"Yes."

"Nice to meet you. Heard about Clive's cock-up. Sorry, Meryl, but your husband can be really thick sometimes."

"You, telling me. Didn't I tell you that he walked into the Meikles Hotel to pick up a client, and he gets booted out for tracking mud and horse poo onto the carpet? I keep telling him he has to stop acting like the whole of the country is one big bush."

"You have a lovely son. He's a real sweetie. Oh, I'm Sandra."

"Thanks."

"He's got really lovely hair, where did he . . . ?"

"*Sandra.*"

"I hope you didn't get offended," says Meryl. "He doesn't mean to be so rough. Just that he was brought up on a farm. You should have heard some of the things that came out of his mouth, I mean for a city girl . . ."

"Oh please, Meryl, *what* city girl? You grew up in Marondera, not exactly . . ."

"Talking about farms, did you hear what Muga—?"

"No, Marge, don't even start with the politics . . ."

And it's as if I've come across Geraldine, Tracey, Dawn . . . all those classmates of mine as grown women, in their inner sanctum.

I pick up the plastic plates, spoons, serviettes and help while the men are out braaing, fishing, and beer drinking, and I think to myself, what the heck. *Chill.*

We're snug full of sausages and steaks and drink in our tent, David between us. Ian reaches his hand across David and I turn, put my hand across David on Ian's, and we go to sleep like this.

"Great Zimbabwe Ruins, heh."

David is already running, scrambling into the conical structures as if something inside him has been sprung loose.

Ian is in sixth heaven, what with the angles and backdrops, the shading, and the lighting.

He wants to climb up to the Hill Complex into the Eastern Enclosure.

"The view must be breathtaking from up there, Lindiwe. The Shonas really knew what they were doing."

I woke up with a sore back and a splitting headache; the last thing I feel like doing is climbing hundreds of steps, no matter the view.

Going up and down the Great Enclosure has been quite enough for me. I didn't tell Ian, but walking through the very narrow passageway that leads off from the Conical Tower, the walls of stone rising relentlessly on either side of me, I'd felt a rush of claustrophobia, panic. I was overcome with thoughts of Maphosa, spirits, ancestors, and for the first time in a long while of Mrs. McKenzie burning. The screech and cawing of an eagle flying overhead seemed to me like her crazed screams.

There is something about this place that's getting under my skin.

Out in the open, looking over the undulating land with its pockets of ruins, my eyes wandering up over the hills dotted with trees, I think of these ancient people, hauling the stones from the hills, setting them on the earth, guided by their gods, it seems to me, for how did they manage this feat without using cement or any binding substance between the stones? There they are artfully constructing their settlement, their homes, creating their kingdom, its fortifications. The work of it. The stones gathering sweat, blood. The children running across the open grassland, getting under the feet of their toiling fathers, the mothers off to collect water, ever wary of wildlife.

Where did they come from? How did they get here, choose this place to settle in, call home?

And why did they abandon it?

Zimbabwe, The Great Houses of Stone.

I look back at the tower again and shake myself awake. These stone buildings were built for the kings, the ruling elite; castles. The povo, as today, had to make do with more humble dwellings; *daga,* mud and grass, long since eroded away, the temporariness of home.

David comes running back, tugging at Ian's hand.

"You two go up, I'll wait here."

I watch them hurry away, hand in hand.

I walk to the gift shop, Matombo Curios, to see if they have some Panadol. I buy some aspirins and sit down at the café. I massage my forehead with my fingers, close my eyes. And in the dark, I'm suddenly gripped by a dense feeling of foreboding, sluggish and wet, working its way through my body. I struggle to lift my eyelids, and when I finally free them, there

is nothing but heaps of tacky souvenirs in baskets, GREAT ZIM-
BABWE stamped everywhere. I go outside into the chilly air. I
look up to the Hill Complex, wonder if I should try going up
the modern ascent. No, I'll go over to the reconstructed Karanga village, a gentle walk. Take it easy.

I watch the supposed Karanga villager pounding maize.

Then there's the singsong and some clapping and a couple
of tourists taking pictures, an invitation to tour the huts by one
of "the village elders."

One of the young male villagers smiles at me and I smile
back, and then I turn and walk towards the museum. I'll go in
there again, cool down.

"I went all the way up!" David shouts, sprinting towards me. He
falls, breathless, into my lap, dislodging me from the outcrop of
rock I've been sitting on, waiting. "I did it, Mum!" As I'm hug-
ging him I look up, and there is Ian, with his camera, *click*.

The next day Ian and David go off for a drive in the park to
see how much wildlife they can come across; they drop me off
at the Great Zimbabwe Hotel, where I read in the gardens and
have some tea.

A shadow falls over me, and when I look up, it's a huge monkey
staring at me with its head cocked towards the plate on the table and
a finger digging in its ear, and then in a flash it has grabbed hold of
the plate with the scone on it and is rushing up across the garden
onto the roof, where it sits, the plate balanced on its haunches, and
scoffs down the scone. I look around to see if there has been any
witness to this, but no, only me, and a surge of emotion sweeps

through me with the thought that I will have a story to tell the boys when they get back from their adventure, an offering.

When we get back to Harare, there's an envelope on the floor that the postman slipped through. Ian picks it up, takes a look at it, and hands it to me.

It's from Jean.

That's all it takes for all the good feeling from the break to dissipate. By even reading the letter, I know that Ian feels a kind of betrayal. I should just chuck it into the dustbin, unopened.

I don't know how to tell him, let him know what Jean says, if I should, if he has any right to it.

Jean is leaving Zimbabwe. He is going to the Ivory Coast.

Ian shuts himself off. For hours after work he disappears, coming home late at night, the smell of chemicals in his clothes, on his hands; he has been at Ilo's studio.

The distance grows between us. I don't know the words, the gesture that will draw us close again.

And David seeks solace, once more, in his giraffe.

9.

David is in the lounge with his new Bible. It's full of pictures. Heaven. Hell. Jesus. Even God. I had felt breathless when I saw it in Kingston, then a flutter of panic when I lifted it off the shelf and saw the price. Ian didn't make any comment when I was wrapping it up, but I could see the annoyance in his eyes; he dutifully signed the card.

The Bible is splayed open on the floor on exactly the same page I opened it to, Jonah and the whale. David is not even looking at it. I've made a mistake. He isn't the same boy we took away. A train set. A bicycle. A ball. A kite. Anything else would have done.

But Ian's got his backup plan. A birthday surprise. *I* don't know what it is. Ian is going to show me how a birthday is done.

We pile in the car and he drives us around the university, where a month ago, I, together with everyone else who wanted to continue their studies, had to sign a piece of paper saying that for the duration of my course, I would respect the governing authorities and refrain from demonstrating against them. We go up along The Chase, past Strathaven Shopping Centre, past Circus Nightclub, and my heart does a dive when I see us go into the grounds of the Old Georgian Sports Ground.

The parking lot is jam packed, and in the end, Ian has to back out and park on the curb. There's a banner stretched up on the gates. BMX AFRICA CHALLENGE.

There are kids all geared up, padded and helmeted, fathers proudly heaving bikes and coolers from their pickups.

Clusters of mothers are talking as they make their way to the tracks. There are uniformed maids bringing up the rear with picnic baskets and infants in tow.

My eyes dart and leap, doing their frantic search—yes, spotted, a couple of black kids, fathers, but I don't see any women.

I look down at David who's staring at two boys. They're pushing their bikes.

"Cool!" one of the boy shouts.

"Let's go and take a look at the action," Ian says coming around to us. "This will be good, my boy. If you like it, who knows come Christmas, heh?"

I walk behind them, smiling like an idiot at the maids I pass who look glumly back at me.

I look at David's hand in Ian's. The shades of father and son.

My heart is in my mouth when I watch the antics of the riders up and down the humps and troughs of the tracks, the bikes leaping into the air and crashing on the dirt again. A surge of anger at Ian for being so irresponsible. David is not going to do something this dangerous. I won't let him.

But then I look over at David, his neck craning in his effort not to miss anything; his eyes wide-open. He gasps; father and son do a high five. Perhaps there are things that Ian knows better than me, things I have to trust him with.

"I'll be back in a sec," Ian says, and he strides off towards the braai area.

When he's gone, I hear behind me, "Man, these Affs," and I feel a dig at my back. I sit stick straight, and then there's laugher and someone saying, "It's disgusting." Another prod at my back. "Siss, man." Then "yuck."

When Ian comes back, he's looking redder in the face. He's carrying two Castles and two plates of T-bone steaks, charred rings of boerewor sausages.

A voice behind him says, "Heh mate, those steaks look good," and Ian laughs and says, "And they taste even better."

He sits down, splashing some Castle on my jeans.

"What's up with you?"

"Nothing."

"Lindiwe, you haven't spoken a word since we got back, what is it?"

"I told you, nothing. I've got an essay to write."

I walk past him and sit down by the table.

"He really had a good time. Come Christmas he's getting a bike. Lindiwe . . ."

"What, Ian?" I say, not looking up from the papers I'm riffling through.

"What is it with you? You blow hot, cold. What's going on?"

"Ian, I have an essay to write. It's already late. Give me room, please!"

I can hear the quaver in my voice. The place is too small for us. Too few rooms for us to storm away from each other. At any one point there must be only two, three meters separating us, so Ian does the sensible things; he leaves.

10.

"Thanks for doing this, Lindiwe."

It's such a formal thing for him to say.

We're driving down to Bulawayo. It's the Christmas holidays. Everything is so dry and barren it seems it could never once have been saturated with any other color but this woeful grayness.

I haven't told my mother we're coming.

"They dumped her there," he told me when he got the notification of her impending evaluation. "They didn't know what to do with her."

She is going to undergo some tests, and if these go well she might be released. She's now living in a more open wing of the hospital, for patients who are considered low risk.

I look up at Ian and brush the crook of my finger on his chin, feel the stubble here. He takes the finger, squeezes tight, nibbles at it.

The thought of our visit fills me with unease; I haven't slept for two days. On Christmas Eve we'll go to Ingutsheni, the three of us, and we will meet her. Ian will introduce her to me, me to her.

I look out the window, at the hacked trees and where the ground has been scorched. I have tried to imagine the kind of trauma being in that fire might have caused; the type of breakdown it might have precipitated. Words and ideas from my studies have leaked out, attaching themselves to the unknown: personality disorder, schizophrenia, psychotic episode.

Nineteen-year-old Ian, coming out of jail, his first visit to his mother, what, who did he see behind those walls? His mother's reality must have shifted so that where she was, where she found herself, became the norm: what kind of adaptations had her mind made to survive?

That was an essay topic last year: does madness really exist or is it just a reasonable response to a set of events?

I look back at David. He's grown. I look down at his feet, at the new Bata tackies we got on Saturday (when I said "tackies," the young shop assistant looked at me with her Big City Girl attitude. "Oh, you mean *sneakers*," she said). I see his bare feet on that morning months and months ago when we lifted his sleeping body out from his grandmother's grasp.

"They need to see that she has some kind of support system," Ian told me.

A support system, I thought. *We can barely support ourselves.* We haven't talked about how we'll manage.

We are staying at, ironies of ironies, the Grey's Inn, former all-exclusive Rhodie Hangout. It is two blocks from The Selborne and caters for the budget traveler. We are refugees in our own town. Looking up at its colonial facade, I think of my schoolgirl self sitting in the car while Ian stood behind a fence trying to connect with an old school friend in Khumalo, arranging to meet here to check out the new contingent of expat chicks.

While Ian sleeps, I go with David into town, his hand in mine, still a surprise.

We go into Woolworths.

"You can have a sweet, David. Any one you like."

I watch him take in the assortment of delights, hazards. The fudge and licorice sticks, the cool cigarettes with their white peppermint stalks and red tips, snug in their packet; Rita would "smoke" them during lunchtimes even though they were forbidden at school, blowing elaborate circles in the air with her exhaled "smoke." I look at the jelly babies, red, white, yellow, orange, and feel the sticky mess of them in my fist.

I look over the counters at the gift packages of men's after-shave and ladies' perfumes. Impulse spray, Shield deodorant for men, the pocket money I would save for my parents' gifts. I think of the day after Christmas when I saw Mummy giving my present away to Rosanna. She wanted the perfumes that came from Europe, that were sold only in Edgars.

"Maybe some chocolate?" I ask him. "Those peanut clusters are delicious."

We stand there together until finally we take the escalator and go upstairs to the supermarket to see if there are any toys there.

I stand upstairs and memory gushes at me: Daddy maneuvering the trolley, the wad of dollars in his shirt pocket, Mummy holding the list, slowly crossing out the found items. I walk up and down the aisles, lifting the familiar objects as if they were artifacts. The same things as in Harare, but here in this place, they seem to resonate with meaning.

There's a selection of balls in one corner, and I notice David eyeing them.

I've bought him a football for Christmas, and it's in the suitcase with the other gifts. Back in Harare there's the bicycle waiting for him; Ian got it on account from Manica Cycles. But I want him to have something now. I want him to have a memory of this moment, me and him together.

"You can choose a ball, David, since you didn't have any sweets."

I almost add "please."

He picks up a red plastic ball, throws it carefully up in the air. And then he puts it down again. He takes hold of my hand. And we take the stairs downstairs.

When we get back to the hotel, Ian's not in the room. I wonder if he has gone to the pub or if he's driven off somewhere. We wait until it gets dark, and then we eat the chicken sandwiches I brought with us and we both fall asleep watching TV.

We drive through the gates bearing gifts: a sweater in baby blue four-ply wool, a pair of yellow socks, a toothbrush and toothpaste, a bar of soap. This time I do not stay in the car waiting for Ian to get back. I step out of the car. David and I find a bench to sit on while Ian goes up the stairs.

"She's sleeping," he says, when he comes back alone.

We sit on the bench, the three of us. I close my eyes and imagine music playing through the air here, something with strings and maybe a flute, something so soft and fragile if you breathed too hard it would shatter.

"I'll go and check again," Ian says, and I notice that this time he takes the gifts with him.

I look down at David and find the giraffe in his hand and David gnawing at the giraffe's head.

I push the giraffe's head away from David's mouth.

Where are all the inmates? Do days like this, days of celebration, make them edgy? Are they given more medication than normal to blot out memory, desire, longing?

As if in answer, a shriek pierces through the silence and David stiffens next to me. At this moment it seems such a foolhardy thing to have brought him here.

Ian returns alone. The gifts are gone.

We spend Christmas in the hotel. We eat the buffet lunch. I don't say anything about Ian's drinking, the Castles cluttering up our table.

Later I go to see my father. Like Ian, bearing gifts.

Mummy is sitting outside by the veranda with Aunty Gertrude.

It is a shock to see Aunty Gertrude there. They watch me in silence as I go inside the house. I go into the bedroom. All the curtains are drawn, and in the darkness I can hear Daddy's raspy breathing.

The room smells, and for a moment I think of Ian's mother, if she might not be in a room such as this, not in size or shape perhaps, but in how it feels.

I go to the windows and gently draw back a curtain, enough for a shaft of light to fall over the left side of the bed, Daddy's side.

I go around the bed, and standing there, I remember that day when one moment Daddy was sitting on his favorite chair in the lounge having his tea, and the next, the cup falling from his hand, the tea spilling onto his lap, onto his slippers, and Daddy's head slumped forwards. And I remember that, while I called the ambulance, Mummy went to the bedroom and I could hear her prayers. Later while we waited for the ambulance, she made phone calls to her Manyano friends, and I thought then how girlish she sounded as she related the calamity that had befallen her.

I lay down my gifts at my father's feet. A scarf and a hat.

I go to the back of the house to the workshop. I find a dog, barely a puppy. I think of Roxy who the vet put to sleep because of the pain he was suffering from a tumor in his neck, and I remember my father's grief at the loss of him; when I came back from school, he told me that he had no choice but to agree with the doctor.

The dog is lying on the mat in front of the door, and when she sees me, she whimpers. I lift her off the mat; she is little more than bones. I go to where the vegetable garden used to be and run the tap. I watch her lap at the running water. I look out at the house next door.

There is no sign of Tess, the cocker spaniel who Daddy got (just before his stroke) and who I'm sure is the mother of the puppy in my arms. She must finally have got herself pregnant, because when she was in heat, she would always manage one escape from the yard, biting right through her leash when she was tied to the gum tree.

Carrying the puppy, I go and see if Rosanna is around. I knock gently at her door. When I push it open, there is a faint smell of perfume but that must be my wishful thinking.

I stand by the veranda trying to find words. Mummy and Aunty Gertrude don't even look at me.

On the drive back to Harare, David sings just under his breath Bob Marley's "Three Little Birds," the track that Ian's been playing at home. He knows the words, I think. *He knows them.* I look at Ian who smiles at me. We were right not to bring him to my mother. It's a gift to have him singing this; The Lord Is My Shepherd spirited away.

The dog sits quietly on his lap.

11.

"Bridgette!"

"Oh, my God!"

"Bridgette!"

"Lins!"

It's Saturday morning, and I'm sitting in the hairdresser's chair when she walks in. I don't see her straightaway because I'm reading *Femina* magazine and my head is bent low because Bea is putting the straightening lotion right at the back. Then I hear, "Hello, I'd like to have my braids undone." I look up, almost knocking the brush from Bea's hand.

"My God, Bridgette, what are you doing here?" I ask her as she drags a chair and sits next to me.

"I've just come back from London. And you, Little Miss Thing?"

"University."

"Of course."

Her "of course" takes me right back to my fifteen-year-old self. How irritating I must have been then and how generous of her to be my friend.

Bridgette reschedules her appointment so that as soon as I'm finished we go upstairs to the Book Café. We order coffees and pancakes.

"So," I say, "fill me in, all the juicy details, please."

"I'm dabbling in import, export. Hair products to start with. I'm thinking of setting up some salons."

"You look great, Bridgette."

And she does with her tight T-shirt and jeans, her sky-high stilettos.

"Thanks. Not too bad yourself. What you're studying and more to the point, any nice Shona specimens over there?"

"I see some things never change."

I tell her what I'm studying. I go on and on about that. How great it is. How interesting it is. How enlightening it is . . .

"Lindiwe, please, move on."

"Okay, I'm also doing part-time work. I'm a production assistant at an advertising agency, which basically means that I—"

"Come on, Lindiwe, I know you're hiding something."

I don't even try to carry on with my routine.

"Well, I'm living with someone."

"I knew it! Well, well, well, so Little Miss Innocence herself has been deflowered, wonders never cease. Details, details."

"And I have a son."

I say that last bit very quickly. She makes an *O* of surprise.

"A son," she says. "Now *this* is unexpected. When, how? I mean, obviously it is a university guy. I hope he's good-looking and gifted in the lower departments."

"Bridgette!"

She waits for me to go on.

How can I? Where do I begin?

"Come on," she says. "I'm dying here."

"He's not a university guy. Bridgette, it's a long story and I'll tell you another day. I just want to enjoy your company today. This is such a surprise. So tell me about these plans of yours."

There were so many rumors when she didn't return for the

second term: she was at a boarding school in London, she was being sequestered in a Convent in Ireland, she had been forced to marry a sekuru somewhere deep in the communal lands, and simply, she was dead. How I had missed her! When my own scandal broke, I finally understood how lonely and desperate she must have felt.

She looks at me and decides to leave me alone, for now.

She talks about how her parents took her back to London and left her in the care of an aunty. She talks about importing and exporting and her hair salons. She tells me about her diplomas and her life in London.

"Why don't you come over to my place for lunch tomorrow?" I ask her as we get ready to leave.

"Yes, yes, I'd like that. Lins, my girl, can you believe it, we're women now."

I give her the address; tell her to come to the small gate, not the black electric gate, which is the entrance to the main house where an Egyptian diplomat lives.

"You'll be introduced to my little family."

"I'm looking forward to it."

"Nice hair," says Ian, when I meet up with him and David at Greenwood Park. "Can I touch?"

"As long as you don't mess the curls."

He lifts his finger, snakes it through some curls. And then he rubs his finger on his jeans.

"It's conditioning cream, Ian."

"Asch Lindiwe, I just prefer you with your hair natural, that's all.

I march off to the ticket counter and buy a whole wad of tickets.

David has a train ride with Ian and then with me.

Then it's off on the trampoline, David jumping up and down on the tarp that is stretched over a hole about three meters deep. I can't stand to look while Ian is busy calling out instructions on how to do a somersault. And then he is in the canoes with Ian, the two of them almost capsizing as they try to take a bend.

We sit down on the grassy patch under the bridge eating ice creams, watching the train make its route around the park.

"They don't sell beers at the canteen," Ian says. "Man, I'm thirsty."

"Water is always an option, Ian. There's a tap, down there."

He stands up and starts fiddling with his watch.

Once Ian's offloaded us at home, he goes straight back out the door. He's meeting up with some guys, watching a rugby match. That's the story.

I look about me for a moment and a wave of despair leaves me immobilized there.

I have an essay to write, due in on Monday, and a dissertation proposal to draw up; I shouldn't have asked Bridgette over. I switch on the TV and I'm in luck. There's *Tom and Jerry,* his favorite cartoon now that he watches TV and Satan hasn't made an appearance. He sits on the couch, the giraffe lying on his lap, his hand on it. I sit down at the dining-room table, arrange my books, and try to write my essay: "Discuss: The Role of Positive and Negative Reinforcement in Interpersonal Human Development." I look at the title for a long time and know that I'm going to have to ask for an extension from Mr. Davidson. There's not any chance I'm going to get even half of it done. I close the books, leave the table. I go on the couch next to David, and we watch Jerry teasing Tom together.

It's ten o'clock and Ian still isn't back.

I think of all the places he could be.

All the Rhodie hangouts, the places I won't go to, the places where he won't take me.

Sarah's Nightclub in town or that place over in Avondale, where a black guy was beaten up, or the Keg and Sable in Borrowdale . . . the little entourage that he's become part of: Heather; Duncan (her lout of a husband); Clive, he of Great Zimbabwe fame; people who drift in and out of the house, making me feel as though I'm a guest or worse still . . .

"Not exactly multiracial, Ian," I try, hearing the edge in my voice, which doesn't escape him.

"Get off your high horse, Lindiwe. They're here, aren't they? You should see how you look at them, I'll get you a picture. What about you and your expats? Here today, gone tomorrow, creating more shit with their solutions. Who's fooling who?"

"*They're* not racists, Ian."

"Lindiwe, enough. One incident and you're still smarting about it. He was just talking."

Duncan, last week.

"Shit," I had heard. "We'll show these munts real tricks, give old Bobs a real right show. You should see how those munts poop themselves when they come to the skydiving club for tryouts. To this day not one has made a jump, speaks for itself, I say."

They were out on the patio, the lounge doors wide open; he didn't see me come in, not that me being there or not would have made much difference to him.

Hearing me, he twisted his neck over the sofa and said, all smiles and ruddy cheeriness, "Howzit Lee, just jolling about Gooks and Spooks Weekend. Oops, I mean heroes. Yes man, all the dead terrs, now we're supposed to be honoring. What about the Rhodesian soldiers? They sacrificed a heck of a lot more. Reconciliation my foot, and what's the other bit of that holiday? Oh yes, Ancestors Weekend, that's a hang of a mouthful if you ask me."

I didn't bother with any kind of answer, and I was moving into the bedroom when he called out.

"Hey Lees, have you heard the latest on Banana, your vice-chancellor, the guy's an out-and-out moff; he's got his you know what stuck up some football chappies over at your varsity. Hell that's what you get for making a banana a president."

Hee hee ha. Hee hee ha.

Beer was spurting out from his mouth. He looked as though he had been dropped in a vat of oil and left out in the sun to dry. His easy familiarity with me made me sick. He was the son of the owner of a building company, but most of the time, he seemed bored and mad as hell that he had been cheated of the war; he fancied he would have made one helluva Selous Scout. Enter the skydiving at weekends and the overgrown thatch on his chin.

Heather was always wearing dark glasses, and her face had far too much foundation plastered on it, even for a Rhodie.

Later, when he was gone, I told Ian that if his friends were going to come over, they should stop with the racist comments.

"He didn't mean anything by it. Don't be so sensitive all the time; sometimes it's just talk."

"Right," I said. "Of course, it's nothing. To him, to you. Kaffir, gondie, munt, boy, etcetera, etcetera; but it means a lot to ninety-nine percent of the population, to me."

"For fuck's sake," he shouted. "Give it a rest, just once."

"You never want to talk about it."

"I know the tune, Lindiwe."

And then he was gone, slamming the door behind him.

Sometimes, I thought, people change; sometimes not enough.

*   *   *

Days, weeks pass like this.

"You think so," he goes on, goading me about my expat friends. "Trust me, they're the worst kind. The Right On brigade. Wait till they ever have to make a choice, a real flat-out choice; wait till their head is put on the wire . . . What do you think they talk about when you're not around, huh? The bloody Africans, the natives, you, me."

Every time when I ask him why he disappears, takes off, he says I should relax; he's just getting a breath of fresh air, as if I'm . . . *we're* stifling him here.

"You wanted this," I shout at him. "We're here because of you, Ian."

"I'm working, aren't I? I'm supporting you. Get off my back. Or you're so used to the expat lifestyle, you're having trouble coping with local rates. How come you're so into foreigners?"

That's always his last card. The thing he flings casually at me. The arrow he thinks finds its target.

"Chill," he says, as if he's still fifteen, sixteen, as if I'm the nagging housewife.

And when he thinks maybe he has pushed it a bit too far and is regretting some of it: "I'm trying, Lindiwe. I'm trying."

As if he's carrying the heaviest load, the responsibility of it. He'll reach out to me, try to draw me close.

And then I'll wonder if it's me who is being judgmental, rigid.

If I shouldn't be more honest. "Yes, Ian," I could tell him, "I miss going out to restaurants and talking about books and movies. Sometimes I can't stand to be in this cottage. I can't. I get a sudden rush of claustrophobia. Is this it? I keep asking myself. Is this it?"

I hear the lock in the door, and I can tell by his fumbling, the dropped keys, that he has had too much to drink, that if I stay awake there will be an argument.

I go quickly into the bedroom, undress, and go to bed.

I hear him open the door, mumble shit, run the tap, and then he's here, on the bed, taking off his shoes.

The room fills up with Castle.

I get up, walk past him, shake off his hand, and go out of there, to sleep on the couch.

"Hi!" I virtually yell out, and Bridgette steps back from my crazed welcome.

I take the bottle of wine from her and usher her in to the lounge where David stands against the couch, Jade between her legs.

"David, this is my friend. We went to school together, Aunty Bridgette."

Jade wriggles her way out and starts running, as is her way, around the room in loops around the furniture, taking nips at the straw chairs, circling David, me, and Bridgette. I have my thoughts about the mental stability of this dog. Then, when she's all tired out, she flops dead at David's feet.

"Hi, David," says Bridgette, going towards him.

"Hello," says David.

He bends down and starts playing the rolling game with Jade. David rolls and Jade, who's risen from the dead, rolls over David.

"Cute," Bridgette mouths to me, and I know that she won't be leaving until all the juicy details have been extracted from me.

We're seated in the lounge when Ian strolls in dressed in yesterday's clothes, his hair all over the place, the smell of stale alcohol about. He glances over at Bridgette who is staring at him.

"Ian, this is Bridgette."

I make my voice as normal as I can; I try to sound as though it's the most natural thing in the world to be here in this cottage with Ian and David and now my long lost school friend, found. As if it's my destiny.

Ian says, "Howzit?"

Bridgette has an amused look on her face.

"Howzit," she says.

If he senses that she is poking fun at him, it flies right past him; he goes into the kitchen and for a moment we are all still, David, Bridgette, and me, as we hear him rummaging about.

"I'm off," he says.

Showered, dressed, and ready to roll, the keys dangling in his hand.

"Cheers."

I don't tell him, but you're supposed to have lunch with us. You're meant to be part of this production. No. I let him go. No worries.

Bridgette doesn't say anything about him, not until after the pasta, and David's fallen asleep on the couch, her hand brushing against his fiery hair.

"Okay Lindiwe," she says, putting down her glass. "Can I humbly ask what in the Lord's name is going on?"

And I'm glad she asks.

"I don't know," I say. "I thought I knew but I don't."

And it's good to say this out loud, to admit that I don't know what the hell I'm doing. I don't know what the hell I've let myself in for.

"Okay miss, shall we at least start from the beginning.

Child . . . how, when, where, who? I've already got the picture, and if that's who I think it is, what is up with you?"

I start smiling and then I laugh.

She looks down at David.

"How old is he Lindiwe? Five, six?"

"Six. Six and a half."

"Lindiwe, that was when I had the . . ."

"After. I found out after you left. It was a one-night thing. It just happened."

"But you were such a *good* girl."

"I know, I know, and maybe that's why it happened. I was kind of infatuated with him. Don't look at me like that, Bridgette. I don't know, I found him really romantic and maybe I felt sorry for him . . ."

"Lindiwe, a romantic k-i-l-l-e-r."

I jump up.

"That's not true, Bridgette! He was cleared."

My heart is thudding, painful.

David stirs.

"I'm sorry, Lindiwe. Come on, sit, or do you want to beat me up?"

I sit down keeping my eyes on David.

"And the setup here?"

I watch her eyes traveling around the room, and I'm embarrassed by the cheapness, the makeshift quality of the furniture: the straw couch she is sitting on, care of the vendors along Avondale road, the table made of crates, the bookshelf balanced on bricks. Suddenly with Bridgette here, it doesn't seem to amount to much, the life I have with Ian and David.

"Lindiwe, khuluma! Speak!"

"I see Mrs. Moyo's classes at school had some effect."

She rolls her eyes.

"Lindiwe, he's a Rhodie!"

"A Zimbabwean, Bridgette."

Another roll of the eyes.

"*Maybe* he's a new breed of enlightened Rhodie, but Lindiwe he's still a Rhodie."

"Bridgette, he's the father of my child, and he's a good person. Don't look at me as though I need a stay in Ingutsheni, Bridgette."

"Okay, then, so what are you going to do after university? You *do* have a *plan* for your *future?*"

"Bridgette, I . . . I just don't know. This has all just happened, I . . ."

"Don't get pregnant."

"At the moment I don't think there's any chance of that."

"So why are you . . . ?"

David lifts his head, looks sleepily around, and slumps down again.

"You should go away, take off. I mean it. Do something for yourself. Leave him with the kid. Come on, Lindiwe. Knowing you, you must be getting top marks. Why don't you do another degree? Go to London. I can get details about scholarships."

"Stop, you're making me dizzy, Bridgette."

"Good, you. Think of it this way . . . the more qualified you get, the more you can take care of him. I mean your son. No offense but your Mr. Right doesn't look like he's exactly rolling in *cash.*"

I don't tell her that he doesn't have O levels.

"Anyway, what does he do?"

"He's a journalist, a photojournalist. He's done lots of work in South Africa."

I don't mention the other work at TV Sales and Hire, the installing of fridges and stoves.

"Lins . . . no, nothing."

"Just say it, Bridgette, you're on a roll. I'm listening."

"Okay. How can you seriously live with a man who . . . who might be . . . Lindiwe, you don't know, not really, how can you ever feel safe?"

I pick up the cork of the wine bottle and roll it in my hand. And then I say, "Come on, let's have some coffee."

When Bridgette leaves, I go for a walk with David and Jade. David is holding onto the leash, which Jade keeps biting at and doing elaborate dances around. I don't know I'm walking so fast until I turn around and see boy and dog, two tiny blobs in the distance; I can't tell if they're moving or still, and for one magical instant, I could just run away, leave, disappear, be free, and then the thought breaks up and I run back to where David stands and Jade sits.

"Mum," David says to me. "Look, I taught her."

And I look at the dog and say, "Good girl, Jade."

I look at the boy and say, "Well done, David."

We walk back home, the three of us.

12.

Mr. Chambers, my psychometrics lecturer, gives me a lift home. We sit in his car at the gate for ten, fifteen minutes, going over some detail about my research project. When I get inside the cottage, Ian is standing by the window, hands crossed over his chest.

"God, I'm hot, Ian. Water."

There are four bottles of Castle in the sink.

I stand there against the sink, looking at his back. I found him this morning face down on the couch. I tried to wake him up so that David wouldn't see him like that. I drove to the school, spying David in the rearview mirror, so small and quiet, his hands pushing against the vinyl seat, his head heavy with all the fighting and tears and silences. I remembered David, the barefoot boy in the pyjamas, whom we stole from his grandmother. We had promised him so much. We owed him so much. We kept letting him down.

When I came back to leave the car, he was still comatose on the couch.

I look at Ian, and everything I've been holding back, I feel pressing against my tongue, lashing at my heart.

"So now we've started in the morning, Ian? Did you even go to work?"

"What the fuck was that?"

"You know what I'm talking about, Ian."

"Don't fuck with me, Lindiwe. What the fuck were you doing in the car?"

I can't believe what I'm hearing. I put the glass of water slowly down in the sink.

"No, what are *you* doing, Ian? You just sit around moping. Look at you. Look at you. You forgot to pick up David twice last week. *Twice,* Ian!"

"Come on girl, has your Jean come back or are you into some other expert these days?"

"You're drunk."

"So are they good fucks?"

The ugliness of his words.

"At least have the guts to actually look at me, Ian. Who do you think you are? What the hell makes you think that you've been making so many sacrifices? Who asked you . . . ?"

I stand there breathless, feeling how empty and stupid it all is.

"I'm going to have a bath."

He spins around, knocks into the couch as he lunges towards me.

I look up at him, splotches of red on his face.

He grabs hold of my arms.

"How much Forex are they dishing out to black chicks these days?"

There is something so tight and sharp in my chest.

"You're hurting me, Ian."

"Do you have any idea what it's like to be doing fricking fuck all while you're off with your boyfriends? Do you want to know how many fricking fridges I fixed today? How many fricking deliveries I made? I am so sick of this shit."

"So you're bored Ian. Grow up."

I snatch my hands from him.

"Fuck you, Lindiwe"

And I feel his words hitting my back, piercing through.

I go to the bathroom. Lock the door. I press my back against the door, waiting. For him to bang at it with his fists. For the handle of the door to jerk up and down. For the fight to go on. For the words to become uglier still, more terrible, more brutal. For us to exhaust ourselves until we find each other again, forgive. But there is nothing. Just the two of us, breathing resentment, hurt, fury on opposite sides.

13.

But it's the attack at Ilo's, two weeks later, that's the last straw.

A demonstration starting at the post office: parents queuing to pay school fees begin a spontaneous protest against the recent 100 percent increase of fees, spreading down to some unemployed youths loitering around, the throwing of stones, bricks, the riot police called in, some demonstrators dashing into shops to take cover, and the riot police flushing them out with tear gas; one canister fizzles open inside at Ilo's where the old man is in the back room.

Ian comes home distraught.

"He's in a bad way, Lindiwe. The gas got into his lungs deep, and with the chemicals, shit. Shit."

When we go to the Avenues Clinic the next day, we find the nurse clearing up the sheets. She shakes her head when she sees us.

"It was too much for him. He could not take it. This is Zimbabwe now. No respect for old people," she says.

Ian walks out before she's finished talking, and when I go out to the parking lot after him, the car's not there. I catch a taxi to town, to the studio, and that's where I find him, carefully taking down the pictures on the wall.

The smell of tear gas lingers in the air.

"Ian . . ."

He doesn't turn around, doesn't answer me. I go to him, try to get hold of his arm, of him.

"Ian . . ."

He keeps working on the pictures, emptying the walls.

I stand there for the longest time, watching, helpless.

"Ian, we have to talk."

He doesn't stop packing his stuff. His gear. He's off, on assignment. I know he's overjoyed to be out of here. He's going to watch South Africa become an independent state. He's going to take pictures. He's leaving this messy life behind.

"Ian, we have to talk."

But he doesn't stop for anything, not for one word. In goes the camera and finally there's nothing else for him to busy himself with. He's ready to scoot off. I should just let him get on with it, he's already missed so much, everything he's had to hear second-hand like everyone else, one gruesome slaughter after another.

"Ian . . ."

He's looking at me. What does he see? His ball and chain probably.

"So talk," he says, standing there with his hands crossed over his chest.

"I said *we* have to talk, not just me."

I sound so juvenile. Desperate. I look at him glower red. I should leave. Let him get away.

"I'm taking David back to Bulawayo," I say. "I can't look after him here."

I don't say, "on my own."

"Lindiwe, it's only for a couple of months."

He looks at his watch.

"I'm off," he says, picking up his bag. Then he remembers something.

"The rent's paid up for the year."

Don't expect me back. Soon. Ever.

And then he's gone.

When Bridgette hears it's me, she says, "Howzit?"

"That's not funny."

"Sorry," she giggles.

"And anyway, you missed out 'hanging.'"

"Hanging?"

"Yes, as in 'howzit hanging.'"

"Oh, my God, Lindiwe, you're not serious. That's how they talk? Howzit hanging? I'll remember that for next time."

"He's gone."

"So you're a free woman. We can have some real fun now. How's David taking it?"

"I'm going to take him to Bulawayo, but Bridgette, I feel so guilty. He's just got used to life here; he's actually made a friend at school and sometimes he forgets about the giraffe and I'm about to—I can't look after him—I have to go out to Makoni communal lands for my dissertation."

"That cooperative thing? Group management styles, group dynamics, etcetera, etcetera . . . ?"

"Yes. I can't drag him around with me. I . . ."

"Listen, Lindiwe, I can do that. When you're not around, I can help. I'm a freelancer; I set my own hours . . ."

"No, I can't."

"Don't be silly. I think he's so cute."

"Bridgette, it's a lot to . . ."

"Think about it, okay?"

"Yes, thanks, Bridgette."

*   *   *

It's the Liberation War Heroes holiday, and we're on the train, David and me, off to Bulawayo.

We're in cattle class, and I'm sitting at the edge of a bench, David squashed up tight against me. The wagon keeps filling up until it's thick with bodies, and I can't see clearly on either side of me. I'm breathing in stale Chibuku coming out in heavy, hot tufts from the gaping mouths of last night's revelers, freshly brewed Chibuku in its brown plastic tubs ready for consuming as soon as the train chugs away into the night, sweaty squashed bodies swaying as fingers lose their grip on the overhead metal bars. The train is already an hour and a half late. I have an urge to bolt out of here, but it's not even possible. We'd be trampled underfoot. It's going to be a long, long ride.

This is our last minute escape from the celebrations. Rumor has been circulating in Harare that the Youth Brigade has been told to go door to door, even in the suburbs, to drag people out to Rufaro to show the president just how much he and the other heroes are loved, and after what happened yesterday in town, it's best to be away. Celebrations in Bulawayo will be a lower key affair.

The train shudders then is still again.

"Hey, man!" someone shouts.

The train shudders again, and this time manages to drag its bulk across the lines.

The ride is fitful, lots of stops and then starts, some short, some long. Chibuku splashes about, and soon the wagon is also filled with the sound of someone retching, someone swearing and shouting, threatening to do damage to someone's organs, but then tiredness seems to settle in all round and the carriage becomes filled with snoring and intermittent murmuring.

David sleeps. I stroke his head and bend over, give him a light kiss on his forehead.

He's been upset that we couldn't take Jade with us; no animals allowed on the train. We left her with the neighbors, distracted by the huge bone we got from the butcher's.

I think of Ian running around, taking his pictures, of the image I've been having: Ian meeting Mandela and giving him that legendary greeting "howzit," and Mandela cocking his head to one side, his face crinkling up into that smile. "Howzit," he says back.

I don't want to think about Bulawayo, what I'll find there.

Mummy, Daddy, Rosanna. And my sister. Half.

I try not to think of the house next door.

I think of the planes that will do the flypast for the president, their acrobatic displays in the sky. Duncan and his merry men landing at Mugabe's feet.

I think about David and me yesterday in town, having hamburgers at Wimpy, First Street. We were sitting watching the fire-eater through the window. He was very tall and very black and dressed in nothing but a loincloth. His body shone and glistened as though he had smeared tar all over it. His teeth were startling white, his lower lip a vivid pink. His hair fell all the way down his back in thick flat pads like the stretched, kneaded dough you could spy from the window at Downings Bakery. We watched him pick up the club, set it alight, and bring the flame to his open mouth. In it went and then out again.

David watched as he sucked the last of the cream float.

Then we watched as the crowd began scampering, somebody falling.

We watched as the youths toi toyed in the wake of the crowd, their berets askew, their VOTE ZANU-PF T-shirts looking grubby and tired.

We watched them kick the fire-eater's drum; grab hold of an old man, give him some slaps; pee on the streetlamps and rip the poster that some brave soul from the Zimbabwe Congress of Trade Unions had stuck on a wall, calling for a general strike against the World Bank–sanctioned economic structural adjustment program.

We watched as three of the youths broke off from the group and sauntered into the restaurant.

"Pamberi ne ZANU!" one of them shouted.

They were greeted with silence.

"Pamberi ne ZANU!" the youths shouted, one of them slamming his fist on a table, rattling the cutlery. There was silence again.

"Eh, eh, Pamberi ne . . ."

"Heh, shut up with your *pamberis,* can't you see we are trying to eat in peace?"

The voice was loud and strong and came from the table behind us. I didn't look back. The youths started moving forwards, and I heard chairs scraping from the table behind. There were four of them, big men. One of the youths backed out and started running out into the streets. The patrons of the restaurant hooted and cheered. There was a scuffle and the fight was carried outside, the two youths looking suddenly small and scared out of their wits, their shirts already torn from the bodies, their pants pulled down, their buttocks exposed; someone squirted tomato sauce on them.

I told David we were leaving. I didn't want to be there when the runaway youth came back with reinforcements. Anyway, the manager came in and started shooing everyone away; the restaurant was now closed for business.

I dragged David home, constantly looking back in case the youths came leaping out.

Home, I locked myself in the bathroom and started crying.

The train stops yet again.

We must be almost there, dawn is beginning to break, rays

of light are filtering through the windows. I haven't slept and my head is stiff and aching. I feel David's weight on me. I shift a bit and he wakes up.

"Hey, sleepyhead, we're almost there."

The train starts again, and around us we begin to hear the stirring of those who've fallen asleep on their feet, shaking the weight back into their legs.

Bulawayo.

I'm too tired and sore to even think of the walk across town to get the bus home. We get a taxi, a run-down Peugeot that smells of engine oil and smoke and whose ancient sound system is crackling "Corruption, corruption" by Thomas Mapfumo.

I look over at David who leans his head against the greasy window, his lips flat against it. I don't say to him, "Don't do that, you'll get sick with all the germs." I let him be.

My heart starts knocking against my chest when we pass the cemetery, then the garage, the bus stop, the turn right, one, two, and there we are in front of the iron gate.

I step out of the car and everything seems eerily quiet. David stands next to me and together we look out to the old Spanish colonial house. I feel his breathing change, his body tense. I take his hand. We'll be all right.

But there are shocks waiting for me, for us.

Mummy is not here. She's been gone for weeks. She just packed her bags and left. The only place I can think of is that she is in Botswana with Aunty Gertrude.

Rosanna has moved into the main house. Her bedroom is the spare room. She is looking after Daddy.

Rosanna's child, Daddy's daughter, my sister, half, looks so much like me.

Maphosa is back in his room. And he has a wife.

I phone Aunty Gertrude who says, yes, Mummy is there with her. I ask to speak to her, and Aunty Gertrude comes back to the phone to say that Mummy has just gone in the bath.

"How is she?" I ask Aunty Gertrude.

"Don't worry," she says. "She is doing well."

Rosanna says that she hopes I am not upset with her for being in the house.

"Your father was in need of care, Sisi, and at night I could not hear him if he had need."

She says this while almost kneeling down in front of me, clapping her hands together.

Sisi Lindiwe, she still calls me.

"It was your mother who sent for me again. She went away as soon as I came, the day after; she was waiting for me to arrive. She said that she did not think that she would be coming back."

I look at her child, my sister, half, and ask her, "What's your name?"

"Danielle," she says quietly, a name she finds hard to pronounce.

My father's name. Daniel.

"Thank you, Rosanna, for looking after Daddy so well. I am grateful. I'm only here for a short time, so we'll keep things as they are. It's quite fine by me."

*　　*　　*

Rosanna wheels Daddy out into the garden under the gum tree. She sits there with him knitting and chatting about this and that. From the kitchen window, I watch her put a blanket under his knees and carefully wipe the drool from his lips. I watch her bend her head towards him to catch whatever words he is struggling with, and I watch her throw her head back in a hearty laugh.

When I look at her, my half sister, Danielle, I have the feeling of falling through a gap in time and finding myself seven, eight again. We are Daddy's girls. She follows me everywhere. I ask Rosanna if it will be all right to tell her that I'm her sister. Rosanna claps her hands and jumps.

"That is a blessing," she says.

"I'm your big sister," I tell Danielle. "We have different mothers but the same father."

She stands there clasping her hands behind her back.

"I am happy," she says and I lean over and give her a hug. I look up and see David watching from the doorway.

Rosanna says that Maphosa has been back for a week or so now. He turned up, she says, wearing that uniform. Maphosa is now a Forward Security guard, and every morning he sets off at five to go off to the patch of field next to Queens Sports Ground to do his drills and then he walks to Cement Side, where he stands guard over the grocery and butcher shop there. Forward Security Company is run as a cooperative by former Freedom Fighters. His wife tends the garden. I don't talk to him during the three days I'm back. The only time I catch a glimpse of him is when one morning I push back the bedroom curtain and see him walking towards the gate in his khaki uniform. His figure looks so forlorn in the mist, as though it might be a displaced spirit, something like that.

Rosanna and I watch the president's speech on TV. He says that whites in Zimbabwe have never reconciled themselves to the black majority. They are responsible for the country's current economic hardships. They control the banks and industry. The land itself. Even food. He says that government forces have exposed rampant racket profiteering by milling companies, which are owned by whites; they are holding back grain to create artificial shortages, selling it off in the black market for exorbitant prices.

Rosanna gets up and says, "This old man is getting more dangerous by the day. He is giving me a headache. Good night, Sisi."

I switch off the TV and sit for a while in the dark.

Tomorrow we'll be going back. David and me.

I phone Botswana. The phone rings on and on until finally someone picks it up.

"Hello," I say. "Hello."

And I know it's Mummy on the other end.

"Hello, Ma, Mummy."

And then I hear *click* and the line is dead.

I take Daddy's hand, hold it in mine. I don't know if he likes it, wants it there. We are sitting on the veranda. Just the two of us.

I hold him, us in another life. There he is sitting on that uncomfortable wire chair, tinkering with something, a broken radio, a TV part, and there I am, on a cushion on the floor, leaning against a pillar reading. *Sue Barton. Nancy Drew. Heidi. Anne of Green Gables.* Now and then the slap of paper as he spreads out and folds his technical diagrams, his eyes poring over the minute details until they grow tired, and he pushes his glasses onto his forehead and rubs the bridge of his nose.

"This one is a challenge," he might say to me. "Come and take a look, see how the See-I-Saws in Magwegwe made a complete mess; I shouldn't even be wasting my time . . ." But then he puts his glasses back down and goes on a marathon session until the item is in good working order.

"Do you want some tea, Daddy?" I might ask him, my eyes swirling with words, images.

And there is Mummy muttering, "What is the point of all this work when your father undercharges all of the time?"

I want to say that I love him, but ever since he has had the stroke, I haven't been able to talk to him, to sit down with him and just say things. It's as if I'm guilty of something, as if I haven't been a good daughter, as if I don't think he has a life anymore.

I tell Rosanna I will be back for Christmas. I give her my phone number in case of any emergency and also that of Aunty Gertrude in Botswana. I ask about money, and she says that every month she takes Daddy to the pension's office for his envelope and that they take his thumbprint.

"Plus, we have the vegetables we are selling," she says. "It is a good thing we have a borehole. Do not worry, Sisi."

I bend down and kiss Danielle and taste the salt of her tears. I give her the wool doll I bought at Jairos Jiri Crafts Centre.

"I thank you, my sister," she says softly.

David stands stiffly at my side. He doesn't say a word.

14.

The bus moves swiftly on the deserted road. I look outside and the landscape is bleak. Stunted maize in fields, the earth parched. Just before we reach Kadoma, a surreal sight, wheelchairs right in the middle of the road so that the bus swerves a bit and stops. I twist my neck back and see men and women in wheelchairs zigzagging along the road, the rims of their wheels catching the light. I wonder if it's some kind of protest since the government has cut welfare payments to the disabled. Then I see their tin cups and plates. The driver gets out frothing and fuming, threatening to beat up one of the guys who is pushing a wheelchair. The sound of plates and tins banging on the metal of the wheelchairs fills up the air. I see thin lame legs coated with dust. The driver gets back in, flings some coins outside, and then we're off again.

I look up and read KADOMA RANCH HOTEL and something in me shifts. I take David's hand and we go into the motel, past the curio shop out to the poolside where we queue up to get our snack. Across the pool I look out and see a table, the table where the three of us must have sat at only six months ago. Does David feel the ghost of his presence?

My son eats his chips, his chicken sandwich, drinks his

Coke. I watch him do these things. It gives me pleasure to see how quickly he eats, how much his body has begun to fill in.

I can't put anything in my mouth.

We go into the curio shop. In a basket by the till, my eyes fall on the jumble of wooden animals Ian must have stopped at, and an ache spreads inside me as I see his large hand delving in there, choosing, wanting something special for his newly discovered son. I tell David he can choose something. He looks around. He stops for a while at the assortment of bottle-top toys. But no, there is nothing he wants, likes.

Home.

I stand inside the doorway and I am suddenly overwhelmed by fear. I'm alone. The thought resonates in the quiet room, and I almost jump when the phone rings.

It's Bridgette. How grateful I am to hear her voice.

"So how did it go?"

"It was fine. We just got in. Everybody's okay."

"And David, is he . . . ?"

"He's here."

"So I'll get a chance to play Aunty after all."

"Thanks, Bridgette."

"When do you have to go to the bush?"

"In about three weeks. I'll have to stay for about two, three days."

"I'm ready and willing."

* * *

I stand over David's bed watching him sleep. He is so still. So perfect. So unharmed. Despite me. I look for the giraffe. I cannot find him and somehow this makes me sad.

What is the measure of a life?

A small cardboard box with a wire elephant stuck on the lid, something he might have picked up in a curio shop.

It's what Ian left behind in my underwear drawer.

In the box, pictures.

One by one I pick them up.

There he is.

The newborn swaddled in his mother's arms.

The young infant sitting on a plaid blanket, chewing on a rattle. Black hands holding him at the waist.

The young Boy Scout scrambling up some rocks.

The schoolboy standing in front of Haddon and Sly, chewing on a licorice stick.

And there he is, the teenage Ian standing with a woman who can only be his mother, Sarah Price. She is wearing one of those cotton Indian dresses and sandals, two loose braids falling over her shoulder, some flowers tucked in them. And I'm startled by her eyes. Ian's eyes staring right through the picture to me, holding my gaze, challenging.

And I can see why she would leave a place like Bulawayo, Baysview, why they might be too small for her, why she might run away with a salesman to Jo'burg.

I pick up the last picture.

That morning in Nyanga; I'm standing in my pyjamas.

I look at it for the longest time. I turn it round and there he's written, "a chick I know," and that makes me smile.

I put the pictures back inside. I close the box. I trace my

finger over the wire elephant and think of him, somewhere out there, courting danger.

"Howzit," he says.

And I start to cry.

"Lindiwe, Lindiwe, hey, what's happening, why ... ?"

"No, I'm ... I'm okay. It's just ... I ... I'm being silly ... it's hearing your voice ... I ... it's just a shock, a ... a good shock ... I wasn't expecting you to ..."

"Things have been hectic here."

"Ian, I'm ... I'm looking at the pictures. Thanks for leaving them here."

"You're always going on about pictures, so I thought I may as well. Not the kind you were expecting, huh? Anyways, I thought I'd give you a bit of history, where I'm coming from."

"Ian, I ..."

"Listen Lindiwe, I was a right asshole. I'm sorry."

"I'm sorry too, Ian."

"I saw a guy getting hacked to death today. Yesterday it was some kid getting necklaced."

"Ian, I ..."

"The thing is, I actually *enjoy* doing this shit. It gives me a hang of a buzz, sick, huh?"

"Why don't you come home? For a couple of days. David misses you. I ... I miss you."

"How's he?"

"He's fine. He's sleeping. We just got back. Like I said he ..."

"Lindiwe, I have to go now, cheers."

And before I can say anything, the line goes dead.

15.

The cheetah's perched on a rock, looking down at us. I can't help thinking that she could easily jump over the fence, one, two graceful leaps, and she would be over at us, having the time of her life. What stops her? The fence must be electrified, but still, it doesn't seem too high; nothing that her formidable limbs couldn't scale. Maybe they're so well fed they couldn't be bothered.

We're at the Lion and Cheetah Park just outside Harare. Bridgette and David are engaged in some conversation over at the other end, where Tommy the three-hundred-year-old gigantic tortoise is. I suppose she's telling him some fantastic, made-up folk-tale. It was Bridgette's idea that we have a day out. We came in her brand-new silver BMW.

"So business is good," I said. "Nice car."

"Yes, business is very good. African women and their hair is a fail-proof enterprise.

I didn't tell her about what Sylvia, a fellow student, told me when she saw me with Bridgette in town some days ago.

"Isn't that girl Governor You Know Who's girlfriend; the one he's set up in one of those luxury flats in Fife Avenue? Everyone says that she's put a big spell on him, and he doesn't even mind that she's Ndebele."

Bridgette's flat *is* in Fife Avenue.

On one of the side balconies, there is a sweeping view of central Harare. Inside, it's all Shona sculptures, wide cream leather sofas, and gleaming metallic surfaces. There is even a waterfall on one of the verandas. It doesn't feel as though someone lives in there that much, and when I opened the monstrosity of a fridge during my first visit, there was only a huge strawberry-and-chocolate cake and a bottle of champagne.

She showed me where David will sleep. The room is bigger than the two bedrooms in the cottage put together. It has a floor-to-ceiling window with a small balcony. She must have seen me looking at that, for she said, "I'll secure it. Lins, there's an enclosed playground downstairs and a swimming pool." She didn't mention the gym and the tennis courts and the sushi bar.

For the first time I took in how sophisticated she was, with her long extensions parted in the middle and pinned loosely on her head with tortoiseshell clips, her high polished heels and tight jeans. She looked like a model. In fact, Precious, one of Bridgette's friends who was the fashion editor at *Mahogany,* was always trying to convince her to do a spread for the magazine. She was beautiful in the way models are beautiful in magazines, glossy and flawless. They wouldn't have to do any retouching. I noticed too that men positively drooled at her, but there was something about her that kept them back. She was too high-class, too fine, too expensive—no, it was more that that, she was too much herself, Bridgette, to put up with any riffraff. And maybe they knew she was combustible matter.

Is she really the governor's mistress? He's notorious for his brutality; there are rumors of suspected rivals being thrown out of windows. Surely it isn't just the material rewards that attract her if all that's true; maybe she's doing it just for the hell of it, Bridgette style. If David is going to stay with her for a couple of days, I have to make sure that her personal life won't put him in some kind of danger. What if the governor comes in one night drunk, wanting to be serviced? . . . Jesus, maybe he shouldn't stay with her, but where else will he go? I could take him with me. That will mean more days missed from school, and what is he going to be doing deep in the rural areas while I interview cooperative workers? He'll be stared at, maybe even laughed at, this boy with his complexion, his blue eyes, his red hair. No, no, it's best he stays. It will only be for two days.

"Lins! There you are. We've been looking for you. Look, look, up there, those monkeys, they're stealing bananas right from people's hands."

Bridgette's pointing excitedly behind me, and I catch the last monkey leaping up the roof of the canteen, joining his mates, munching away, looking for all the world as though they're the ones watching the animals in the zoo.

David is watching wide-eyed, his hand in Bridgette's.

"Aunty Bridgette, a monkey stole Mummy's scones."

Bridgette lets out a squeal. "Scones, David, that's funny. But why not? They're our cousins, after all. Did he also get hold of some Five Rose tea?"

David looks away from Bridgette to me and says, "But . . . but monkeys aren't humans. They don't talk, only in cartoons."

Months ago Ian and I took David and two of his classmates to watch *The Lion King*. In the car Ian entertained us with his rendition of the theme song and lots of "Hakuna Matatas" were flying about. I got into a ridiculous argument with Ian while the boys were playing table football in the ice cream parlor.

"Typical," I said.

"What?" said Ian who was itching to join the boys. At school he was the table football champion, and he received "mahobo hidings" for sneaking out and playing and honing his skills at the back of Baysview bottle store with garden boys and tsotsis.

From the way he talked about it, it sounded as though he were a legend in his own lifetime.

"Of course, it had to be the baboon with the African accent."

"What?"

He was half-sitting, standing.

"Sit down, Ian. The baboon with the thick African accent. Rural, primitive, undeveloped, lower down the evolutionary pole, bush."

"Lindiwe, you're not serious." He was standing now, his hands deep in his pockets, looking down at me.

"Ian, sit." It felt like I was ordering a dog about.

"So now a cartoon is racialistic," he said, pushing his bottom on the very narrow chair.

"It's not just cartoons, Ian. Fairy tales, folktales, movies, how come anything to do with evil is always black? How come the lion king, boy, whatever, had the with-it American accent while . . ."

"Lindiwe, it's an *American* movie, and the lion king was the main character. Simba, Mufasa, check, African names, and I really dug that hornbill, what's his name, Zaza . . . I don't even believe I am having this conversation about a cartoon."

"Exactly the point I'm trying to make, Ian. African names, fine, for African animals, and so why not African accents? It's happening in Africa, but no, they can't have the lion king, the top dog, be African. And don't say, 'it's just a cartoon'; it's about messages, a philosophy, it's the image . . ."

"Lindiwe, how about we joll it the other way? The baboon, and I'm not even sure it's a baboon, minds. Anyways, the baboon is the wise elder, Mother, okay, Father Africa, cradle of civilization, positive. And man, he was a fricking majestic baboon."

"Ian, please, you Rhodies have been calling blacks, that's us, majestic Africans; you've been calling us monkeys, baboons, and don't start changing history and saying that it was all a misunderstanding and it was said in praise and adulation as in 'as wise and clever and enterprising as monkeys,' huh?"

"History, Lindiwe, history. The Past. Feenished. But one thing I agree is that they should have left the entire singing to Africans, Ladysmith Black Mambazo. It sounded like them, they were sweet over all that wilderness, really gave you the heart of Africa. Man, that chorus at the beginning gave me chills down my spine, and then we have that chick and then Elton John. Please, man, not in Africa, at least get Johnny Clegg, the White Zulu, to belt out that shit African style. Come on, Lindiwe, please chill. Too much education, that's your problem. It's just a cartoon, entertainment, no great shakes. Hakuna matata."

"For you."

"Not that again; it's like a stuck record with you."

He made to get up and then changed his mind.

"Okay, how about Scar, the baddie? Definite hoity-toity British accent there, and the hyenas, I checked a British one . . . On the other hand, I think you might have a point there . . . hyenas, British . . . yes, man . . . come on, Lindiwe, crack a smile . . . please."

"Lins!"

I look up at Bridgette.

"Where were you at girl?"

On the drive back we stop at Nando's and have quarter chickens. Then we move to the ice cream parlor next door and Bridgette treats us. I see Heather in the queue wearing her dark glasses.

And here is Duncan.

Great.

"Howzit," he says.

"Hi," I say.

"So heard anything from Ian?"

"Yes, he phoned. He's fine. Very busy."

He grunts.

"Well, don't you get up to any hanky-panky," he says and gives me a grotesque wink and a wag of the finger.

I watch him muscle his way in the queue, snatch the slip of paper from Heather, shove it into the hand of the ice cream parlor attendant.

I watch Heather edge herself out from the crowd. She stands by the stools looking at herself on the mirrored walls. Then she turns around, sees me, or maybe she doesn't. She walks straight out of the room and waits outside.

And here is her husband, victorious, two cones in hand.

"Heather, where the fuck . . . ?"

And he, too, is out the door.

I wonder if Heather ever wishes that one day the parachute doesn't open, that one day his great, bully body falls in one heavy mass, obliterates itself on impact.

"You like Aunty Bridgette, don't you, David?

David nods.

"Well, how would you like to stay with her while I do some work out of Harare?"

His breathing changes, his body tenses up.

"It will only be for two days."

He stands there, already defeated.

"Yes," he says at last.

I pick up the other thing Ian's left behind for me, the tattered schoolboy's exercise book that could have notes on a subject such as history, geography, or English or its pages could be filled with bored scribbles and doodles, sketches and comic strips, anything to pass the time while a teacher drones on and on.

But there is no innocence on these pages. I know this.

I open it and begin to touch the fragments of his life; so many years past when he was a boy alone with a stepmother while his father went off for months at a time to fight in the war.

I close the book and sit on my bed, the book on my lap, the pictures moving furiously in my head.

16.

In the bus going to Rusape, my head throbs with the single thought, I should have taken David with me.

I see him standing there in his pyjamas, the giraffe in his hand again. He looked like he wanted to cry. And I put on a show. All hustle and bustle and distraction (just like Ian). And then I dropped him at Bridgette's and ran away. I didn't even kiss him good-bye. I could hop out of the bus, hitchhike back. I could . . . but I don't. I carry on sitting there, here, letting the bus take me further and further away. It's only for two days. He'll be all right. I'll ring as soon as I can get hold of a phone.

"Bonjour, mademoiselle," Herbert says, taking my bag.

It's good to see him.

The cooperatives I'm going to be interviewing are dotted around the Makoni area, and Herbert, who has been working with them for the rural market project, introduced me to them. "Your questions might motivate them," he said. "Improve their output and enthusiasm for us."

"Do you know," he said, the last time I saw him at the Alliance Française with Jean Pierre, "the whole infrastructure at the Nyamidzi market was stolen over one night, door frames, window frames, roofs, bricks. I'm sure it's Mrs. Masasa who has been very successful in her campaign to stop us."

Mrs. Masasa was a legend in the area. A ZANU-PF stalwart, who had threatened to beat up all those little boys from Europe, who had come to disrupt her profitable rural shops where the markup for anything was at least 200 percent. She had long ago driven out the Indians.

"That shopkeeping lady is tough. But one must remain optimistic. The whole thing is ridiculous, of course; everyone has been quite happy to sell their one, two, five tomatoes in the open, on the ground, along the road, until the experts come along. But this is the nature of the aid business in Africa. At least we give a little employment."

It was the only time I had ever seen Herbert downbeat.

I get into the Land Rover, which looks like it has been involved in yet another accident.

Herbert catches me looking at the smashed-in rear door.

"Nothing, nothing. A little fall into the Mucheke riverbed. Nothing to worry about, my dear; I have improved very much recently."

"I certainly hope so."

"First we get a little to eat and then we are off. We pick up Wilfred at one o'clock."

We drive out to The Crocodile Motel. I order a cheese sandwich, Herbert a steak with chips. The water of the pool is yellowish green.

"Not very inviting," says Herbert. "Chlorine *is* very expensive these days."

I'm thinking of Ian and me sitting here; it seems such a long time ago.

"How is Marie?"

"Good, good. She is painting again. You will see her this evening. She is preparing a grand dinner in your honor."

I wait for Herbert to say something about Jean, but it's me who finally says, "Have you heard from Jean Pierre recently?"

He thinks something over and then he says, "He has told me a little of what happened. You are happy, yes?"

I don't know how to answer that.

As we get up to leave, he adds, "Don't worry about him, you understand?"

"Good afternoon, madam!" Wilfred greets me cheerfully. He's the office messenger at Herbert's NGO and he is going to act as my translator.

He is old enough to be my father, perhaps even my grandfather, and even though I have repeatedly told him to call me Lindiwe, somehow being with the expats makes me an irrevocable "madam."

"Good afternoon, Wilfred."

Wilfred insists on sitting at the back. I give him the pack with all the questionnaires to lean against.

"Ready?" says Herbert.

"Ready," I say. "Please don't fall into any riverbeds."

Herbert laughs and puts on his Humphrey Bogart hat, and then we're off.

The members of the Poultry Cooperative are waiting for us at the school. I greet Mrs. Chiwana and the others. I thank them all for participating in the project. I hand out the questionnaires, which have been translated into Shona. Then one by one, Wilfred gives them a quick interview, which I record on a tape recorder. Afterwards Mrs. Chiwana thanks me for my interest in their small cooperative. She also thanks the most wonderful French people who are helping them with funds. Herbert says that the French people are very happy to be part of development in the region. Everyone claps and is happy.

Things also go smoothly at the Uniform Sewing Cooperative.

At the Bakery Cooperative there is pandemonium. Mr. Maxwell, the husband of the energetic chairwoman, has absconded with the bakery's savings, the money that they were collecting for a new oven. Mrs. Maxwell is sitting on the floor, smacking her head with her hands. Some of the other members are commiserating with her. I stand at the door. Herbert steps inside.

"Oh, Mr. Herbert, it is a disaster, a disaster."

Mrs. Maxwell looks up, struggles to her feet.

"He has betrayed us," she wails. "All the hard work. Everything, it is over."

Herbert pats her on the shoulder. "These things, they can happen. You must not panic. How much money is left in the savings?"

"He took all of it," cries Mrs. Maxwell. "All of it. I was going to take the money to Rusape tomorrow, oh, oh."

One of the younger members of the group, who is standing by the old oven, mutters something, and Mrs. Maxwell looks sharply at her; she starts banging her hands on her head again.

"Oh, oh," she cries. "Now I am being accused to be an accomplice, oh, oh."

"Shush, shush," remonstrates a woman next to her. "It is not so. We know you are a good woman; it is only the men who create problems."

I don't give out the questionnaires. We don't do any interviews. We'll come back another day (if the cooperative is still in existence).

In the car Herbert scratches his head.

"They are finished now. They cannot compete with Lobel's. Their prices are too high. The locals complain that their bread does not look nice and straight. Imagine, my dear, in Europe people are willing to spend much more for homemade bread? Life."

"I wonder if they'll report him to the police."

"I hope not. It will completely destroy poor Mrs. Maxwell, and she has six children to support. I must try and find some way to help, look for another donor, maybe the Swedes; I'll talk to Stefan this evening."

We end at the Soap-Producing Cooperative. All goes well, and we leave with a bar of soap each.

"If they could only get funds for packaging; they could sell this in France. Organique, c'est en vogue, très chic. I have to bring Marie here. She could help."

I can't imagine his Parisian wife and the cooperative ladies getting on, but stranger things have happened.

"I'll try and arrange a meeting with a pottery-making cooperative tomorrow and you also have the other two to interview."

"Thanks, Herbert. You are so Bogart, the way you rescue damsels in distress."

And with that endorsement he takes the Galois from behind his ear and lights up.

I give Wilfred an envelope.

"A small something for all your help today, Wilfred. I'll see you tomorrow."

"Thank you, madam, thank you, madam, you are too kind. Christmas is come too early now," he says, clapping his hands.

Herbert drops Wilfred off at his house, Number 203 Vengere township, and soon children are swarming the car calling out, "Murungu, Murungu." Herbert cheerfully waves before covering them in a swirl of dust as the Land Rover takes off across the Mutare Road into the suburbs.

"Ah, Lindiwe, darling."

"Marie."

She gives me three air kisses. She smells of red wine.

"Come, come," she says. "I'm finished in the kitchen. Herbert can take over."

"Mmmmm, it smells delicious."

She shows me to the spare room.

"I will leave you to get ready. It is such a pleasure to see you again."

Tired, I sit on the bed for a bit. I should have asked her if I could phone Harare. I'll do it later. I'm tempted to fling my body on the bed, but I know that if I do that, I'll go straight to sleep.

There is Stefan and Astrid, a Swedish couple who work for the Swedish International Development Agency (SIDA—an acronym that Herbert has told me is well deserved because the Swedes are a hard-partying lot and are well-known and appreciated regulars at "TK," Terreskane Hotel, in Harare, otherwise popularly known as Brothel Central); Benjamin Murape, a lawyer who has represented trade union officials. Marie told me, in the kitchen, that he has been detained by the CIO several times and has spent some nights in Chikurubi. There is also a British journalist, Paul Redmond, who is making a documentary about his travels in sub-Saharan Africa and is sporting a FREE(D) MANDELA T-shirt.

"People are tired," says Benjamin, as I'm walking in. "This Economic Structural Adjustment Package of the World Bank is really an unmitigated disaster."

"Ah, ESAP," says Herbert, "Extra Suffering for African Peoples."

Benjamin doesn't acknowledge the joke that's been doing the rounds; Zimbabweans seem to have this limitless capacity to theatrically personalize World Bank acronyms.

"The ZCTU wants to organize a mass stay away," Benjamin marches on. "The government suspects something, that's why the nefarious charges."

"Mugabe won't let them organize," says Herbert.

"Look, we Zimbabweans are famed for our goodwill, but I tell you, cometh the hour, cometh the man. Even Smith didn't think his hour was coming . . ."

Varsity days. Student Union meetings. Demos. Manifestos.

The same recalcitrant tone, a mix of Marxist bombastic overload, and a real passion and recklessness for justice. I'm pretty sure Benjamin was a student leader perhaps a couple years before I got in.

I want to ask Marie about the steel sculptures she has dotted around the garden, where she gets them from. I also like the steel candleholders she has speared into the lawn.

It's such a beautiful night. There is the heady scent of lilies and irises drifting in through the screened windows. I wish I could slip away, do something silly, like walking barefoot on the lawn.

". . . which reminds me of this interesting chap I met last month in Johannesburg," Paul's voice filters through. ". . . free-lancer, a photojournalist."

I drag myself back to the conversation. I look at Benjamin, who is staring morosely at his drink. Stefan and Astrid are slouched on the couch, a haze of smoke around them. Herbert is looking at Marie, who is looking decidedly bored. This is not the kind of soiree she had hoped for. I should step in. Bring up a book I've read. This is my role here. An infusion of culture.

". . . taken some amazing pictures of the troubles in the townships. But also some superb portraits of the residents there. They were showing in a gallery in Johannesburg. He's a white Zimbabwean of all things. What do you call them here, Rhodies?"

Benjamin snorts.

I am very quiet, very still.

The night contracts until all I hear is this one voice.

"That's what he calls himself. A white Zimbabwean. He took me down to Soweto to show me the sights, and on our way back he goes into lecture mode. About the Historical Perspective."

"From *a white Zimbabwean*," says Benjamin, "that must be very interesting."

"According to his take, and remember this is him, not me. According to him, the problem is that people get hung up about what's happening now, as though it were the first time ever in history that something like this has ever taken place."

"Like what?" demands Benjamin.

Paul, who has had a few drinks, doesn't seem to notice Benjamin's tone. He should stop now.

"Sorry mate, you know, colonization. According to him the only difference now is that it was a tribe of people who happened to be white who went and subjugated; although if I remember, he used more colorful language: a tribe of people who just happened to be black. This thing's been going on since time immemorial. His thesis is that if people bear that in mind they wouldn't get so jittery about moving on, forgiving and forgetting. You see . . ."

"What utter rubbish," jumps in Benjamin, spilling part of his drink on his white shirt.

"And this so-called history is supposed to justify oppression."

"I don't think he meant that," I hear myself saying.

"What?" he swivels his head in my direction, spilling more drink on the carpet.

"I don't think he meant to justify anything," I plod on, even though I should know better.

"So now you are with the oppressors."

"Oh please. I think he meant that in the end these kinds of crimes have always been committed and that they are not the preserve of any one particular group of people, in this case, white people; that conquest and humiliation of another group of people is the nature of humanity; no one's hands are clean, and if we recognize this we can, I don't know, lower our expectations of each other and be more realistic."

Benjamin looks as though someone has forced him to swallow a rat. No, two. "What did you say your surname was?"

Marie steps in. "Dinner's ready," she says.

Benjamin puts his drink down on the table and gets up. "Excuse me," he says, "I have to prepare the defense for our *historically oppressed* union members, good evening." And with that, he leaves.

Over dinner we talk about small things and I laugh too hard.

It's too late to make a phone call. I'll do it tomorrow.

My head feels as though someone has been pounding away at it throughout the night, probably Benjamin. I look at my watch and it's already ten minutes to nine. Paul has offered me a lift to Harare, and I can hear his voice and Marie's just outside my door. I don't have time to phone Bridgette. I'll give David a surprise. I've cut my visit short; in a couple of hours, I'll see him, tell him how much I missed him.

As we're passing The Crocodile, Paul says, "I hope I didn't make a complete ass of myself last night."

"No, you didn't."

"I should steer clear of the hard stuff. That Benjamin chap was pretty wound up."

"Yes, he was."

"I'm not supposed to alienate the nativ— sorry."

"You know that guy you were talking about yesterday, the Zimbabwean . . . ?"

"Yes, I wish I had never brought him up. He was quite a bloke, though."

"I know him."

"Really? How?"

"He's my—" (What are you, Ian?) "—we have a son."

The car almost lands on a tree by the roadside.

"Careful."

"You're serious?"

"Yes."

"I could kick myself. Why didn't you say anything?"

"I . . . I . . . don't know. A mixture of things. As he says, it's the history of things. I guess I felt intimidated and embarrassed."

"You mean if Benjamin wasn't there you might have said . . . ?"

"Maybe."

"Tell you something, I've spoken to a few white Zimbabweans, and he came across as different. You know what I mean?"

"I think so."

"He's not so damned sure of himself. I think that's it. I gave that Benjamin chap the wrong idea about him. Down there in Soweto, he has quite a following. And he's a straight shooter, once he gets round to talking, that is."

And that makes me smile.

"And then when he gets into that Rhodesian dialect . . ."

"Rhodesian dialect," I say. "I like that. That's good."

*   *   *

I start pulling faces at the mirror in the sleek, futuristic-looking lift, and then I start worrying about hidden cameras and one-way mirrors.

I should have brought him something. Damn. A ball. A proper football. We'll go into town; have a treat. Yes. Him and me.

I press the doorbell. I hear it ringing. I wait to hear the sound of footsteps. Someone calling out, "I'm coming!" Nothing. No one comes. I press the bell again. And again. They might be out by the pool.

I'm about to leave when the door is flung open. And Eunice, the maid, stands there, her hands dripping water on the floor. "Oh, it is you, you are here at last. I was washing the bathroom; I did not hear the first time. The madam has been calling and calling, asking if you have come here."

"What's wrong? What's the matter? What's happened? What . . . where's David, David . . . ?"

"The child, the child is not well," the maid says. "He is in the hospital. He was very hot. The madam says you must go to Avenues."

I run all the way.

I find her in the children's ward; her head bent low, her hands clasped tight.

"Bridgette, what, David . . . ?"

"Oh Lindiwe, thank God, thank God. He's in there, intensive care. The doctor says he has acute bacterial meningitis. It was all of a sudden. He's on a drip, antibiotics . . ."

I hurry past her.

I push open the door. "I'm here. David, Mummy's here." I whisper the words over and over. "I'm here, David. Mummy's here."

The long night passes, and I stand there, watching him breathe.

The doctor says that he should make a full recovery, but that there might be long-term effects. Only time will tell. There might be hearing loss, epilepsy, or some level of brain retardation. Or he might be completely unaffected.

I take him home. I lift him out of the taxi (how light he has become again), and I take him into the cottage. I sit with him throughout the night, watching him drift in and out of sleep, the antibiotics leaving him washed out.

Bridgette comes the next day. She wants to talk about what happened, how he suddenly got sick, but I don't want to hear it.

"Bridgette, it's no one's fault."

The words come out forcefully, strong and bitter, full of accusation.

The doctor said he was in a very bad way when he got in, he should have been taken to the hospital much sooner.

My heart is beating so loud, but it doesn't drown out that little voice, *you knew he didn't look too well, you knew that, and you still left him behind.*

Bridgette stays for a while looking at David, stroking his head, and then she gets up.

"I'll call you, Lins."

I don't say anything back.

I sit in the lounge counting the breaths from him. Until night comes. My beautiful, beautiful baby.

PART THREE

Mid-1990s

1.

"That's one hang of a behind," he says, and even though I'm cross with him, I can't help smiling.

It *is* one hang of a behind. And boy does it belong to our new First Lady, First Shopper, the indomitable Grace Mugabe, swathed in designer chiffons and silk, the white queen, the Air Zimbabwe fleet ever happy to whisk and carry her off for fittings and excursions for this, the most important of all days. But why, oh why, does she appear so glum? Is it the hordes of villagers who are kicking up dust with all their dancing, spoiling the dress, the hair, the handbag? A castle would have been a more fitting setting surely, the one allegedly acquired in Scotland perhaps?

There it is, courtesy of ZBC (the Station of the Nation), the Wedding of the Century, the Mother of all Weddings. There it is as foretold by the government spokesman: "it will be a quiet, classy and royal-like affair." *Indeed!*

There goes the open-top Rolls-Royce and horse-drawn carriage, too.

There go the delectable First Children. We knew you not. But now, there, there you are.

There goes Mandela looking bemused in his trademark paisley-print outfit. Twenty years of incarceration and look, look where I find myself, his look seems to say, what I've been missing all those years cooped up in Robben Island.

There goes the best man, Joachim Chissano.

There go the minions.

There go the forty thousand well-wishers

And with them the thirty-eight slaughtered cattle, the God knows how many pigs, goats, sheep, chicken . . . the truckloads of maize (oh, in this season of drought, the many who've come to get their one proper meal of the year, and of course, to wish the First Couple many, many happy returns).

And there, there goes our beloved president and intrepid First Traveler (the African Vasco da Gama off to discover lost worlds, as the Student Union secretary-general so gloriously termed him and his quest) all decked out in the finest of livery, looking as gleeful as a schoolboy. And why not? Why not, indeed? A life of service to others must surely, surely one day be rewarded. Justly so.

Oh, how romantic! Look, look, look at them, how they snuggle up close to cut that multitiered wedding cake. Isn't that so cute, so endearing? If only Grace could squeeze out a smile. But oh, how the open-mouthed drooling must annoy her so, how hot it must be in the tent underneath all that Parisian couture, how cool Harrods is, if only, if only . . .

There, there it all goes. Two million pounds of his money. *No, really. His.* Okay then.

The gift of a grateful nation to him. Because he's worth it.

"Switch it off, Ian. I can't watch anymore."

"You see how pissed off she looks. I reckon she had second thoughts, but 'sorry, honey, no second thoughts with Bob.'"

Technically, I'm not speaking to him. Not since yesterday.

"But they're, you're so beautiful, Lindiwe. Can't you see it?"

"You promised, Ian. You said they were just for you."

This last bit makes me hot.

"Lindiwe, sorry, I couldn't resist. And you should see the reaction to them."

"Ian, I'm naked!"

"Come on, Lindiwe, relax, there's nothing on show. It's not Scope. It's your back, maybe a bit of breast in profile . . ."

"Ian!"

"It's Art."

"You broke your promise. That was the only reason I let you take them."

"And there's me thinking you would love them up there."

"What! Are you crazy? You could at least have warned me, not drag me into a warehouse for me to find everyone gawking. Ian, it's not funny. I'm really upset."

"Yah, I see. Well, some American wants to cart the whole set off for his private collection."

"No."

"Yes. Fifty thousand, and I'm talking U.S. dollars, not our bog roll."

"N. O."

"Yes. He told me hims—"

"No, Ian. I mean, you can't sell them. No."

"But Lindiwe that's what an exhibition is all about, to drum up interest, to . . ."

"Jerk off."

"Language, my girl."

"Ian, I'm naked."

"Lindiwe, don't be such a wuss. You're part of the animal kingdom, nature . . ."

"Thanks."

"Now, don't get all worked up, what I mean is—"

"So I can take naked pictures of you and plaster them all over . . ."

"Be my guest."

"Oh, get lost, Ian."

"Language, language. Anyway, we can celebrate, Bob Style."

"Mum! Dad!"

"Yes?"

"You're supposed to be sleeping, David."

"Are you fighting?"

"No."

"Just play fighting, my boy."

"Go back to sleep."

"Okay. But can you play fight quietly? I can't concentrate on sleeping."

"Okay."

"Good night."

"Good night."

Those first few days when Ian came back, we were, are still, so gentle with each other. Almost losing David jolted a fission of sense into us, made us both grow up, both step back from ourselves and see the other "warts and all" as Ian says, and accept, be kind, generous. We don't say these things. But I feel them, know them to be true. I see them every time he looks at David, every time his eyes find mine. And there is the hard evidence. The drinking has stopped. The camera has been picked up again, used.

After sending out his portfolio, he's been called in for assignments with the local *Independent* including a photo spread on nightlife in Harare's streets, which inadvertently caught a senior government official accepting favors from a lady of the night in the arcade of Karigamombe Centre. And the lady of the night turned out to be a transvestite.

He has recently signed up with Sygma, the biggest and most prestigious photo news agency in the world, based in, of all places, Paris. Herbert introduced me to a friend of his who was visiting Zimbabwe and who just happened to know someone who worked for Sygma. Ian swallowed his pride and showed Herbert's friend his pictures; impressed, the friend took them with him to Paris, and days later, Ian received a phone call.

He's a great find for the international press as the government is making it very difficult for foreign journalists to get accredited, accusing them of being spies and rabid colonialists. Mugabe's recent rants against gays (accompanied by the destruction of the GALZ stand at the book fair by ZANU-PF youth militia captured by Ian) and his "love story" with its excesses has piqued interest in Zimbabwe. We have always been considered the success story of Africa, a stable, economically sound democracy ruled by an intelligent Western-educated, soft-spoken liberator, until now.

The growing unrest brought on by ESAP, the liberalized economy demanded by the World Bank in exchange for loans, has left large numbers of Zimbabweans unemployed, unable to afford basic commodities like bread whose prices used to be state controlled. Government subsidies have been taken away from health and education, leaving everything to market forces. Children are being withdrawn from schools, and people are left to die in their homes because they can't afford the new clinic prices. Strikes have been organized by the trade union, and there has been some small-scale rioting in the high-density areas, which are full of young, unemployed men. Ian says he's seen that kind of hopelessness before. South Africa. He has the pictures to prove it.

He is fearless, scaring me with his tidbits from the battleground, but I see that he is happy: he is his own man, someone he respects again, and I know that he can take care of himself.

The government doesn't seem to know what to do with this highly visible white Zimbabwean male stalking about, snapping pictures.

*　　*　　*

And there was the surprise of the studio, Ilo's gift, a few lines on a piece of paper, signed and dated, legally valid as a last will and testament. The studio where Ian developed *my* pictures, in secret.

"This is so depressing. First the presidential elections, now this."

"I'll tell you what's what: now that he's got the young chick, no way he's giving up power any time soon. You think she doesn't want to stretch out the First Lady production? Look at him, next to old Madiba there, he's fresh fresh, ready for the next round."

"Ian, I haven't forgotten or forgiven."

"Come on, Lindiwe."

"Come on, what?"

"Okay, if you really don't like them, I'll take them out."

"Really?"

"Yah, yah."

"I didn't say I didn't like them, it's just that I thought they were going to be private. It's funny to think of them in some stranger's place. I don't know, it feels kind of grubby."

"Man, you're tight. I thought you were the sophisticated fundie."

"Maybe it's a white-black thing; you don't understand."

"And now who's being a racist? And anyway, don't give me that bullshit. There's lots of bums and tits in African sculpture."

"Now who's being the fundie?"

"Fifty thousand big ones, Lindiwe. Think what we can do with that."

"We?"

"Yah, *we*."

"It's your money."

"Jeez, soz, but think what *we* can do with *my* money then."

I don't say anything.

"Come on, think!"

"I . . . I don't know, Ian."

"We can buy a house, that's what. Somewhere with a big yard for David to play in proper."

He stands there looking at me.

"We can go upscale. Highlands, Borrowdale, Chisipite. Swimming pool. Tennis courts. Thatched gazebo for entertainment purposes. Braais. The works. We can pay cash for it. No mortgage, nothing. One go, it's ours."

"It's yours, Ian. Yours."

"Why do you have to be so hard, Lindiwe? I'm doing this for us. I want to."

The words leave him breathless. Then red.

"Lindiwe, what's wrong?"

"I'm tired, that's all."

He lets me get away with that. He lets me go to bed. He leaves me alone.

I'm lying in bed when I hear loud banging on the front door. I sit up. I hear Ian calling out, "Hey, hey, who is it? What's the matter . . . ?" And then after a couple of seconds, I hear him open the door. "Jesus, Heather, what . . . ?" And then I see her. "He beat the shit out of her" is what they would say.

She stands there shaking by the door. Her face swollen, black and blue, a gash on her lip, eye; her right hand limp, hanging. Ian is looking at her, mouth open. I go to her. "Heather . . ." She backs away. "Heather, it's me, Lindiwe. I think you should sit down. Come." I don't know where to touch her.

"I . . . I . . . ran, he's going to come, I . . ."

I steer her to the couch, and as we're sitting down, what she fears happens. We can hear him. "Close the door, Ian. Ian, close the door!"

"Mum . . . ?" I look up and see David standing in the doorway.

"It's okay, David, there's been an accident. Go back to sleep." He looks at me and then at Heather. "Did a car hit her?" he asks.

"Go to bed, David. We'll talk about it tomorrow."

"Where is she? Where is she? Where's the bitch? I'll teach her a . . . !"

"David, go to bed, it's okay."

"Duncan, calm down. Calm down, man. I'm coming. Step away from the door, I'm coming out. Yes, she's here. Calm down. I'm coming out."

"Ian, no."

He opens the door.

Duncan's hand lunges inside. Ian struggles to keep him out. "Hang on, Duncan man, let's talk outside." The door closes again. I don't know if I should lock it. If I should call the police.

"He wants to kill me. He wants to kill me. He thinks I'm having an . . . oh, God . . ."

I don't know where to start, what injury to attend to. The arm is probably broken. We need to go to the hospital. I try to remember first aid, how to make a bandage, a sling.

"Heather, I'm going to look for a shirt or something. We need to support your arm."

As I get up, she cries, "Don't, please, don't leave me alone. He's going to come back; he wants to kill me. He thinks I've been sleeping around, oh God . . ."

I sit down again, try to arrange her arm on the cushion. She whimpers.

"We should disinfect those cuts, Heather." I think she's going to need stitches, on the side of the eye for one.

The door opens. Heather jumps.

"He's gone. Jesus, he's plastered," says Ian.

"We have to take her to the hospital. I think her arm's broken, and the eye looks bad."

"I'll take her. Keep the door locked. Come on, Heather," he says.

"I . . . I . . . he's going to . . ."

"He's gone, Heather."

His voice has shards of irritation, impatience flicking off it.

"Heather, you need to go to the hospital," I say.

I help her to her feet.

"Lock the door," Ian says.

I lock the door. I go into David's room and find him sitting bolt upright on his bed. "It's all right, David. It was an accident."

"It's Granny," he says.

And absurdly, I find myself looking around the room as though she might be somewhere here.

"What about Granny?"

"She . . . she said Dad did something bad."

I hold my breath.

"She said he killed his mum."

My breath comes out sharp and fast, so sharp and fast it hurts my chest.

"No, David. That's not true."

"Granny said."

"Granny didn't mean it. The woman in the house wasn't your father's real mother, and your dad didn't do anything, okay?"

"She said he burnt . . ."

"It's not true, David. It was a horrible accident."

"But Granny . . ."

"Sometimes grown-ups say things when they're upset with another person that are very hurtful and are not true."

"She said Dad was going to hell."

"Listen, David, your father would never, ever, not in a zillion, gazillion, bazillion years kill anyone, never, ever, ever."

He's trying to believe it. He wants to believe it.

"Granny doesn't like him."

"No, she doesn't. Sometimes grown-ups don't get along, just like you and other children. You don't like everybody, do you?"

"Yes. I mean no. But he likes you."

"Yes."

"And you like him."

"Yes. And we both love you very, very much. Now time for bed. School tomorrow."

"Mum, where's Dad's mum, his real mum?"

"She's . . . I . . . I don't know David. She went away when he was a baby."

"Oh."

"Good night, David."

"She didn't love Dad."

I don't know what to say to this.

"Good night, David. You'll be tired tomorrow if you don't go to sleep now."

"Good night, Mum."

I stand looking down at him until he opens his eyes and says, "You can go now, Mum. I'm okay."

Ever since Ian's been back, he's been telling me to relax about David.

"It's been yonkers now, Lindiwe; he's okay. Check how he's all over the place."

In the first weeks I kept asking Ian, "Do you notice anything different about him?" and what I meant was, "Do you think he is . . . does he act brain damaged to you?"

And Ian's reply: "Yah, he's a heck of a lot more lively. The lightie got sick, that's all. It happens, Lindiwe. Shit, I got a burst appendicitis when I was nine; I was this close to . . . the bitch just let me, wouldn't take me to the doc . . . but that's another story."

"He almost died, Ian."

And I don't say, "*I* almost let him die."

The doctor says he's fully recovered. I can relax. I *should* relax. But I still awaken sometimes at night, and I have to rush to his bed to check that he's there, breathing, whole.

It took me four days to get hold of Ian. He took the first flight out.

"How's he?" I heard behind me.

"He's sleeping," I said turning around, and something in me gave in, some pressure collapsed as he drew close to me. He cupped my face in his hands, kissed me.

And it was Ian who called Bridgette, unknown to me. He invited her over to lunch. And finally I could tell her what I had been agonizing about, ask her to forgive me for my coldness towards her, my wish to apportion blame, how Daddy was always doing just that and . . .

"Oh, shut up, Lins," she said, breaking through my words, "this is not a fricking confessional," and her eyes were moist with tears.

Ian was busy showing off his braaing techniques, using a cutout steel drum, to David who was sitting on a deck chair, laughing with his friend Titus.

I looked at Bridgette.

It had been over a month since I had last seen her.

She was wearing a pair of jeans that were bunched at the waist with a red shiny belt. The green tank top hung off her body.

"Are you on a diet?" I asked her.

"Diet?" she said. "Since when have we Africans gone on diets?"

She was drinking a Zambezi, not looking at me when she spoke. I wish I had stopped then.

"But you're not a true African. You're a British African,

haven't you been listening to Mugabe? You guys come back, your culture forgotten, importing all kinds of retrograde ideas."

Bridgette should have laughed here and come back with a good retort, but she just kept looking out to where Ian and the boys were.

"Anyway," I went on, "it's just that you're looking so slim . . . ," and that's when our eyes found each other, Bridgette just looking at me. She put her drink down.

"I'll go and see what's taking your man so long. I'm starving," she said and left me alone on the veranda.

It's about four in the morning when Ian gets back.

"Shit," he mutters, throwing the keys on the table.

I'm shocked by how tired he looks. The only thing I can think of saying is "Do you want something to eat?"

He looks at me like I'm completely nuts. "No," he says, slumping down on the couch. "He was there waiting for us at the clinic."

"No."

"Lucky he'd sobered up a bit. Scared shitless we'd called the cops."

"So?"

"So, he was all, 'Forgive me, I'm sorry, honey, it will never happen again . . . ,' what a load of bullshit."

"And . . . ?"

"I left them to it . . ."

"You *what?*"

"Lindiwe, she was practically begging me to get lost. He took her to Emergency, and last time I saw, she was getting her arm looked at. And to top it off, she's preggies."

"Oh no, you think she'll be all right?"

He shrugs.

"I'm hammered."

I go to him, put my hands on him. I kiss him. And the words come out like a choke, a sob, "I love you"; I say them into his chest, bury them there, and I don't think he hears, or if he hears, he says nothing but holds me and then there is the shock of his heaving chest. At first I think he's laughing. "What's so funny?" I'm about to ask, scold him, and then I realize he's weeping, holding me so tight as though I'm the only thing that keeps him there . . . my darling, beautiful Ian.

2.

"*Ian!*"

I follow him into the bathroom. He looks a mess. His shirt is torn at the sleeve, and there are cuts all the way down his arm.

"Shit, Lindiwe, it's bad."

He takes off his shirt, takes a look at his arm, runs cold water over it.

"What's bad? What's going on? Here, I'll get the Betadine."

I begin to smooth the Betadine on his arm with cotton wool.

"Ouch."

"Sorry."

"It's mayhem; the police are kwapuling people downtown. And I reckon I heard gunshots. There's mahobo police with AKs. Don't venture anywhere near town. Got chased down an alley when they spotted my camera. You should have seen my fall; lucky for me the goon got distracted. Hope the thing's not broken."

He turns the camera in his hand. "Looks okay, I'm going to take a look at what I've got."

He starts moving to the shower, where he has set up a temporary developing room.

"What's going on?"

"Can you believe, it's about tomatoes and bits of vegetables on tin plates? The city council police were chasing some of the vendors from their spots at the corners, busy kicking trays of tomatoes, stamping on stuff, and some of the vendors got riled up—shit, that's people's livelihood right there, and everyone knows that those municipal guys are freeloaders. Anyway, they started beating up one of the guys, then some aleck called in the cops who've barged in there like it's Gaza."

"I'm going to get David."

"No, leave him, he's all right. It's town. I tell you what, Lindiwe, this country slowly but surely is going to explode. Mark my words. South Africa's on the way up, and we're on the way down. Bread's become a luxury, and what do they go and do? Blow a stack of Forex on luxury Mercs for ministers; Bob's so out of touch with his trips and what with that chick of his, he knows shit all. I mean, I hate to say this, but no one starved under Smith, and just the other day, I heard someone cracking a joke, a black chap, that they were going to organize a petition for the return of Rhodesia in double-quick time."

On the news the reader talks about minor disturbances, but on the BBC, there are reports of at least ten dead and the wounded being dragged out from their beds at Parirenyatwa Hospital and the Avenues Clinic, bundled into unmarked vehicles. Ian's contacts tell him of an anti-police demonstration being organized for tomorrow.

I drive David to school. Everything is quiet in Mount Pleasant. I drive along the university road. Nothing. But as I'm turning left, I see in the mirror a truckload of soldiers turning towards the university's main entrance. They probably want to seal it off. At home I keep the radio and TV on while I work on the text of the pamphlets for SAFE, an organization that advocates for children's rights and is currently campaigning for the banning of corporal punishment in schools. The work is funded by SIDA and the cosignatory of my contract is none other than Stefan Larsson, whom I met at Herbert's house (connections!). It was quite funny when I went up to their offices to find him sitting in the conference room looking very businesslike and serious; that evening at Herbert's he was completely chilled out on some good quality dagga he'd picked up at Rusape market, and he spent the whole time on the couch trying to undress his wife. He told me that the lawyer who'd been there, too, Benjamin, had died a week later in a mysterious car crash; he had, the previous day, filed some papers against the attorney general implicating senior government officials in the torture of trade union members.

Stefan didn't want to talk very much, and later, out on the pavement, he said that they routinely found bugs in the office.

"We were supposedly debugged this morning," he said, "so it should be safe. It's the secretaries."

I pick David up early and find other parents doing the same thing. There's talk at the gates about the city center being up in flames and the riot police running amok. On the local news there's Mugabe's latest trip. BBC and SABC have reports of rioting spreading out from the city center. Army trucks are rolling into Chitungwiza and Mbare. Ian hasn't been back home since he left in the morning. With his camera.

Ian doesn't come home for two days. I phone around for news. No one knows anything. An eerie calm descends on the city, helicopters hovering, seeking out would-be trouble-makers.

Rosanna phones. She says that there is some trouble. Maphosa has moved into Number 18 with his wife. They are living in the main house. They have been joined there by other war veterans.

Ian's editor at the *Independent* phones. Ian has been charged with spying and is in Harare Central. "Don't worry," he says. "They won't dare lay a finger on him." Too much bad press. He is a journalist. A *white* journalist.

Five days later Ian is released. He is interviewed by BBC and Sky TV. "I am a Zimbabwean," he tells the international viewers, "getting on with my job." They ask him if he was tortured. He says no. He was treated quite well. No electric shock. No beatings. Just some screaming intelligence officer, ranting and raving about white colonialists and their agents. And then the international press loses interest in the story despite the fact that three other (black) journalists were indeed tortured and one of them is in Avenues Clinic with severe head injuries.

He'll have to go to Bulawayo to sort things out, find out what Maphosa and his goons are playing at. If push comes to shove, he'll call the police in. They're squatters; they'll be evicted. The law's the law.

He hires a lawyer in Bulawayo who files the necessary papers in court. One eviction notice passes. Then another. And yet another one. The war vets remain put. The police say they have "no transport." And that's that.

I phone Rosanna and she tells me that one of the war vets came to the house and strutted around like he owned it.

"You should have seen him, Sisi, his bottom was almost touching the sky; he was pointing at this, at that, and when I gave him tea, he was putting the tea bag in his mouth to eat it . . . and Sisi, they brought a nyanga who killed one of our chickens, and he sprinkled the blood on the inside of that house to drive out the bad spirits. The war vet said that the house is now good and that they can now dwell in it with no issues; he said that since our yard is so big and underutilized he is ear-marking stands for resettlement. He said he is going to come back with pegs."

"Have you seen Maphosa, Rosanna?"

"No, no, Sisi, that one is keeping a low profile; when I see him, I will have something to tell him that is for sure; for a relative to behave this way, it is a disgrace."

"How is Daddy?"

She is quiet.

"He is fine," she says at last. And then, "But I think he is feeling lonely, that is all."

"Slow down, Ian."

He stops the car and shouts, "If you don't like it, get out and walk."

"Ian, okay fine, let's just go."

He starts off very fast, and then just after Chegutu, drivers going to Harare start flashing their lights at us, which is the Universal Zimbo Signal for Speed Trap ahead. So he slows down.

We drive without talking, just swallowing up the road and Otis Redding filling up the silence in the car until he, too, is quiet.

Last night I tried to talk Ian out of going.

"You don't know who's behind them."

"It's your gook relative."

"Maphosa? Maphosa's being used. I don't think he . . ."

"He moved in didn't he?"

"Yes but . . ."

"They better not have, shit, which other fricking country . . ."

One part of me doesn't understand how he can be so upset about the whole thing. The house is abandoned; he hasn't been able to sell it. The house has bad memories. "Let them have it," I want to tell him. "Let them deal with all those spirits."

He drives right past Number 16 and swings over to next door, the tires kicking gravel, almost hitting one of the gateposts. He gets out of the car, leaves the door wide open. I get out, too. "Stay here," I say to David. "Don't move."

I look at the gate and read the cardboard sign hanging from a dirty pink string on the latch:

> HEADQUARTERS OF THE PEOPLE'S
> LIBERATION COOP.
> TRESPASSING WILL BE PROSECUTED.

Ian reads the sign, too, and snatches it from the gate. He drops it on the ground and kicks it.

"Ian . . ."

He turns around.

"Just be calm, okay. Don't provoke them."

He looks at me, and I can hear his unspoken question, "Shit, whose side are you on?"

The rusted gate makes too much noise as Ian pushes it open.

He takes two, three steps inside when all at once, "Hey, hey, who is, what are you, foosake, this is Private Property, out!"

They come stumbling out from the caged-in veranda. Ian stands very still and then he lets rip. "This is *my* Private Property. *You* are trespassing. *You* get out."

"Ian . . ."

He doesn't hear me, or if he does, he's past caring about anything I might have to say.

"I have a title deed for this place. You must get the hell . . ."

Two of them start pushing Ian; one of them is holding a mug, home brew spilling out of it.

"Get your fucking hands off me."

"Ian!"

There are bodies slumped on the veranda and the pungent smell of home brew coming from a steel drum on my left.

A couple of women have joined the two men. They are real mamas, one of them wearing a T-shirt with Mugabe's face plastered over her gigantic, braless breasts. They are carrying pots and wooden spoons.

"The property has been resettled," says the one with the mug.

"The white man is no longer wanted in Zimbabwe. African aliberate Zim-ba-bwe. Now foosake."

"Ian, please, let's . . ."

"And you, what are you doing here?" says the woman wearing a bush hat. "Are you his prostitute?"

The other bodies on the veranda are starting to stir.

"Ian, please . . ."

"I see I cannot help you," Ian says.

The men and women are confused by this, by Ian's change of tone, his voice now soft, almost gentle, like a parent who's done with remonstrations, who's ready to give up; he has tried his best.

"Yes, I came here to help, to warn you. You know that a white woman died here?"

The one with the mug is swaying, this way and that.

"Yes, we know all that," says the other woman, "the nyanga . . ."

"*Nyanga?*" says Ian. "I hope he is the nyanga of a paramount chief. I am telling you the woman who died here had a very powerful medicine. Why do you think I am not living in this house? The woman has very big ma jealous. She loved this house and said that she would never leave it. So I am telling you, be very careful."

The two women step back from Ian and start banging on their pots, shuffling their feet, and wailing. One of them begins tearing at the loose plaits of her hair. I watch as the president wobbles up and down the woman's breasts.

Ian turns around, and I notice how he fiddles with the pocket of his trousers, and then he spins around, opens his fists, and throws something in the air—ash, pepper, sand—which the wind blows into the faces of the two women who run yelping and crying onto the veranda.

"We are being bewitched, we are being bewitched, the white man is bewitching us!"

In the car, Ian keeps banging his hands on the steering wheel. "*Bloody fricking kaffirs, goons, munts, gondies . . . ,*" over and over. David and I leave him there, alone in the car, we walk back to next door.

"Come on, let's go swimming, David. It's hot."

I fish around in the storeroom and finally find my old school navy blue swimsuit. A little bit of stretching and it will fit. The last time I used it must have been when I was eleven, twelve, at primary school when swimming lessons were compulsory and we had to trek down to North End Swimming Pool every week. Anyway, I have no intentions of getting wet. I'll leave that to David.

"Are you coming?" I ask Ian who's in the lounge sitting in that chair like so many years before.

"Asch, why not?" He stands up and then he slumps back down again. "Asch, you go."

I take Daddy's Cortina and drive to Haddon and Sly to get a pair of swimming trunks for David.

North End Swimming Pool has been closed for ages because the local council has run out of funds to keep it up; the strict water rationing put in place by the city because of the drought means that fresh water can't be pumped into the pool, so we have to go to Borrow Street Swimming Pool in town where the water is recycled back into the pool.

* * *

This is the first time I've come here; the girls in the senior school swimming team would train here. When I was at primary school, it was Whites Only.

David struggles a bit with the ancient turnstile but finally manages to get through.

And then, as it happens ever so often, after pushing myself through the turnstile, I step into *Rhodesia:* an enclave of immaculate nostalgia.

Oh, time stand still and it does.

Heads turn. Eyes dart up and down. Thoughts sharpened, mulled over, whispered into glossed lips.

School gave me enough practice.

"David, do you want to change with me?"

"No."

I point him towards the children's changing room, and I stand there watching my growing son rush off, on his own.

I choose a cubicle with a red door and squeeze myself into the very unbecoming swimsuit that smells so musty, and I'm overwhelmed by a sudden heady rush of the torture of school swim days, where the only way to get out of them was to feign severe period pains. I must look ridiculous. I should have bought a new one, too. But I *never* swim. Still, it's embarrassing to be wearing this tatty thing. I wrap my Zimbabwean flag towel (why, oh why, did I bring this threadbare relic here, Daddy's purchase to mark Zimbabwe's Independence Day).

"You took *sooooo* long, Mum!" complains David who's been running up and down the pathway, poking his head under doors, looking for me.

We pass two girls on the veranda flicking through magazines who both stop, give me the once-over.

Come on, I can do this.

David jumps and splashes in the water. I marvel at how athletic he has become. He won a gold medal for the breaststroke at the school's intersports this year.

I give him twenty dollars, and he goes off to buy chips and cream sodas at the kiosk.

I'm lying on the grass, my towel wrapped over my breasts like a chitenga, when a shadow falls on me.

"So you're not even jumping in, what a wuss."

Ian sits down next to me, and I glimpse the girls on the veranda shooting us looks and chattering away.

"I almost drowned once at school."

"Really?"

"Yes, and I almost drowned another student, my rescuer. I was swimming in the shallow end and drifted off to the deep end; when I tried to put my feet down, panic station."

"And your PE teacher?"

"She had to jump in, fully clothed, wasn't at all amused."

He puts his hands behind his head. He takes a look around.

"Best pool in Bullies. Makes North End look like a fricking pond. I reckon it's Olympic size, this one. Used to come here for interschools. Some lighties would have towel fights and jeez, man, the warden would throw a major kadenze, threatening to chuck everyone out of the pool and ban the whole lot of us."

"Dad!"

"So, my boy, this is what you do when I'm not around, heh, cream sodas, chips, man . . ."

I watch the girls on the veranda transfixed. Ian looks up at them.

"You forget this place when you're up in Harare; a village, everyone into everyone's business."

"Watch, Dad, watch. Check this dive, from the top one."

And he's already running off.

"David, I don't think . . . !"

"Leave him, Lindiwe."

"Do you think he should wear sunscreen?"

"Sunscreen! Man, that was for moffs."

"Ian!"

"What? No one put that stuff on when I was a kid; come to think of it, sometimes we'd really get fried and then we'd just slather on margarine. Boy, did that hurt."

David climbs up the stairs of the high diving board. He gives us a wave when he reaches the top.

"I wish he wouldn't. I could never do that."

"To tell you the truth Lindiwe, me neither; I'm shit scared of heights."

David, our son, knees tucked up to his chest, whoops and jumps fearlessly into the water.

He shakes the water off his body and goes up again.

"The old man was a heck of a swimmer. Told some stories about swimming across rivers underwater to ambush the terrs. Watched him once here swimming a whole length underwater. Hardcore."

"What are you going to do, about the house?"

"I don't even want to think about it; man, did I give them a fright."

The girls leave the veranda and come down to the pool. They choose a patch of grass a couple of meters from us. They pull over their tunics and parade their bikini-clad bodies. They jump gracefully in the water. I look at Ian.

"So, I reckon I'll just leave it."

The girls climb out of the water, spread their bodies on the concrete, put their fingers under their bikini bottoms, snap them back into place.

I think of Bridgette and me at Geraldine's house.

David comes dripping water on us, and he and Ian have a fight with the towel, pulling and tugging at it until they're both rolling on the grass.

The girls turn their heads.
And a single thought erupts in my head.
He's mine!
No, two.
So there!

The drums beat throughout the entire night.

"They are trying to chase away the bad spirits," says Rosanna.

In the deep darkness I lie on my childhood bed next to David. Ian's stormed off. He can't bear to stay near the house; he's over at the Holiday Inn.

I lie listening to David's breath, heart, and the drums until I fall asleep.

"Sisi! Sisi! Sisi!"

Rosanna's screams pierce through my sleep. She is standing in the doorway, clutching her head.

"Sisi!"

"What? What? What is it? Rosanna!"

"They are crying, she is dead. She is dead. She is dead."

"Who? Who? Rosanna, who?"

"Oh, oh, mai weh! Mai weh!"

"Rosanna!"

"Maphosa's wife. Maphosa's wife. She is dead. Oh, oh. Ufile. Ufile. She is dead. Mai weh. Mai weh."

We check that the doors are locked, all the windows closed, the curtains drawn. After some moments, I think to phone the Holiday Inn.

"Ian, you have to come and get us quick. Maphosa's wife has died during the night."

"Shit, shit. I'm there. Five minutes."

*　　*　　*

Rosanna can't stay still. She starts hitting her upper arms with her palms, moaning, groaning, in the hallway. And then banging her head rhythmically on the wall.

"Rosanna, stop. Please, stop. Rosanna, go and see if Daddy's fine. Go."

David sits on his bed, his eyes scanning the walls in the dim light.

"Are they coming to kill us, Mum?"

"No, no, don't be silly."

"Did Dad kill her?"

"Kill? Who? Maphosa's wife? Of course not, David. She was sick."

"Why didn't she go to the hospital?"

"I don't know, David. Sometimes people are afraid to go to hospital."

"Maybe it was too dark."

"Yes, maybe that was it."

"Is Dad coming?"

"Yes, so we have to get ready. Let's get dressed, okay?"

He nods solemnly. "Yes, Mum."

My ears are strained to hear, catch any sound, but the morning seems very still.

No bird. No dogs. No cars. No screaming. No chanting. No drums.

The tense expectation of something terrible, retribution. Biblical words resound in my head: *Vengeance. Is. Mine. Saith. The. Lord.*

Then a sound so loud, so catastrophic that either the house is being shaken at its foundation or The Lord has Spoken.

Thunder.

Only thunder.

Rolls of it, one after the other, as though God doth speaketh.

The slow patter of rain on the red tiles of the roof soon turns into a roaring barrage. We are Noah, in the ark, tossed about in the tumultuous waves of God. El Niño is being banished for this one moment by greater, stronger spirits, Amadhlozi. The spirit world is in mighty turmoil, uproar.

I find Rosanna under Daddy's bed, her hands clasped over her ears, whimpering, "Eh, eh, eh . . . Amadhlozi, Amadhlozi . . ."

I lie on the bed with Daddy (and David sideways, at our feet), two question marks on the bedspread, lulled by Rosanna's moans until finally Ian comes.

We drive in the storm in our getaway car, fugitives, fugitives from justice. Off, off, away we go, all along the familiar landmarks, all the way up until we reach the Harare Road, all the way to Cement Side, and there we are at last surging on the open road. The rain pouring down, smashing into the metal of the roof, so fragile it seems the torrent could so easily crush us.

It's so cold in this car.

"Lindiwe," I hear Ian, "you're shivering."

The car swoops and swoons, the road plays with the car, and the rain tumbles, relentless.

Ian stops the car, puts his hand on my forehead. "Jeez, you're burning. Shit, I hope it's not malaria."

"Is Mum sick?" I hear from far, far away and I don't hear Ian's answer.

I feel Ian parting my lips, pouring rain into them. "Easy, Lindiwe, not so fast."

The rain has gone and now it's the sun beating fiercely, terribly on me, us. It wants to burn us up, twist the metal.

"I'm too hot, I'm too hot," I say over and over, and I don't know if anyone hears or understands for suddenly I am no longer there, but running as fast as I can, something dark and rapid snapping at my heels.

Lindiwe, Lindiwe, it's me, Ian. Lindiwe, you're dreaming, it's a dream . . .

And I'm scrambling, clawing myself out of the earth, breathing, gasping, flash, eyes, wide, open, shut . . .

Lindiwe, it's me.

. . . Eyes open, flash . . .

"Ian," I say. "Ian," I say in the still, still room.

"Has it stopped raining?" I ask him.

"Jeez, man, you've been out for two days."

My lips, dry, hot.

"And Lindiwe," he says. "You're pregnant."

And there, here, he is, with the widest, flashiest, whitest smile, as if he is on a Colgate extra-strength advertisement or he is a crocodile or a hyena or a shark, something, something that will gnash its whitest teeth, eat me whole.

But three weeks later, the baby dies.

It could be anything.

The fever, a genetic defect, stress, fright at the all too white Colgate smile. . . .

He (in my head, it is a he) comes out in drips and drabs, throughout the day.

I go to the Bronte, rent a room.

No, Ian, I want to be . . . alone.

And standing, in the bathtub, legs apart; hands pressed against the wall, on my stomach; lips clenched tight, not a cry, not a single cry.

Ian's baby.

My baby.

David's brother.

Wordlessly (no, there's *Kojak* on the TV sound turned low), disappears.

And then I drink.

Half a whole bottle of red full-bodied wine.

And pour the rest in the drain.

Rosanna phones to say that the war vets have left.

"Sisi," she says, "Mother has come back. She is now at church."

3.

"Sorry, I'm late, Bridgette." I sit down, look at her.

"Don't do that, Lins."

"Do what?"

"That. Checking for symptoms. I'm fine. The pills are working. My blood platelet count is good. So relax. I'm not about to D-I-E."

"I'm sorry."

"And don't do that, either. It's irritating, you being sorry all the time."

"Is there anything I can do?"

"Be yourself."

We order two cappuccinos.

"So where've you been, Lins? I don't see much of you these days."

"I've just come from the German embassy. I got a big contract."

"Doing what?"

It's difficult for me to tell her that I'll be writing pamphlets on AIDS prevention.

"They're even sending me to Uganda next week. They're way ahead of us in tackling the . . . the epidemic."

"Lindiwe, excuse me, but this sounds like it's going to be another well-intentioned but futile exercise."

"What do you mean? It's going to educate, get people talking about it, focus on . . ."

"Oh please, Lins, that's so tired. Educate who? Do you think it's actually going to change anything? Who's going to read them? And do you honestly think African men are going to accept condoms? And also, which Zimbabwean is going to come up and say, 'I have AIDS'? That's a pipe dream, anything but—tuberculosis, pneumonia, a long illness, whatever. Don't even go there, do something real with your brains, please."

"Real? Like what?"

I'm trying so hard not to look at her, not to give her *that* look. I wish I hadn't brought up the subject.

"Bridgette, there has to be a start," I say softly.

"A start! A start maybe when it has infected all the government ministers, their wives, their girlfriends, their sons, daughters, maybe then, but don't hold your breath. For now it's you go and see a nyanga who tells you all's fine, you just have to go and rape a virgin and you'll be as good as new."

Her voice is trembling with contempt, anger.

She jerks her head back and then gives me a bright smile.

"Look Lins, look who's just landed, over to the left. Mr. Black Empowerment himself. That loud shiny suit of his probably matches his Pajero."

"Shush, Bridgette."

"And there he goes with the latest cell phone, and now we are all going to get bombarded with his First-Class business deals. God help us if this is what indigenization means."

"Bridgette! You'll get us arrested."

"Don't worry girl, I have connections. By the way, guess who I bumped into in London on my last trip? One of the old schoolgirls who gapped it."

"Who?"

"That Geraldine girl."

"Oh, her."

"Yes, and it was at Tooting Bec tube station of all places. I was coming back from the market with all the hair extensions I'd got, and there she is by the ticket machine."

"Did you talk to her?"

"Of course, my dear. My word did she look haggard. She lives in Tooting, and I'm telling you, Lindiwe, Tooting is no Matsheumhlope, a long, long way away from swimming pools, gazebos, and whatever else they had going down there. Remember those boys at her party?"

"Yes."

"So, how's your Mr. Howzit? I haven't seen him for a while."

"He's good. Since he won that big award in the States with his pictures of the Nigerian oil delta and the rebels there, he's the man. Everyone wants him; actually, he's supposed to go to Bosnia next week, but I think he's tired of all the running around. He's thinking of doing more studio work."

"Oh yes, like those celebrated infamous nudes!"

"Don't remind me, Bridgette! Half of Harare has seen my breasts!"

"Oh Lins, you don't tell me that underneath all that grown-up attitude still lurks the Miss Goody Two-shoes. My, my, I would never have guessed and really, my dear, they are very fine breasts."

"Very funny. By the way, David's been asking about you."

"That boy, he's smart, Lins. I bet you his IQ is somewhere up there."

"He must get that from me."

She shakes her head. "You know, he's a good guy, your Ian, Rhodie or not."

*　　*　　*

When I get home, the boys are making a production of dinner.

"Smells good," I say. "What is it?"

"Spaghetti Bolognese!" shouts David.

"I thought so, just checking. I hope you didn't use ketchup instead of tomatoes."

The silence is all the answer I need.

"It smells great. I'm going to have a bath."

We're sitting, the three of us, having dinner.

"Delicious," I say.

"Good thing you're not a—a vegetarian anymore."

"Mum, we used ketchup."

"Oh, so *that's* the secret ingredient!"

And we all burst out laughing.

4.

"Howzit, doll?"

It's a surprise to have him there, here. A good surprise.

He gives me a full-throated kiss right there in the Arrivals Hall, lifting me off the ground.

When I finally come up for air, I hand him the duty-free gorilla.

"Nice," he says.

In the car I can't stop looking at him, smiling. I've only been gone for five days.

And I'm suddenly swept by the sensation of being that sixteen-year-old girl once, more and I am alone in the car with Mr. McKenzie/Ian.

"It's quiet," I say when we're waiting at the traffic lights in front of the Coca-Cola company.

"Here, it's quiet. The action is down in the townships, Chitungwiza, Mbare, after dark. Door-to-door sweeps, like I said. Anyone caught with any new goods, shoes, clothes, guaranteed one hundred percent beatings. Government's running shit scared. Didn't reckon docile Zimbos had it in them to go about rioting, vandalizing Private Property. ESAP is doing its job. And the war vets are adding their two cents: that Hunzvi chap's got them all riled up about their right to more dosh from the country they liberated; we owe them big-time. I got some good shots of them prancing around ZANU headquarters. Don't look at me like that; I used a long lens."

We don't talk about his mother. Not until we're turning into our cul-de-sac. He stops the car right there. We're half in, half out of the bend. It's a dangerous place to be.

"So Lindiwe, like I said on the phone it's a temporary thing. Until I can find something. I'm looking. I couldn't let her stay in that place anymore; there were cockroaches crawling all over her when I went to see her, I . . ."

I put my hand on his thigh.

"It was so overcrowded in there. They were happy to let her out, I . . ."

"It's all right, Ian."

"Listen, Lindiwe, she doesn't look, she doesn't look too good, her face is . . ."

He's holding onto the steering wheel, looking straight out ahead.

"It's all right, Ian," I tell him again.

She is sitting on the veranda. Her hands are resting on her lap, her back straight, her head inclined to her left. Seeing her like this, it seems she may be sitting for a portrait or simply be one of those people who can wait without having to pretend to be occupied by something. Her hair falls over her shoulders. She seems so self-contained, and I wonder if, in there, this was what she looked like, who she was.

"Ma," Ian says walking towards her. "Ma."

He kneels down beside her, takes her hand gently in his.

"This is Lindiwe," he says holding out a hand to me.

"I told you about her. She's been away. She lives here. She's David's mother, my . . ."

He looks up at me, and I see that he's biting at the inside of his cheek.

"She lives here."

"Hello," I say.

She raises her head and slowly twists herself around. She looks up at me, her head perfectly still, and I have the strangest feeling that she is giving me a chance to look, to gape, to have my fill, just this one time.

I stand there not daring to move, to look away.

"I'm very happy to meet you," I say at last into those eyes, my words ludicrous and somehow insulting, offensive to my ears.

"Mum . . ."

"Mum!" I look up and see David sprinting from next door, Jade leaping and barking at his feet.

I watch him do that Indiana Jones thing of his of leaping over the stream, while Jade wisely scrambles up onto the wooden bridge.

"Mum!"

He dashes up the steps, tripping on the last one, and then he's up again.

"Mum!"

And as he dives into my arms, I catch sight of her hand raised, her fingers splayed, brush against his head.

He wriggles in my arms, turns around.

"Gran!" he laughs.

PART FOUR

Late 1990s

1.

Ian's mother is sitting at the kitchen table, drawing circles with the tip of her finger. I stand there for a moment leaning against the door, watching her.

There are times when I wake up in the morning with the feeling that she has stood by my bedside during the night; when I breathe, it's her breath I take in. I haven't told this to Ian because I'm not sure if it's real, if it's not my imagination getting carried away, my fear taking over.

It's taken me a while to admit it. I'm afraid of her, of her quiet. Of her eyes that seem bluer than they were in that picture when she was young; I don't know if this is because of the contrast between them and her shiny, scarred skin pulled tight over her bones.

There are moments when she seems to me the stereotype of a madwoman, when she's pulling at her hair or scratching her scalp, when she's mumbling words to herself or walking in what looks like some kind of pattern up and down the garden.

But when I catch her eyes, I'm not so sure. There's something there. They're alert and, perhaps it's my imagination again, sometimes it feels like she's amused. That's the word, amused.

She raises her finger and draws something in the air. No, she's writing something. Letters. M-O-R-T-U and then she turns and looks at me. It feels as though she's known I've been there all the time, spying.

"Good morning," I say.

There won't be an answer, I know this. She hasn't said one word to me. Not one.

It's David she talks to. Long, whispery monologues. I wonder sometimes if she thinks she's talking to Ian.

I'm amazed at how unfazed David is by her, taking everything in his stride. Maybe he's had the practice, knows all about dealing with otherworldly grandmothers.

She gets up from the table, and a book slips from her lap to the floor.

She doesn't seem to notice because she walks around the table, opens the kitchen door, and steps outside, and I watch her walking in the garden in her white nightdress, floating, like Wilkie Collins's *Woman in White,* the ghostly apparition disappearing into the mist.

I shake myself free from what I used to call the heebie-jeebies when I was a girl.

I go to the table and take the book from the floor. It's Ian's notebook. I sit down by the table and open its pages once again. I see that in a very soft hand with a pencil she has drawn a spidery web over his words.

I think of what Ian has told me. The four years he lived with her in South Africa. She had just been recently divorced when he found her. She was living in a squalid flat in Johannesburg, supporting herself by doing housecleaning work. She was a poor white. She had the old yellow Sunny, one of the few things she'd been able to take from her marriage, which had made that journey to Bulawayo once upon a time.

I open the book again and look at the pictures of a boy falling over the edge of a cliff, blood spewing from his lip; another of the boy standing on the same cliff, an eagle swooping down, its claws so near to the boy's head; another, the eagle's claws digging into his shoulders, and somehow the boy's chest has been cut open and his blood is bleeding out into the air, but the boy wears such an euphoric smile as if he's being set free at last.

As I hold the book in my hands, I know one thing with absolute certainty: Ian's mother has been in our bedroom. She has opened my bedside drawer and she has taken this book out. She has done it perhaps while I was sleeping, and as I lay there, she must have for a moment stood there over me, watching.

I go back to our room where Ian is just getting up. I take the deepest breath of my life, it seems to me.

"Ian, your mother . . . ," I begin, wading into treacherous waters.

He is rubbing the sleep from his eyes. He looks so much like a boy, a kid, his hair all rumpled, his head still in the warmth of his blankets.

"Yes, my mother . . ."

"Ian, I don't know her. I don't know who she is, what . . ."

He is standing up, stretching, and he's starting with his stretch and touch my toes routine.

"Ian, I think we should . . ."

I try the words out in my head: *I think we should keep her locked up at night in case; it's for her, to keep her safe . . .*

"Lindiwe, stop worrying. She's fine."

It's as if he's gone right through my head, extracted the nugget of thought there, and is giving it back to me.

"No, she isn't Ian. She should be seeing someone, a doctor."

I can't even say the word *psychiatrist*. I remember those years ago when he was right about David and the psychologist. But he's not right now. He can't be.

"Lindiwe, she was locked up for all those years, and now you want me to put her in a position where some clown is going to say she needs to be put away again or that she has to be dozed up on pills? No, Lindiwe, it's not going to happen."

"Ian, she went through my drawer. She . . . she just stands there. . . . I . . . I don't feel safe."

He drops his arms.

"You don't feel safe."

He says the words slowly as if he is trying to fully comprehend their substance, what may lie behind, in them. I can't bring myself to say about the fire. How yesterday I went through the kitchen drawers and took all the matches, the lighters, and I drove to Sam Levy's Village with them and dumped the lot in a dustbin.

"I would never endanger this family. *Never.* You either believe that or you don't know me, Lindiwe."

I want to believe him.

"Ian, did she start the fire?"

It's as if a bomb has detonated in the room and then I throw another one.

"Did she do it on purpose?"

Ian looks at me and then sits down on the bed.

"You won't let that go will you, Lindiwe? It's always there, that story, no matter how many years pass. It always comes back to this point."

"She is living here, Ian. There's David to think of."

"And you think she's going to go after him?"

"Ian, it works both ways, trust."

"Lindiwe, my mother found out about all that shit that was happening in the house. She found out on the day of my dad's funeral. I was so mad with the bitch; the way she comes over drunk when we've just put the bastard under the ground and goes on about how I'm trying to steal her inheritance. Your father was there . . . and I lost it . . . sobbed the whole sorry story out to my mother. Every bit of it. The men who'd come there.

Everything. So, you see, I'm responsible for what happened. I should have left well alone, drove us back to South Africa, but my mother said, no, no, we had to stick around to deal with all the legal shit, and then that evening we had come to discuss the house with the bitch and . . ."

He rubs his eyes with the heels of his hands.

I sit down next to him.

"Anyway, she was out cold drunk when we got to the house. I went out back to check what was happening with Mphiri. I don't know, it must have been ten or so minutes, and there was shouting coming from the house. As I'm rushing back in, she . . . she comes running out on fire. I froze, Lindiwe. I froze. And then my mother's out there, and she's trying to put out the fire except she catches on . . . God."

We sit there together in the room. One.

And yet, a single thought elbows its way between us, *the story always changes.*

2.

Bridgette breaks the news to me at the Italian Bakery.

I'm not sure, watching her walk to the table, if she has gone plain mental or is making a fashion statement that only people in the know are privy to. The long white skirt and blouse. The white doek. My first thought is oh, my God, she's joined the apostolics, and then I see the belt in green and yellow cloth tied at her waist and the woolen Rasta hat tucked into it. She looks both odd and impossibly stylish. People keep turning around to look at her. I expect her to say at any moment, "jah, man."

"You like?" she says, giving herself a twirl.

"I like. What's the occasion?"

"I've found the Promised Land, Lins."

Her eyes are cloudy. Her movements lazy. I wonder if she's been smoking dagga, if she's floating on rainbows. The long skirt doesn't hide how skinny she's become. I tried once to ask her if she needed help getting some of the drugs, and she got angry and said that all she needed were natural foods and vitamins. The chemical shit was messing up her body.

"Listen girlfriend, I'm off. Jamaica. ASAP. One love."

"Jamaica, Bridgette? When?"

"Wednesday."

"Wednesday? Next week? Wednesday? You mean in five days' time?"

"Yes man, I've been given a place at the University of the West Indies. Clever me."

"You serious?"

"Jah man. I'm going to see the ocean, Lins, have some red, red wine. That's where I want to . . ."

She shakes her head, banishing the thought.

Even though I can hardly believe her, I say, "We have to have a party, Bridgette. Blast you off with some quasi-homegrown reggae, Lucky Dube and company."

I find David at the bottom of the garden, sitting on the borehole, dismembering a locust. Even from here I can hear Ian's mother snoring out by the gazebo. He looks up at me while his fingers keep working on the locust. And then, he chucks the bits of locust away and stands up.

Even the neighbors must be able to hear Ian's mum.

"You know, she reckons she's a ghost, so it doesn't matter what bad thing she does because she doesn't exist. That's what she told me yesterday."

"Well, she's a very noisy ghost, David, that's for sure."

We exchange shy grins.

"She's just talking. Old people do that sometimes."

That brings out a stretching of the lips which I take for an introspective smile.

I put my hand gently on his wrist (how long his limbs are).

"David . . ."

He stands so still then. Just his soft breathing. In and out, in and out.

And before he can be off again, I tell him about Bridgette.

We stand together there, quiet. The sun is beginning to set. The day is coming to a close, and I am standing here with my son. The thought seems incredible to me at this moment. He scratches his right shoulder, pulls at the sleeve there. I can't be-lieve how much he's grown. I'm looking *up* at him. He's wearing sports shoes one size smaller than Ian's. And he's got muscles now. He can outrun me. Sometimes his manliness intimidates me. I thought that he was going to be one of those nerdy kids, his head always in a book, perpetually afraid, timid. I thought I would have to deal with bullies.

"We can visit, right?"

"Yes, yes, we can. It's far, but of course, we can visit."

"So we'll see her again."

"Yes, yes."

"She's sick isn't she?"

"Yes."

And it's as if for the first time, I'm acknowledging this to myself.

"Jamaica. Cool. I could learn to surf, water-ski."

"Great, another reason for me to get a heart attack."

"I wish we could head off to Bulawayo. I'm bored here, Mum."

I wait for him to say something more. He waits for me.

"We will. Sometime, soon."

I can smell the locust off his hands. He rubs the smell onto his jeans.

He's about to wander off when I remember something I've been meaning to ask him for some time.

"David, over at the gardens, what do you guys do?"

"Stuff."

"Stuff?"

"Yeah. Just stuff, stuff."

A thought strikes me.

"I hope you're not smoking."

"Oh, please, Mum."

And then another thought that sends my heart racing.

"And I hope it's not girls."

"Mum, enough already."

"Well, okay, I just hope you're not messing about at the back, you know, over the fence. You know you can't go there. It's a restricted area. You've seen the signs."

"You mean where the army is?"

"Yes, David. You're to stay in the gardens, okay? Doing whatever innocent thing you're doing."

I wait for him to say yes.

"What do they do there anyway? Lots of activity, trucks coming in and out, packed with—"

"David . . ."

"Okay, okay, Mum . . . chill."

I try to think of all the boys I know. Not much. The Secret Seven. The Hardy Boys. What do boys do? They get up to mischief. They have adventures. They build tree houses . . . I think of my father. What did he do as a boy? Terrorize the countryside with his homemade catapult? Herd cows, yes, now that would be a great help!

"Are you building a tree house?"

The thought fills me with so much hope.

David looks at me with something like pity, and then he offers me a lifeline. "I'm taking pictures. Nature."

Now this, I can believe in, happily live with.

It's either the Walkman or the camera, sometimes the two of them in tandem, a double act. The camera, one of Ian's old ones, the one Ian says of, "I tell you, my boy, if that camera could talk, the things it's seen . . ."

"For the class project. Environmental Science."

"Good. Just stay in the gardens, okay? Or you'll have me tagging along."

He pulls a face.

"So about this school camp, are you sure you want to go?"

"Definitely."

"A *whole* week?"

He stretches out his hands in a long, extravagant yawn.

"Definitely, definitely, definitely *fucking* sure."

And then he bursts out laughing and runs away.

When I phoned this morning, Rosanna said they had received a visit from some youths demanding that they show their ZANU-PF party cards.

Luckily, said Rosanna, she had Maphosa's card which he had left behind.

I thought of the Unity Accord signed in the late '80s that had finally put a stop to the Fifth Brigade terror in Matabeleland and effectively demolished Nkomo and the opposition. How Nkomo had been accused of selling out the Ndebeles by former Ndebele fighters like Maphosa, and yet now, so many years later, some of the same fighters had maneuvered themselves in good positions in the unified party. They virulently supported Mugabe in his sporadic attacks against white farmers and his default revolutionary cry to wrench the land from them. And now, there are reports of farmers being harassed and chased off their property.

"The youths are so ignorant," Rosanna said. "They did not even read the name. Anyways, they were drunk and they were satisfied that I gave them some chicken and bread."

She said Daddy was sitting up these days, more and more, and that he was writing things with his right hand.

"You must come and visit, Sisi. He would like that very much."

I felt a stab of guilt. It's been almost a year since I last saw him.

"He is missing little David. How is he?"

"He's fine, Rosanna. What about Danielle?"

Peals of laughter from Rosanna. "She is fine, fine, fine, Sisi. She is doing so well at school; she is in Form Two now. She is catching up. Thank you for the moneys that you are sending for her education."

"I'm glad it's helping. Has Mummy called?"

She had taken off again to Botswana. And every time she left, she took more and more of the furnishings of the house with her. It was as if she was moving away in bits and pieces. When she came back, she would throw Rosanna out.

There was a little silence, and I imagined Rosanna nervously twirling the cord between her fingers.

"No, Sisi. Not at all."

Ian finds me on the veranda.

"Guess who called? You won't believe."

"Who?"

"The President's Office."

"What? You're joking."

"Listen to this one."

"Yes, what?"

"They want me to take some portraits."

"What?"

"Tomorrow. Can you believe it?"

"What did you say?"

"*Say?* I had no choice in the matter, girl. It was a summons, not an invitation."

"Presidential portraits?"

"Ugha, and I'm thinking now, maybe these are the ones that are going to be anointed with the 'all-seeing eye.' Jeez, man, I'm good."

"Maybe you can say you're sick or something."

"What! You know how much I'll get paid? It's not like we're exactly swimming in dosh, is it? And don't look at me like that. Principles, my foot. About the eyes, I'll try to get Bob to look down, or I'll do something when I develop the things, maybe an Andy Warhol kind of thing, you better believe. I'm supposed to get my ass over at State House nine sharp tomorrow. Maybe I'll get to see Grace and the kids. I'm going to Graceland, Graceland . . ."

"Try not to get shot while you're there."

"No worries. He's got enough issues, what with the war vets camping outside State House. I hope they get me in through a back door; I don't fancy a confrontation. By the way, we're jolling tonight, you and me dolly bird."

"Jolling?"

"Jolling, for sure, over at that fancy place at Highlands, Amanzi, where all the Pajeros, VIPs, expats, and local fundies hang out."

"Now you're joking."

"No, my child. I've booked us a table and everything. Don't look so shocked. We're talking class here."

"And what's the occasion?"

"*Occasion?* What? I can't just take my chick out? Okay, but you're really chissering me. You mean to tell me that you've forgotten our anniversary."

"Anniversary?"

"Anniversary, for sure, now you're *really* burning me."

"What anniversary?"

"You don't even remember. Man, I'm burnt."

"Ian!"

"That day at the bus stop. That day I picked you up in your netball getup."

"Oh, I . . ."

"It's official, an anniversary. Fifteenth anniversary, if you please, plus or minus. You have two and a half hours to doll yourself up."

"What about David?"

"All taken care of. He's spending the night at Charles's."

"Your mother?"

"Ma Patience is coming over."

"A well-planned operation, I see."

"Yes man."

Ma Patience comes in with her customary heaving and sighing.

"Hello. Hello. I am here now. Where is that big boy known by the name of David? Where is he right now?"

David, of course, has long gone. He has had more than enough experience of getting squashed up in Ma Patience's ample hands to hang around.

"Hello, little madam. I have come. I have come. As you can see, I am here."

Ever since Ian's mother has moved in, I have become the "little madam."

"I will go and see madam now. You can go. I am ready. Have a good time now, you young people."

And with that she giggles into her fist and heaves and sighs out of the room to find the (big) madam.

"You look nice," he says, opening the door for me.

I don't say, "what the . . . ?" although I'm tempted to.

"Thank you."

*　　*　　*

Even though it's a Tuesday, the restaurant car park is almost full. The guard directs us with a flourish of his baton to an empty space.

"Stay right there," says Ian jumping out of the car.

He darts around to my side and flings open the door.

What the . . . ? "Thank you."

Ian tells the young lady standing behind the dais his name and the time of his reservation.

The lady looks at Ian and then me and says, "This way, sir."

Ian fairly vibrates with importance.

I've heard about this place. Bridgette's told me. But nothing has prepared me for the fairy-tale display of light, water, and foliage, which spreads out before us, as we sit on a table on the veranda. There is the sound of running water, lights shimmering along its path as it darts in and out of the green.

"Wow."

"Can you believe, Enterprise Road is just behind all this?"

We are with the beautiful people. *We* are the beautiful people.

I reach out and squeeze Ian's hand.

The waiter takes our orders. A Thai curry for me. Lamb for Ian. A bottle of red wine. An extravagance.

I feel not myself, as if I'm on a stage set. I wonder if Ian feels the same.

"Here, I got you this."

He takes the packet from his jacket pocket, puts it on the table between us.

"Can I open it?"

"Sure, why not."

I wait until the waiter pours the wine and leaves.

Inside, a single golden heart.

A locket.

A teenage boy's gift. Lockets and lip gloss, daisy chains,

whispered intrigues in the back of the class. Something to wear under your school uniform, to steal peeks at between lessons, feel its lovely coldness against your skin, to sneak out in the toilets, in the changing rooms.

Ian and his gestures. The flame lily earrings, the box of pictures, the notebook. The owner's deed he made me sign, "It's this way or no moving on up, babe . . . ," he said, and there were our names, side by side, newly minted homeowners.

I lift the locket out from the box, open the gold heart. Inside, a paper folded and folded, over and over again, until it fit in the golden heart; Ian with his large, bruised hands doing this delicate task.

I work on the paper. Over and over. Until there it is open in the palm of my hand. I read, a single momentous word; *Us.*

There is such an ache in me. Something so sharp and terrible. So tender. So brutal. "Ian . . ."

And then, the moment is shattered by the explosive frenzy of masked men rushing in, upturning tables, the crash of glass, plates, shouting: "Wallets! Money! Cell phones! Car keys! Valuables! Rings, necklaces, earrings! Watches! Move! Come on, move!" The blur of a man wearing a balaclava; another one, something dark in his hand; another wrenching a watch from a hand. "Come on, I said, move," a voice behind me shouts. Clink of cell phones, keys, jewelry. Slap, slap of wallets. A hand swiping them off the tables into a black bag. "Down! Down!" A gloved hand pushing a man on the floor; bodies scrambling off chairs. "Down! Down!"

And then, feet rushing, a car engine, engines, starting; squeal of tires followed by silence. Just the sound of the water trickling between the fairy lights. A woman sobbing, "Oh, oh, oh, oh . . ." A man shouting, "Fucking bastards!" A fist on the table, shattering glass. "Calm down, shamwari." "Don't tell me to calm down, white boy; this is not Rhod—" "Oh, foosake man . . ." "Ian, please, please, just . . ."

I'm shaking, shivering; I can't seem to stop. "Lindiwe. Lindiwe. Look." He opens his hand, and there resting in its cradle, a golden heart. "No ways was I letting them get away with it, not a chance."

He holds me tight in his arms, squeezing the breath out of me into him. He holds me there.

It's early morning when we finally get home, after giving the police statements. Ma Patience is sleeping on one of the couches in the lounge. She sleeps as she moves. With a lot of heaving and sighing.

Ian puts me to bed. He pulls the duvet right up, but I can't stop shaking, shivering. He tucks in a blanket and sits on top of the covers, his hand on my head, nursing me.

I don't know when I finally sleep. When I wake up, it's past midday and he's gone. There is a note on the bedside. He scribbled it in a hurry: "Sorry. President. Late Already. Stay in bed. Rest." He started another word but scribbled it out so hard that he made a hole. I sit on the bed listening. For something. Anything. The house is quiet.

I get out of bed. I wait, my heart thumping. I stand up. I wait. The shaking, shivering is gone. My head feels heavy, that's all. I look down on the night table and see the locket with its message. I go into the bathroom. I step into the shower. And that's where the shaking and shivering begins again. I press my body against the wall, ignore how much it hurts. I press and press until finally the shaking and shivering stops. I don't know how long it takes, but it is where Ian finds me. He runs the water. Over me. *Us.* And then he puts me in bed again, and when I wake up, it's morning and he is there.

"How did it go?" I ask him getting up. "The president . . ."

He's looking at me in a strange way. He looks so pale. His face contorted so.

"Ian, what's wrong?"

That's when he tells me about Bridgette.

She is dead.

It was a frenzied attack. Multiple stab wounds. Her blood all over the house.

Mavis, her new maid, and the complex's gardener have been arrested. Mavis confessed. She had made copies of the keys, given them to a cousin. Bridgette surprised them.

"People are desperate," everyone keeps saying. People are desperate. We are fast going in the way of South Africa. Hijackings and the like. The young ones see all these Pajeros, and they want to get rich quick, too. They see corruption and stealing among their elders, so why not them? Why must they starve, sacrifice, be fools like their parents? Why must they lose out? No. Not a chance. They will get what they want fast, fast. If the government cannot find employment for them, they will find it for themselves.

I can't go to her funeral. I can't go down to Bulawayo, watch her getting buried. I can't see her like that.

I go out to find her alive. Here. In Harare. The Sunshine City. I go to one of her hair salons, the one by Eastgate. There's a note stuck on the closed door. I do not read it. I know what it says. I cross the square, sit down at a table. The waiter comes and I ask for an espresso. I sit down looking at Bridgette's place. I look down and watch my hand shake.

I slap it down; push it hard on the table, so hard I might just crack a bone. Slowly, drifts of voices from a table behind me find their way. "I mean, what a slut . . . Ndebele . . . She spread her legs for anybody . . . What did she expect . . . ?"

I close my eyes. I drink the espresso. I don't wait for the bill. I leave some notes.

I walk. As far as my legs will carry me. And then I'm running, running, as far, as fast as my legs will carry me, running so fast that the feet pounding on the ground bounce, leap, and I'm up, breathless, far, far away, going, going, as high, as fast as I can . . .

"Iwe, stupid!"

The commuter bus driver leans so far out of his window that his spit hits my face.

Before I can catch my breath, he's off, blasting his horn.

I look around me. Faces staring back at me; penga, they must think. Running into the road like that. Where does she think she is, in the bush? What does she think she is doing, a marathon? Practicing for the Olympics? Waves of heat. Legs trembling. A blur of color and sound. Silence. Absolute silence.

I take a taxi home.

I go into the bathroom. I take a long, hard look in the mirror. I pick up the electric shaver and run it through my hair. I take a shower. And then I go to bed.

3.

I wake up to the sound of someone humming in the house.

In the kitchen there is Heather drying a cup, Ian sitting at the table, scratching the back of his head with a pencil.

"Jeez, what did you do to your h—?"

Heather looks at me openmouthed.

I put my hand on my head, scalp. I'd forgotten about that.

"Coffee?" asks Ian.

"Yes, thanks," I say, going over to the table.

I haven't seen Heather since the fight with Duncan. I notice her hand posed on her stomach as she leans against the sink. She had a miscarriage.

When her back is turned I mouth to Ian, "What is she doing here?"

Before he can answer, she sits down, too, and says, "If you wear hoops, you'll look fine."

It takes me a moment to realize she means earrings.

"Heather has found a place for my mother. They've just opened. That complex on the Borrowdale Road."

"Dandaro," says Heather. "It's assisted-living accommodation. There's a full-time nurse on the premises."

"But isn't it way too expens—?"

"I can get you guys a special rate."

"Heather's working for the company that owns it."

I nod.

"I'll get everything sorted before I leave. She'll like it there. She might even make some friends. Anyway, I just came over to tell."

"So where're you off to Heather?"

Ian's leaning back on the chair with that look on his face that dares "entertain me."

"Oh, that's another reason why I came over, so that you didn't hear it over the grapevine. We're emigrating. Australia."

Ian and I exchange a look.

"Australia," he says. "So they're still taking Rhodesians then."

Heather darts me a look.

"Skilled. I have family there. We're having a party on Saturday. Next week. You must come. Anyway, I have to go now. I'll phone about things."

Ian takes Heather out, and when he comes back, he stands against the fridge, his arms folded over his chest.

He looks at me.

"What?"

"What happened to you yesterday? I couldn't find you anywhere. I was worried sick."

"I had to get out of the house. Ian, where's David?"

I see him standing there, thinking how much he can push anything.

"Camp, remember?"

"No, Ian. You didn't let him go, not after . . ."

"Lindiwe, he wanted to go."

"What if he wants to talk? He loves Bridgette. What, what if . . . ? "Oh, God, Ian, oh . . ."

Ian tries to hold me, but I push him away.

"Just leave me. I'm fine. Fine."

I swipe away the tears with the sleeve of my nightdress.

I give Ian a smile. *See.*

"I didn't tell him, Lindiwe. I didn't have the heart. He was so keen on the camp, I . . ."

"You did the right thing, Ian. I wanted to see him, that's all."

I don't want to talk anymore about Bridgette. To remember.

"So are you going to show me those portraits or what? That's if the war vets let you in."

Ian opens his mouth and closes it.

"Lindiwe . . ."

"Ian, please, not now . . ."

"Okay then, come with me, my girl."

And there he is, our dear leader, all spread out on our dining-room table.

I don't pick them up. I look from afar.

"Ian! What did you say to him? What did you do? Look, he's smiling. And that one, look at his laugh. Ian!"

"Don't go on about it. I'm in a real fix."

"But they're good, great, so human."

"Exactly, like I'm running his ad campaign. I mean, I couldn't take one shot that says ruthless African dictator, bloodthirsty tyrant; no, there he is looking like a decent chap in all of them. Asch man, I'm screwed."

Somehow, I must smile, somehow.

"What's so funny?"

"Just tell him they came out bad, that they aren't any use."

"No, he won't fall for that. Like the Americans say, the man's got game. He wants me to deliver the pictures personally. Man, I'm knackered."

"What about Grace, the kids?"

"Not a sign. I actually felt sorry for the bloke. Looked as lonely as hell when I got in there."

"That's why he must have appreciated your company."

"You know who popped in? The police commissioner. He was huffing and puffing about "urgent, disturbances, townships, war vets." Something's going on. Bob waved him away like he was a mozzie. Listen, are you going to be all right today here? I want to head down to the studio, do some tweaking on these."

"Yes, yes, go. I'm fine. Promise."

For lunch I eat a slice of brown bread and I open the wine that Bridgette gave me for my birthday. I drink it all and then I go to bed.

I wake up; I go into the bathroom, throw up. I wash up, change.

I stand outside Ian's mother's room. I push the door open. She is sitting by the dressing table, head bent down, pulling at the strands of her hair. Her hair fascinates me, the abundant luxury of it against her scarred, shiny pink skin. A stranger looking at her from the back might mistake her for a young and vibrant beauty. She looks up, our eyes meet, lock, something passes. I don't know who gasps. Me? Her? Us? I close the door gently behind me.

I go out to the gazebo, and I sit there until it gets dark.

4.

David comes home from camp with a cut above his left eyebrow and a black eye. When I ask him what happened, he says, "fell," and goes into his room without another a word.

"Ian, he looks like he's been in a fight; what did the teacher say?"

"He was very vague; according to him, David and some boys were fooling around, and well, boys . . . I'll talk to him."

It comes out. Some boys calling him names: "dirty colored," "half-breed," "a wannabe honky." Ian looks as though someone's punched him right in the stomach, winded him.

"He doesn't even *look* like a colored, Lindiwe."

"Oh, so, he's white then."

Ian stands there looking at me, and it hits me that he has always thought of his son as white. I'm stunned.

"He shouldn't hang around that gardener's boy."

"Robinson? Why not?"

"He should be friends with kids his own level."

"Charles is his friend, too."

"Others also. He's always with those two."

"Others like who?"

"Asch, I don't know Lindiwe, kids in his class, good kids."

"So you think if his friends are white, then maybe people will think he is white, too? He is colored, Ian. Colored in Zimbabwe, South Africa; mixed race in Britain; black in America. There is no place on earth where he would be classified as white, Ian; in case you've somehow forgotten, he *does* have a black mother."

"Oh, so now you're black. Weren't you once a goffle?"

Ian looks at me as though he's seeing me for the first time. He makes me want to hit him, throw something at him, shake him.

"Ian!"

"What? I'm not thick. Ever since those war vets have started going on about getting back the land, finishing off the Chimurenga, chasing the white man out . . . asch it's like there's been no bloody progress."

I don't know how the war vets have suddenly leapt into this conversation.

He can't get over his own flesh and blood being a victim of racism. Welcome to planet reality, Ian!

"Don't start talking to him about race this, race that. I mean it, Lindiwe, I don't want him getting hang-ups."

"Oh, and you don't think that hearing himself being called a dirty colored is not going to give him hang-ups?"

"He beat the kid, didn't he?"

"Ian, *he* got beaten up. He can't fight everyone who calls him names. He's going to grow up with that kind of abuse. It's everywhere, Ian."

"Yes, Lindiwe, I'm a Bhunu remember? The lowest of the low. I know all about racism."

I don't know what to say about that, so I keep quiet.

"He's *not* a goffle."

"That's right, Ian. He's our son. My son. Your son. But out there where they put people in boxes, categories, he is a race."

"Asch man, maybe the Afrikaners have the right idea. Everyone must keep to their own race, avoid complications."

"That's right, Ian, as soon as things start to get a bit difficult, uncomfortable, all of a sudden apartheid seems like a jolly good idea."

"I'm just sick of everything being about racialism. Those war vets blew their compensation fund big-time and now it's back to scapegoat number one—whitey. It's *not* whitey who stuck his paws in the pot and doshed themselves millions for nonexistent injuries. The thing was looted by their own fricking ZANU-PF chefs, and now Hunzvi and his war vets even have Bob dancing to their tune, telling him that they'll take matters in their own hands if he doesn't cough up. And it is all the fault of the white man, of course, jeez man."

"And you don't think I'm sick of it, too, Ian?"

"So why do you keep going on about it, heh?"

"You know what, Ian? Here's an idea. Why don't you find a white girl like, like Heather fricking whatever, get a white son, and go off in the fricking sunset in fricking Australia."

Now *he* looks stunned, again.

"Man, Lindiwe, that's harsh."

And he cracks up laughing.

"It's just that I don't want to see him suffer. It really tears me up."

"I know."

"As long as he knows where we're coming from, I suppose he'll be okay, huh?"

I don't ask him where we are coming from. I nod.

"You know what he asked me in the room just now? It really threw me."

"What?"

"What happens to the three of us if Bob decides to throw all whites out of the country? It really hit me Lindiwe, what with all the noise the war vets have started making . . ."

I know what he wants me to say, what he hopes I'll say.

"I hope Bob really likes your pictures" is all I can manage.

Ian gives me a long, hard look.

"God, you're so full of it sometimes," he says and turns away.

Ian takes his mother to Dandaro. When they are gone, I go into her room, open the two windows, and I start cleaning. Ian finds me vacuuming. I feel as though he's caught me with some kind of incriminating weapon.

"Thanks for sticking it out."

"I was feeling restless," I say, feeling obliged to explain the vacuuming.

He's wearing the jeans I got him for Christmas last year. Fashionable Levi's instead of the hard-wearing local ones that he's had for years, which never fade and have a permanent iron crease in the middle of each leg. He's got a great butt. He was complaining yesterday that already there are holes appearing in the jeans. "They're meant to be like that," I said, and he looked at me with that "asch, man I'll just amuse the chick" expression of his. The T-shirt is another piece of image makeover sneaked in as a gift from David. It fits just right, not baggy and not too tight, a nice change from his collection of POWER SALES, EXPRESS, RADIO LTD, DEES GARAGE ones, buy one, get one free.

The shoes are fellies from Bata, farmers' shoes, but I'm working on that.

His hair has been stylishly cut by Les, the moffie at the West-gate Salon.

I finally managed to drag him there on New Year's Eve and the thought of him sitting on that chair squirming, sus-piciously eyeing Les's well-manicured fingers as they whirled and twirled in front of his face; him listening to Les's excited babbling about what a divine haircut he was going to give this gorgeous boy, makes me smile.

"No moffie hairstyle, highlights, streaks, or what you may

call it," he had warned me before stepping into the salon. "Otherwise, I'm straight out of there."

I let Les work his magic.

I'm amazed that he has kept up with it, that he and Les have formed quite a relationship.

And so here he stands. Ian. My man. The father of my child. He looks very handsome. He doesn't look like a Rhodie at all. He could be an expat. A foreigner.

Later, after the haircut, he said, "Maybe now you won't be so shy to show me around, huh?"

"I think she is going to be all right over there; it looks pretty organized. Everything spick-and-span."

The voice, the mannerisms, though. No mistaking those.

There is no one else in the house. I'm sure that if I'm still enough, I might hear our hearts beating. I'm still holding onto the vacuum cleaner. It would be good if he kissed me now. If he took the one step and kissed me.

"I'll be back a bit late today."

That's all he says.

To prove something to Ian (and myself), I ask him to come along to a barbeque some guys from the Swedish International Development Agency are having. I don't say anything about the outfit Ian's chosen. Local jeans, POWER SALES army green T-shirt, and fellies.

At the barbeque he lays on the Rhodese pretty thick: "Yah, it's fricking hot today, you telling me . . ."

Thankfully I spot Solace who works as a guest liaison officer at the Sheraton and who always has some juicy gossip about Harare socialites. She is in the middle of telling me about a prominent black businessman, who has been spotted on First Street in the early hours of the morning donned in killer heels and a hot pink miniskirt, when I look up and see Ian engaged in a conversation with a pretty-looking blonde.

Solace finishes telling me the story, and Ian is still with the blonde, who flips her locks off her shoulders.

I have a drink, another one, and they are still together.

I go to the toilet, and when I come back, I am in time to see the woman write something down on a piece of paper and give it to Ian, who puts it in the front pocket of his jeans.

He doesn't say anything about the woman or the note on our drive back, nothing when we're in bed, until finally I give in.

"Who was she?" I ask him.

"Who?" he says innocently.

"That girl, the one you were talking to at the party?"

The lights are off, so I don't see the splotches of red on his cheeks, forehead—the imprints of guilt, shame.

"Oh, her," he says.

I wait in the dark for something else.

"Ian?"

"What?"

"The girl. Who is she?"

"Which girl? Oh that, just some chick who knows me from way back, wants me to take some pictures."

And then he rolls over, goes to sleep.

In the morning he gives me a long kiss.

"What's that in aid of?"

He looks at me and starts to get out of bed. I reach out my hand to pull him back, but it's too late. He goes into the bathroom. I spy the jeans on the chair. I stop myself from going to them, sticking my finger in that front pocket.

He comes out of the bathroom, a towel around his waist.

"Ian . . ."

Please, please, kiss me again. Please.

He puts on his jeans. I think of the note in that front pocket.

When he'll remember it, if he already remembers, when he'll call her.

Please, please, kiss me again. Please.

He put on his T-shirt, runs a hand through his hair. He sits on the bed, puts on his socks.

"Ian, it's just that— Okay, I'll say it, the note, from yesterday, you're not going to call her? I mean, you and her. I just want to know if you were talking for a long time, do you like . . . ?"

And it all comes out in a rush, leaving me breathless, standing there in my nightie that's covered in teddy bears.

He looks at me.

"Maybe you want, Miss White Hair, feeling it . . ."

And it doesn't help that I have a sock on my head to keep my braids from getting messed up.

"Yah, yah, just like in the Sunsilk advert, Lindiwe, silky, soft, shiny hair. Yah, I miss running my fingers through that. Man, Lindiwe, how many years and you're still thinking this shit? Come here, you dunderhead."

But he comes to me.

And he pulls off the sock, puts his fingers between my short braids.

"Sometimes, I think you'll go off with a white . . ."

"Man, now you're really going to get me really mad, and what about you and your university fundies?"

I reach out my hand, draw his face towards me.

"I'm allowed to be jealous, aren't I, Ian? You being such a charmer?"

And he smiles and lets me kiss him.

"Lindiwe," he says when I let him go.

And he whispers the words, slowly, in my ear.

I   love   you.

And then, in case I haven't understood, he says them again in Ndebele and then he adds a bit of Shona: *chete,* only.

"So did he like the pictures?"

"Shit, Lindiwe, you spooked me."

"Sorry. You're reading."

"Yah."

"What?"

"It's nothing."

"Come on, show me. Don't be shy."

"Asch man, you may as well know."

He lifts the book, hands it over. *Rhodesians Die Harder: Selous Scouts in Action.*

"Nice. Any particular reason?"

"Check out the inscription, first page."

"To Comrade Ian, from Bob . . ."

"Bob? Who's Bob?"

"Bob Bob."

"No!"

"Oh, yes, Bob Bob. *That* one."

"You mean *he* gave this book to you."

"That's right. Wish it ain't so but . . ."

"Why? Why would he . . . ?"

"Got to hand it to the man, he has one helluva sense of humor. Check the pictures, round about the middle."

"Selous Scouts. Nice. 'The infamous rotting baboon that starving recruits were forced to eat.' Nice."

"Check the one at the bottom. The one where he's standing over a dead gook."

"Jesus, Ian."

"Read the caption."

"'The legendary Captain Ian McKenzie overseeing the body search of a dead terrorist for intelligence.'"

"Captain Ian McKenzie? Ian, not your . . ."

"Yes, Lindiwe, my father."

"Jesus, Ian. *He* gave you this book."

"Yah, yah. He knows everything. You got to give it to those guys at the CIO. They've got their facts, that's for sure."

"What are you saying, Ian? You mean they have a file on you?"

"Me and every fricking . . . you know he thought it was one great big joke. He starts asking, 'How is your son? David it is? . . . And your beautiful African wife. Ah, but excuse me, you are not yet married.' . . . That really got me spooked . . . man."

"What? You don't think he was, I mean, threatening you."

"You know the stories that fly around about him. He has this way of looking at you, and you think, jeez, I'm going to get fried, man, and you know he's just enjoying himself big style, watching you sweat it out. Then he hits me with the book."

"Well, they say he has dirt on everyone. That's why no one . . ."

"Dirt! Read the chapter on Operations. Ian McKenzie, a fricking bloody legend in his own lifetime. I thought all his talk about contacts and kills was bull, trying to show how tough he was, what a man . . . Read, Lindiwe. Then as he's walking out the room, he comes out with, 'I'll be in touch, Mr. McKenzie.' Man, I'm thinking of gapping it for sure."

I take the book outside and read.

I read what Captain Ian McKenzie has bequeathed his son, Ian.

In 1973 Ian McKenzie was one of a troop of Selous Scouts (four Africans, four Europeans, Special Ops) that took part in a clandestine mission to kidnap several ZIPRA terrorists from Francistown, Botswana. Posing as a Polish journalist, he managed to sweet-talk his way into ZIPRA headquarters and to conduct interviews with high-ranking officials. After he gleaned intelligence information from his "interviews," the targets were captured by his team after being lured into a rendezvous with the promise of good times with some Polish girls at a local hotel.

After various other operations (internal and external), his bravery and willingness to do just about anything for his country caught the attention of Lieutenant Smith-Avery and he was reassigned to Mashonaland. It was here where he truly thrived and his survival skills and instincts for a kill were fine-tuned and highly valued.

Operation Take Down is where Ian McKenzie made a name for himself. November 1976. Together with black Selous Scouts, they disguised themselves as FRELIMO fighters and raided a ZANLA training camp in Mozambique. In a matter of a couple of hours, well over a thousand terrorists were exterminated with no injuries sustained whatsoever to the twenty Scouts. On their way back across the border, the Scouts still managed to have enough energy to ambush two Land Rovers loaded with ZANLA big shots, adding to their kills.

There is other stuff I can't bring myself to read. I skim over the words. Manuals on how to extricate information from living terrorists. Manuals on how to use torture methods effectively. Manuals on how to prepare for a kill. Quickly. Quietly. Efficiently.

I ruffle through the pages. I look at the pictures. At Ian's father who looks so much like him. I think of Ian, how it must have been like to have him back home, after all those months his father spent away, killing. If his father had had nightmares.

"The legendary Captain Ian McKenzie overseeing the body search of a dead terrorist for intelligence." There he is, cigarette in his mouth, just another day on the job, time for a drag.

I put the book down on my lap, then pick it up again.

I look at the pictures and stop again at *"The legendary Captain Ian McKenzie overseeing the body search of a dead terrorist for intelligence."*

I look at Captain Ian McKenzie rakishly smoking his cigarette. I look at the dead terrorist. I look at the Selous Scout who is doing the body search of a dead terrorist for evidence. And then I look up from the dead terrorist to a figure to the left of him. I look up. The face is twisting away from the camera, but still there's enough to see.

Maphosa.

I think he must be a terrorist, terr, gook, guerrilla, Nationalist, Freedom Fighter. He must be a Prisoner of War.

Then I look closer and see that Maphosa has an FN and he's giving the foot of the dead terrorist a kick.

When I get up again, it's dark. I put the book on the dining-room table, walk as far as the kitchen, come back, lift it, and look for some place to put it away. I'm standing in the room when Ian flicks on the switch.

"Second time you've spooked me today, Lindiwe. What the hell are you doing in the dark?"

I don't want to keep secrets from him.

"I . . . Ian, that picture with the baboon . . . I think I saw Maphosa."

"Maphosa?"

"You remember, the war vet who used to live with us. He's in the picture. Look."

He takes the book from me, finds the page.

"Shit, Lindiwe, is that him? Are you sure? What's he doing there? And shit he's all decked out in Selous Scout gear: bush shorts, camouflage T-shirt, beard; man, he's looking rough."

"I know, I . . . I don't understand."

"He must have turned. Lots of terrs turned once they'd been captured and been wined and dined by the Rhodesian Army."

"I think I'm going to be sick."

"It's Ancient History, Lindiwe. That generation has got blood on their hands all round."

"I think I'll go to Bulawayo this weekend. I haven't seen Dad for a while. We'll catch the bus."

"With David, you think that's safe?"

"Ian, Maphosa wouldn't . . . I don't believe it. He's a relative."

"I'll come with you."

"No, Ian, remember last time. I don't want to provoke anything."

He drives us to the Ajay Motorways depot early on Friday morning. As the bus pulls away, I watch him walk towards the car and his figure, alone in the early morning, hurts.

David puts on his Walkman and is lost in Bunny Wailer. I haven't really talked about Bridgette with him. What is there to say beyond the reality of her death, the brutality of it? We didn't even hug. I don't know what he is carrying in his head. Ian says he's dealing with it in his own way; when the time is right, it'll come out. This is my, our, first visit to Bulawayo since she died. I should go to her grave. Maybe even David should come with me. But I don't know if I can do it. Stand there looking at a tombstone with her name etched on it, with the parameters of her life fixed forever between two dates.

I take out some work. I nudge David. He's singing along to Bunny. He takes the earphones off. "What?"

"You're a bit loud."

"Oh," and he puts the earphones back on and bops his head to Wailer.

I look at the twists of hair he's growing, much to Ian's annoyance. I smile. *My boy.* I look down at the papers. I turn them over, try to concentrate, but my head goes back to Maphosa. Did he infiltrate the guerrillas? If he did, how many men did he betray or kill? For so long, Maphosa has been one thing and now he is another. How utterly wrong I, we, have been. Maphosa, my eccentric, colorful relative is now, what? A killer. But he was that before, wasn't he? Does it really matter, what side? A traitor. He is a traitor. It was a dirty war. Notorious for it. Civilian planes shot down. Survivors hacked to death. Whole villages mortared. Babies shot. "Ancient History," Ian said. Gone. It was gone. But Maphosa and his war veterans? My head throbs against the window.

I look at David, who's fallen asleep, his lips puckered open. I try to smooth down the twists of his hair, and I switch off the Walkman.

"Tell me everything," I say, watching him breathe. "Don't keep secrets."

6.

Daddy is so thin. I lift his hand; the lightness of it—its lack of weight, substance—shocks me. I look up at Mummy busy smoothing the cover at the foot of the bed. She must feel my eyes on her, but she refuses to meet them.

"Mummy, why is he like this? What happened? Why is he so th . . . ?"

She won't look up.

"Mummy . . ."

"It is his stomach. He cannot keep anything in. He must have an operation, but he doesn't want. He is tired."

I look down at Daddy. He is asleep, the breath coming out of him so shallow.

I will leave behind a blue jersey and a hat, my guilty offerings. In less than a week, he will have yet another birthday in this bed, and I will be gone. I look away to the door, to David who stands there, the Walkman earphones dangling from his neck.

When we were standing outside the locked gate, he had been so jittery; he'd wanted to climb over it, already his feet were on the fencing.

"David, no. Come on, get down. Be patient. Look there's Granny. . . ."

"Gran!" he shouted to the figure marching up to the gate. I was struck with how much stronger she looked. How hard she seemed.

"Gran!"

She didn't even look at him. She undid the lock, left the chain still hanging around the gates, and marched off again.

David stood there next to me.

"Jeepers Mum, she looks pretty mad," he said softly.

I knew what he meant, upset, angry, but the literal translation seemed to me spot-on. She *was* mad. Penga. How did such a sweet boy get two nutcases for grandparents?

I was struggling to unwrap the heavy chain. "She's just getting old. Old people get confused."

Finally the gate was free of the chain. I pushed it open.

"Maybe it's my hair."

We made our way to the house. I was shocked by how desolate it seemed, as if any moment, ghosts might come waltzing through. There was no sign of dogs, life.

"And you've grown so much. She remembers you when you were just so high."

We were both trying so hard.

I look up once more at Mummy, then down at Daddy, and then I turn away and go to my son, closing the door behind me.

"Come, let's go and explore."

We walk through the dark passageway into the kitchen, open the wooden door, and stand outside on the concrete doorstep, the two of us squeezed together. It is cold in the shade of the loping eaves. I step onto the sparse grass. I don't look left. I'm not yet ready for that house. The chicken coop is deserted, feathers caught in the fencing. David walks over to the dog kennel, peers inside, nothing. He walks towards the girls' kaya, stands in that place between it and his grandfather's workshop.

"I don't think Rosanna's around," I say.

He turns, screws up his eyes, scratches his forehead with his middle finger, and bites his lip, looking so much like Ian then. I wait for him to say whatever is playing in his head, but he makes a little shrug and turns again, the palm of his hand moving along the rough wall.

I don't know how much of Rosanna he holds close.

I follow him to the girls' kaya. There are spiderwebs and deep cracks, crevices, running all along the outer wall. Daddy blamed the apostolics for their shoddy work, and every year after the rainy season, he would spend a week plastering and filling in the cracks with cement. Mummy would stand by the kitchen complaining that he was wasting money.

Standing here with my son, I am seized by shame at its shabbiness, how we could have allowed dear Rosanna to live in here.

I don't know how long Mummy's been back. What arrangements she's made with Rosanna. The other times Rosanna's been expelled she's always gone to Uncle Silius to seek refuge, but last time I talked to her, Uncle Silius and his family had been evicted from their flat in Pelindaba for nonpayment of rent.

I walk around the workshop, and my eyes sweep past the gum tree away to the far corner, where an outbuilding that used to be partially hidden by rows of maize plants squats.

"Maphosa lived down there," I say to David, who is crouched on the ground jabbing a stick at an anthill. "He was our gardener. Let's go and take a look."

We walk silently in the dirt. Not a single sound. It's like walking in a devastated zone. The earth scorched and abandoned.

We stand outside the zinc door, which is just open enough to give a sight of the blackness inside.

I am suddenly gripped with dread, but before I can tell David we should leave, he has already pushed the door open wide.

Something scurries on the floor, and I let out a yelp and jump backwards.

"Chill, it's just a lizard, Mum."

There is nothing in the room, not even a mattress.

What did I expect to find? Evidence. Of what? The Great Lie?

"He lived in *here*? It's so small."

"Come on," I say. "Let's go." I try to shut the door, but the warped zinc springs open. The latch has been long broken and rusted. "Let's go and have a sandwich, and then we can go into town for a drive. No, actually, better idea. Let's go for a pizza or a chicken at Nando's, and then we can go and take a look at the museum. You haven't seen the animal exhibit; it's good."

David eyes me cynically. But he's also amused as evidenced by his right eyebrow cocked higher and his lips swinging to one side, his dimple deeper.

I'm frantic with the desire for distractions.

We both stand staring at Daddy's treasured Ford Cortina. There is rust and dirt, things Daddy would never have tolerated. I wait for David to make some comment, but when I look at him, I'm shocked by how gentle and sad his face seems to be. What does he remember?

"Okay, then, let's get going."

David opens the front passenger door.

"Back," I say.

"Mum!"

"Come on, you know the rule."

"Mum! I'm not a kid."

"Humor me."

My beautiful son glares at me and then flings the door shut; the car rattles in protest.

"Dad's right; sometimes you're the gestapo."
"Seat belt."

Bulawayo, as ever, seems to be stuck deep in another century: the genteel, fading, faded grandeur of the colonial past. Sleepy Bulawayo with its wide, wide roads that Rhodes had constructed so that horse-drawn wagons could make a complete turn. Ancient models of cars chugging along, some of them seeming to come from the turn of the century, old, beaten down, driven with infinite care and pride by their equally antiquated owners. Harare has all the glitz. Harare is fast, Bulawayans fresh from their travels to the Sunshine City gossip. "Too, too fast," they say, sinking into the welcome torpor of Bulawayo while still feasting on the hectic rush of life that is Harare. Too fast, as if that city, that foolish, reckless metropolis with its good-for-nothing Shonas, will one day simply run away with itself, with its good times, get rich vibrations while Bulawayo, good old Bullies, ever solid, reliable, dependable, boring, dull, will survive for all time. But it is also Bu-la-wayo. The place of killing, isn't it? Bloodletting is in its history. The beautiful wide, wide streets are seeped in blood.

"Mum!"
"Yes, what?"
"You're going as fast as a snail on sleeping gas."
I readjust the rearview mirror until I can see him.
"This is Bulawayo pace."
"Yeah, right."
"That's right."
I flash him a smile. He sighs, flings his back hard on the seat rest.

I press down a bit more on the accelerator.
"Is that better, more Formula One style?"

I watch him for a moment. The earphones are back on. His forehead is pressed against the window. What on earth does he make of it? The utter wretched barrenness of it. The dry patches of wasteland. The shacks all over that field, where sometimes I would watch boys kicking their plastic footballs. The land has been reclaimed, and everywhere there are cardboard houses. And next door to all this, the crumbling houses of the once Whites Only suburbs. What had the whites said as the hordes of blacks moved in and claimed possession of the well-tended gardens (if they hadn't been spitefully uprooted by the fleeing white owners): oh yes, "wait till the munts move in; wait and see what a dump they'll turn these places into, just wait."

And how angry it makes me to see how right they've turned out to be. Everything is falling apart.

What did Daddy himself say?

"The problem is, we blacks, we move into these big houses with big yards, and we don't have the money to upkeep them. We want to be seen to be living like bosses. And then all the relatives descend. It becomes a mess, the whole thing. People living one on top of the other; it is a recipe for disaster. I'm telling you, very soon we will have cholera outbreaks like in Zambia."

There's no longer the *thik, thik* of sprinklers as they water lawns or flower beds—instead, patches of anorexic maize straggling over broken fences.

And now, to top it off, the smell of sewage entering through my open window.

"What a pong."

"It's the river," I say closing the window.

Daddy was always complaining to the city council about all the illegal dumping that was going on upriver at Trenton. If you caught the bus at certain times, you would have to share it with a goat or a pig from one of the squatter camps there that was beginning its long, miserable journey to the lands.

Main Street.

"Look, David, there's where Grandpa used to work."

The Main Street Post Office building, I'm relieved to see, is still there, sturdy and reliable with its thick red stone and straight lines despite all the internal havoc and machinations of its occupants: the never ending strikes, the go-slows, pay and labor disputes, firings, rehirings, court cases, pending court cases, tribunals, and the decline of all the services rendered by the Post and Telecommunications Corporation.

"I remember it," he says, craning his head out of the window. "Grandpa used to take me to his work. The machines were gigantic, and there were pictures of naked ladies on the walls."

That must have been the main telephone exchange down at the basement of the building. How many times had Mummy allowed Daddy to take him there? He had taken me, too, sometimes straight from school when he got called out on a fault, and I had seen those pictures, Miss January, Miss June . . . which some of the younger guys had tacked onto the walls. The older pin ups were from *Scope* magazine, the newer ones, with black girls with clothes on, from *Drum*. There is a pang of sorrow when I think of David with Daddy. I can see them walking down those stone steps in the gloom, Daddy steadying David on the uneven stairs, David reaching for his Granddad's hand.

"So, pizza or chicken?"

"Pizza."

"Right then, pizza it is."

Pizzarama is still in existence. Shabbier than I last remembered it. The blackened-out glass front, which has always made the place look like an illegal nightclub, seedy and downmarket, is covered in dust, and I spy several flies in the casement. I'm already having misgivings but I'm also very hungry.

It's gloomy inside. I can't remember if, once upon a time, this was an atmospheric gloominess; at the moment it feels more like an economic strategy as hard times have befallen the once-grand Pizzarama.

Laughter rings out from the table to the left of the door. Some teenagers. Their pose and laughter sweeps me back into Grasshut (Grasshut!) with Bridgette.

David glances at the table and feigns lack of interest at the two girls there, who are staring at him virtually openmouthed. I think schoolgirl Bridgette would have called it, drooling.

We get a table right in front of the door so that at least we have some light. David looks at me with what I take to be a new interest. *So this is what Mum thinks is a nice restaurant. Interesting.* His head is bobbing and only now I notice the music. Rap. The waitress comes. She looks very bored and tired and also irritated with us for giving her work to do.

"Yes?" she says, scratching her weave with her finger.

"Two pizzas," I say. "Can we see the menus?"

She digs her finger out of her weave, points to the table next to us, and waits for us to grab the grimy menus and look through them.

"One Margherita with lots of olives," says David.

"O-leaves," says the waitress, yawning. "We don't have o-leaves."

David bops his head as if he is agreeing with her.

"I'll have a Margherita, too. And can we have some bottled water?"

She looks at me as though I'm crazy. A black woman asking for bottled water, in Bulawayo, well . . .

"Thank you," I say.

She shuffles off.

David's taking a look around, his eyes flitting over the two girls, who appear not to have changed posture at all.

The door opens and a well-dressed young couple walks in. They swivel their eyes over the joint. The woman whispers something to the man, and they both turn back, straight right out of the hole. This is not a place to be seen (caught dead in). Not even in Bulawayo.

After what seems like forever, the pizzas finally arrive. David looks down and then up at me with his "Is this a pizza? Are you joking?" expression.

He's right to ask.

The bread, dough, whatever, is awash in a Day-Glo yellow substance that I presume to be cheese. Islands of uncooked tomatoes are stranded in it. Rings of onions charred around the border.

"Pizza, Bulawayo style. We can go to Nando's."

David sighs and gingerly picks up one end and bites into it, the cheese slopping down his chin onto the plate, taking a forlorn tomato with it.

"The taste's not too bad," he claims.

I could hug him for such fortitude.

I bite, too. And swallow. Just the one slice.

We take a walk to the city center. It seems amazing to me that I can be walking on the pavements of Bulawayo with my teenage son. But here I am. And here he is.

A board on the pavement is advertising Ndoro Company and the arrow points to stairs going up. I am attracted by the photographs of traditional Ndebele beaded jewelry and animal figurines, and David by the pictures of wire cars and motorbikes. Sometimes he surprises me with what *isn't* too young for him; what's so gauche, it's hip; what's so old-fashioned, it's retro, happening.

"Cool."

My hand is deep in the basket of beaded animals when I hear behind me, "Lindiwe, c'est toi?"

I release the animals, and there, here, is Jean. For a moment I can't remember his name, that's how stunned I am. And next to him is a young woman cradling a baby.

"It is you, Lindiwe. What a surprise."

I finally find the power of speech.

"Jean. Wow."

"Yes, 'wow' as you say. How are you?"

I have the impression of standing there with my mouth gaping; I wish there was a reflecting surface to check.

"Lindiwe," he says again.

The woman next to him shifts the weight in her arms.

"Lindiwe, my wife, Clara. We have met in Côte d'Ivoire."

"And you have a baby," I blab. "Wow," I add for extra measure. (Two *wows* so far, wow.)

Thankfully, David barges in. Bless him.

"Mum, that motorbike's supercool."

"Is that little David?"

"Yes, that's him."

"David. How much you have grown. You cannot remember me, of course. Hello to you."

"Hi," says grown-up David.

We stand there in a jittery silence, as if any moment someone might drop something and start screaming.

"Is she a girl?" I ask the woman.

Clara smiles down lovingly at the child.

"Yes, she is a girl, Santini."

"Congratulations."

"Mum . . ."

"Okay, David, I'm coming."

"Kids," I say to no one, anyone.

"It was good to see you, Lindiwe. We are en route to Johannesburg. We leave tomorrow."

Too much information.

"Well, have a great time. Take care." Are these my words? Really?

"You, as well."

"Bye."

I turn away from them and concentrate hard on the mechanics of David's cool bike.

"See how it moves, Mum, and look at the light, cool, and the pedals; it's got a motor, look at—"

"Okay, okay, I'm convinced. Let's take the thing home," I say as I listen to the sound of Jean's steps on the stairs, taking his family away.

"We'll go to the museum tomorrow," I say while putting the key in the ignition.

I'm exhausted. I want to talk to Ian. I need to hear his voice.

The engine tries to start, chortles off. I try again. And again. I hit the steering wheel with the edges of my palms. I spy David through the window with a "could you get a grip" expression on him. One last try and this time we're off. I turn around to say something reassuring to David, but he's leaning back, eyes closed, completely chilled.

*　　*　　*

I phone home. Four times altogether, the last try at eleven thirty. No one answers.

I draw back the curtains of my old room, and I'm shocked by the bare visage of the house next door. The trees that used to dot the length of the fence between the two houses have been chopped down for firewood, and now sitting up, I can spy parts of the McKenzies' veranda. There it stands.

I took the keys with me. I found them in one of the kitchen drawers.

They should tear it down. Build something new and sparkling on top of it. Something modern with lots of windows like the new buildings sprouting up all over Harare. Yes, that would be something, quite an attraction, deep in the boondocks here. Or Ian should give it away. Donate it to somebody. The Social Welfare Department. Have it used for good deeds. Atonement. An orphanage. A homeless shelter. A refuge for abused women, single mothers, street kids.

I sink back into bed.

I'm ready to leave today. But the ticket's only for tomorrow afternoon. A whole free day ahead. It was crazy for me to come running back here. What was I hoping to achieve? A confrontation with Maphosa?

I get up. I tiptoe past David's room into the bathroom, and then I go to the kitchen. I run the cold water gently, fill the kettle, put it on, and wait by the sink, my hands cradling my elbows.

In the quiet, I know clearly, sharply, exactly what I want. I want Ian to be here, to be tapping at this window above this sink. To see him mouth, "no ways are you getting rid of me so easily." I want him to take us home.

I finger the locket on my neck, rub it with my thumb.

I push the curtain to one side expectantly, as though miracles can happen at whim, at one's bidding, but there is no tapping at the window. All is still. All is quiet. There is the tree under which Daddy and the chief constable sat discussing the fire and I . . .

"Mum!"

Just as with Rosanna, so many years ago, the cup slips from my hands.

"Sorry, I frightened you; you're up early."

"You, too, mister. Did you sleep well?"

I get the broom from the corner and sweep the pieces there.

"Okay, the bed's small. Midget size."

"You were a midget once, my dear."

"So you think Dad's awake?"

"Umm, what time is it? Eight, eight thirty, maybe."

Not if he's been up all night, elsewhere.

"We'll try a bit later. We might wake up Granny and Grandpa if we use the phone now."

He sits down, jabs his ever-lengthening limbs under the table.

"Shit," he says, vigorously rubbing his knee.

"You have to stop growing."

"So I can fit on the fucking midget bed?"

Time for that serious talk.

"David, I don't think it's necessary to use that word as a form of expressing yourself. You have a very well-developed vocabulary; you don't need it."

He gives me his "what the?" look and then he twigs on. "Dad says it all the time."

"No, he doesn't."

"Yes, he does."

"It's *fricking,* that's what he says, fricking."

And I know exactly what David is going to say to this.

"That's just like *fucking.*"

"No, it isn't."

"Yes, it is. Ask Dad."

"In any case, Dad happens to be an adult."

David smiles at that and gives me the "oh, really?" mug-shot.

I resort to blackmail. "If I don't hear that word from you all week, I'll give you eighty dollars."

"Ninety."

"Eighty-five."

"Done."

That settled, he stretches out his arms and indulges himself in an elaborate victorious yawn.

"I wish he was here."

"Me, too."

He gets up, tries to open the kitchen door. I fetch the keys from the nook where the telephone is. He steps outside.

"You're going to catch a cold. There's dew."

His chest, exposed by the *V* of his striped pyjama shirt (he only wears the thing when I pack it), seems so ridiculously vulnerable.

"Can we go next door?"

I almost drop the kettle.

"Next door?"

"It's Dad's, isn't it? We can *explore*."

I know he's making fun of me for yesterday with that exaggerated "explore."

"No, I don't . . ."

"Come on, Mum, it's major, major *boring* here."

"Let me think about it, okay? Remember we have the museum today."

"Get a hold of the major excitement on my face, Mum."

*　　*　　*

I try to phone at nine o'clock and then at nine twenty and then nine thirty-one. Nothing.

"Come on," I say to David who has been standing behind me. "Let's get a move on. We'll have a brunch over at Wimpy's and then we'll go to the museum."

I sound like a stuck record about this museum.

Mummy comes out of the bedroom wearing a threadbare nightie, which reveals the outlines of her heavy sagging breasts. I'm embarrassed for her.

"How is Daddy?" I ask her.

She walks past me into the kitchen, and I listen to the water running.

I put my hand on the door handle, press slowly down, inch the door open. It's dark. It smells musty and medicinal. I listen (for what?), to hear Daddy's breathing?

I gently close the door.

"Remember to take the extra set of keys with you. I'm going to Manyano this afternoon," Mummy says coming out of the kitchen with two cups of tea, one black with lemon, the other very milky.

"What about . . ." but she's already elbowed the handle down and disappeared into the darkness.

Surely, she can't leave Daddy on his own? There must be someone who comes, but why would I need the keys? What if there's a fire, or he needs something, how can she . . . ?

"Mum, let's go. I'm starving."

The phone rings.

I wait for Mummy to pick it up.

After the fourth ring, I do.

"Hello."

"Howzit?"

"Ian! We've been trying to phone you all yesterday and this morning. Where've you been? Oh, hold on, Ian, David wants to speak to you."

I hand the phone over to my son, and he gives me his "could I please have some privacy?" look, so I disappear into the lounge.

After about five minutes, David comes in.

"Mum, Dad said he had to go. He'll phone later."

We have two plates of very thick pancakes with cream and syrup. David wolfs his down as though he hasn't eaten for days and days. And then two tall glasses of chocolate milk. And then he burps, which earns him a look from me.

"Excuse me, mademoiselle," he says pulling on his earphones.

I look out of the window.

Opposite the road is Woolworths, owned by ZANU-PF. All along its pavement are beggars and cripples and a couple of women selling bits and pieces: chipped enamel cups, some thread, pieces of faded material, scrawny-looking tomatoes, some sweets. How it has changed from my schooldays when the pavements were uncluttered.

Just outside Wimpys, right by the stairs, we had to jump over a blind man and his infant son, and even from here, I can hear the rattle of his tin cup on the stairs. In last night's news, there was something about the homeless settlement in Killarney, just outside Bulawayo, being trashed by the army. Street children have been rounded up in the city center and dumped in various detention centers.

Already, there's a queue for a consignment of sugar that is rumored to be on its way that stretches from upstairs in the supermarket at Woolworths, around the counters downstairs, to a side entrance and out onto the pavement.

There is a discarded newspaper on the table. The front page is occupied with a car hijacking in Morningside and an old white man at the Edith Duly Nursing Home found dead, beaten, his TV taken. Even in Bulawayo crime is on the rise.

The MDC offices downtown were ransacked two days ago and several homeless people who had taken shelter there were beaten. Like in the rest of the country, inflation, corruption, lawlessness, are all taking their toll on Bulawayo.

David looks up, removes his earphones, and takes a look around and then his eyes settle on me.

"Mum, can I be brutally honest?"

"Yes, of course, what?"

"You're the bomb." And he makes those funny hand movements that must come from the music videos he watches.

And then the earphones are back on again.

My son doesn't seem that impressed by the carnage on display in the Animal Section.

When Daddy used to bring me here, I would be filled with expectation and dread as I waited behind him at the Admission's desk, sneaking looks into the narrow stone passageway, dimly lit, where, on both sides, glass cases were filled with animals in the wild, tearing apart other animals. There was blood and intestines, the lion's fur matted with red, the poor once-elegant impala shredded, and I would feel through my trembling hands and legs that those predators might just be able to break through the glass and get me, too.

And then there was me and Ian, standing here, too, a long time ago.

But here is my son, already out the other side in the cavernous hall, where in the middle is a huge Styrofoam whale looking utterly displaced and worse for wear.

"You didn't enjoy it, the animals?"

"Mum, they're *stuffed*."

"Well, in case you haven't noticed this *is* a museum; next time I'll take you to Hwange."

I'm tempted to add "duh." I sound crosser and more annoyed than I feel. What's wrong with me?

We go up the long spiral of stairs.

A stop at the reptiles, and these do make a better impression.

The cobra. The black mamba, also known as the three-steps snake, one bite and one, two, three steps, you're dead. Then over across to the Hall of Man, the big mural on the wall showing the Ascent of Man from his apelike ancestors to his supposedly more intelligent and refined present-day incarnation. A few steps and we are in the Hall of Chiefs, and this one seems to capture David's imagination, earphones now dangling from his neck, neck craning to see artifacts from the battlefields in Matabeleland and Mashonaland, the business of how men go about killing each other. The meticulous display of weaponry: guns, axes, spears, shields; horns to sound out an impending attack; a bullet that got imbedded within a Bible on a soldier's chest pocket (and there is the very Bible), a soldier's life saved by the holy word. And look, there is how a country was bought and sold: the Great Indaba, Lobengula, sitting on top of a kopje and Rhodes and his men exchanging a few guns and gold for a simple *X* on a piece of parchment.

Out again, and as we walk out, I turn to see the bench that Ian sat on, looking out of the window, how *he* turned around and saw me. I watch David walk along that same bench and jump gracefully off it.

Into the butterflies and birds. How sad these casements have always made me feel: small, delicate creatures trapped forever, some of the wings of the butterflies rubbed away by not-so-delicate fingers and time.

And just like that, an image of Bridgette lying so still inside a wooden box holds me.

Into the spooky tunnel showing the mining of minerals, and David, on cue, makes ghostlike noise, *ooooo, ooooo,* and I, too, respond, on cue, *shuuu*. And then we're down the stairs again, outside. I blink my eyes in the bright sunshine.

"Let's go for a stroll in the park. We can get something to drink at the bar by the train rides."

Centenary Park.

Ah, the pleasures of Saturday afternoons, strolling up the long thoroughfare, bumping into other families, coming and going. The thrill of treats awaiting. On special occasions, perhaps a birthday, the train rides, perhaps even two, on the miniature steam train run by the Rotary Club of Bulawayo; the conductor walking along the open carriages, punching tickets and making jokes about picannins; the train starting, steam shooting up in a straight column; the pulse and pace of my heart quickening; Daddy curling up, shoulders bent in the seat next to me, his head scraping the wooden roof, ducking under the long, long narrow tunnel, where if you're brave enough you can touch the walls with your outstretched hands; up some bridges; *oh, look,* a pond of ducks; watch your outstretched hands on the thickets and then back again to the waiting platform.

The frantic scramble onto the huge models of an airplane and a tank, children shooting and calling, *vroom, vroom; pa, pa, pa, pa.*

The run up to the playground, a haven of swings and slides, *look, look what I can do. Look!* And the swings that can go so high that the sky seems to be about to crash on you, and coming off, legs shaking.

"That's where I got this," I say to David, turning my head and tapping a finger to the scar above my right eyebrow.

"On that?" he says, eyeing the slide.

"Yes. I was seven, maybe eight. It looked so high, scary. The big kids would go down whooping. I was with Thandi, one of Uncle Jacob's kids. She had gone down a few times already.

She was the same age as me and they lived in some flats in Lu-veve Township, which I thought was very exotic."

David starts fiddling with the Walkman.

"Anyway, I finally worked up the courage to go on it. I can almost feel myself going up those steps, biting my lips, wanting to cry; the other kids, bigger kids, pushing and prodding be-hind me, *move, go, move.* So I'm finally right at the top, my legs have managed to carry me up those, what? twenty steps, and when I look down, Mummy and Daddy seem so small. I squeeze my eyes shut, my heart is racing. I'm holding on for dear life to the sides. I can barely hear Mummy, Daddy, Uncle Jacob, maybe even Thandi calling out encouragement. And then, suddenly, I'm off. One of the bigger kids behind me must have given me a shove. I open my eyes, big mistake. The sky seems to be falling. I will never stop. I'll keep going, going . . . and so, to make myself stop, I swerve to the right just as I get to the bottom, and I hit a bit of the metal edge that's jutting out. Lots of blood. I had to have stitches."

David looks at the rusty slide again with a newfound re-spect, and then the earphones are back on.

I don't tell him how Daddy had to blame someone as usual. Mummy. Or that there were specific times when black chil-dren were allowed in the playground.

Centenary Park.

What a grand affair it used to be. And now look at it.

The Christmas lights, famous throughout Africa. And then Harare stole them for First Street. The fountain where before independence, rowdy whites would jump in and splash about while the few brave blacks, garden boys and garden girls from the surrounding suburbs, Burnside, Khumalo, Morningside, Ascot, on their one day off, watched from the road. And now, the smell of feces from the receptacle, its sides stained yellow.

And here we are at the aviary. For a moment, I watch Ian

grab hold of the fence with his bruised hands. It was the first time he told me about Khami Prison.

There are no birds anymore. I would like to think that they have finally been set free but it's more likely that those tame birds have all been eaten. In fact, throughout the park, I notice patches of charred grass and sticks.

Behind the aviary there used to be a wild park full of impala, ostriches, and a giraffe. The impala and ostriches must have long become "inyama" and as for the giraffe, who knows. One ostrich would come right up to the fence and jab its beak at it. Daddy said an angry ostrich could easily kill a man.

The Horticultural Society of Bulawayo planned and tended the gardens, and there were intricate beds of flowers, which fascinated Mummy, and she would try to remember the arrangements so that she could do a bit of the same at home.

"The whites, they really know how to beautify," she would say bending down to examine a particular flower.

The colors! Purples, oranges, reds, all of them so vivid and startling. Hydrangeas, sweet peas, roses, chrysanthemums, flame lilies . . . Daddy would be standing impatiently behind her muttering about how expensive seeds were and "unnecessary expenditures." Sometimes he would tug on a seedling, even though it was forbidden to take any plant life from the park and if you were caught the fine was a hundred Rhodesian dollars and maybe even time in jail.

The flowers are long gone; trodden ghosts of beds and dirt remain. Benches missing planks (firewood again).

We walk back to the museum car park.

"Do you feel like an ice cream, David?"

I have to ask him again, shouting through his music.

"Yes," he shouts back without taking off his earphones.

So we drive to Eskimo Hut next to the Trade Fair Grounds where they have the best soft ice creams in Bulawayo.

As usual there are carloads of youngsters and families. And vendors milling around selling Ndebele jewelry and some replica pots and carvings from Khami Ruins.

For a moment I think I must be wrong. I must.

We see each other at the same time.

She looks up from talking to a man with a black rucksack. I'm handing David his cone.

Her face breaks out into a wide smile. "Sisi!" she calls out. "Rosanna!"

And then I see *her*. My sister. Half. Danielle. (How small she is. How much David towers over her.)

The man with the rucksack gives Rosanna some money; he clumsily folds the lace tablecloth and shoves it into his rucksack.

We meet each other halfway. "Sisi!" "Rosanna!"

For a moment we cannot say anything but hold each other's hands. And then we move to a patch of grass and we sit on the bench there.

We watch David and Danielle look at each other, and the thought strikes me, they are cousins; no, no, that's not right, if she's my sister then, oh, my God, she's David's aunt. David's her nephew!

"You are looking so fine, Sisi. Harare is too, too sweet for you." She giggles into the palm of her hand.

"But you, too, you are looking good, Rosanna."

Rosanna laughs.

We both know that I am lying. She is much thinner and the chitenga cloth hangs limply on her.

"I am keeping busy, that is all. Surviving."

I notice the swollen blackened area below her left eye, and she raises her hand to hide it.

"Where are you staying, Rosanna?"

"I was staying for some months in Killarney, but the army came and destroyed everything. Now I am here."

"Here" I know is the streets.

She puts a hand on my knee, lowers her voice.

"Sisi, I must tell you this. Maphosa is busy terrorizing people. He is the number one war vet in these parts. His gang killed that white farmer over at Nyathi. He is looking for your white man. He must not come to Bulawayo."

I look up from her hand back to the children. David has given Danielle the ice cream. The tip of her tongue darts in and out as she licks the cold. David stands there with his hands in his pockets, trying to look so much like the man of the world. So much like his father.

"He is saying Number Eighteen is Headquarters and Interrogation Centre. He is saying that the fighters are going to truly liberate Zimbabwe now. He is going to the Indians in Lobengula and getting money; otherwise they beat the Indians and take from the shops anyways."

She lets out a long sigh. "People are changing, Sisi."

Someone calls her name, one of the vendors. "I have a customer, Sisi. I must be going."

I sit for a while watching Rosanna negotiate with the elderly white lady who is holding a doily in her frail fingers. Rosanna takes the doily, carefully folds it, and gives it back to the lady. The lady digs in her purse and gives Rosanna some coins. Rosanna stands there, looking down at the coins in her open palm, and then ties them up in a handkerchief, tucks the bundle in her chest.

Ashamed of myself, I give Rosanna all the money that I have despite her protests. I ask her if she still has my Harare number. She says yes. If you need anything, I tell her, just call. "Thank you, Sisi," she says. I know that this is not right. I should take her back to the house. Have it out with Mummy. But I am a coward. So I leave them there. Rosanna and my sister, half.

*   *   *

When we get back, I try to phone Ian again.

This time I startle awake. I draw the curtains to one side. As though I've expected this all along, the glow of orange in the dark does not surprise me. I turn to Ian, but he is not there. I feel the smoke and heat in my mouth, eyes. I get out from the bed. I walk out of the room, the house, and stand outside in the dark, watching the house next door burn, and then there is a figure running towards me lit up, whirling and twirling in the night . . .

I jolt up and find Ian standing at the foot of the bed.

"Hello stranger," he says.

7.

David and Danielle are sitting, whispering at the back.

I keep seeing Rosanna's face when she stood by the car and raised her hand to wave good-bye to her daughter.

"You must be a good girl," she told Danielle. "Don't bring shame to me. You are now with your little mother."

Ian had stayed behind the wheel, nothing said between him and Rosanna.

"Yes, Mama," Danielle replied and sat down quietly, her hands folded on her lap.

David had his earphones on and was looking out his window.

"She will be fine," I said to Rosanna. "Don't worry."

She had phoned early in the morning.

"Please, Sisi, take my Danielle with you. It is only till I find a place to live. It is not good for a girl to be living in the streets. The government will take her. Also, there are some gangs from South Africa who are coming after young girls. Please, Sisi."

It's only when David and Danielle are both sleeping, their heads lolling on the backseat that Ian opens his mouth.

"Now don't get all worked up about it, but I had a visit from the spooks."

"What?"

"The spooks. CIO."

"Ian!"

"I told you, don't get all worked up about it; they just took me over to headquarters, for a discussion."

"A discussion?"

"Yes man, listen to this one. Someone's got hold of a negative and is busy adding horns and a pitchfork to Bob's portrait."

"Ian . . ."

"Don't get overexcited. They just gave me a couple of slaps. I reckon they know it's not me. A white man these days wouldn't dare try that one. They just wanted to be seen to be doing something."

"Is that why you weren't home?"

"When? Oh, yah, kept me there overnight, got on good terms with the blimming roaches. It was like being in a bad movie. The dialogue. The looks."

"Ian, what did they say?"

"The usual, people can be made to disappear, accidents can happen. Come on, Lindiwe, don't look so shit scared; anyway, I reckon it's an inside job. I gave all the negatives to the President's Office so someone's playing a fast one."

"So they just let you go?"

"Yes man. Dropped me off at Mbare with zilch dollars. Had to walk home like the masses. But I haven't even mentioned the classic they pulled. In the car they say Bob likes me and wants me on board for the campaign. I'm to report to duty first thing on Wednesday over at ZANU-PF headquarters. You're looking at a party man, my girl."

"Ian, you're not going to . . . ?"

"What were you phoning about?"

"Answer my question, Ian; you're not going to work for . . . ?"

"You first."

"Ian . . . !"

"Come on, Lindiwe, be realistic now. You don't honestly think that Bob's going to hand over the fricking country, no matter what the voters say, to a former Trade Union guy, that's if the bloke actually has the balls to take on Bob with his, what's it called, Movement for Democratic Change. You're not really thinking that 'chinja, chinja' is coming. Please, the same old, same old is coming. Bob's here to stay. Didn't you hear what the army chief said? If all else fails, they step in. The only people qualified to run the country to the ground are former liberation fighters.

"Ian, it's propaganda; you'd be selling their propaganda, you can't, all your work in Soweto . . ."

"Oh, Lindiwe, please. This is Africa. I'm going to be taking some pictures, that's it: Bob waving, shaking his fist, kissing children, kissing the delightful Miss Grace, who the hell cares. . . . It's a campaign. It is democracy in action. Just like in the U S of A."

"Ian . . ."

"Are we almost there?"

"Only forty K's, my boy."

I turn around and I see Danielle sitting straight up, tears rolling silently down her cheeks. I turn to David who gives me a scowl. I look over at Ian. What have I, we, let ourselves in for? I think of all the things I could say to Danielle. It will only be for a little while; you'll see your mother soon; don't worry, don't; it will all work out; just wait, you'll love Harare; you won't even want to come back to sleepy Bulawayo . . .

"Are you guys hungry?" I say instead.

Danielle has on the headphones and is moving her head gently back and forth. David gives me his "you see" look.

I look at Ian and imagine his body cramped in a filthy cell, faces bent over him, fingers clenched, unclenched.

I put my hand gently on his thigh and I leave it there until he finds it, and we drive the rest of the way back to Harare like this.

8.

The day before Daddy's birthday, I decide, on an impulse, that I'll go down to Bulawayo, surprise him. I think of taking him out in his wheelchair, maybe even going to the park, just the two of us; him feeling the sun on his face, breathing in the scent of grass. Or we can sit on the veranda. The image of him lying on the bed, his hand so thin, his breathing shallow in that musty, dark room, spurs me on. I want to do something for him.

"I wish I could drive you, Lindiwe, but there's mahobo work here and . . ."

"It's fine, Ian. I'll take the bus. I just need to see him. I *want* him to see me. I didn't talk to him last time. I feel as if I've let him down."

"Lindiwe, they're our parents; we're the kids, remember."

And hearing him connect my father to his mother like that is like a miracle, the wonder of our story: how far back we go, how far we've come.

"How is she, Ian?"

"I think she actually likes the joint; doesn't say much, but her face seems relaxed, and yesterday, when I was up there, she was wandering in the vegetable garden with a wily looking old-timer, male."

"I don't think I've ever told him I love him, Ian, not once."

*　　*　　*

When everyone has gone, I phone Bulawayo.

When Mummy hears my voice, she cuts in, "Your father passed away. Two weeks ago. He was sleeping. I'm selling the house. I'm going to Botswana. Come and get your things."

I stand there breathing, the receiver tight in my hands.

A memory sears itself: Daddy and I walking along a zebra crossing; the feel of his hand too tight on mine and the sound of the road trembling underneath me and him, airlifting me up, up away from the monster truck that had no interest in yielding to me. He stood on the pavement, then bent down to me and wiped down my dress with his shaking hands as if I had fallen in some dirt. We walked again hand in hand along the pavements of Bulawayo.

"Mummy, what? I, when . . . ?" The wretched tumble of my meaningless words.

But she has already left.

I put the receiver down. I squeeze my eyes very tightly and I try and think of him, my father, but when I seem to have him in focus, the image peters away.

There is only the weight and fury of Mummy's revenge. Her words biting, merciless.

She buried Daddy alone, without the people who cared for him.

All those years he contributed to their funeral policy: the tall white man coming every end of the month for his check, how Rosanna and Mummy, even wouldn't go anywhere near him, and how they rubbed some foul-smelling ointment on everything he had touched. Maphosa called him nothing but a robber, a crook, another settler.

I go into the lounge and look at Danielle, who is lying on the couch, earphones clamped on.

In the afternoons I've come upon her sitting outside by the gazebo, writing the lyrics of the songs down in a blue notebook. It's Bob Marley; hip-hop, of course; but also some of Ian's tapes, jazz, the blues, Ella Fitzgerald, Mahalia Jackson, Louis Armstrong, all the greats that Ian once surprised me with. I've tried to ask him where, how he discovered that kind of black American music, but it's always the same nonanswer he gives me: *"What? Even racialists know good vibrations; don't be so racialistic, Lindiwe. You should check out even the hard-core farmers when Mapfumo, or even better, Mtukudzi comes on and..."* I know it touches something very deep, tender, and raw in him. I've spied him listening to it when he thinks he is alone, and there is so much gentleness and anguish in his face, in him, then. For moments, while the music plays in his head, he lets go. And I try to think if he even sees the irony of it: he, the son of oppressors, finding release in the music of slaves.

Once when I picked up the Walkman and put it on, I was shocked by the tragic, sad, pure sound of Billie Holiday's "Strange Fruit," and I wondered if Danielle understood the meaning of the song, of the strange fruit of black men swinging from trees in the American South.

I've seen her leafing through some of Ian's books, old books he has found in markets in Mbare and Johannesburg which are full of black-and-white pictures of the old-time greats playing in clubs and bars. Now and then I've caught her humming and sometimes even singing snippets of songs, and as soon as she sees me she, gives me a shy, nervous giggle.

"You have a very sweet voice," I told her once.

Most of the times it feels more as if I'm a mother, an aunt, not a sister, half.

And seeing her now, her eyes closed, her lips moving silently, I don't know where to begin.

She opens her eyes, sees me, and pulls the earphones away.

She starts to get up, and I say, "No, it's okay, Danielle, I..."

And I know, from looking at her face, that my voice sounds odd, broken, so I go to her and take her hand, hold it gently in mine, and then I hug her and there is a single thought in my head: did Daddy ever hold her, know her?

I go in the bedroom and begin to pack, then stop, the clothes limp and horrid in my hands. I lie on the bed, wait for Ian, David, my hands crossed over my heart. I reach out a hand, spread it over Ian's side, seeking comfort, touch.

I put my fist in my mouth, bite at it, bury the sounds coming from me into my flesh, my body heaving.

I look at my watch and the numbers slide and fall. I wipe my eyes and the numbers glisten: eight thirty. The house is quiet, as though like me it's absorbing the news, holding its breath.

David's still not home. He's supposed to be in by seven on school nights.

I ask Danielle if she has seen him. I phone Charles's place. I go next door, to the boy's kaya, to ask Robinson. I go into David's room and stand there among his things looking for something. Anything. How neat he is for a teenage boy. His bed made up with army corners just like Ian showed him when he was nine, ten. His jeans hanging over the chair. His army jacket slung over them. His tennis racket and hockey stick in the corner. Bob Marley on the wall.

I get down on my knees, check under the bed, as if he might be there playing hide-and-seek.

I sit on his bed, trying to quiet the racing of my heart. I turn over his pillow.

"I'm going to the gardens," Ian says when he gets home.

It's nine thirty, and I've made five other phone calls.

"I'm coming with you."

"No, Lindiwe."

"I'm coming."

"Did you get the torches?" Ian asks as I'm climbing into the car.

I jump out of the car, frantically open kitchen drawers, tears streaming down my face, until I find them at last in the corner behind the toaster.

Danielle stands there, and I tell her to lock the door.

I get in the car, and we drive to the Botanical Gardens.

"Don't worry yourself," Ian says. "He's just being a boy, no sense of time. He's grounded for a month for this stunt."

There is no other car in the parking lot.

We walk along the narrow path, past the gazebo used for lectures and seminars, into the open expanse of savanna territory, my eyes straining for any glimpse of the boy and his bicycle, my boy and his bicycle, in the eerie dark.

We walk quietly, quickly, Ian far ahead of me; I almost have to run to keep up.

We walk along the edge of the pond, and I know that Ian is doing the same thing as me, looking *in* there, searching the dark depths for our boy, the beams of the torch swooping over the water . . .

"David! David!" I call out, my heart jumping, racing.

"David!"

Ian turns to me.

"Don't panic," he says, but there is something in his voice, something subdued and held closely, fluttering.

We walk into the rain forest, Ian pulling me along; then out into the wide-open space again.

And then I see it, the torchlight settling on its metallic surface, propped up against a boulder.

A bicycle.

Ian reaches it first. It's David's.

I'm about to shout his name when Ian tugs my hand hard. "Shhhh."

We are at the park's boundary.

On the other side of the fence, the army camp.

We are still, hearing the murmur of voices, singing, chanting. "Shit."

We walk along the fence's boundary, trying to find a way through, but in the dark, our torches off, it's impossible. Ian falls into a ditch, and I think of our boy lying there, heart racing.

We find our way back to the car park, Ian wheeling the bike, and we drive silently home, and inside I feel as though I've abandoned David, my boy, my son, that I've let him terribly, terribly down.

I'm opening the front door when I hear the phone ring. I dash inside. I pick up the receiver.

"Hello, hello," I say into the quiet.

There is a gasp, a whisper of some word, and knowledge snaps in my head, painful.

"Hello, hello, Sarah . . ."

And it's as if we're both shocked by what I've just done, said, for there is such a stillness between us, and yet so dense and physical it is that we could be in the same room, looking at each other for the first time really.

"He's with me," she says at last.

We find him sitting on the cot bed, his face turned to the wall. Ian's mother sits on a chair in a corner of the room, David's camera on her lap.

"David," I say gently. "David."

I put my hand on him and his body pulls away.

All along his legs are scratches, some of them turning into welts, a nasty one along the inside of his right leg, blood congealing. There are blackjacks in his socks, and there is an image of him so clear in my head of him crouching, running through bushes, catching his breath in his hands.

There he is cutting through the park in the dark, stumbling out of its perimeters into Alexandria Park, zigzagging though the roads, and by luck, by luck he doesn't wander into Gunhill suburb, where Mengistu the former bloody dictator of Ethiopia has been given asylum, living in a luxury villa, protected by the Zimbabwean army, until finally he finds the highway and he is running all the way up, up Borrowdale Road, the place where his legs carry him to, his feet pounding the earth, his breathing ragged, choked up with fear, the camera beating again his chest.

I look up to Ian.

"Ian . . ."

I want him to make whatever is wrong right.

"David," he says.

His boy is shaking, and when I touch his forehead, it's damp.

"David, David." That's all I seem able to say.

"He keeps going on about pictures," she says.

I look up at Ian who lifts the camera from his mother's lap.

David suddenly shoots up from the bed and then goes limp; Ian is there to keep him from falling. My boy, my son, is crying in his father's arms.

I look up at Ian again.

"He's seen something," he says quietly. "Something's happened."

And then seeing him standing there, holding his son with the camera in his hand, *his* camera, the camera that has witnessed so much that is brutal and unforgiving, so much killing and slaughter, I know too well what he is saying. I understand. Our son is traumatized. He has been a witness.

We take him home.

I take off his clothes.

The shock of his warm body in my arms.

"Let's run you a bath," I say. As though he were five, six again.

I go to the bathroom, run the water.

When I come back, he's asleep.

I put him under the sheets and draw up a chair, watch him in his sleep.

"Mum," he says. "Mum."

"Yes, David, I'm here."

"I saw them," he says.

"Who, David?"

"I saw them."

And that's all he says.

Ian won't show me the pictures.

But I find them.

It's the camp out at the Botanical Gardens. He stumbled onto their little playground.

It's the thought of him, my David, my boy, my son, seeing the heavily booted foot on an old man's head; a trail of boys, their pants down, defecating on their elders; a blood-splattered face . . . and more and more, fragments of reality, real life in a democratic nation . . . which takes the breath out of me, makes me tremble with rage.

*   *   *

David won't speak. He is camouflaged once again in the silence of his Walkman. A film of resolute defiance over his eyes.

"We have to leave," Ian says. "This stuff is explosive. We get this in some British papers, heck, even South African, and there's mahobo explaining to do."

Awe and bewilderment, slivers of pride, all spilling out of Ian: his son, his boy, has done this; the audacity of it; a chip off the old bloke, that's for sure.

"You're in good books with the ruling party these days, Ian. Remember: you're their advertising genius."

He staggers back as if I've hit him.

"I haven't *done* anything for them, Lindiwe. I told them I had AIDS. Shit, you should have seen how spooked they got. I reckon all of Bob's portraits are being burnt as we speak. Haven't seen one up."

I don't know whether to laugh or to cry. Whether to be angry with Ian.

"Quick thinking," he says, tapping his head.

"And where are we supposed to go exactly? We can destroy the pictures, Ian. No one will ever know."

"David will know."

"Oh, please, Ian, don't, just don't."

"Don't what? I'm just saying that he saw what he saw. We can't change that. He took those pictures, Lindiwe."

"And what's that supposed to mean? He's a child, Ian, in case you've forgotten. We have to protect him."

"Lindiwe, we have to use those pictures. . . ."

"We? Who's 'we'? It's you, Ian. You. Fame and glory. Award-winning stuff on the back of your . . ."

It happens so quickly; the look of pain, shock, rage, disgust.

"Don't you *ever* accuse me of, damn it, Lindiwe, he is my son. How can you . . . ?"

"Ian, I didn't mean . . . Ian, I'm sorry; I'm scared, that's all. Ian, please, let's talk."

I watch him standing there.

"Ian, please . . ."

"Leave it, Lindiwe, not now."

He turns from me.

"My father's dead, Ian. He's dead. Mummy told me yesterday. She's already buried him. I, we . . ."

He is standing so far away from me, looking at me, through me, the color drained from his face, his hands holding David's pictures.

"You're right, Ian. I'll take Danielle back to Bulawayo. You go with David across the border. I'll . . . I'll join you later. You fly out."

"No, we'll all go together, I'm not leaving you . . ."

"Ian, it will look less suspicious if it's just you two. A little holiday with your son. Just staying for a couple of weeks."

"*You* should go with him, Lindiwe."

"Ian, you've got all the contacts for the pictures. I . . . I need to go to Bulawayo. I have to, my father, I . . ."

"Shush, Lindiwe, it's okay. Don't, we'll work it out, shush."

9.

I drive them to the airport, watch them at the ticket desk and then a last glimpse as they walk through the narrow passageway to immigration. Danielle and I could go upstairs and watch them board the plane from the balcony there, but I can't do it. I should wait to see that they do actually board the plane, that they are actually on the plane when it takes off, that they are not hurled off by bulky men in overcoats, but I can't stay. I can't watch them leave.

From the airport I drive straight to Bulawayo.

I park the car outside the gate. I look up at the house.

"Let's go," I say at last to Danielle.

I swing the door shut and I wait for Danielle.

I turn around and there is Maphosa.

"Oh," I gasp.

"You have come," he says.

In this moment, a sense of this man as a form of spirit flitting from one life to the next seizes me.

"Yes, I have come," I say.

I try to find the Maphosa I know, knew. My childhood Maphosa.

Sunglasses are clasped to his eyes.

Maphosa's lips move and twist. It is hard to tell what they mean to convey. A smile? Scorn? Irritation?

"We are doing serious business here."

Whiffs of dagga. Petrol. Diesel.

I look down at his hand to the jerry can there and think of the farmer he must have got that from, the terrors that must have been inflicted on him and his family.

"Yes," I say.

And now I see the two looted Land Rovers over at the McKenzies stacked high with their scavenged bounty.

He turns his face to Danielle who has been standing rigid against the car door, her hand clasping the door handle.

The jerry can knocks against his leg, and petrol spills out on his trousers onto the gravel. There was a piece in *The Financial Gazette* about disgruntled war vets running amok at petrol stations, creating home depots in the townships where they sell fuel in the black market.

"Is this one Rosanna's?"

"Yes."

Danielle keeps her eyes clamped to her feet.

"That one is no good."

I try to think that here is a man, a killer, but I also think, here is Maphosa, a relative. A *distant* relative, I hear Mummy.

He peers into the car. "Where is the boy?"

It takes a moment to know who he means.

"He is in Harare. At school."

I watch Maphosa push a finger under his glasses, scratch. It is his bad eye.

"We are cleaning the area."

We stand silently, facing each other.

Is this a warning then?

Don't bring your white man here. He is not welcome. We will deal with him.

And then he turns around and walks slowly up to Number 18, the jerry can knocking against his leg, spilling petrol, and the sound of the latch of the gate clanging down fills my ears. Like a spirit, Maphosa disappears.

There are two suitcases lined up against the wall in the passageway.

I find Mummy sitting in the lounge, waiting.

She gets up from the couch.

"Good," she says.

I watch her smooth down her black skirt and then pat the black doek on her head.

"I'm waiting for the taxi. Here are the keys. When you have finished, give them to the estate agents. I have written down all the details by the telephone."

I hear a hoot.

"That is the taxi. I am going now."

I will never see her again. I will never see this woman who is my mother, whom I call Mummy. This is it.

"Mummy," I say. The word is there out loud between us.

If she could only say, "Daughter, my child." Something.

She stands still. And I am sure she will give me something. Some thing.

She looks up, sees Danielle pressed against the doorway.

"Just like him," she says. "A face of a man."

I look up at Danielle, and for the first time, I see Daddy's nose, his squashed chin. Daddy who is gone.

Danielle steps back from the door. Mummy walks past, and I watch her dragging the suitcases to the gate.

And then she, too, is gone.

I'm afraid to be in the house, to go into Mummy and Daddy's bedroom, so we drive to Eskimo Hut to find Rosanna.

She is not there. There are no vendors.

We ask one of the waiters, and he says that the army came and cleared up the area. We should try at Cement Side. There are some camps deep in the bush there.

I buy Danielle a chocolate cone. While I'm paying, the waiter leans over the counter, whispers to me. "You must be careful with the girl. The soldiers give too many beatings and even shootings. They are mad from the DRC. You must not leave her alone."

We sit down on one of the benches, and there is nothing but the sound of Danielle slowly licking her ice cream, the Walkman tucked in her hand. The sound is on too high, snatches of Billie Holiday's "He's my Man" filter out. I think of how David left it on the kitchen table, and when I told him not to forget it, he shrugged his shoulders and said, "Danielle can have it."

I look towards the Trade Fair Grounds. The queues used to be so long during the fair that sometimes it took three hours to get into the grounds. Daddy would always say I was two years younger than I was so that I would get in for free. Mummy would pinch me to make me smile at the ticket lady.

"Come, Danielle," I say, getting up. "Let's go to town."

I know I can't keep delaying. Soon I'll have to face the house. I'll have to face Daddy. But for now we can drive into town. We can be tourists, visitors.

Bulawayo has always been slow, but looking at Main Street now, it is no longer the quaint slowness of country people where everything is next time or tomorrow, but a brutal nothingness as though time itself has been vandalized, savaged. There is nothing to see.

The streets are deserted, emptied. Down past Haddon and Sly, Woolworths, up to OK Bazaars, right past Truworths, Edgars, Meikles. Nothing. Bulawayo's soul has been ripped out and here lies the dead body.

It has only been six months since I was last here with David. What is happening? What is happening?

I park the car opposite what once was Kine 600 and has now become the Apostolics of God's Freedom Hall. Old kung fu posters are still pasted on the walls.

I get out of the car. I have eyes. I must see what cannot be seen. What once was.

No vendors. None at all. No street peddlers with their scotch carts laden with tin pots, vegetables, old shoes, clothes. No street children shuffling between shoppers. No beggars on the pavement. No street entertainers. No old men sitting, playing the blues or country on Olivine Oil tin guitars. Nobody at the bus depot opposite the City Hall selling flowers and curios. No young men loitering in corners, whistling and calling, "Sisi, Sisi, you are too nice." No sounds of high-pitched laughter, exclamations.

"Let's go to Lobengula Street," I say to Danielle.

There is always something happening by the Indians' shops.

We get in the car and I drive downtown. Surely we will find the old Bulawayo there. Something to stand and stare at.

But today, nothing.

No crackle and blare of music from dimly lit, musty interiors. No hot, tangy smell of curries and samosas. No Indians standing outside calling out, "Come, madam, just to take a look." No zigzagging along the cracked pavement, trying not to trip and fall on all the enterprising individuals squeezed on the ground: card sellers, shoe shiners, button sellers, scrap of material sellers, certificate sellers. . . .

And if I close my eyes, there is Lindiwe walking down these streets with her friend Bridgette who needs help.

All is quiet. Still. The shop fronts closed.

I open my eyes. What *is* there to see? Look! Look!

VOTE ZANU-PF OR DIE scrawled in blood red all along walls.

MAKULAS OUT spray painted on a window.

BACK TO INDIA scratched on a dustbin.

The blackened, charred wooden storefronts.

The Bulawayo of Ian McKenzie and me.

Driving through the dusk, it hits me that this is it. The country's been shattered. For the first time I take in how serious things are, how far gone, how much is lost. How this country, my country of eternal optimists—live and let live; next time, things will work out; tomorrow—has come to this.

And so I drive on, on to the house of my childhood, the fading Spanish colonial, to the place that grew me. To the house I must say good-bye to, to the father I must leave behind. For I don't belong here. I have a home and it is not here.

I turn into Marula Drive and for a fleeting moment I see the schoolgirl in her netball uniform standing against the bus stop, waiting. . . . She is grown. I am grown. I know this now.

There is a pack of frozen boerewors in the fridge, some bread, a couple of tomatoes. I put the boerewors in a pot of hot water for a quick defrost.

We eat the boerewors sandwiches in front of the TV. We watch *Mvengemvenge,* which used to be a showcase for local music and was very lively but is now full of government-sponsored groups extolling the virtues of all things Bob, and the Women's League choir. I try to switch to ZBC2, but there is no reception from Harare. The satellite has long been disconnected, so no SABC or MNet. Danielle seems fascinated by the program, though, chewing her bread slowly, her eyes glued to the screen.

Danielle goes to sleep in David's room.

*   *   *

For an hour I fiddle with tidying things around the lounge and the kitchen until there is nothing else but to go to Mummy and Daddy's room.

The mess of it shocks me.

The bed unmade. The cupboard doors flung open. Papers and clothes littering the floor.

I breathe in the smell, hoping . . .

I pick up Daddy's pale blue jersey, my birthday gift.

I stand in the room.

I sit down on the bed, just at the edge where I would have sat if Daddy was lying . . .

I look up to where Daddy would be resting his head.

I turn quickly away and look up to the opened cupboard.

Daddy had all his papers in the black briefcase.

Birth certificates. Marriage certificate. Diplomas. Burial payments.

His will.

Mummy must have taken it.

I look at the chair in front of the cupboard that she must have climbed on to look, check that she had everything she needed.

I get up from the bed. I get on the chair. I stretch my body, arm, so that it reaches far into the last shelf. I'm taller than Mummy, I can reach further. I swipe my hand this way and the other. Nothing. I stretch until I'm almost falling off the chair. Some thing. I drag it carefully towards me. A photograph covered in dust.

I sit on the edge of the bed.

I hold the picture in my hands.

I pick up the sleeve of Daddy's blue jersey and wipe the dust and grime away.

There is Daddy. In the bush. In his army uniform.

Standing beside him, Mr. McKenzie and Maphosa. They are wearing Selous Scout uniforms.

Daddy is holding a gun. The bayonet out.

I look at Daddy. I look at Mr. McKenzie. I look at Maphosa.

I look at Maphosa.

I bring the picture closer, closer, until I see.

Maphosa's eyes.

Both of them looking straight at Daddy who is holding the bayonet.

Both eyes wide-open, clear, seeing.

I turn to Mr. McKenzie.

Help me!

But he's not interested in Daddy or Maphosa.

He's looking down at the dead terr.

Except the dead terr is a woman with a baby strapped on her back.

I sit down on the bed.

I turn the picture in my hands. "*Rhodesia. War.*"

And I know Daddy is asking me to understand.

How that war, the bush, twisted everything, what you believed was right or wrong, and made every man who fought in it its victim.

I start awake. The wail of a gate, which gets louder, louder, until it becomes bloodcurdling screams. Instinctively, I draw the curtain aside.

The house next door is alight.

I wait on the bed to awaken from this dream.

Like I have done so many times before.

I wait and wait.

I look outside in the dark.

The house next door is alight.

I get out of bed. I walk in the dark passageway. I stop. I go back. I slowly open the door to David's room.

"I am awake," I hear Danielle.
"Stay here," I say. "Don't leave the room."
I close the door.

I stand outside and watch the house next door burn.
The smell of petrol thick in the plumes of smoke.

The house will crumble into ash.
The fire brigade that has no fuel, no water, no trucks, will not save it.

It will take with it its secrets.
The story of that night, so long ago now.

AFTERWORD

Here we are.

In this city with its pristine storybook lake and snow-covered mountains, its international bureaucrats and bankers.

We will call this place home, until the time comes for Return.

The three of us, displaced, like so many others here. And like others, a family: A Work in Continual Progress.

No worries.

I look up at Ian who can't believe he's ended up living with Frenchies. But he's making a go of it.

You wouldn't believe, he's always telling me, some new thing he's found out about these Frenchies and their easy life.

I wouldn't believe how much he knows.

Who'd have thought he would be fluent in French in months.

That he would cut such a dashing, incongruent figure, heads turning in his wake.

That he would become quite the skier, David and him whizzing effortlessly down the Jura.

* * *

I think of Danielle, my sister, half, whom we'll pick up at the airport tomorrow, what she'll make of it all, this strange land with large white birds that glide in the water and the jet of water that rises day and night from the lake, her hands lifting the personal CD player David picked out for her, which lies wrapped in festive red on the dining-room table, Marilyn Manson the first CD in David's selection.

"Tell her to bring a packet of biltong," Ian mouthed to me while I was on the phone making the final arrangements with Rosanna. "Jeez, I could kill for that stuff."

We have our mementos.

The cover of *Time* with one of David's pictures on it. The picture that has won him two major awards.

An enlarged Zim dollar with Bob sporting horns, and Ian finally confessing to me that yes, he did have some hand in it, together with some mysterious others who are in Bob's inner circle.

The book of photographs that Ian's putting together in between all the freelance work he does, a tribute to Ilo Peretti.

I have found work here too, with UNICEF, and in a week's time, I will be going to Kosovo to help collect information on the state of the children there.

I raise my hand and look at the ring on my finger,
    A single Zimbabwean emerald full of promise and light.
    Dug out from the soil by black hands like mine.
    He slipped it on my finger this morning, and before he could ask, I said yes.

*   *   *

I turn the dial of the stereo louder, let Johnny Clegg, the White Zulu, and Savuka flood this room so far away. "...*And we are scatterlings of Africa. Both you and I*..."

David looks up from his Game Boy and slaps his forehead in mock despair at the gaucheness, the utter rural sentimentality of his parents, and I think how tall, how tall he's grown, how handsome....

And Ian leaps up, starts doing his African township jive, "tshaya ndoda, tshisa mama," heels clicking, in this room, and he sweeps me in his strong African arms, this boy, the boy next door, mine.

ACKNOWLEDGMENTS

Many thanks to John G. H. Oakes whose kindness and grace led me to Paul Bresnick, my wonderfully astute agent who found exactly the right editor, Judy Clain who with great charm and intellect nurtured both the story and the storyteller.

To my sisters: what can I say except, yes, your prayers were finally answered!

Ian's work as a photojournalist in South Africa during the early nineties was inspired by the feats of a group of photojournalists known as the Bang Bang Club. Their story can be found in *The Bang-Bang Club: Snapshots from a Hidden War* by Greg Marinovich and Joao Silva (London 2000).

And to Fabio, my first reader, thank you.

To everyone at Little, Brown for making this debut a thrilling journey, in the best possible way.

About the Author

Irene Sabatini spent her childhood in the laid-back city of Bulawayo in Zimbabwe, gobbling up books from the public library. After university in Harare, she ventured across continents to Colombia, excited by the chance to live in, learn from, and be inspired by a new culture. One early morning she found herself in the lush countryside outside Bogotá, sitting on the veranda of a former Dominican monastery: in the quiet, she opened a red notebook and started writing. She has yet to stop.